AMOR ACTUALLY

A HOLIDAY ROMANCE ANTHOLOGY

ADRIANA HERRERA   ALEXIS DARIA
DIANA MUÑOZ STEWART   MIA SOSA
PRISCILLA OLIVERAS   SABRINA SOL   ZOEY CASTILE

Cover illustration: Chloe Friedlein

Cover design: Natasha Snow Designs

Editor: Mackenzie Walton

Proofing: Michelle Li

Print edition of all titles: December 2021

To everyone searching for their own love story

A NOTE FROM THE AUTHORS

Back in the simpler times of 2019, the seven of us gathered in Upstate New York for our first ever Latinx Romance retreat. Despite having known each other for years online, in conferences, and critique groups, this was our first time away together. Over the course of the weekend, we workshopped outlines, untangled plots, roasted several chickens, and discovered that rose flavored syrup turned any cocktail into magic. The following year—well, you know what happened.

In 2020, we turned our retreat virtual and after hours of talking, wine, and dreaming of the upcoming holidays, *Amor Actually* was born: nine stories full of holiday joy and romance, ranging in style and heat level, so there's something for everyone.

Join us for a Nochebuena.

Love,

Zoey, Alexis, Adriana, Diana, Priscilla, Sabrina & Mia

MAKE THE YULETIDE GAY

ADRIANA HERRERA

After a string of broken engagements, an international Latin Pop Star finds love in her sexy and constant manager. Days before her big live holiday special, Vivi wonders if the woman of her dreams could finally be hers.

CHAPTER 1

TWO MONTHS UNTIL NOCHEBUENA

VIVI

"Will the sixth time be the charm? Hide your men, ladies, Vivi G is back on the market!"

"Grrr," I growled as I read through the pack of lies being peddled as entertainment news on a popular celebrity gossip site. Under the headline was a photo of me and Mark, my real estate agent, walking out of Lucali's after a business lunch. We'd been playing phone tag for months, and when he miraculously happened to both be in Manhattan and free for lunch, we jumped on it. It had been a lovely lunch. He'd told me a joke, so I put a hand on his shoulder while laughing, which apparently was enough to engage me to the man, at least according to Page Seven.

"I fucking hate tabloids," I grumbled, holding my phone in front of my face as Eddie, my makeup artist, did my lashes.

"Lids down, mujer. If I take your eye out, Leila is going to cut my balls off."

"And you need those, Pa," offered Yanelis Paniagua, a.k.a. Bad Kitty, the powerhouse female rapper, from her own makeup chair next to mine.

"My man would have words with the management for sure if I showed up missing the family jewels," Eddie said with a laugh, and I just shook my head, still fuming.

Bad Kitty and I were both getting ready to do a promotional photo shoot for our upcoming holiday special. It was a pretty big deal, not only because this would be the first-ever show of its kind with two Latina headliners, but because it was also my first big appearance after I'd broken off my engagement to baseball superstar Patrick Grant nine months earlier.

You'd think after five engagements and twenty years of covering my seemingly endless misadventures in love, the media would have moved on. Well, you would be wrong. At forty-five, it seemed I was still the gossip blogs' favorite disaster. A multiplatinum pop-super-star-with-a-perfect-ass disaster, but a disaster nonetheless.

I sighed again, intending to sink further down the online gossip rabbit hole when a golden-brown hand scooped my phone out of my hands.

"Oye, I need that," I complained as Leila Baez, my long-time manager—and life wrangler—smoothly slid my phone into her royal purple bomber jacket pocket.

She waved a finger in the air in the universal signal of *heellll NO* and handed me my e-reader. "Nope, you don't need those hacks putting you in a shitty headspace before the shoot," she told me while pulling out a can of my favorite flavored seltzer from another pocket. The woman was a magician. "Hydrate, Miss Guerra. I'm going to go confirm what time they want us in the studio."

Eddie made a sound of approval at my manager's efficient de-escalation of what would've almost certainly devolved into a meltdown.

"See," he told Yanelis. "There is no better manager in the game than this bitch right here." He pointed one of those super-long tweezer-looking things he used to apply my lashes at Leila. "She gets shit handled."

"She sure can," Bad Kitty said appreciatively as her big brown eyes followed Leila stepping out of the makeup room. A weird feeling churned in my stomach at the greedy look the rapper was sending my manager's way. Once Leila was out of sight, Bad Kitty turned back to me. "Tell me again, why is it you're still fucking around with dick when you literally have a goddess looking at you like you hung the moon?"

I balked at that, snapping my head back, which had Eddie howling.

"Keep your head still, Vivi!" he cried, voice carrying a hint of humor. "Yanelis, don't blow her little mind like that, mami. She's totally oblivious to it." That part he said while looking straight at me in the mirror.

It? What *it?*

I was so damn confused.

"What are you talking about?" I asked.

"Ay, mija," Yanelis said with a roll of her eyes, her pointy claws fluttering in front of her, obviously relishing whatever she was about to apprise me of. "That woman"—she directed a black matte fingernail at the door—"is crazy about you." It sounded like *aboutchu*, which made me smile, even as I shook my head in denial.

"What? No," I spluttered, thankful that Eddie had moved on to my eyebrows, because I was starting to fear for my eyeballs with all the head-shaking I was doing. Leila looked at me like... ? No. No. Not going there. "She's a kid, Yanelis!" I protested, which prompted an eye roll.

"Girl, you are blind. That woman is fiiiiiine, and the ass in those skinny jeans is definitely not a kid's." She literally licked her lips as if she were imagining said ass at that very moment, and weirdly, a hot stab of possessiveness almost leveled me. I didn't like the way she was looking at Leila, like my manager was a double scoop of her favorite ice cream.

And where was this possessiveness coming from?

It was none of my business how anyone looked at Leila. If only I could just convince the throbbing in my temple of that fact. I was ready to throw hands over a look. I needed to get my shit together

ASAP. This was not it, at all. Thankfully, Yanelis's voice dragged me back from whatever had hijacked my common sense.

"If it wasn't for the fact that I am extremely happily throupled up, I'd try it."

I suppressed the growl threatening to come out of me. Yanelis was a friend, and I didn't need to get all territorial on her.

I needed to *calm the hell down*.

Still, I kind of envied how free Yanelis was. She loved to joke around, and she was always an open book about her love life and her sexuality. She was proudly bisexual and in a poly relationship, which had been the talk of the town right before my engagement disaster.

She was fearless.

She was so free. And she seemed happy. Sometimes, I felt a little jealous of how open she was about what and who she wanted. Just the thought of doing it for myself, of exposing myself to people's hateful opinions, scared the shit out of me. But mostly I was freaking out a little bit about the butterflies in my stomach at her suggestion that Leila was looking at me with interest.

"She's way too young!" I protested again after a long moment, needing to cement that simple fact into this conversation. Eddie—Mr. Nosy AF and soon to be my former best friend—sucked his teeth as his big hands daintily shaped my brows.

"She's thirty-two, Viviana, and a grown-ass woman making power moves all over this industry for a decade now, so please stop with the ageist BS or implying you're ancient, because I'm a year older than you and I'm in my prime."

"Tell her, Pa!" Yanelis leaned over to fist-bump—more like elbow-bump—Eddie for his little speech while I sat back, mind reeling.

"She works for me, Eddie. Not to mention she's Carlos's little sister."

Eddie only scoffed, as if that was a minor detail. But Carlos Baez, a Panamanian producer who worked with me on my first album, and I went way back. That's how Leila had come to me, through her brother. Ten years ago, when he'd told me his youngest sister had recently graduated from USC and was looking for a job, I interviewed her, and within hours had hired her as my new PA. It was still the best decision I'd ever made.

"One," Eddie proclaimed, waving a mascara wand in the air, "Carlos is not the type to be micromanaging his sister's life. And two, she works for you because she *wants* to." I wrapped my top lip over my teeth because Eddie was now in full lecture mode. "You know damn well she gets offers every six months from other pop stars telling her to name her price. She stays with you because she wants to be here. She doesn't need this job." This was true. Leila did get offers all the time, and she always turned them down.

Why had I never stopped to wonder about the reason?

"Maybe she *likes* working for me?" I sounded a little petulant, but dammit, I made a point of not treating my staff like crap. People in this industry were notorious for their narcissistic-bordering-on-cruel behavior to their staff. I took pains never to be that asshole. I always reminded myself that the people who worked for me had lives outside the insanity of running my day to day.

Every member of my staff got consecutive days off *every* week, they got paid generous overtime, they could bring their kids and partners on trips that were longer than a week. I paid them all extremely well so that when they were running around getting what I needed, they didn't have to worry about how they were going to afford rent. I split my time between LA and New York—both of those places had extremely high costs of living. I wasn't going to be lounging in a mansion while the people who made sure I looked the part were surviving paycheck to paycheck. A few years back, on Leila's suggestion, I'd even started subsidizing childcare for those in my personal team with children.

"Of course she loves working for you, you're an excellent employer," Eddie reassured me. "That doesn't mean she's not attached to you in other ways, babe." This was said in a much gentler tone than the earlier comments. Again that hot, tight thing in my chest pulsed.

I sat with that for a moment, letting myself hear what he and

Yanelis were saying. I loved Leila. I depended on her. She made my life easier. She made me smile with her kindness and grounded me with her no-nonsense approach to life. But I had never dated women. I'd been thrown into this world at twenty-one, and with a fat ass and big boobs, the easiest label to stamp on me was that of man-eater. I refused to be ashamed of the fact I'd used it to my advantage. Hell, I'd run with it. So yeah, it wasn't something I'd considered for myself.

But it wasn't like I couldn't be open to it. I knew enough about desire and sexuality to understand all of it was a lot more fluid than I was taught to believe growing up. And maybe that was my problem: I let other people's expectations make my decisions for me. Why did I keep getting involved with the same type of guy when they disappointed me again and again? Maybe it was time for me to do things differently.

But was it fair to add Leila to my mess?

"I think you're wrong," I stubbornly told Yanelis and Eddie, who both responded with glares and shakes of their heads.

"Don't play yourself, Vivi," Yanelis said after a moment. "You should be getting your back broke by that fucking goddess on the daily instead of fucking with all these man-babies with big dicks."

Eddie cackled so hard he had to take a step back from applying my eyeliner. I only shook my head, trying not to laugh because yeah, Yanelis was a lot.

"Maybe because the last thing Leila needs right now is her boss wanting to get all bi-curious on her," I whispered.

"Listen, Vivi. You know I love you," Yanelis started.

"Oh boy," I said, only half teasing.

She looked around, but it was just us in the small greenroom. I braced myself, because if the woman was actually making sure we couldn't be overheard, I was about to get the top of my head blown off.

"I'm serious," she said, gently pushing my shoulder. "When I started five years ago, you were one of the few Latinas in the game who would even give me the time of day. I came into the scene openly dating a woman, unapologetically flaunting my Blackness, and you

8

took the time to give me advice, point me to the right people, even told me who to stay away from. I will never not be grateful to you." She *was* dead serious now. Not a trace of humor in her eyes. "I also know that if I would've started out when you did, I would've never had a chance. It just wasn't possible to be a queer woman living her life openly like this." She pointed at her engagement ring, which was made of three intertwining bands. "And as much as I love being Dominican, it's not like it's exactly okay to be gay in our culture, you know? Not with the heavy dose of patriarchy we get served with every meal." Yanelis's words were making me slightly uncomfortable, but I didn't think it was a bad thing. I kept listening to her in silence. "As women we're taught to suppress our desires, not to examine anything that might be different from what is acceptable, which is always some misogyny-tinted mess."

I was certain my eyes were bulging out by then, and she laughed with a sigh, patting my hand. "What I mean by that rant is that maybe you hadn't considered there might be more to your sexuality because we are basically brought up to accept that whatever the patriarchy wants us to have, is what we get. It's a lot to unlearn, friend."

She wasn't wrong about that. I hadn't stopped to think about my own needs in my relationships in a very long time. I kept dating these men who looked great on paper but never made me feel cherished.

Yanelis tipped her chin in the direction of Leila, who was standing in the hallway, talking to one of the production assistants. She never hovered over me—she said I needed space to do my "pop star" thing, though I knew a simple glance would have her by my side in seconds.

"You shouldn't have to settle for someone who just looks at you like you hung the moon." Yanelis waved that thought away. "That's basic. What you *deserve* is someone would go and take the stars right out of the sky, and one by one hang them around your neck." My heart fluttered at the image. Of having something that big, that deep with another person.

I'd never had that. Not once.

I was still struggling with a response when the subject of our conversation walked back in.

"We're on in ten—is she ready, Eddie?" Leila said as she came in with Yanelis's stylist on her heels.

I took a moment to look at her. All business, as she always was. Undeniably beautiful. Medium-brown skin a shade lighter than hazelnut, big brown eyes, high cheekbones, and perfect lips. She never wore much makeup, only a little mascara and gloss, and her hair was always cropped short. Tight fade on the sides and back and longer on top. A riot of mahogany curls cascaded over her forehead. She had tattoo sleeves on her arms, which were covered by her purple bomber jacket. On her tight, slim form she had a black tee, black skinny jeans, and purple, gold, and white Air Force 1s on her feet. They were of the many pairs she owned, the woman was a complete sneaker head. I'd personally added dozens of Jordans to Leila's collection.

Butterflies flapped papery wings behind my sternum as I took her in. As if I were looking at her for the first time. And yeah, this self-possessed, powerful, confident businesswoman was most definitely not a kid. Leila had been a lifelong athlete, with dreams of a career in the WNBA before a shoulder injury in her sophomore year of college closed that path for her. Her second passion was Latinx pop music—so she'd come to work for me and had made my life her home court. Beautiful, talented, passionate, funny, ambitious, Leila Baez had stayed here with me when she could've had the world.

Why?

"Vivi, did you hear me?" Her voice pulled me in, dragging me out of musings I had no business indulging in. Things happened in my body as I met her eyes. Molten heat coiled in my lower belly.

Girl, get a hold of your damn self.

"Yeah, I'm ready," I said with a smile, and in that second, I felt like I was talking about a lot more than the photo shoot. She gave me a weird look as she took the empty can from my hand and passed me a lemon-lavender mint from my favorite candy maker in Paris, from whom she ordered in bulk for me.

Always taking care of me.

"Are you sure you're all right?" she whispered close to my ear, making me shiver. I was trembling from something she'd done a million times before. But suddenly, my awareness of her was overpowering.

"I'm good," I insisted for her sake, and for mine. "Let's do this." I pushed the barrage of emotions down as I went to do my job. But I had a feeling that from now on, I would be looking at Leila Baez in a whole different light.

CHAPTER 2

ONE WEEK UNTIL NOCHEBUENA

LEILA

"I'll be right over there, behind the camera guys," I told Viviana Guerra, Latina superstar and gorgeous, perfect human. The woman I'd been in love with for a decade now, who also happened to be my boss.

"Okay," she said in that soft voice she only used in private. In front of the cameras, for the world, Vivi G was a larger-than-life bombshell who loved the spotlight. In private—the way I knew her—she was a gentle, almost shy woman who spent too much time on her own.

"Do we have anything else after this?" she asked, turning her attention away from the hosts of the morning television show she was about to go on to promote her upcoming live Nochebuena special. It was the first of two dozen appearances we'd do in the next five days.

She already looked exhausted.

"No," I said with a shake of my head. Knowing it usually took her a day or two to adjust to the flurry of intrusive questions—and at times, unkind comments—I'd made her schedule lighter on the first and last day. "Just this today. Later we have a wardrobe check and then your sister is bringing the kids for a couple of hours."

"Oh, good." She turned fully around then and smiled at me, that soft one I only ever saw when those she loved were involved. "I thought I wouldn't get a chance to see her before they left for their cruise."

The "cruise" was a private yacht Viviana had rented for a seven-day trip in the South Pacific as a twentieth anniversary present for her sister and brother-in-law. It was an extremely generous gift, but she didn't expect her sister to stop by and say thank you before she went on it. That's how she was, selfless, and I hated that only a few people knew that.

"Five minutes!" the production assistant informed us as she walked across the sound studio to where Yanelis and her two partners were currently canoodling. She'd been in a heated conversation with Viviana before I'd walked up, but she left us alone the moment I returned. That had been happening a lot lately, lots of secretive, hushed conversations that seized as soon as I was within earshot.

"I confirmed they received the disclaimer asking not to mention anything connected to your personal life," I reassured my boss in a whisper, my mouth not too close to her ear, where I could accidentally brush her skin, but near enough that I could see the smattering of freckles on the nape of her neck and shoulders. I leaned back a bit more, just a fraction of a centimeter, and swallowed hard as I got a whiff of her scent. She used a special body wash that smelled like cloves and orange zest, and I was addicted to catching little traces of it through the day. Everything about her was delicious and decidedly not mine.

Not. Mine.

I was so in my head I missed what she said, and then when it registered, I was certain I got it wrong.

"What did you say?" I asked, very careful not to run my finger along the edge of her slouchy, bright-red blouse, which was revealing a whole lot of supple, sun-kissed shoulder.

"I said, I don't mind if they ask me about what I want next." There was something to her posture, the intense way she was looking at me that made my blood rush between my temples.

"I don't understand," I answered dumbly as she flicked those long, curly lashes at me. She shifted in my direction, and I was pinned under that new way she looked at me sometimes. Like she wanted to extract every thought from my brain. It had been happening for weeks now, and I still could not figure out what was happening, other than every time she did it, my entire body went rogue on me. Mouth dry, hands sweating... heart racing. Chaos.

Because something was absolutely up with my boss. Viviana had always looked at me with fondness. She'd been kind and loving to me from the first moment we met. We were close, more than close—I knew her better than anyone else in her life. I was aware of every single thing she loved and loathed. I took care of her. It was my job; more than that, it was my pleasure. But in ten years together, she'd never given me the impression she saw me as more than her friend.

But now, whenever she locked her eyes on me, I felt like I was being torn open.

"I'm serious." She leaned in a little, her proximity making goose-bumps break out all over my body. From that angle, I could see the lacy edge of her red bra under the blouse, and my mouth felt like I'd eaten a fistful of sand. "I don't care if Ruben wants to ask me about my love life. He can ask." She waved her hands, as if the kind of questions she'd obsessively avoided for years were no longer consequential. "Oh!" she exclaimed while I stood there, stunned. "Will you have dinner with me tonight, after Gloria and the kids leave?"

I made myself blink as I struggled for a response, knowing she was about to be called on set. "Uh, yeah. Sure," I mumbled, confused as hell. "You need me to order something? Carbone or—"

"Nope," she said with a shake of her head, then winked at me. My entire lower body felt like it had morphed into Jell-O. "I'll cook. I put an order in this morning."

I forced my mouth open and pushed out words despite being certain I was hallucinating. "*You* ordered groceries?"

Another bright smile, this time paired with a sneak peek of the tip of her very pink tongue between her gleaming white teeth. "I sure did. You know I love ordering stuff on the phone." She held up the latest model of iPhone in her hand like she was presenting me with Exhibit A. "It said it would arrive between noon and 2:00 p.m. So it'll be waiting for us." She did like to personally buy treats for her niece and nephew when they came over—they were eight and ten and loved their sweets—but that was different than buying groceries for dinner. Dinner she would cook for me...

"What are you making?" I fought the urge to narrow my eyes at my boss. Reminding myself of my seven-figure salary did the trick.

"Your favorite."

"My favorite?" Why did I keep responding to everything like a question? Viviana just laughed a twinkling laugh like I was cracking her the hell up.

My favorite food was caldo de bolas verdes, which took hours to make, so...

"Actually, more like your second favorite," she corrected, interrupting my thoughts. "The caldo takes too long and I'm a little rusty, so you'll have to be happy with rice and peas and bistec picado."

As discreetly as I could, I pressed my palm to the left side of my chest, just to make sure my heart didn't burst out of its confinement. I had no idea what was happening, *none*, but my body would not be able to take much more of it.

"In ten!" yelled the PA, and before I could ask Viviana what exactly was going on with her, she and Yanelis were headed up to the stage and greeting the hosts of *Breakfast Bochinche*.

I stood in the spot I'd said I'd be and watched Viviana play the role of Vivi G. The studio was fully decked out in a holiday theme. There were tall silver Christmas trees around the dais where the hosts did the show. Fake snow and lights sparkled all over. She looked radiant among the holiday décor in custom Alexander McQueen cream slacks and red blouse. On her feet were strappy Louboutins, which were embellished with an eye-watering sum of real freaking diamonds. She had her signature hoops on, made of platinum and tiny diamonds. She'd gone for a sleek, high ponytail, baby hair laid in perfect little swirls. Her face was fresh and young, her caramel skin glowing as she smiled at the adoring crowd. She looked to me just like she had the first year I'd started working for her. Only now there was a serenity to her that hadn't been there until recently.

"You've had a big few weeks, ladies," said Ruben Ruiz, the male host of the show, looking between the two pop stars. Viviana grinned at him while Bad Kitty stuck her tongue out, her signature move.

"The new Latina holiday queens," said Carla Camilo, former Miss Universe and co-host of *Bochinche*, with an enthusiastic nod. "You all have the number-one song in the country. 'Navidad with You' is the most streamed holiday song this season."

"That's right," Yanelis crowed. "Me and my girl Vivi showing them how Latinas do." She shook her shoulders with her usual brashness, and the audience loved it. The rapper was a newcomer, but she'd made big moves in the last couple of years. Vivi G's career, on the other hand, had seen a dip. She was a veteran now, part of the old guard to some. Even with this special and new single putting her back in the spotlight, things just weren't like they used to be.

I knew that stuff bothered her, that she'd been worried about being redundant. That she didn't know what she would do with herself if she lost her career. Except right now, as I looked at her, the usual unease at not being the center of attention was not there. She only smiled indulgently at Bad Kitty's antics, content to be in the background for once. Eventually the hosts turned their attention back to her, and she took her time responding to their question.

"It's been a good year," Viviana finally said, and I grimaced at the opening she'd just given Ruben, who was notorious for using any excuse to go for the jugular.

"It didn't start off *that* great," he said with that benign smile. The man had verbally eviscerated thousands of guests while deploying that "sweet abuelito" expression. "I heard you even made a vow of celibacy for your New Year's resolution."

That cabrón.

Furious, I took a step forward, not caring if anyone heard me. He knew perfectly well the breakup was off limits. Ruben was not going to make a fool out of Viviana, not on my watch.

I unclipped my walkie-talkie from my belt with every intention of forcing them to go to a commercial break when Vivi found my gaze and gave a shake of her head. Nothing anyone watching at home, or even in the live audience would've noticed. But when your every waking moment was spent anticipating Viviana Guerra's needs, you learned to recognize when she was giving out a distress signal and when she wasn't.

"I think we should focus on the positives—these are the holidays, after all," Yanelis told Ruben with a pugnacious smile on her face. But Vivi once again didn't seem to find the man's words upsetting.

"It's fine, Kitty," Viviana said, then turned to Ruben and Camila. "The truth is my year got off on a seriously wrong foot. Once again, what I thought was my happily ever after turned out to be not so happy," she told them with such vulnerability I choked up. I hated this. Hated that she was putting her heart out there like that for people who just wanted to drum up some juicy sound bites for clicks. "And it's true..." She laughed then, waving her hand. "Well, not about the celibacy." The audience laughed, and she beamed. She wrecked me without even trying. "But I did take this year to reflect on what I wanted. I also made a point to practice some gratitude for the many riches I already have."

She turned so her entire body was facing the audience, but her gaze—that golden, warm gaze—was locked on me. I had to remind myself to breathe so I didn't black out.

"I've been blessed with a long career in a business that rarely allows women like me in. I've done things my way, and at times that's meant I've rubbed some people the wrong way." She cupped her hands around her mouth and fake-whispered, "Men. I've made a lot of them real mad." This time, the audience roared. She had them in the palm of her hand. "I've decided that I'm ready to make some drastic changes, to reach for the gifts that have been offered to me that I have not been smart enough to take."

Her eyes were burning me now, my skin prickled under her attention. *What was happening?*

"I'm ready now." She said it looking in my direction, as if the words were meant for me.

I was not the only one sensing that, despite the casual demeanor and easy smile, Viviana meant every word she said. That whatever was coming would be monumental. For a beat, the audience, the hosts, and Yanelis seemed to be frozen, as if we were all holding our breath for her big reveal. But after a moment, she tapped Ruben on the knee and laughed.

"You're not getting the exclusive, Ruben." He pouted, and she grinned evilly. "Let's talk about the Nochebuena Special! That's what we're here for!"

After that, both Vivi and Yanelis launched into the details of the production happening in a week. They both smiled for the camera and even teased a few of the original songs they'd do together. By the time she walked offstage and came looking for me, I could passably fake like whatever I had seen in her eyes hadn't upended my world.

CHAPTER 3

VIVI

Just ask her, you dummy. You've done the electric slide with Obama—you can ask this woman a simple question.

"This was really good," Leila said from across the small table in my kitchen. "Thank you for making it." She still sounded kind of confused, but was rolling with it.

"You're welcome. Thanks for eating with me."

She didn't respond, just looked at me with those piercing brown eyes that in the last two months had become an obsession. She'd been unusually quiet while we ate. Actually, she'd been quiet since we'd gotten out of the *Bochinche* studios.

At dinner, we'd kept to discussing the appearances for the next day. We always ran over details the night before. Busy days could be unpredictable, and I liked to have a plan. Leila did too—that's why we were so good together.

But surprisingly, something that had yet to come up was what I'd said during *Breakfast Bochinche*. The hosts had gone off script, and that was usually the kind of thing she would be heated about, the sort of faux pas that would have her on the phone to executives in a hot second, but she had yet to mention any of it. I could not help but think that her silence was connected to what I was itching to ask her.

I'd been hyping myself up the entire time it took to make the food —once I figured out how to turn the oven on, that is. It had been at least a couple of hours since my sister and her kids had come through, and I still could not make myself do it.

I stood abruptly, reaching for her plate, but she swiftly moved it out of the way and plucked mine off the table, to boot. "Nada de eso," she said with a shake of her head.

"But you're my guest." I balked, panicking at the idea that she'd clean up and head home before I could work myself up to telling her.

"You cook, I clean. That's the rule." She made quick work of cleaning up the table and was at the sink in seconds. That was Leila: take care of A before getting to B. "Keep me company," she said in that raspy, low voice of hers. The sound crawled up my spine, tickling every nerve.

It was funny, this thing that was happening with Leila. Usually, the moment I decided I wanted someone, I could not keep it in. I'd shout it from the rooftops before I had to time to truly think about what was happening. I threw myself into it, buying over-the-top gifts. I'd bought custom Lamborghinis for men after the first date. I'd thrown parties in private islands to commemorate a one-month anniversary. I did the absolute most, eager to take big bites out that rush of falling for someone before it wore off. With Leila, I wanted to stop, take my time.

I'd spent days mulling over what it was about the way she drank her coffee that made my heart skip. Why the one curl which never seemed to want to stay in place on her forehead made my chest all warm and gooey. Why suddenly everything about her made me deliriously happy. I could feel the difference in me. I wanted to do this; I wanted her. But this feeling was like a good Dominican sancocho. I knew if I let it simmer longer and let it develop fully, once I tasted it, it would be so damn good, I'd be ruined for anything else.

Yeah... I would freak her out if I unloaded all that on her. I wouldn't even hold it against her if she ran out on me.

"Viviana, you're tired." Leila said, pulling me from my thoughts. The next thing out of her mouth would be *go to bed*, and my moment would be ruined.

"I don't want to go to bed yet," I blurted out as she closed the door to the dishwasher, the kitchen neat and orderly in a matter of minutes.

"Okaaaay." She dragged out the word as she dried her hands on a tea towel. Her mouth was pursed and her eyebrows knitted together as she looked at me. "We have a long day tomorrow, though." She glanced at the clock. It was barely 9:00 p.m.

Do it. Just ask her, dammit. If you let her walk out of this house, you won't ever do it.

"Why are you spending your Saturday night with me and not out on a date?" Oh yeah, prying into her private life with a defensive tone was totally how I would woo my manager into this holiday romance fantasy I was cooking up.

I braced myself for the awkwardness that would follow, but I should've expected Leila to handle things with all the chill.

"Por que, you asked me to dinner." She sounded amused enough, but her eyes were practically drilling a hole in my forehead. Leila was much taller than me, an inch under six feet tall. I was five-three in my stockings. We were still in the kitchen, her leaning on the counter, me sitting on the island a few feet away. Everything about her stance evoked repose, total and absolute calm, but if you knew what to look for—teeth gnawing on her bottom lip, knuckles gripping the countertop a little too tightly—you could see the tension there.

She was in one of her casual fits. Dark green joggers and matching hoodie, black crew socks. I was wearing the exact same set in Christmas red. I imagined what it would be like if I just went to her, stepped into her space. Would she hold me? Would she kiss me?

The very thought made my skin tighten, flush with heat. How could something I'd rarely thought about before consume me like this? *Days*, I'd spent days wondering what it would be like to press up to her, part my lips, and feel her tongue slide inside. Guessing whether she'd make a sound of pleasure when I carded my hands through her hair. Whether she'd make the same one if I pulled on it while I kissed her.

Focus, Viviana. FOCUS.

"I didn't mean just today," I said, flustered, and saw something flash in her eyes. Something wary but hopeful in her expression. "I meant that you could be out at clubs, dating, spending all the money you make, but most weekends you're here with me."

"That's not true," she retorted, a bit guarded. "When you've been involved, I'm usually not around on the weekends."

Ouch. Also, truth.

She pushed off the counter and took the two steps to get to me. My breath caught when she placed her hands on either side of my hips and looked at me. I held my breath so she couldn't see how fast it was coming.

"I like spending time with you," she said in an easy, breezy tone. She was as unbothered as she always seemed to be, but when I glanced at her, I saw it. She was shaking a little bit, and her throat kept moving, like she was trying to swallow, but it wouldn't take.

"But you don't date," I countered.

"Who says I don't?" she offered in that infuriatingly vague way of hers.

"Are you seeing someone?" I asked more forcefully than I had any right to, and her mouth tipped up into a knowing smile that practically screamed *gotcha!*

"Why are you suddenly wondering what I do with my time outside of the job, Viviana? What's this really about?" I had a feeling she already knew the answer. Her nostrils flared as she looked at me.

"I..."

"You...?" she asked, her voice strong now and very serious. Our faces were only inches apart. God, she was so beautiful. It's not like I hadn't been aware of it. Leila—with her height, that strong nose, lush mouth, and perfect cheekbones—was striking. That plus the self-assured, no-nonsense way she carried herself—she was not a woman to go unnoticed. But now it wasn't something I was merely aware of. Now she was the only thing I could see. She flooded my senses. I was too aware of her. Of how much I wanted her, and I just... I had to know.

"I don't want to ruin things between us," I finally said. She simply angled her head to the side and waited.

"You're going to have to say it, Vivi," she pushed, using the shortened version of my name. She rarely ever did that. Maybe that meant something, and I would probably figure out what that was if I didn't keep getting distracted by how good she smelled. Like cedar soap and the yerba buena from the mojito she'd made for us.

"I want you. I'm attracted to you," I finally whispered, my voice so small I could barely hear it. "But I don't want to make you feel uncomfortable. I don't want you to feel weird about it." I was totally freaking out. I put my hands to my face and squeezed my eyes. "Dammit."

"Vivi." Her strong voice hit my nervous system like a live wire. Every nerve ending was fully awake. "Look at me."

I spread the two fingers covering one of my eyes and looked at her. She was grinning at me, her face flushed, eyes bright, and my heart was beating in my chest like a drum.

"This isn't bad news." She looked... happy?

"I'm your boss," I moaned.

"Because *I* want it that way," she told me. "It would take one text message, and I could have half a dozen offers for work. I work with you because I respect you. I believe in what you do, in the art you make. Because I have never met anyone with the work ethic you have." She winked at me and pushed just a tiny bit closer. I was still hiding behind my hands. "I need you to know something."

"Okay." Was that mousy thing my voice? I had headlined Coachella, for fuck's sake!

"If we do this..." Her heat was melting me. I wanted to touch her so bad. "It's going to be *a thing*."

"A thing?"

"A kissing, fucking, keep you horizontal for days, bring you breakfast in bed just to keep you in it kind of thing."

My breath hitched in response to the possessive heat in her eyes, at the graze of her fingers on my ass. She glanced down at the apex of my thighs and licked her lips.

I was getting wet... from a look.

"What if things don't work out?" I croaked. "My track record is not exactly stellar." Self-mockery was the only weapon I had at the moment. But she rolled her eyes as if all of that was inconsequential.

"None of those men knew what they had. They wanted Vivi G, the fantasy. I want this," she said, running a hand over the inside of my thigh. "I want Viviana Guerra. That's who I've wanted for years now."

"Years?" I couldn't help it—I whimpered then, pressed myself to her touch.

"So many." Her smile turned a bit sharp at whatever she was thinking.

"Why aren't you weirded out or pissed off that I'm getting all bi-curious on you?" I asked, and that time her head did snap back in surprise.

She gave me a long, considering look, and before she answered, she gripped my butt and brought me forward so I was flush against her. Just in case I was wondering where the conversation was going.

She was so fucking hot. I felt like I was on fire. How was I the novice in this situation when I had a full decade on Leila?

"For one..." She frowned, no longer amused. "*Bi-curious* is a word for people still hanging on to binaries and shit that I have no use for. Two, people's sexualities, people's *desires* are complicated." It was hard to focus when she kept rubbing circles right on the pulse point of my throat, but I did my best to listen instead of begging her to kiss me and put me out of my misery. "Viviana, you grew up in the DR in the '80s and '90s. How many Dominican women that you knew were out as bisexual? How many times did you hear the adults around you saying horrible homophobic shit?"

None and *all the fucking time* were the answers. "But maybe there were, and I just didn't look. I just hid this from myself." It was something I'd been thinking about almost as much as I'd been fixating on how much I wanted Leila. Maybe I'd avoided thinking about it because, in a lot of ways, defaulting to being "straight" made my life easier. I knew it was true, none of these things were simple, but I still felt guilty. Like I'd let myself down.

"No," Leila snapped, making me look up. She was frowning, her expression full of concern. "Whatever is going through your head, put it out right now. Coming out to yourself is not on anyone's timeline."

Coming out. A breath shuddered out of me. I wasn't scared, though. I knew what fear felt like, and this wasn't it. But there was definitely something happening inside me that I hadn't experienced before. Leila leaned in, brushed the back of her knuckles over my cheek, my lips. I shook with need.

"There is no wrong way to do this. Just *your* way. I'm not surprised you didn't explore that part of your sexuality. People see you, and they assume something, and sometimes it's just easier to go with it." Was she reading my mind? "We're socialized to be one thing, and it can be a journey before we're ready to challenge that. When exactly would it have been safe for you to explore that side of you, with your ultra-machista dad saying you needed to find a good man and make some babies all the fucking time?" That truth almost took me out.

I winced, thinking about my dad. He loved me, yes, but he was conservative and antiquated and still did not approve of my "life choices." Even when those choices provided not only for him, but for our whole family.

"By the time I was coming up, things were not great, but they *were* better," Leila said, pulling me out of my thoughts. "The truth is that I didn't have to look so hard to answer the questions I had about who I wanted. You didn't have that growing up. The important thing is that you're here now and you're open to new things. New possibilities. I'm not just saying this because it's with me either. I'd encourage you no matter what. I mean that."

"I know." And I did.

She smiled wryly and ran her hand over the mop of curls on top of her head. Just a little self-conscious thing she did when she was trying hard to show she was in control but was in over her head. She wasn't the only one who paid attention. And honestly, knowing this was getting to her too made me feel better.

This mattered to both of us.

"I don't want to mess things up," I confessed, burning up for her already.

"You won't," she assured me, and I desperately wanted to believe her. Because this whole thing was starting to feel a lot like my Christmas wish.

"I want to kiss you real bad," I blurted out. I could barely think from how much I wanted it.

Without a word, she helped me down from the counter and led me to the luxurious white couch in front of the fireplace. The lights were low and it smelled like fresh pine from the garland and wreaths. Through the windows, the Brooklyn Bridge shone with its own white flickering lights. It felt like the kind of night when a Christmas miracle could happen.

We stood on the plush carpet holding hands, and then Leila brought me closer. I shivered, though the room was toasty.

"Come here," she said quietly, like she didn't want to spook me. I let her hold me and something electric licked up my spine from her touch. She was slender but strong, lean muscle and sinew. I was all curves, with boobs and a butt people talked about like they were separate entities from me.

I'd grown used to the men I dated going straight for them. Groping, squeezing, getting to touch that ten-million-dollar ass other guys fantasized about. But Leila was focused on my face, her hands tight on my lower back.

"I'm going to kiss you, Vivi," she said breathlessly, and I nodded, swallowing hard.

I pushed up to reach for her, circling my arms around her neck while she gripped my waist. My heart skipped and skittered while what felt like a swarm of bees took residence in my stomach. I gasped at the friction of our chests brushing against each other. She lifted a hand and palmed my cheek so tenderly, I choked up from emotion.

"Tan bella," she said, awe in her voice, and my heart thumped so hard, I thought I could hear it. My mind flooded with *kiss me, kiss me, kiss me.*

She leaned down agonizingly slow, as if giving me a chance to change my mind. I clutched the sides of her sweatshirt, my way of telling her that I wasn't going anywhere. I strained up to reach her mouth, eager to feel it crushed against mine.

"Leila," I said, need roaring inside me. Her eyes burned as she looked at me, and when I licked my bottom lip, a pained groan escaped from her.

"I want to make this good for you," she confessed, biting the inside of her cheek. I could not take it anymore.

"Besame, Leila!" I growled, making her laugh, then grabbed the back of her head with both hands and pressed our mouths together.

I parted my lips, inviting her in, and she slid her tongue inside, coaxing mine. I felt that kiss in my core, the thrill of it pulsing through my body. Leila kept her hands on my hips as she took my mouth with breathtaking expertise. She would pull back and glide the tip of her tongue along the seam of my mouth and lick in again. As if she wanted to explore every corner. An invasion, a conquering.

I was aggressive, needy as I kissed her, sipping and biting, learning her taste.

"Mm." I gasped, needing things I didn't know how to ask.

She dropped down onto the couch, bringing me with her. I surprised myself by sitting astride her lap. I was typically cautious when things got physical. People likely thought I was happy to be naked with as much as I showed my body, but I was weirdly self-conscious about it. For all that I was the vixen in the videos, under the clothes and shapewear, there were scars from surgeries to make my body perfect for the cameras.

Still, there were stretch marks and dimples. There were imperfections, and over my career, I'd learned the hard way that for some, imperfections were unforgivable. But Leila knew those scars. She knew the ones that couldn't be seen too. With Leila, I wanted to get close so much, I didn't care. I couldn't remember the last time I'd felt this free, this turned on. She sucked her teeth as I circled my hips into her. Grinding together, it was so good. For once I felt free.

"I want to see you," she whispered in my ear, then moved that hot mouth to my neck, grazing skin with teeth as her hands possessed every inch they touched.

I leaned back, looking at her, and lifted my sweatshirt over my head, and the panic that usually came with having someone see me this close with the lights on never came. I was too focused on the way Leila was looking at me. I had on a soft bra with a zipper front. Leila sucked in a breath as she lowered it. My breasts popped out of the enclosure, bouncing heavily.

"They're too big." I wasn't even sure why I said it, but she only shook her head.

"Viviana, you don't know. My mouth is watering, baby." Her eyes were locked on the hard brown tips of my breasts, hands cupping me. My clit throbbed, liquid pooling between my legs. "I'm going to suck on them, okay?" She was so straightforward about it, so direct. She wanted me and was asking if she could have me.

I could not say yes fast enough.

Oh God, her mouth. She kneaded both my breasts in her hands and just looked at them. I gasped as she touched me. She brushed her thumbs over my nipples, eyes fixed on what she was doing.

"You like that?" she asked as she tweaked a nipple, then flicked it with a short nail.

"Oh shit," I moaned, thrusting my hips. "You found a live wire between my nipple and my clit." I gasped, and she did it again. Then she laughed a dirty, wicked laugh and added her tongue to the mix. She took one of my tits in as much as she could, tongue flicking and swirling around the nipple.

I threw my head back, pushing up into that wet, filthy caress. She slowly pulled off with a pop, then went back in to suckle it again.

"Your skin tastes so good." Leila's lips moved against the hard tips of my breasts when she spoke. Her eyes were hazy from arousal, her lips bruised from her efforts. I didn't think I'd ever seen anything sexier than Leila Baez poised to wreck me with her mouth and hands.

"Taste the other one?" I asked, a little bolder now.

"Greedy." She grinned as she kept tweaking and pinching, then with the flat of her tongue, she lapped at me like I was a lollipop.

"I could only imagine what that tongue would do to my pussy."

She laughed again, and oh... yeah, I said that out loud.

I didn't care.

I was already addicted, and it had only been a few minutes. While other lovers made a show of having me, almost as if they were performing, Leila's sole focus was my pleasure. If I moved into one of her caresses, she'd do it again and again. Then she'd try something new until she had me writhing against her. She made love to my tits until I was practically weeping, then slowly lowered her hand to where I needed her.

She palmed me over my sweats, and I wondered if her hand burned with my heat.

"Can I?" she asked, looking straight into my eyes.

"Ah," I gasped, as she pressed the heel of her hand into my clit, making a sweet shiver course through my limbs. "Yes," I told her, and in an instant, I was being pulled to the bedroom.

"I want to do this in a bed," she answered before I could ask the question. "I want to take my time, this first time."

"You really want this?" I sounded like some silly teenage girl, but God, no one, not ever, had looked at me like that.

She only shook her head, a helpless little laugh escaping her lips. "Baby, I want it all."

I knew what I looked like—I was no stranger to being lusted after, to having men's hungry, possessive eyes on me. If I was honest, I got off on it. I liked having that effect on people. It was bit of a power thing for me to stay aloof, to see the other person heated and frantic while I remained collected.

With Leila, I was poised to be fully undone.

CHAPTER 4

LEILA

The dream had been good, but reality was much *much* better.

Like Christmas miracle–level fantastic.

That was the truth of it. The other truth was that I knew this was going to wreck me. This night, with this woman I'd been in love with for ten years, was going to ruin me, and I would kill anyone who tried to stop me from having her.

I led her into the bedroom that I'd been in hundreds of times, and it was almost surreal to be here with her like this. I'd been here the day she moved in, thinking this would be the apartment she would live in with the TV producer who'd turned out to have a wife he'd forgotten to mention. I helped her buy a new bed when the one he'd slept on had been donated to Goodwill. I knew the thread count on the sheets, and I knew there was a sleep mask and a satin bonnet under the pillow.

I knew *everything* about this woman, and yet it felt like I was looking at the four-poster king bed, packed with fluffy white pillows, for the first time. And it was a first time. I didn't dare hope for more nights like this, but I wanted them. I wanted her so much, I shook from it.

We'd lost a lot of the clothes between the living room and the bedroom, but there was still a bit of lace and satin covering her pussy. I wanted to rip it off with my teeth.

"Sit on the edge of the bed for me?" I asked. She moved slowly, languidly, as if she was aware of every muscle in her body. Her eyes were low-lidded and dreamy when she finally looked at me. Her chest rose and fell as harsh breaths sawed out of her.

"Are you turned on, chula?" I asked, sounding more confident than I felt.

"So much." Her voice was clear, unashamed, and my whole body swelled with love for her. For her open and brave heart.

"Can I tell you what I want?"

Another nod, and I went down on my knees for her.

"I want a taste." I placed the palms of my hands on her knees and pulled them apart.

"Yes." Her thong was a dark burgundy and I could see a spot of wetness there. She'd soaked her panties already and was panting. I had to breathe through my nose. I was so turned on, my skin felt like it was on fire.

"First, I want to see." I slid my hands up her inner thighs until I was framing her cunt with my hands. "Pull the thong to the side with your finger," I ordered, and she tugged on it.

She was... she was everything. Smooth and bare brown labia, and that pink bud engorged and begging for my attention. Dewy lips and folds that I wanted to suck and lick for hours.

I was going to gorge myself on her. I wouldn't stop until she was screaming my name.

"Fuck, Vivi," I breathed out, swallowing hard. I ran my thumb over her labia, then dipped it into the furrow. "Hot and slick. I can't wait to eat this cunt."

She groaned and swiveled her hips like she wanted to fuck my fingers.

"Save those good thrusts for when I sit you on my face later." She clenched on my finger.

Our eyes were locked as I touched her. I played with her while I watched her reactions. I ran the pads of my fingers over her, dipped them in, and clit got harder and her harder. Then I went for it.

"Juicy and throbbing for me," I moaned as I rubbed her the little bud in tight circles, and her mouth went slack. I dipped another finger inside and she rocked into it. I was desperate to put my mouth on her.

"Leila," she gasped, holding the back of my head with her hands.

"You're gorgeous," I said in a reverent whisper as I touched her with trembling hands. She leaned back, and those beautiful tits swayed with her breaths. I would have to go back to them soon. But now, this. The very core of her was the only thing I could think of.

I snaked my tongue over her furrow gently, ready for more...

"Wait," she said, and I immediately retreated, my heart trying its best to lodge in my throat. By the time I glanced up at her, I could tell something was wrong. She seemed worried.

Disappointment flooded me, but I made myself say it.

"Viviana," I said, pulling back so there was some distance between us. "We don't have to do this if you're not sure."

"No, please, it's not that." She shook her head furiously and reached for my hands as she squeezed her eyes shut.

"I have a confession to make..." She paused there and took a few breaths. Whatever it was, she was mortified. What could possibly make this woman, who I'd seen face down boardrooms full of men, look like she wanted to disappear? I suspected it was some asshole's fault, and I was ready to fight somebody.

"It's okay, babe," I said soothingly, caressing her palm with my thumb.

"I just..." She gulped, eyes still closed. "I have a really hard time reaching orgasm. It can be frustrating for my partners."

"Oh, babe," I said, furious on her behalf.

She extracted her hands from mine then, covering her face, an embarrassed laugh coming out of her. My heart and gut clenched for her.

"This is so pathetic—I'm a forty-five-year-old woman who has made a career out of being a sex symbol and I can't remember the last time I had an orgasm during sex." She looked so miserable, and I seriously wanted to go and look for the assholes she'd been sleeping with and ask them what the fuck was wrong with them.

"Sweetheart, that's fine," I tried to reassure her, but misery was rolling off her in waves. "Not everyone can come on command—every body is different, the mood needs to be right, you're under so much stress all the time." Her shoulders relaxed somewhat at that. "You have to be *on* all the time. I'm not surprised it can be hard to let go."

She shook her head again, hand still over her eyes. She looked so adorable, I just wanted to put her on my lap and rock her.

"It's not just that." She sounded so miserable. I fucking hated this for her. "Whenever I'm with someone new, I keep thinking that if they see the real me, they'll feel cheated or something." She sighed, hands falling to her sides.

"Because you feel like you have to give them Vivi G."

She nodded, a shaky breath escaping her lips. "It's so exhausting."

I knew right then and there I'd kill for this woman.

"Can you come when you're on your own?" I probed a bit, and instead of answering right away, she reached for my hand. Her cheeks flushed a little, and I bit back a smile. "You're blushing."

Viviana Guerra's shy smiles were a fucking life altering revelation.

"I can." She kept her gaze on the place where our hands were joined together. "Come on my own, I mean. I... ah... I've kind of been exploring that lately." She let the words drift, and I had to work very hard not to push. I was vibrating with the need to hear exactly in which scenarios she could orgasm, especially when she was giving me those shy looks.

"Oh?" I finally asked as my heart began to race.

"I've been looking at some adult content, to figure out the things I like."

God, that was so fucking hot.

"What kind of content?"

"Just figuring out what turns me on." Her blush had deepened and there were two little red circles on the apples of her cheeks. Her neck was flushed pink too. Yeah, I was barely hanging on to control.

"Do you touch yourself?" I asked, taking a chance.

She sucked in a breath at my question, and her fingers gripped mine almost painfully.

"Yes."

My clit throbbed and I could feel my nipples hardening against the cotton of my bra. This was the most erotic thing ever and we were barely touching.

"Your clit? You spread your pussy and touch yourself until you fall apart?"

I got a quick nod and deeper flush on her cheeks. I was into the game now, though.

"Do you use toys?"

"Mm-hm." She cleared her throat. "Yanelis sent me that box with all the stuff from her line," she explained, and shot a glance at the table by her bed. Bad Kitty's adult toy brand had launched recently, and everyone was talking about it. I'd gotten a gift box too but had yet to try them. But Vivi seemed to have partaken, and I approved whole-heartedly.

"There's one I like a lot." She closed her eyes again and this time, pointed in the direction of the bedside table.

"Can I see?"

Another shy nod. As far as foreplay went, this was A-plus content. Fuuuck.

I untangled our fingers and walked around the bed to the drawer. I smiled when I pulled it open because everything was so neat and organized. There were a couple of toys still in the box with the plastic, and there was one little black velvet pouch which I assumed was the one she'd been using. It was a clit stimulator from the look of it—round, lavender, and shaped like a huge ring. I turned it on, and Leila jumped when the toy started quietly buzzing. And yup, the little ball next to the power button applied some serious pressure. The thought of her watching porn and pressing this toy to her pussy was... damn.

"How hard do you make yourself come with this?" I asked, intentionally casual. Like we were talking about shoes or something. Her legs splayed open a little wider.

"So intense," she said breathlessly, eyes closed again, head thrown back. "I watch my favorites and then I imagine it's us. That your hands are the ones working me. Your thumbs pinching my pussy lips, and your tongue flicking my clit." Holy shit... yeah, I should've known Vivi wasn't going to let me down. "Your head between my legs and your fingers inside me. I go off like a rocket, every single time." She moaned like I was getting her off right then, and I clenched my teeth to keep from pouncing.

"What else do you do?" I asked, mouth dry. I couldn't swallow if I tried.

"I pinch my nipples... hard."

"Will you let me see?" I blurted out. My mind was a blur of X-rated images, starring Viviana Guerra.

She hesitated, the softness in her posture going rigid just for a moment.

"I... all right," she finally said.

"It's okay if you don't want to," I hurried to reassure her, already regretting making her feel pressured. "We can take this as slow as you need to. We can stop for now—"

"No," she said, reaching for me. "I don't want to stop."

I was not strong enough to refuse her when she was buck naked and pulling me into bed with her. Especially not after that play-by-play of how she worked her pussy while thinking of me.

"Okay, but if you'd rather close your eyes or leave the light off, we can do that too."

It hurt to say that, but I also knew this was a lot of uncharted territory for her. Maybe she could do the fantasy on the screen but wasn't quite ready to touch or fuck with a living person with a pussy.

"Stop it, Leila," she said, voice hard and strong. "Whatever is going through your head, I guarantee you it's not it." This was the voice of the Viviana Guerra I'd seen dress down heads of music studios. "I want to do this with the lights on, with my eyes wide open. I want to be with *you*. It's just I want to be good for you too, and I know I can be a little weird in bed."

I would happily punch every man who'd made this woman feel like their issues were her fault right on the fucking mouth.

"Babe," I said, leaning on the bed until I could reach her. I kissed her then, tongue sliding inside. Without hesitation she took me in hungrily, teeth scraping a little as she sucked on my bottom lip.

Mmm, shit. Yeah. It was on.

I pulled back, shaking my head. Shivers running through my body.

"I'm almost coming just from seeing your nipples all tight and rosy from my teeth," I told her, and she laughed. I angled my head in the direction of the bathroom. "I'm going to wash that toy, and then we're taking care of this." I palmed her crotch and slid my thumb between her labia just a little, knowing the scrape of the lace would feel good.

She hissed and I pinched her mons.

"I'm going to own this kitty tonight," I warned, and Viviana's eyes glazed over.

I made quick work of washing the toy, and by the time I came back, she was sitting against the headboard, legs spread wide. From the foot of the bed, I got a full view of her wetness. I wanted to dive in face first and let her ride my tongue until she came on it.

But this needed to be *only* about what Vivi wanted. For now.

"I want to see you too," she said, swirling a finger in the air.

"You want to see me naked?" I asked as I peeled myself out of my joggers and briefs. "This too?" I had my hands on the hem of my bra.

"Por favor." Her voice was sweet as honey. If I thought I was in trouble before, I was truly screwed now. No way I could deny this woman anything.

"Since you asked so nicely."

She moaned at the sight of my breasts. I'd had a reduction in college and was a little self-conscious of how visible the incisions were, but Viviana knew all about scars and the visible traces of what women's bodies endured.

"Come closer," she said, beckoning me with a crook of her finger, and for the first time that night, the power shifted in the room.

Suddenly, I was the prey.

I crawled on the bed, the toy in one hand, and got close enough that she could reach me. She looked at me as she cupped my breasts, feeling them tenderly, sweetly touching.

It was an achingly gentle exploration. One hand slid down between my legs, and I trembled. I was not bare like her, but I kept things trimmed down there. She rubbed her hand over it.

"I like this," she said, as I rolled my hips into the touch.

"You can have it," I told her breathlessly. "You can have anything you want."

She already did. Had my heart and likely my fucking soul too, but that was a lot to bring into this moment. For now, I wanted to watch her come.

I lifted the lavender toy, and she grinned. "How are we going to do it?"

"I'm going to sit behind you so I can watch." I was taller than she was, and with her leaning on me, I'd get a great view.

"Okay." We moved around until my back was pressed to the decadent velvet headboard of her bed, and she was sitting between my legs. She put her own legs over my thighs, spreading them wide for my view, toy in her hand.

"Can I play with your tits?" I asked as she leaned her head on my shoulder.

"Yeah."

I cupped one, taking the nipple between my fingers, and started massaging. "Let me see you work that pussy." I sounded like I'd pounded ten shots of bourbon in a row. With two fingers Viviana spread her labia wide; her clit was red and engorged. I swallowed down a moan at the sight.

"Mm," she moaned, and bucked into me the moment she pressed the toy to her clit.

"Those little sounds you make get me so fucking wet," I told her before bending to kiss her neck.

She gasped as I licked her skin, and she let her legs fall open a bit more. My eyes were locked on what she was doing. With one hand, she was tugging up her mons, exposing her engorged nub, and with the other she pressed the toy to it. She moved the ring in circles and pushed her hips into the toy like she was fucking it. It was so damn hot. This body I'd seen move on stages for so many years was now in my arms, doing an erotic dance that was just for me. My skin was tight and hot from lust.

"That's so sexy, baby, look at all that cream." I licked my lips and pinched a nipple. "I want a taste—can I get a taste?" I begged, and she nodded. I swiped my thumb over her furrow and then popped it into my mouth, sucking on it next to her ear.

"Mm, you taste so good, I can't wait to eat it," I growled, and felt her stiffen. Her breath caught and her legs started to tremble. "Fuck yeah, those sounds you make, mi cielo." I was holding her open now so she could slide two fingers inside. "That's good, get it ready for me. I'm gonna do you with my tongue." I bit her neck, just a little bit, and she bucked against me. "Gonna get so deep inside, I'll be tasting you for days."

"Oh my God," she moaned, then gasped, chest rising and falling. "I'm coming already." Her voice was reedy and full of surprise. She rocked against me, the toy tightly pressed to her clit as she let out these little cries that drove me crazy.

"That's it, sweetheart. So pretty." I hooked one of my hands under one of her knees, opening her wider. I was dying to add a finger to hers, watch it go in and out of her, but I wanted to leave the control of this orgasm to her. It was so fucking hot to see her like this, chasing her climax, lost to it. Her back bowed as it hit her, her eyes squeezing shut, and she screamed. I almost came right then too.

After a few breathless moments, she slumped, boneless and sated. "Mm," she groaned as I circled my arms around her. "That was amazing. The best orgasm of my life." Her voice was full of awe and my heart both ached for her and soared at once. I was so fucking happy I got to do this with her.

"That was hands down the sexiest thing I've ever seen in my life," I told her sincerely.

She opened her eyes and looked at me dreamily.

"Are you feeling okay?" I asked, a little self-conscious.

Her mouth tipped up into a blissed-out smile, and my heart kicked up in my chest.

"I am amazing. I want more," she said cheekily, and it felt like the blood started flowing in my veins again.

I sank into the bed with her and took Viviana into my arms. Our legs tangled together, breasts bumping against each other as we learned how to be joined like this. I'd touched this woman for years, felt like there was very little of her I didn't know. Yet when we lined up together and she could kiss my neck, it felt like discovering the secret of the universe.

Her hands moved on me, fingers tentatively grazing my skin.

"Touch whatever you want, babe," I said as she lightly tapped one of my nipples.

"Anything I want?" she asked, brazen, sitting up so she could straddle my thighs.

I couldn't stop looking at her pussy.

"You see something you like?" she asked as my tongue swiped my lower lip, searching for a trace of her. Her pussy was a little rosier now that she'd touched herself. I was dying for another taste.

"I'm going to have some of that later," I told her as I pierced her with my thumb, dipping into that scorching heat.

"I want you to." She let me touch her some more for a few seconds, then pulled away. "Wait," she said, blocking my hand and palming herself with the other. She looked so damn cute. "I want to do you now. It's only fair."

"Oh yeah? Where are you planning to start?" I asked, bringing my arms behind my head as my core clenched at the thought of Vivi's hands on me.

"Do you like having your nipples touched?" she asked, getting a fucking gold star in consent.

"I do," I admitted. She raised an eyebrow in question, hand hovering over my breast. "Go for it."

And boy, did she.

That's when the Viviana Guerra who twenty years ago had taken the entertainment world by storm made an appearance. This was a woman who never half-assed anything. That very included her first foray into kissing a woman's breasts.

She started with little cat licks that had me fisting my hands. Then she cupped one and brought it to her mouth and blew my damn mind. She would suck and then flick my nipple, swirl her tongue around the areola while tweaking and pinching the other breast. Used her teeth on the tip and blew on the sensitive skin. Again and again she did this until I was writhing under her, on the cusp of orgasm just from her playing with my breasts.

"Mm, I love that," she said, going in for a kiss. I opened for her hungrily. I wanted more, but I didn't want to freak her out—this was all new to her. I would not pressure her into something she wasn't ready for, so I kissed her hard, letting my hands roam down to her ass and palming it as she rocked into me.

"Can we?" Vivi asked against my mouth, moving so our pussies were lining up.

Where the hell did she even...?

She pushed up, sitting so that we were locked together, and laughed at whatever she saw on my face. "Porn exists, Leila. The thought of doing this with you didn't just pop into my head today. I told you, I've been looking into things..."

She was going to kill me.

"Is this okay?" she asked as she rolled her hips into me, our folds rubbing deliciously.

"Yeah," I grunted. "That's good... it's great." She went from slow, tentative movements to a steady back-and-forth that had me on the verge on coming within seconds.

"Don't stop, baby," I begged through gritted teeth as she braced herself on her hands and fucked in earnest.

"God, this is so good, and you're so hot down there," she gasped. "My pussy's tingling from the friction," she said in awe. I would very likely not survive this night. The orgasm started in my groin as we thrust into each other. I reached up and rubbed that little nub between her legs, making her moan. Waves of pleasure turned my limbs molten, and soon I was sinking into it, brain whiting out from sheer pleasure. I heard myself cry out as stars burst behind my eyelids.

After a moment, I felt Vivi slump into me, pressing kisses into my neck, my jaw, my cheeks, my eyelids.

"You are the best Christmas gift," she whispered, and she sounded so content my heart lurched in my chest.

"Christmas isn't for another week," I said as I fumbled for the covers, lifting them on top of us.

"Santa came early this year, then," she said, then after a moment burst out laughing. "I didn't mean it that way!"

CHAPTER 5

NOCHEBUENA

VIVI

"Come here a second, I have to show you something," I coaxed Leila, who was sitting on the other end of the backseat of the Escalade currently driving us to the studio.

We were only hours from the live airing. The buzz for the show had snowballed in the last week as "Navidad with You" stayed on top of the charts—it would be a big night for me. But all I could focus on were the red, lush lips of my lover, who was currently grinning at me like the cat that got the cream. She looked edible today in black-on-black skinny jeans and a sweater, the pair of Lucky Green Jordans I'd gotten her for Christmas a couple of years ago on her feet.

My very own super-hot, super tall, goth Christmas elf.

"You can tell me from there," she teased while I debated whether or not to take my seatbelt off and throw myself on her lap. It would not be the first time that had happened in the past seven days.

"I have to tell you here," I lied.

She pursed her lips in the universal "Who do you think you're fooling?" expression.

"You want to rile me up before we get to the studio, and it's not happening," Leila told me with a laugh. "You got plenty of attention this morning."

My core throbbed at the mention of what we'd gotten up to in the shower. Leila had propped my leg on the bench in the shower and gone down on me like a fucking champ. She'd tongued me for what felt like hours. I'd lost count of the times I came; my limbs were liquid by the time she was done.

I glanced up when I heard her laugh. "You're thinking about it, aren't you?"

"Maybe," I hedged, squirming.

"Is your pussy dripping for me?"

How had I been living day to day with the hottest, most perfectly filthy woman on earth and never knew it?

"All day, every day," I told her without an ounce of shame. It was the truth.

"Good." She winked at me, and every muscle in my body clenched. "If you behave, maybe I'll do it again tonight." I groaned, ready to whine, but she just leaned in over and gave me a peck on the cheek. "You have a long day ahead—let's get through it and then I'll make it all better at home."

I knew she would too. God, I melted for her when she got bossy like that, and she knew it. I clenched my thighs and nodded as heat flooded my body.

I could safely say that this had been one of the best weeks of my life. The live show we were doing tonight definitely had something to do with it. And some of it was likely the excitement that I always felt around the holidays. I was one of those people who loved the songs, the snow, the decorations. I adored all of it.

But mostly, it was Leila. There was an easiness between us from the first night. It felt so natural, so right to be with her like this. I had never felt this relaxed, this *myself*, at the start of a relationship. As though missing pieces of the puzzle of my life had finally locked into place. I woke up craving her and went to sleep with her taste on my lips.

I could not get enough.

I couldn't remember being this consumed by anyone, and yet I wasn't fretting. I didn't wonder what she thought about me, my career. Whether she was intimidated by my success or resented my money. I *knew* she didn't. I was certain that she not only respected me as a businesswoman, but she was also proud of my success. It was heady to be able to fully throw myself into something, into someone, without any reservation. I wanted this to work.

I wanted this to last.

She was still cautious, though. I could tell by the way she never asked about plans beyond the holidays. Leila was a planner, always looking to what was next. And yet there had been no questions of where I wanted things to go with her. I suspected she was trying to hedge her expectations. Not get in too deep when she wasn't sure if I'd be up to revealing to the world that I was falling for a woman. And though the idea was a little scary—not because I cared what people thought, but because the media was vicious—I knew for sure she was the one for me. I had to make it clear to her I was all in.

"Are you going to Gigi's this year?" Gigi was Leila's cousin who, every Nochebuena, threw a huge party for everyone and anyone who didn't have family to spend it with. Leila was close to her folks, but she just went to their house in Westchester on Christmas Day. She usually spent Nochebuena with Gigi. I did whatever I did. Which, in the last few years, had not been much.

"You remember Gigi's party?"

"I listen to you," I protested. "You've been going to your cousin's house every year since I've met you. So, are you going?"

"I was planning to, yeah." Leila knew me too well not to know there was more to my question than I was letting on. She put down the tablet she'd been tapping on and turned her full attention to me.

"Can I come?"

"Are you serious?" She widened her eyes, clearly surprised. It made sense—I was very particular about where I went. You had to be when you lived under constant scrutiny, when even a run to the drugstore for toothpaste turned into news.

"Don't you have Marbella's party?"

She said the woman's name like she'd bitten into a lemon, and I could not blame her. Marbella Bustamante was *problematique*, but she was also an institution. She'd hosted the most popular daytime Latinx television show for decades, which she then turned into a portfolio of streaming services. The woman was a powerhouse. She was like the Spanish-speaking Oprah, except Marbella's views on certain things were not as evolved. She also hosted an ultra–VIP Christmas Eve cocktail party every year at the Peninsula, which was the most coveted invite in Latinx celebrity world.

This year was the first time I'd ever been invited in the twenty years of my career. If I was a no-show, I'd never be asked again—and Marbella would not be okay with me bringing Leila as my date.

It was one of those things that when I was still on the come up, I would've done anything for. To feel like I'd arrived, that I was being validated by my community. These days, I mostly wanted to be wherever I didn't have to be fake the whole time. And sure, it would be good publicity for people to spot me entering the Peninsula for the yearly bash, but was it worth letting down Leila?

The answer came instantly and unequivocally: No.

"I would rather spend it with you," I said, a little self-conscious now.

"You know how Marbella is. She takes everything personal." This was true. The woman *was* petty. She acted like that open bar was tantamount to an invite to the Buckingham Palace.

I shrugged. "I don't care."

"This will be the first of many times that you will have to make a choice like this, Viviana," Leila warned in that infuriatingly sensible way of hers. "I don't want to be the reason that you rush into a situation that later might feel too complicated." She seemed completely casual, pose relaxed, but I knew her. I could see the brittleness in her eyes. The tightness around her mouth. She was trying to let me off easy. Anticipating I would see any changes or adjustments that came with being her as too high of a cost.

I knew what this was, and still I was hurt.

"If you don't want me to come with you to Gigi's, just say so, Leila."

"That's not what I said at all." She leaned in, but she didn't reach for me. I regretted ever starting this conversation. "I just don't want—"

The car halted as our driver lowered the partition, cutting off whatever Leila was about to say and shattering our last moment of privacy for the next few hours.

"We're here, Ms. Guerra," my driver announced as I stared at the screen of my phone and the text from my publicist asking that I let her know when I planned to arrive at the Peninsula that afternoon. I didn't want to go to Marbella's party, but it didn't seem like Leila was thrilled about me coming with her to Gigi's either. So, I held off on answering.

"Let's go," I said, tucking the phone in my bag.

The show had to go on.

LEILA

Once we got into the studio, I was not able to exchange another word with Vivi that wasn't about the show. She was tense, and I didn't have to wonder why. She'd been hurt by my apprehension, and yeah, I was being sort of a coward, but dammit, I could get really wrecked by this. We both could. It had only been a week and I was gone for her. If that made me a coward, then so be it, but it would be irresponsible to pretend there weren't difficult choices ahead if Vivi and I became a couple.

And her image would be impacted by coming out. Not necessarily in a negative way, not at all. But things would be different for her.

I knew that as much as she loved the way I made her come, once reality came knocking, she might change her mind about how much she wanted me. Because the truth of the matter was that despite the progress we had made in LGBTQ+ rights, even in the Latinx community, Bad Kitty's career had taken a hit when she came out as poly. She was a popular rapper, but she was a "gay rapper." I hated that it was the way of the world, and I would not encourage Viviana to be reckless with a career she'd worked so hard to build.

Despite the awkwardness between us, the show went on without a hitch. Both Vivi and Bad Kitty were spectacular and managed to hit every note and every dance move better than they had in rehearsal. I was in the front row, enraptured by the way my woman could still dominate the stage. She left it all up there, blood, sweat, and tears, and she kept you on the edge of your seat the entire time.

It was sometimes hard to believe she was human when she was in her groove. So much power, talent, and beauty in one person. I shivered, thinking of how I'd owned that body only hours before, how she'd trembled under my touch, how she'd begged for more.

My attention returned to the show when I heard the first notes of Vivi's solo. She'd been nervous about singing it—it was a song she wrote not long after her breakup with Patrick. One night she'd confessed that she wrote it for the lover she knew she had yet to meet. The one she hoped was still out her and just for her.

Her soulmate.

I was not foolish enough to go anywhere near that delusion, so I focused on Vivi. She moved to the microphone, which had been placed at the front of the stage, her eyes searching the crowd until they landed on me. Her gaze hit me like a punch to the solar plexus, knocking me the fuck out. I was still trying to catch my breath when she began to sing. Her eyes locked with mine like we were the only two people in this place, in this world.

I recognized what I heard in her voice, what I saw in her expression. I could see it clearly because it was identical to what was burning in me. It was love.

I loved her. I had loved her for a long time. I'd love her forever.

When the last lines fell from her lips, I could almost believe they were meant for me.

Because this season, the reason, is you. Esta navidad y siempre, el amor, mi amor, eres tu.

I sat with the words and the way I'd felt hearing her sing her heart out while she looked straight at me, and I wished that we could make this Nochebuena the first of a lifetime of them. After the solo, the show wrapped up and the cast took their bows, and I made my way backstage to wait for Vivi. I would tell her that I loved her. She deserved to know.

Once I got to the dressing room area, I found Cathy, Vivi's publicist, waiting.

"What are you doing here?" I asked her, surprised to see her there. Cathy was excellent at keeping boundaries when it came to her work/family life balance. Seeing her on set on Nochebuena was a surprise. Something was up.

"I figured I'd stop in and see what she wants to do about Marbella's party. I knew you'd both be off your phones back here, and I never got an answer from her before she went live."

Cathy could be a bit pushy when it came to events that would "keep the brand strong" and could sometimes forget Viviana was not a machine, but she usually got the message if I told her to back off. At that moment, for the first time, I hesitated in doing my job, because this thing with the Marbella party was about my personal feelings and not about me doing the best for my client.

I was still grappling with that new and game-changing development when Vivi sauntered up to us, looking edible in her red-and-white bodysuit and thigh-high black boots with a faux fur trim. She didn't offer her usual warm greeting when she saw Cathy. Something about her expression was guarded, but she didn't say a word before pointing to the dressing room. "I have to change. I'll be out soon," she told us.

"Do you need any—" I started to ask, but she just shook her head, walking off without a backward glance.

"Is she okay?" Cathy asked as she looked after our boss. I was about to make up an excuse but decided to talk to Vivi first.

She and I had to figure out what we were doing. Though it was part of my job to run interference for her, the reality was if we decided to stay together, things would be different. We'd have to establish a new way to balance our work relationship. I was willing to do that. I was willing to do whatever it took. I needed to know if she was on the same page.

After what felt like an eternity, Paola, one of the PAs—Vivi's favorite—walked up to me with a knowing grin on her lips.

"The boss wants to see you." She then gave Cathy an apologetic look. "Just Leila, sorry," the younger woman clarified as I excused myself.

I'd been summoned.

Suddenly everything felt way too serious, too real. Still, I made myself move. If Viviana had changed her mind about us, I'd be fucked up, but at least at Gigi's, I could get hammered listening to La Lupe and eating pernil.

I knocked on the door with my heart in my throat, bracing myself for the "it's not you, it's me" speech. For Viviana to do her best at letting me down easy. To tell me that being with me was just too complicated.

"Come in." Would her voice ever not melt me to the very core?

I stepped inside and froze.

"What are you wearing?" I asked dumbly as I took in her jeans and red sweater with a pair of simple ankle boots.

"Is this too dressed down for Gigi's?" she asked sweetly, as if nothing was the matter.

"But what about the Peninsula? Aren't you going to Marbella's?"

"Are *you* going to Marbella's?" she asked in response.

"No."

She only shrugged as she pumped some perfume on her wrists. "Then I'm not going." She looked up then, her eyes roaming over me possessively, and my heart raced. "I am in this with you, Leila. Are you with me?"

"I just thought..." I barely knew what to say.

"You just thought that I'd let you put everything on the line like that, risk your job, and then turn my back on it." She wasn't even hurt, just pissed. I fucking loved this woman so much. "When have you ever seen me not give something that I wanted my all?"

"Never," I answered honestly, unable to wrap my head around what she was telling me... And then I didn't have to because she told me.

"You're all I want." She stepped up to me and wrapped her strong arms around my waist, her big brown eyes warm and full of something that took my breath away. "You make me happy, Leila. I won't throw that away because of what people might think."

"I..." I floundered, scared to believe this could be real.

"Will you do this with me? Ride or die?"

That question only had one answer.

"Siempre, siempre," I promised with everything I had.

"Then we're good," she said simply before lifting her arms to circle them around my neck. Then she kissed me. Her mouth was so familiar, so necessary already. Like we'd been doing this for years instead of days. "Let's go celebrate with our people and drink some coquito, baby. Make some first memories," she whispered against my mouth, and I knew then I was done fighting this.

"If you're sure," I said for the last time, and my love, the woman of my dreams, smiled and kissed me again.

"Utterly and completely certain. For the first time in my life."

Sign up to my newsletter for a free book, updates and exclusive excerpts.

If you liked *Make the Yuletide Gay* be sure to check out *Mangos and Mistletoe*. A F/F foodie holiday novella. Read it now.

ALSO BY ADRIANA HERRERA

DREAMERS SERIES

American Dreamer

American Fairytale

American Love Story

American Sweethearts

American Christmas

LAS LEONAS SERIES

A Caribbean Heiress in Paris (May 2022)

DATING IN DALLAS SERIES

Here to Stay

On the Hustle (October 2022)

SAMBRANO STUDIOS SERIES

One Week to Claim It All

Just for the Holidays...

STANDALONES

Mangos and Mistletoe

Finding Joy

Her Night With Santa

DON'T MISS MY NEXT RELEASE!

Sign up for my newsletter for updates and a FREE book.

OR VISIT ADRIANAHERRERAROMANCE.COM

ABOUT THE AUTHOR

USA Today bestselling and award-winning author, Adriana Herrera was born and raised in the Caribbean, but for the last fifteen years has let her job (and her spouse) take her all over the world. She loves writing stories about people who look and sound like her people, getting unapologetic happy endings.

Her work has been featured in The TODAY Show on NBC, *Entertainment Weekly*, *The New York Times*, *Oprah Magazine*, *NPR*, *Library Journal*, *Publishers Weekly* and *The Washington Post*. Her debut, *American Dreamer*, was selected as one of *Booklist*'s Best Romance Debuts of 2019, and one of the *Top 10 Romances of 2019* by *Entertainment Weekly*. Adriana is an outspoken advocate for diversity in romance and has written for Remezcla and Bustle about Own Voices in the genre. She's one of the co-creators of the Queer Romance PoC Collective. She lives in New York City.

Sign up for Adriana's newsletter here!

twitter.com/ladrianaherrera

instagram.com/ladriana_herrera

ONLY YOURS

SABRINA SOL

For six months, New York City Mayor David Lucero has worked side by side with Natalia Menendez, the community liaison for Major League Women's Soccer, to bring a new women's team to the city. For six months, he's tried to deny his attraction to the curvy brunette because he didn't want to jeopardize the deal or give his opponents a made-up scandal to use against him. They have one more publicity event together before Natalia flies back to Los Angeles and David decides it's time to go after what he wants. But once the event is over, she is nowhere to be found. So, he embarks on a Christmas Eve search, with his bodyguard in tow, to find the right door that could lead him to Natalia once and for all.

CHAPTER 1

EL REGALO

(The Gift)

Were Santa hats always this sexy?

Probably not. But if they were on top of *her* head, then abso-fuckinlutely.

The bright white furry trim was a stark contrast to Natalia's smooth, dark hair. The hat's red trunk leaned sideways to the right as the white pom-pom dangled near her gold hoop earring like a wayward ornament. It was the perfect bow to top off her festively sexy look, which included a dark red fitted wrap dress and knee-high black leather boots.

As if she knew I was thinking about her, Natalia glanced up and caught me staring. But she didn't seem to mind. Instead, she gave me one of her warm, infectious smiles—the kind that had rendered me nearly speechless the first day we'd met, almost six months earlier.

57

That day, I'd had a couple of meetings, conference calls, and a ribbon cutting, which had kept me busy from seven in the morning to almost two in the afternoon. Basically, a normal weekday for the mayor of New York City. When Natalia and three others from Major League Women's Soccer had walked into my office, my normal day quickly became anything but.

Natalia was introduced as the league's new community liaison, replacing an affable fellow named Henry who'd moved into another position within the organization. I'd been so struck by her kind eyes and genuine smile that I didn't say a word at first when I'd reached out to shake her hand. In response, she'd quickly rushed out, "Hello, David. Oh, shit. I mean, Mayor Lucero."

Her candor quickly put me at ease, and I couldn't help but laugh before saying, "Hello, Natalia."

From then on, we were on a first-name basis. Our easy working relationship evolved into an easy friendship. But over the past few weeks, something had definitely shifted. Something that made me notice how the tiny double dimples on her right cheek seemed to deepen the bigger she smiled.

Something that gave me a brand-new appreciation for Santa hats.

I continued to watch from across the hotel's ballroom as Natalia handed out gift bags to the kids who were waiting in line to see Santa Claus. She took time to bend down to each child's eye level and talk animatedly to them for several seconds instead of just rushing them through the line.

I was still impressed by how quickly Natalia had pulled this event together. Originally, the plan had been to hold the holiday party at the community center last Saturday. It was supposed to be the first joint event between New York and MLWS. Our deal had been announced last month and we figured we'd squeeze every last drop of publicity out before the end of the year. Then a pipe burst at the community center, and the water damage was extensive. Definitely not the kind that could be cleaned up with just a mop and a bucket. Luckily, Natalia was able to negotiate some kind of promotion with the Park Central Vista so we could use their ballroom as a last-minute alternate venue. The catch was that we could only use it today—Christmas Eve. I wasn't sure how she'd done it. Natalia still got nearly every vendor and community group to show up, and the party was turning out to be quite the success.

Smart. Capable. And sexy? No wonder I was so attracted to her.

"For God's sake, David. Will you just ask her out already?"

I turned and saw Roger, my friend and head of my security detail, standing next to me, looking in Natalia's direction.

I glanced around to make sure no one was listening. "What are you talking about?" I said quietly, just in case.

"Don't play innocent with me, man. I've spent the past several weeks enduring the puppy dog stares and poor attempts at flirting. And she's been almost as bad."

I opened my mouth to argue, but changed my mind because I knew I couldn't get anything past him. He was a former NFL defensive lineman, after all.

I let out a big sigh and faced Roger. "She goes back to Los Angeles today. It's too late."

His face scrunched up in confusion. "It's not like Los Angeles is in another solar system. And I'm sure there are going to be more and more meetings next year leading up to the team's first season. It's not too late."

Another frustrated sigh escaped my lips. "I think she's seeing someone else."

It pained me to admit the possibility. Real ripping-my-heart-out-and-kicking-it-in-the-gutter kind of pain. Not that I had any fucking right to feel the way I did. Sure, we'd had some deep conversations and found out we shared lots in common, including our love of soccer. Plus, the sexual tension—in my mind, at least—seemed as thick as the dulce de leche I sometimes put in my morning cafecito.

But we'd never said anything to each other about pursuing something more than our professional relationship. And honestly, I'd tried hard to not even consider the thought. The deal with MLWS to bring another women's team to the city hadn't come easy. No way was I about to give the naysayers another reason to tank it. An affair between me and someone from MLWS before the contract was signed would have proven to be "muy escandaloso," as my abuelita liked to say.

The figurative ink on that digital contract, though, had been dry for at least a month now. But I had still convinced myself it wouldn't look good, wouldn't be smart. I told myself it would be a mistake to risk tainting the project with even a hint of impropriety. The contract didn't guarantee it would be smooth sailing from now until the team's first game next year. Especially since MLWS had also included some funding dollars for a new youth sports complex.

So, I'd offered nothing but friendship to Natalia until I finally admitted to myself a few days ago that it was no longer enough.

She was the only thing I wanted for Christmas this year.

And now it was too late.

Roger motioned for me to follow him to the one corner of the ballroom that didn't have some sort of food, activity, or giveaway station. I headed over, even though I dreaded answering the questions I knew he had.

"I thought she told you that she didn't have a boyfriend back in LA," he said as soon as I joined him.

I nodded and then shrugged. "She did. But I think she met someone here."

"She told you that?"

"No. I saw them here last night."

Uneasily, I reminded Roger how I'd gone in search of Natalia the night before, after we'd shown up unexpectedly to help with any last-minute setup needs. "When I came back, I told you I couldn't find her. But that wasn't true. I did find her."

She had been in the kitchen adjacent to the ballroom. I watched her from the door for a minute or so as she emptied boxes of fruit snacks into plastic containers. Her hair was up in a high ponytail, and she wore a black-and-white polka-dot sweater, dark jeans, and furry black boots. The jeans were what made me not want to interrupt her so quickly. They fit her like a glove, emphasizing her curves perfectly. Part of me wanted to go to her and pull her into my arms and tell her everything I'd been feeling for the last few weeks. And I almost did. Until I saw that she wasn't alone.

"Daniels was there?" Roger asked after I finished explaining that Borough President Ed Daniels had appeared out of nowhere.

"Yeah. I guess he had the same idea I did." *The pinche pendejo.*

"That doesn't mean they're dating."

"He came up to her and put his hand on the small of her back."

"So?"

"Then he leaned down and whispered something in her ear."

"And what did she do? Did she fall into his arms and kiss him?"

I crossed my arms against my chest. "No. But she didn't push him away. And she laughed at whatever it was he said."

"Then what?" Roger pressed.

"Then she turned her head and saw me standing there."

Even now, I could still see the look on her face. Guilt. Or maybe it was embarrassment. Either way, the color drained from her cheeks and she had stepped away from Daniels. The asshole also noticed me and had the nerve to smirk. I should've known it would be him. Out of all of the borough presidents, he'd been the one who had insinuated that there was something going on between Natalia and me. I'd thought it was because he'd wanted it to be true so he could use it as ammunition to shoot the deal down. Not because it was a bad deal, but because I was the one getting credit for it, not him.

It turned out his curiosity was because he'd wanted Natalia to himself.

And last night, it looked to me as if he'd gotten her.

Before either of them could have said something, I did. "Just thought I'd stop by to see if you needed anything," I'd said in a rush. "But it looks like everything is under control. Have a good night and I'll see you tomorrow." Then I'd speed-walked back to Roger and told him we were leaving.

"And you haven't spoken to her since?"

I dropped my head and studied the marble pattern on the floor. "We've talked today. Sort of."

The conversations had been short and limited to what was going on during the event. A few times, I got the feeling that she'd wanted to say more, but we were always interrupted. I did notice that Daniels was nowhere in sight, though.

"Listen, David, I don't know what you saw. But I know what I've seen with my own eyes, especially in the past week or so. There is something between you two. And I think if you let her leave without having a real conversation about what that something is, you're going to regret it."

I turned to watch Natalia again. She was talking to a couple of the volunteers, and the small group's combined laughter echoed throughout the ballroom. I smiled just because I saw her smile. And the fact that my pulse immediately sped up confirmed that my feelings hadn't changed. But could I risk telling her about them, especially when there was a good chance that I'd read everything all wrong?

"I don't know," I told Roger. "She's flying back today and it's Christmas Eve. Maybe this isn't the time or place to have that conversation."

He shook his head in disappointment. "For a smart man, sometimes you can be really dumb."

"You know I'm still your boss, right?"

For the next hour, I tried not to worry about what I'd seen last night and what it meant or didn't mean. Instead, I kept busy, taking photos with families, serving pancakes to attendees and volunteers, and chatting with some of my constituents.

I had just finished speaking with a new resident who had moved to the city from Puerto Rico. I was about to tell Roger that I was going to sneak into the kitchen and answer emails. But before I could pull out my phone, Natalia was standing in front of me.

"Hey, stranger," she said, giving me that golden smile again.

"Hey, Santa," I said back, nearly dropping a "sexy" in the middle.

Natalia laughed. "I wish. Based on the weather, I might need some reindeer and a sleigh to get me back to Los Angeles tonight."

"Is your flight delayed?"

"Yep. Right now, it's only two hours. But we both know that could change any minute."

"I'm sorry."

She looked surprised. "Why?"

I shrugged. "We didn't have to have this event on Christmas Eve. We could've canceled."

"We could've. But then you'd be stuck with a thousand make-your-own-reindeer kits in your office."

That made us both laugh. Still, I couldn't shake the nag of guilt. "I hate that you're stuck here instead of spending Christmas Eve with your family. What would you be doing right now if you were in LA?"

Natalia checked her watch. "It's almost eleven? Hmm. Probably right now I'd be at my abuela's house waiting for the first batch of tamales to be done cooking. After that, I'd go home to finish wrapping presents and then head back to my abuela's for our traditional Nochebuena dinner. I usually spend Christmas Day with my parents, but my dad just retired, so he decided to take my mom on a cruise. I was just planning to visit some friends, watch some Netflix, and eat my weight in tamales and buñuelos. So, no need to feel bad if I'm a few hours late getting back to LA. I can still do those things on December twenty-sixth." She paused and then added, "Besides, I don't mind the company."

She smiled again, but this time it was different. It wasn't wide or bright. It was the kind of smile you gave someone when you knew something they didn't. It was sly and seductive. Heat rose up my back and then traveled down my front.

Neither of us said anything for a few seconds, which gave us both permission to compose ourselves. I shifted my feet, hoping my ill-timed arousal wouldn't be too noticeable. Both fortunately and unfortunately, my memory bank decided to replay the scene of Daniels whispering in her ear last night.

I cleared both my throat and that image from my brain. "Well, I can't help with the buñuelos, but I do happen to have at least five dozen tamales sitting in my fridge at my office."

"That many?" she said with a laugh.

I nodded. "Apparently, I mentioned in an interview once how

much I missed my abuelita's homemade Mexican tamales de pollo con chile verde. Now, that's what I get for Christmas every year."

"That's kind of sweet, actually. And what are your Christmas plans?"

"Well, tonight I'm meeting my sister Eneida and some of our friends for our annual Nochebuena party. And then tomorrow we'll take our parents to Mass in the morning and we'll spend the rest of the day with them and her kids."

"Sounds like a pretty great Christmas," she said with a quick smile. Then her expression turned serious. It took her a few seconds before she responded. "David, I wanted to talk to you about last night. I feel like I owe you an explanation."

I held up my hand to stop her. "You don't owe me anything, Natalia. There's no need to—"

"Hola, Mayor Lucero, hola!"

The loud voice made me stop mid-sentence. I turned to see Doña Ramirez walking toward us carrying a large plastic container. The eighty-four-year-old lived next door to the community center where the party was originally going to be held. She was also one of the project's most vocal supporters. Which meant she was someone I always made time for.

But not today.

I still wanted to talk to Natalia. She was leaving soon and I'd have no excuse to see her again for another few months. I wanted to make the most of our time left together and share more stories about our childhood Christmases or our favorite foods or even about the goddamn weather. I just wanted to keep hearing that voice and seeing that smile.

Natalia touched my arm just as Doña Ramirez arrived next to me. "I'll let you two talk."

I wanted to protest and almost reached out to grab her hand. But the politician in me finally woke up and let her go.

"Feliz Navidad, Mayor Lucero." The older woman presented me with the container.

"Feliz Navidad, Doña Ramirez. Are these what I think they are?" I teased.

She beamed with pride. "My tamales. I told you I make the best ones in all of New York."

"Yes, you did. I can't wait to try them."

"I brought you two dozen. That way you freeze some so you can have for dinner later on those nights when you work too late. Because you have no wife at home, I worry our bachelor mayor is going to get too skinny working so hard."

I chuckled at the nickname: bachelor mayor. It was one I'd heard before. My marital status had been the subject of several articles during the election. A reality show producer even approached my publicist about the possibility of following me along as I went on dates.

Problem was, I never went on dates. It was rare when I didn't have some meeting or business dinner on nights during the week. I tried not to work on the weekends, but I usually failed. After all, I was barely going into my second year as mayor, and I had a lot to prove and accomplish. I'd run my campaign on neighborhood improvements and bringing jobs to the city. Most importantly, I had wanted to make sure the kids in our city had access to sports programs and safe outdoor spaces. The deal with MLWS was a chance to make good on all of it. So, yeah, I had been willing to sacrifice my love life for it.

And then Natalia walked into my office and made me rethink it all.

Not only was she damn good at her job, she was one of the most genuine people I'd ever met. She was never afraid to voice her opinion and she listened intently when others voiced theirs. And while she was very serious about her responsibilities with the league, she also knew how to joke and have fun. It wasn't long before I found myself missing that laugh of hers in between our monthly meetings. So much so that I'd call her just to tell her a silly joke or story. It wasn't unusual for one of our quick chats to turn into an hour-long conversation if my schedule allowed for it. And even sometimes when it didn't. Only Roger knew I'd canceled a handful of important appointments just so I could talk to Natalia a little longer.

As Doña Ramirez chatted on about how much she and her grand-children had enjoyed the party, I couldn't stop wondering where Natalia had gone. She said her flight was delayed, so that meant I had at least another two hours with her. We still had time to grab some lunch, or even coffee.

We still had time.

But a few minutes turned into ten and then another five. Finally, Doña Ramirez realized that the party was over. She told me she had to get home and check on the last batch of tamales she'd left steaming on her stove.

The ballroom was just about empty now. The festive holiday music blaring over the speakers was drowned out by sounds of chairs being stacked and tables being dropped onto the floor to be folded. I made my way back to Roger, who was sitting on a chair next to what had been the registration table.

"What kind of tamales are those?" he asked as I took the seat next to him.

"Chicken," I said.

He sat up straighter. "Okay, how about a deal? You give me the tamales and I'll give you the present that Natalia left for you."

I whipped my head in his direction. "You talked to Natalia?"

"She came over and told me she didn't want to pull you away from Doña Ramirez. So she told me to give you this." Roger held out a tall, narrow gift bag with one hand and reached for the tamales with his other.

I was about to give him the container, then stopped. "Wait. If the gift was already for me, then why am I trading it for tamales that were also for me?"

"Do you really want to waste time arguing about this or do you want to find out what she got you?"

I answered by taking the bag from him and putting the container on the table where he could grab it.

I removed layers of green and red tissue and uncovered a bottle. Carefully, I pulled it out and discovered it was my favorite brand of tequila. I couldn't help but smile at the memory of the time I had first told Natalia about it. It was the day that the deal had been announced. And the first time I almost kissed her.

We'd spent hours together as I fielded various press conferences and media interviews. A group of us had gone to dinner to celebrate, which included a few rounds of tequila shots. The younger ones had wanted to continue the party at a local club. But Natalia had said she was going to go back to her hotel, so I offered her a ride. Roger drove us the few blocks north while Natalia and I continued to chat and laugh. I teased her about only taking two shots compared to my five.

"Tequila gives me a headache," she'd said.

I had shaken my head in protest. "Then you've been drinking the wrong kind. The one we had tonight was pretty good. But you need to try my favorite, Casa Milagro. It's made with agave azul grown in the Los Altos region of Jalisco. It's so smooth and rich. If we had had that tonight, I definitely would've had a few more shots. And Roger would've had to carry me to the car."

We both laughed at the image in our heads.

"Then it's a good thing the restaurant didn't have it or you didn't bring it."

I had sighed. "Not too many restaurants order it. And, unfortunately, I only have a few drops left in my bottle at home. I'll have to remember to order another bottle one of these days."

"In between your back-to-back meetings, lunches, dinners, breakfasts, special events, and the million other things you do every day. You work too hard, David."

The softness in her voice had conveyed a concern I hadn't expected. That was the thing about Natalia: Every encounter with her revealed yet another layer to her kindness and warmth.

I tried to brush it off. "It's what I signed up for. I'm one of the youngest mayors of New York in recent history, and I'm Mexican *and* Puerto Rican. You know as well as I do that I have to work harder and better than everyone else. Mistakes are not an option and that means I have to be very careful about everything I do. I can't give my critics any excuse to crucify me."

They were the exact reasons why I hadn't reached out to touch her, caress her cheek, or squeeze the knee that had been resting against mine for most of the ride.

They were the reasons why I didn't do a lot of things I wanted to do.

That's when she'd reached out and grabbed my hand from my lap. "I get it. I just want to make sure you don't get so busy trying to fix the lives of everyone else that you forget to enjoy yours."

Our eyes met, and the whole city seemed to drift away. She bit her bottom lip and I had the sudden urge to bite it too. And just as I began to lean in, reality came roaring back in the form of Roger honking the horn at the car in front of us.

There weren't too many moments in my life that I regretted. But that one was now at the top of my list.

"There's a card." Roger's voice pulled me back into the ballroom.

I put the bottle of tequila on the table and took the white envelope off the front of the bag. The first thing I saw when I pulled the card out was a pretty green foil tree on the cover. Inside was a simple printed message: *Wishing you all the joys of the season.*

Then I noticed the handwritten message on the inside cover. I began to read:

Dear David,

¡Feliz Navidad! I hope all of your Christmas wishes come true. My Christmas wish is for you to think of me every time you enjoy this tequila. I know what you think you saw last night, but I want you to believe me when I say that there is nothing going on between me and Borough President Daniels. Although he would like for there to be. I have never given him any reason to think that I ever wanted anything from him except his support for our deal. Because the truth is, my heart and my body already belong to you.

Only yours,

Natalia

One long breath left my body, but it might as well been all the oxygen in the world. I had to read the message again. And again.

Only yours.

Natalia did have feelings for me, just like I had feelings for her.

In that moment, I realized that it was more than just an attraction or my poor neglected libido. It was deeper. Stronger.

I had fallen in love with her. My heart and my body belonged to her as well.

I jumped to my feet and scanned the almost-empty ballroom. "Roger, did you see where Natalia went?"

CHAPTER 2

LA BÚSQUEDA

(The Search)

She had disappeared.

¡Ay, carajo! Why had I spent so much time talking to Doña Ramirez today of all days?

Roger and I couldn't find her in the ballroom, or the kitchen, or the small foyer outside the main doors. Panic set in, and I prayed that she wasn't already on her way to the airport. Her phone went straight to voicemail after I tried calling it a few times. Either she had forgotten to turn it back on after the party ended, or it was dead.

It might have seemed ridiculous, but I couldn't shake the thought that I needed to see her before she left. I couldn't let her spend Christmas thinking that I didn't care. That I didn't want her.

I was seriously considering having Roger drive me to the airport when I spotted Steven, one of the other staff members from MLWS. I ran up to him and asked if he'd seen Natalia.

Steven, who was someone's assistant, thought about the question for a moment. "Not in the last few minutes. But the last time I saw her, she was walking down the hallway toward our staging room."

Relief swept through me. She had to still be on the property. "Where is the staging room?" I asked, trying not to sound too urgent.

"It's one of the conference rooms on the other side of the hotel. I don't remember the name of it, but it's on this same floor. You have to go past the elevators and a couple of the other rooms. We used it to store all our equipment and supplies for the party. She's probably there, helping pack everything up."

"Thanks, man. Merry Christmas."

Before he could say anything else, Roger and I made a beeline for the conference rooms on the other side of the hotel. And then we stopped in our tracks as soon as we found them.

Because there wasn't just one or two rooms along the hallway. There were at least a dozen doors. And I had no idea which one Natalia would be behind.

"Where do you want to start?" Roger asked.

The third frustrated sigh of the night escaped my lips. "If I could, I'd start all the way back to this morning so I could pull my head out of my ass and tell Natalia that I'm in love with her before the party even started."

As soon as I said the words, I braced myself for his reaction.

He slapped my back and yelped, "What? In love?"

I closed my eyes and took a deep breath. "Yes, Roger. I love Natalia."

Another slap. Another yelp. "Wow, man. I had no idea. I just thought... well, you know what I thought. That's very cool."

That surprised me. "It is?"

"Sure it is. I think she would be good for you. It's about time."

Roger's approval renewed my sense of urgency. "Okay. Let's start looking for her."

We decided to skip the first two rooms located immediately next to the elevators since Steven said we had to go past them. The next room turned out to be empty.

Door number four turned out to be some sort of chair storage area.

Door number five led to a conference room that still held the leftovers of another holiday party, complete with shreds of wrapping paper on the floor and a tray of half-eaten cookies on a nearby table.

Disappointment needled at my nerves. I tried not to let myself think about the possibility that the search would prove pointless. Then I remembered that sexy smile of hers and allowed myself to imagine what it would feel like to finally touch and taste her. It spurred my anticipation and my hope.

Door number six opened into a bigger meeting room—with some sort of meeting still going on.

"Oh, hello, everyone," I said sheepishly as everyone turned to look at me. "So sorry. Didn't meant to interrupt."

"Mayor Lucero!" the woman standing at the front of the room said. "Is everything okay? Did you need something for your party?" That's when I noticed her nametag. She worked for the hotel, which probably meant the others in the room also worked for the hotel.

"No, no," I repeated. "The party is over, actually. I was just looking for someone."

"Did you want one of us to help you?" she said, then motioned for two of the men to stand.

I held up my hand. "That's okay. No need to disrupt your meeting. I'm sure we'll find the person shortly. Thank you, though."

She didn't seem convinced even as the men sat back down. I wished them all a merry Christmas and walked backward out of the room.

Door seven led to another empty room and another wave of disappointment.

"You're going to find her," Roger said, sensing my frustration.

Unfortunately, Natalia wasn't behind door number eight either.

Instead, a young Latino man, wearing a very stylish white tuxedo, jumped to his feet and said, "I'm sorry. I know I'm not supposed to be here. I'll leave."

I shook my head and waved my hand. "No, I'm the one that's not supposed to be here. You stay, I'll go," I told him.

He studied me for a moment. "Wait. Do I know you? Are you Marissa's tío?"

I chuckled, wondering if Marissa's tío also had a habit of checking hotel meeting rooms. "Not that I know of. Who's Marissa?"

"My fiancée. Well, she'll officially be my wife in a few hours."

The man radiated happiness when he said that. Which made me curious as to why he was all alone in this room instead of with his bride-to-be. "Congratulations," I said as I stepped further into the room. "A Christmas Eve wedding, huh? That sounds pretty nice."

He nodded. "We met on Christmas Eve three years ago. And I proposed to her on Christmas Eve last year."

"Like I said... pretty nice. But is there a reason why you're here and not where you're probably supposed to be right now?"

The man sat back down and let out a big sigh. "I guess I just needed a moment to myself before, you know, it all becomes too much."

I probably should've wished him luck at that point and gotten the hell out of there. After all, I was the last person to be doling out relationship advice. What if I said the wrong thing and poor, sweet Marissa was left at the altar on Christmas Eve?

Still, I couldn't help myself. I took the seat next to him. "Are you having doubts?" I asked, even though I didn't really want to know the answer.

The man looked like I had slapped him. "What? Oh my God, no. Not even. I want to marry Marissa. I've never been more sure of anything in my life."

I scratched my temple in confusion. "Then why are you hiding out here in this conference room?"

"I'm not hiding."

"You're not?"

"No. I just wanted a little bit of time to myself, that's all. I know it's going to get kind of hectic in a little while and I guess I just wanted to take a few moments to really take it all in. This is going to be the best day of my life. I don't want that to get lost somehow."

His words sounded genuine, and I finally understood. "You want to honor it," I said.

He nodded enthusiastically. "Yes, that's it exactly. It wasn't easy to get to today. Marissa and I have been through a lot together and there were times when I wasn't sure we would make it. Now that we're here, it's kind of hard to believe."

Suddenly, I was the one who needed the advice. "How did you do it? How did you two make it to today?"

The man shrugged. "We told each other that if things ever got so bad that it would be easier to walk away than stay, then we owed it to the other person to leave. No matter our issues, I could never imagine my life without Marissa. And it was the same for her."

It sounded simple enough. Maybe because it was the reason why I had decided to finally go after Natalia. It would've been easier to read her card and then go about my day as if her words hadn't meant anything to me. It would've been easier to keep pushing my feelings to the side.

But the more I thought about not being with her, the more I realized how hard it would be to go on pretending. Walking away wasn't going to be easy at all. And that's why I needed to find her. Fast.

I stood and told the man that I had to be somewhere.

"Yeah, of course," he said, and stood up as well. "Thanks for listening... I'm sorry, I didn't get your name."

"It's David."

"Thank you, David. I'm Mando."

We shook hands. "Nice to meet you, Mando. I wish you and Marissa all the happiness in the world."

He smiled and nodded. Before he left, he turned around. "Hey, if you're free later, our reception is going to be in the Valencia ballroom at five. You're welcome to stop by and have some drinks and dinner."

If it had been any other day, I probably would've gone. I declined instead. "Thank you for the invite. I wish I could, but I have other plans."

"No worries, man. Thanks again."

Roger walked in after Mando left. "What happened?"

I shrugged. "Nothing. The man had a wedding to get to. And I have a woman to find, so let's get moving."

There were four more rooms to check. Although I wasn't as hopeful as I had been, I wasn't about to give up.

Then I walked through door number nine and reconsidered.

A cacophony of voices in various pitches filled the room. The voices belonged to a group of about ten people who looked to have appeared straight out of a Dickens novel. The women wore bonnets and large cloaks, while the men were dressed in long coats and top hats. The cacophony, though, fizzled to a lone soprano once I was noticed by the majority of the group.

"Mayor Lucero! How nice to see you," one of the men said. As he came closer, I recognized him as Paul Sullivan, chair of the city's transportation committee.

"Hello, Paul," I said, and reached out to shake his hand. Then the rest of the group approached me, and I noticed a few more familiar faces.

After all the greetings were done, part of me wanted to rush back out the door. Still, I wondered what they were doing at the hotel and asked.

"We're going to be singing carols down in the lobby in a few minutes," Paul explained. "We've been making the rounds at different events all over the city the past few weeks. So this is kind of like our grand finale."

That's when I remembered that I had seen them perform at a recent holiday dinner. "That's right. Wow, you guys were amazing at the chamber's party a few nights ago. I'm sure everyone at the hotel is going to love hearing you sing."

Paul beamed with pride. "We were just about to practice our opening number, 'Winter Wonderland.' Hey, why don't you join us?"

I froze. Not only didn't I have time for a concert, but I also had no tone or rhythm. A fact my very musically inclined Latino family loved to remind me of every chance they got.

"Oh, I don't think you would want my frog voice to get mixed in with your beautiful, melodic ones," I explained. "Trust me."

"Nonsense," one of the women I didn't recognize said. "We would love to sing with you. It would be an honor, Mayor Lucero."

Others in the group agreed and I knew I couldn't leave without having to bare my most embarrassing quality—all in the name of getting out of there and back to my search for Natalia. "Well, okay then. Let's do one song," I told them.

Everyone cleared their throats in preparation, so I did the same just for show. I knew the absence of phlegm wouldn't suddenly make me be able to carry a tune. No, there would be no Christmas miracle for this tone-deaf mayor.

Paul counted down, and then we began to sing.

At first, I barely mumbled the lyrics in hopes that my off-key voice would be lost among the more harmonic ones next to me. But as we continued, I got caught up in the spirit of the song. I could even picture Natalia and me dreaming by a fire, conspiring and making plans because I wasn't afraid of "what if" anymore. The words to a song I'd heard millions of times in my life suddenly made sense to me. And I wanted everything it promised. I wanted to walk in a winter wonderland—or whatever came close to it in New York City—with Natalia by my side, damn it. So, I sang louder and with more enthusiasm on the slim chance that doing so would make my dream come true sooner. Any self-consciousness I had before melted away. Until I belted my last note at the top of my limited range—almost as if I were a hoarse Bruno Mars. That's when I noticed the wide eyes and uncomfortable expressions.

"Uh, that was great, Mayor," Paul said after a few seconds of stunned silence. The others offered their own kind comments. They were liars, of course. Every single one of them.

I shrugged. "Well, you can't say I didn't warn you. I'm surprised we didn't find ourselves surrounded by an audience of amorous stray cats."

That made everyone laugh and any awkwardness disappeared. We wished each other a merry Christmas and a happy New Year. Then I swore Paul to secrecy before saying goodbye.

"Don't say a word," I also warned Roger, who was red-faced and probably using all his strength not to dissolve into laughter.

As I paced the hallway, I pinched the bridge of my nose. What on earth was I doing? I wanted to find Natalia. I really did. But how many more times did I have to mortify myself doing it? And what if, at the end of it all, she was already gone?

Roger sensed my increasing frustration and stopped me in my tracks. He held up three fingers. "Three more doors, David. That's all."

Nodding, I headed to door number ten. Before pushing it open, I rolled my shoulders and took a deep breath. She was worth all of this. I just had to remember that again.

There were a few people inside the room, surrounded by folding tables, boxes, and luggage carts. Everyone seemed busy doing things, so I decided to venture a little farther and look around.

And then I saw it. The sexy Santa hat.

She was standing just a few feet away with her back to me. I couldn't see exactly what she was doing, but she was by herself.

"Natalia." Her name fell out of my mouth on its own as if I had been holding it in like one last life-saving breath.

The next time I said it, I made sure she could hear it.

"Natalia!"

CHAPTER 3

LA REUNÍON

(The Reunion)

"Hi."

"Hi," she said back.

We walked toward each other. "Hi," I repeated when she was just a few inches away. "You're a hard woman to find."

Natalia smiled and tilted her head. "You were looking for me?"

"I was." *I think I always have been.*

"Did you get my gift?" she asked.

"I did. Thank you."

Her cheeks flushed with a pink glow, and I noticed she bit her bottom lip before asking, "Did you get my card?"

"I did," I said in a whisper.

I watched as her chest rose with a deep breath. "Oh. Good," she said as softly as I had.

We stood facing each other for a few more seconds without speaking. At least not out loud. I could see clearly now that Natalia was telling me she wanted me as much as I wanted her. The filters I'd forced myself to look through in order to seal the MLWS deal without a hitch had finally come off.

The only thing standing in my way now was this busy conference room.

"Can we go somewhere?" I asked.

She nodded. "I have to go up to my room to get my suitcase. I need to check out of the hotel."

"Let's go."

We both headed for the door, with Roger lagging behind us. But as I reached to open it again, my intentions of finally kissing Natalia on the other side were thwarted by a five-foot, blonde, very animated marketing executive named Sasha.

"Are you checking out now, Natalia?" Sasha asked as she walked with us out of the conference room.

Natalia glanced in my direction before answering. "Um, yeah. I just need to grab my suitcase."

"Perfect! I need to go to my room too!"

I cleared my throat, and that's when Sasha noticed I was still walking with them toward the elevators. "Oh, did you have a room upstairs too, Mayor?"

Yes. It was going to be Natalia's.

"No, uh, I offered to give Natalia a ride to the airport. It's going to be hard to catch a cab or an Uber right now."

"Aww. That's so nice of you," Sasha said. She pressed the up button and the elevator doors opened immediately.

I should've stayed behind and offered to wait for Natalia in the car. But I was too greedy now. If there was any chance of us being alone, I was going to take it. So I walked into the elevator and Roger had no choice but to follow.

As starved as I was to finally find out if Natalia would taste as sweet as I'd imagined, the politician in me couldn't stay quiet. "Sasha, did you need a ride to the airport as well?" I asked. Roger coughed and I knew he was calling me all sorts of names in his head.

Sasha's face brightened with a big smile. "Oh, yes, please. Thank you so, so much. Once you mentioned how hard it was going to be to get a cab, I started to worry. You are a lifesaver, Mayor Lucero."

Well, I was *something*, I guess.

The doors opened onto the twentieth floor and the four of us walked out of the elevator. Roger and I followed behind for a few doors when I finally admitted to myself that it would look very suspicious if I went into Natalia's room.

It wasn't going to happen. At least not today.

"We'll just wait by the elevators while you ladies get your things, okay?"

Sasha nodded and continued walking. Natalia looked back at me, and I could see the disappointment written all over her face.

I'm sure my expression was just as depressed. I shrugged at how unfair the universe could be. But in my head, I was giving it the finger.

When both were inside their respective rooms, Roger and I began walking back toward the elevators. "You just had to offer the other one a ride, didn't you?" he accused.

"Yes, I did. I'm going to be working with Sasha again and I don't want her telling everyone at MLWS about the time the mayor of New York gave Natalia a ride but left her stranded."

"You're so fucking dramatic," Roger groaned. "And a masochist. You actually had a chance to have a *very* merry Christmas and you blew it."

We sat on the small couch across from the elevator.

"It's fine," I said, bending to brace my arms on my knees and clasp my hands. "Natalia knows how I feel now. I can let her get on that plane because I have every intention of flying her back for New Year's Eve."

Roger sighed and leaned back. "That's six days away. And she's here now. So make your move, man."

I threw up my hands. "How exactly?"

He was quiet for a few seconds, which meant he was analyzing the situation in his head. When he turned his body in my direction, I looked up to meet his very serious expression. "Red one," he said.

I sat up straight. "Red one?"

When I hired Roger four years ago, I knew having a former football player as head of my security detail would come with certain advantages. Mainly because he looked intimidating, and it was pretty obvious he could hurt someone with just his pinky finger. What I hadn't expected was his insistence on creating a playbook for possible emergency situations. He named the response to each of those situations just like plays run during a football game. I had to memorize them so we could communicate safely and efficiently in the middle of possible chaos.

Red one was the play where Roger left me alone.

It was supposed to be a last resort, to be used only in situations where it was safer for Roger to stay and fend off the threat and give me a chance to escape on my own. Trying to get me and a woman alone in the middle of a five-star hotel didn't seem to qualify.

Yet all I kept thinking about was the phrase *Put me in, Coach!*

"I have an idea, but it's got to be quick," Roger said.

"Are you sure? I mean, I appreciate you trying so hard to make this happen, but I also don't want to be foolish."

"We're not being foolish. I've analyzed all the possible scenarios and the risk is low. I think we can do it."

A rush of excitement ran through me. Even though I had no idea what the plan was, I was still up for it. Anything to have just one minute alone with Natalia. Just us. No distractions. No misunderstandings. No worrying about what it would mean for my career.

I was done waiting. I was done getting in my own way.

It was time to go for what I wanted.

A few more minutes later, Sasha and then Natalia walked out of their rooms, each pulling one suitcase behind them. Natalia wore a long black coat over her dress and a red scarf wrapped multiple times around her neck.

Sadly, the Santa hat was gone.

Roger and I stood to meet them. On purpose, I stayed still as Roger walked over to Sasha and offered to take her suitcase. She let him, and then I offered to do the same for Natalia. He pressed the button to call the elevator and it arrived after a few seconds. Four other people were already on it when it arrived. As Roger and Sasha walked inside, I grabbed Natalia's hand to stop her from following. She was startled, so I winked at her to let her know I had a plan.

I called out to Roger, "I don't think there's room for us, so we'll just catch the next one."

He nodded and gave me a rare smile.

The doors closed, and I was finally alone with Natalia.

Red one was officially in play.

CHAPTER 4

EL ROJO

(The Red One)

My immediate urge to lean in and finally kiss her, however, was dashed by the ding of another elevator.

The doors opened and I looked over Natalia's head to find a group of about seven or eight people staring at us. Roger and I hadn't figured on the second car arriving mere seconds after the first one.

"We'll wait for the next one," I said with a wave.

"Is that the mayor?" a voice said.

"I think it is," another voice answered.

A tall man wearing a dark green beanie and matching scarf stepped out of the elevator. "You can fit, no problem," he told me.

A chorus of voices agreed.

All of a sudden, I was frustrated that this hotel was full of so many people. Why couldn't they be off doing all their Christmas cheer somewhere else? Why did they have to be decking the halls here? And why couldn't they just take the damn stairs?

Que chingada. I had become Scrooge.

Everyone nodded at us with huge smiles as we joined them inside, and all I could do was smile back and pretend that my body wasn't on fire. It was as if every nerve tingled with anticipation. It was excruciating being so close to Natalia in the packed elevator without being able to take her into my arms.

The elevator stopped at the next floor, and we moved so a man could step off. As everyone else watched the numbers go down on the display screen above the door, I nudged Natalia with my arm in a signal to back up until we were both positioned behind everyone else.

I moved my hand until it brushed against hers. Just for a second at first. Skin on skin. Warmth against warmth.

The next time, though, my hand lingered. I took my time, becoming familiar with the sensation. And she let me. We both kept our heads forward, not daring to move or let on what we were doing. When I began to pull away, she stopped me by looping her pinky around mine.

I stepped an inch to the side, just enough so I could take her hand. Lazily, as if we had all the time in the world instead of mere seconds, I stroked her palm with my index finger.

Two more people left on floor number eight.

Feeling braver, I maneuvered my hand so it could slide between her coat and her waist. A little gasp escaped her mouth when I reached the spot where her back met the arch of her ass.

When the elevator stopped on floor number two, I reluctantly dropped my arm.

That's when the universe finally did the right thing.

The last two people began to walk out. One of the women turned around and said, "Feliz Navidad, Mayor Lucero."

"Gracias," I said with a big smile. "Feliz Navidad."

As the doors closed, my politician side warned me not to do anything too rash, too reckless. The politician in me told me to wait.

But I was done waiting. Just as the elevator began its descent to the first floor, I hit my palm against the emergency button, bringing the car to a complete stop.

"What are you doing?" a startled Natalia asked.

I spun around, wrapped my arms around her waist, and pulled her hard against me. "What I should've done weeks ago."

My mouth slammed into hers, hungry for the taste of her. She responded as if she was just as ravenous for me. I couldn't help myself. Couldn't get enough. I moved her into one corner, and then another until we found ourselves once again against the back wall of the elevator. It was a dance of lust and desire, and she let me take the lead. The sound of the elevator's alarms mixed with our mutual gasps and heavy breaths. But then she pulled away.

"The cameras," she whispered. I watched as she unwrapped her scarf from around her neck. It was wider and longer than I had expected. She handed it to me and then nodded toward the single lens protruding from the right corner of the elevator's ceiling. I got the message immediately and was able to easily throw the scarf over it.

"Roger will get the footage later," I said, right before I took possession of her soft lips again. I locked away any nagging worry about what would happen if Roger couldn't do what I'd just promised. I didn't want anything to distract me from the pleasure that was the sweetness of Natalia's tongue.

A thrill ran through my body and electrified every nerve. I was heated from head to toe—especially everywhere in between.

"Touch me," she moaned.

Without saying a word, I moved one hand from her hip and slid it over her right breast. She gasped in pleasure, and I could feel her nipple harden underneath my palm. It wasn't enough. I pulled at the vee of her dress until it exposed a lacy black bra. Then I slipped my hand inside to bring out one ample breast. Immediately, I covered it with my mouth.

"Oh my God, yes." Her words tumbled out breathlessly, revving up my arousal even more.

The elevator's alarm continued to blare, but it didn't distract us. If anything, it spurred on our desire like a frantic siren. It was urgent. So we were urgent.

"Fuck, you taste so sweet," I said with a groan after several minutes of exploring every curve and valley. "I can't wait to taste the rest of you." My cock pulsed with need and I ground my pelvis into her thigh. Then she was there. Rubbing me through my pants.

I nearly broke.

I was losing control.

And I didn't care one fucking bit.

While one hand groped the breast I wasn't sucking on, the other grabbed a handful of one plump ass cheek. She returned the favor by squeezing my shaft. My vision blurred as pleasure swept through me.

Familiar tension began to build. I wanted so badly to come in her hands. And the fact that I was actually considering doing just that was what finally made me realize that we needed to slow down. Because I wasn't some horny teenager desperate for a hand job. Natalia needed to be savored. I wanted this to mean something.

I reluctantly tore myself away from her perfect breast and lifted my head so I could meet her eyes. "I need to tell you something," I said.

Her eyelids were heavy with lust and her lips were swollen. In that moment, I knew I'd carry that image with me always. She was so beautiful and vulnerable. It made me more determined to tell her the truth.

"I'm only yours too."

Her eyes brightened as if she were seeing me for the first time. In a way, I guess she was. This was the real me. Also vulnerable, and even a little afraid about what would happen tomorrow or a year from now. As a politician, it was always a good strategy to hold back a little. That way, you could appeal to every side. It was always a bad strategy to show all your cards so early in the game.

With Natalia, I knew I had to be all in. Starting now.

I reached up and cradled her face in my hands. "I'm in love with you," I whispered before kissing her again. It was a soft and sweet promise. An unspoken oath that from here on out, we were going to be together.

This time she pulled away first. "I'm in love with you too, David," she said.

I took her into my arms again and kissed the top of her head. "Stay. Come with me to the Nochebuena party and then spend Christmas morning with me."

"Really?"

I smiled into her hair. "Yes, really."

As I moved to kiss her again, another voice filled the small space.

"This is the New York City Fire Department," the voice crackled from a speaker near the doors. "Is everyone okay in there?"

I cleared my throat and announced, "Yes, we're fine. What's going on?"

"We're not exactly sure. Are you able to pull the emergency lever next to the speaker?"

"I think so. Hold on a moment."

We broke apart and I helped Natalia fix her dress and her hair. She grabbed a tissue from her purse and wiped her lipstick off my mouth. "Guess it's time to get back to the real world," she said, a little hint of sadness in her tone.

Taking her hand, I placed it against my heart. "But this time we're going back together as us. And something tells me it's going to be a pretty fantastic Christmas. Are you ready?"

She met my eyes and gave me one of her infectious smiles. "I'm ready."

I squeezed her hand and then pulled the lever. The elevator jolted into action, then came to a stop within a few seconds.

The doors opened.

And for the first time that day, it truly felt like Christmas.

ABOUT THE AUTHOR

Sabrina Sol is the chica who loves love. She writes sexy romance stories featuring strong and smart Latina heroines in search of their Happily Ever Afters. Sabrina and her books have been featured in *Entertainment Weekly*, *Bookriot's* "100 Must Read Rom-Coms," and *PopSugar's* list of "8 Up-and-Coming Latinx Romance Writers Who Should Be on Your Radar," and her *Delicious Desires* series made *The Latina Book Club's* Annual Books of The Year Lists in 2015 and 2016. Sabrina's common themes of food, family and love are woven into intricate plots that all connect for a powerful read that lingers in the hearts of readers. She is proud of her Mexican-American heritage, culture, and traditions—all of which can be found within the pages of her books. Sabrina is a native of Southern California, where she currently lives with her husband, three children and four dogs.

Sign up for Sabrina's newsletter here!

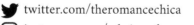

twitter.com/theromancechica

instagram.com/sabrina_theromancechica

MEET ME UNDER THE MISTLETOE

PRISCILLA OLIVERAS

Challenged by his friends to find a plus one to Nochebuena dinner or else, widower Héctor Gutiérrez isn't sure he's still got any good moves left. That is until he strikes the right chord with his son's music teacher, Cristina.

CHAPTER 1

Bring a plus-one to Nochebuena dinner or suffer the consequences.

His best friend Eneida's latest ultimatum, one of many delivered via text, screeched like a howler monkey in Héctor Gutiérrez's head.

Frustrated, he jabbed the lever on the toaster with more force than necessary. The basket lowered with an angry scrape of metal that grated on his agitated nerves. The red flare of the heating coils mimicked the firestorm of guilt and loneliness burning in his chest as pieces of his recent conversation with Eneida played through his head.

"Look, I've made a decision, and..." Her voice had trailed off on a shaky breath that carried through Héctor's cell phone, dragging a long-suffering sigh from him.

"I need a wingman. Don't make me go it alone," Eneida had pleaded. More like coerced. "¿Me oyes?"

Oh, he'd heard her, all right. Half of him raised a fist in solidarity. The other half remained plagued by doubts.

"You *have* to get out of hermit mode," she had argued, going on to play the ace she held up her sleeve. "It's been two years since Marielena died."

Like he didn't already know the number of years—days, even—

since his wife of thirteen years had passed after a brief, valiant, yet brutal battle with ovarian cancer.

His wife's dearest friend had been Héctor's rock during Marielena's sickness and in the years since, despite the troubles Eneida had faced in her own personal life. The woman was pushing him out of his comfort zone for his own good. Like his mami and tías.

But unlike his mother and her sisters, Eneida knew the promise Héctor had made his wife before she died. One year of mourning. No more.

Still, after you met and married and then lost your other half, was it possible to find that again? Especially when you'd been out of the dating game for over fifteen years?

Marielena wouldn't have wanted him to crawl into a cave and hide away. And truthfully, lately it was uncertainty more than mourning that had him sticking close to home, focusing on his son. Helicoptering, as Eneida accused him of doing.

The thud of plodding footsteps above him on the second floor of their Brooklyn Heights brownstone jerked Héctor back to the weekday rush. His son was still in early morning slow motion, despite Héctor's "apurate" call a few moments ago. "Hurry up" and mornings didn't mix in Luisito's lexicon.

Héctor glanced at his watch and muttered a curse before calling out, "Oye, Luisito, you have ten minutes to eat or you'll miss morning recess."

Suddenly, a herd of wild buffalo led by his eleven-year-old stampeded down the hardwood stairs. Luisito bounded into the kitchen, his sneakers screeching on the black-and-white tile, his face a mask of horrified accusation only a preteen could pull off.

"Papi, middle schoolers do not have recess." He smoothed a hand down his school uniform's burgundy plaid tie and white button-down and puffed out his chest. "Ya no somos bebés."

"I know you're not babies anymore, but recess—"

"It's *social time*," Luisito clarified, clambering onto a barstool at the island. "And I can't miss it."

The breakfast pastries popped up in the toaster.

"That's breakfast? Again?" Luisito's black brows angled in a fierce scowl above his nearly black eyes. "Pa, this is such an injustice to my taste buds!"

Ignoring his son's dramatics, Héctor sipped his café con leche, turning to stare out the back window at the small courtyard behind their brownstone. The round metal table and matching scrollwork chairs where his wife used to enjoy sipping her morning café sat empty. Dusted with snow. Unused. She would hate that.

Luisito's heavy sigh behind him echoed in Héctor's heart.

"I miss your homemade French toast and omelets. And you haven't made inkblot pancakes since..." Luisito's voice trailed off.

Guilt reached in with both hands and ripped the gaping hole in Héctor's heart wider.

He stared mutely at the stark, bare branches of the cherry blossom tree in the courtyard's far corner, its late December limbs devoid of the sweet-smelling flowers that would carry on the spring breeze and decorate the cobblestone path and patches of bright green grass with delicate petals.

What could he tell his son? It was as if Marielena's passing had whisked away his joy of cooking for his loved ones. Of rolling up his sleeves and dirtying his hands with flour and water as he mixed pastelillo dough. Or filling the house with the musky scent of crispy bacon and sautéeing garlic while he peeled and sliced and fried green plantains for his special shrimp and bacon mofongo. Or opening the oven door, letting sweet steam billow out as he removed a batch of mini flans for a familia movie night treat.

Cooking for others had been a love language learned at his mami's side from a young age. While his mind worked in numbers and spreadsheets and market values, skills that led to his rise up the ranks at the bank and his current position as VP of Distress Trading, his heart bled an orange-red tint from the sazón and achiote found in many of the Puerto Rican recipes he had mastered and revamped over the years. Until...

The slap of sneakers hitting the tile floor alerted him to Luisito's approach. Reaching his side, his son pulled the boxed pastries from the toaster.

"It's okay, Papi, you'll get your mojo back." Luisito patted Héctor's arm, then took a super-sized bite of a tart. Crumbs tumbled onto the speckled countertop.

But unlike the indecision twisting Héctor's insides, Luisito's eyes gleamed with certainty.

"Speaking of mojo," Luisito said, his tone serious. "I'm working on mine."

"You are?"

"Uh-huh. There's a new girl at school. Jennifer. And she's... she's..." His son's tanned complexion darkened with a blush.

Alarm bells clanged in Héctor's head. His coffee mug plunked on the counter, the dark tan liquid nearly sloshing over the rim.

Coño, Luisito was only eleven. It was too early for that all-important discussion about your body's natural reaction to someone you found attractive. About mutual respect, using protection, and the healthy aspects of pleasuring yourself. Wasn't it?

"So, this, uh, Jennifer. She's nice, huh?" Héctor ventured, tiptoeing into the conversation like a man on the shore of Lake Michigan readying himself for a mid-winter polar bear dip.

Luisito rolled his eyes, the epitome of a preteen exasperated by an adult.

"Papi, she's *way* more than that. Jennifer's smart and pretty. She has this great laugh. And her voice." A hand talker like his mami, Luisito's hands fluttered in the air with his excitement. "I was in the band room for drum practice when Jennifer was next door auditioning for choir. ¡Diantre! She sings like a freakin' angel. Like how I used to imagine the angel on top of our tree would sound!"

He pointed to their six-foot Douglas fir, set in the center of the expansive living room window overlooking Pacific Street. At the top perched a dark-haired angel with tan skin, hazel eyes, and fluffy feather wings. She wore a long, billowy white dress and waved a Puerto Rican flag in one hand. Héctor's gaze traveled down the decorations, ranging from fancy blown glass orbs to the ones Luisito had made from construction paper and glitter in preschool. At the tree's base nestled an empty manger, waiting for Nochebuena, when El Niño Jesus would arrive. Right after they returned home from their annual Nochebuena dinner with his goddaughter Lily's familia and some of their closest friends.

The same dinner Eneida was needling him about bringing a plus-one to. A date he wasn't even sure he was ready to go looking for.

¡Embuste!

Yeah, he *was* lying to himself.

A steadily growing part of him wanted to find someone. Craved it, even. Especially late at night when the house was quiet, and he was assailed by memories of the intimacies he and his wife had shared.

Having a partner. Someone who accepted you, flaws and all. Your person. Coño, how he missed that connection.

Was he supposed to just be thankful he'd been lucky enough to experience it in the first place? Many people never did.

Dios, what a depressing thought. One he knew would have Marielena, Eneida, and every woman in his familia shaking a chancla in his direction. Also one his lonely heart rejected.

". . . so I signed up. I just need your help paying for the private lessons, okay?"

Luisito gazed up at him expectantly, and Héctor realized that while he'd been throwing himself a private pity party, he'd missed most of what his son had just said.

"Pa, were you even listening?" Luisito sucked his teeth at Héctor's blank stare. "I wrote a song for Jennifer and I'm singing it in this year's Christmas Talent Pageant. Ms. Pagán said she could help me with the chords on my guitar, but we have to—"

"Wait, you wrote a song? And you plan on getting up in front of the entire school to serenade this girl?" Héctor's pulse raced as if his son was asking *him* to perform.

"Jennifer. Uh-huh." A self-satisfied grin split Luisito's pastry crumb–sprinkled mouth. Hands deep in the front pockets of his khaki uniform pants, he rocked back on his heels. "Mami always said if there's something you want, hazlo con ganas. So that's what I'm doing, going for it with gusto."

His son's gung-ho attitude, so different from Héctor's deliberate, think-first-act-later mentality, had his chest swelling with pride. Maybe even a little envy. When had his Lego-loving little boy gotten so grown up?

"So can you come to the band room after school?" Luisito strolled through the open dining area and into the living room, where his backpack sat on the black leather sofa. "Ms. Pagán said she has to clear it with you before my first lesson."

Ms. Pagán.

The temporary—also appealingly memorable—band teacher who had started mid-fall semester.

Héctor had only met the woman once, at the band parents' meeting when she was first hired after the long-time teacher's emergency heart surgery. Either Cristina Pagán was a child prodigy who'd earned her master's degree from NYU's School of Music in her teens, or she was older than her youthful energy, enchanting smile, and flawless skin made her seem. Talk about a first impression that had left him bamboozled!

Sitting in an industrial-grade plastic chair, surrounded by other parents crammed into the room, Héctor had shifted in his seat, uncomfortably aware of his body's instant response to the engaging teacher who had strolled into the room with a swish of the floral skirt that skimmed her shapely calves.

Héctor had left without speaking to her, disconcerted by the throbbing awareness her lilting voice and warm personality had awakened inside him. He hadn't seen her since. Though he'd certainly heard enough about her from his son, who regularly raved about the Broadway musician now at the helm of the music department.

"Can you, Pa? She wants to see you," Luisito pleaded.

She wants to see you.

There was no reason for Héctor to read any subtext into the words.

But he did. Especially the secret part of him that had been wanting to see her again too.

"Okay, I'll be there."

"Sweet!" Luisito snagged his backpack, then headed for the foyer to slip on his winter coat.

Sweet? More like sweaty palm–inducing.

Eneida and the rest of the women in Héctor's familia wanted to hip-check him back into the dating game. Maybe talking to a woman who quickened his pulse, but in a mundane, comfortable setting like the school, could be good practice.

The clock was ticking, and he was running out of time to find a suitable plus-one for Nochebuena dinner. If he were lucky, Cristina Pagán might be the key to helping both Gutiérrez men fulfill their romantic Christmas wishes.

CHAPTER 2

"Mami, por favor. I already explained why I can't come home for the holidays." Cradling her forehead with one palm, Cristina swallowed a sigh and leaned back in her creaky desk chair.

Guilt at her mom's disappointment weighed on her, but it was quickly brushed aside by her own frustration. ¡Coño! She had been pushing herself for the past five years. First as a student in NYU's musical department, earning her master's degree. Then doggedly trying to land a permanent spot in the orchestra pit of a Broadway show. Subbing on the fly whenever anyone called her to fill in. Selectively building her private lessons side hustle. Teaching here at Saint Cecilia's because she'd been assured it was a great way to make contacts with people who knew people who knew people.

Yet despite her dedication to her dream, her parents and entire familia back in Puerto Rico didn't understand. Hence the passive aggressive and flat-out aggressive badgering for her to hop a flight back to the island for the holidays. Preferably for good.

Instead, as she had for the past three years since graduation, she stuck around NYC, ready to race to a theater should she get an emergency call from a show.

Her phone buzzed, and she pulled it away from her ear to check the notification.

Calendar Reminder: Parent Meeting: Héctor and Luis Gutiérrez

Her breath hitched.

While her mom's nonstop lament droned on in a decent Charlie Brown's teacher impersonation, Cristina finger-combed her hair. She pressed the back of her hand to her chin, nose, and forehead, blotting her T-zone. When she started reaching for her purse to touch up her lipstick, she drew to a flustered halt.

This was a parent meeting, not a date. So what if it happened to be with "the Catch," as some of the single—and not-so-single—band booster parents had dubbed Héctor Gutiérrez. For good reason.

She'd only seen the man once, at the meeting when she'd been introduced. He'd sat in the back row, silent but fidgety, almost broody, oozing a magnetism she hadn't been able to forget.

"Mami, me tengo que ir."

Her mom sputtered at the abrupt interruption and Cristina repeated herself, tacking on an explanation to appease her mom's complaints. "I really do have to go. My student should be here any minute."

"Ay, por favor, nena, think about what I said. We miss you."

The sorrow in her mami's voice rained like vitamin-fortified water on the seed of homesickness buried in Cristina's heart. Fertilized, the seed sprouted a tiny forget-me-not bud.

"I'm sure Padre Francisco would rehire you as the church choir director," her mami insisted. "Plus, I saw Franco grocery shopping at the mercado the other day. He misses you too, nena."

Her mother's words snipped the newly sprouted bud with shears sharpened by past disappointments. The seedling withered and was immediately swept up by the turmoil swirling like hurricane winds in Cristina's heart.

She didn't want her old job back. Or her cheating ex. Both only led to dead ends filled with regrets and what-ifs.

She wanted a new life here, in the boroughs of New York City. Even if striving for that meant holidays away from home, ready to answer the call from a Broadway show in need of a last minute substitute in the orchestra pit. Being a dependable sub strengthened her reputation as a talented, reliable musician deserving of a full-time gig.

A knock sounded on the band room door. Her pulse picked up its tempo, moving into an alegrissimo.

"They're here," she told her mom.

"Llámame mas tarde."

"Fine, I'll call during my walk home. Te quiero." She hung up without waiting for her mom's answering "I love you," then rose on shaky legs. Pressing a hand to her jittery stomach, Cristina sucked in a slow, steadying breath.

In her short time at Saint Cecilia's, she'd never been nervous about a parent-teacher meeting. Yet with Héctor Gutiérrez about to enter, she found herself wiping her sweaty palms on the skirt of her dark green sweater dress.

"Come in," she called.

Luisito Gutiérrez poked his head inside. His expectant expression lulled the swarm of Puerto Rican harlequin butterflies anxiously flapping their wings in her belly, slowing them to a languid beat.

"Are you ready for us?" he asked.

For him, or any of her students, the answer was yes. She was always ready to help a budding musician.

For the tall, broad-shouldered man standing behind the boy... the hunk who looked like a Brooks Brothers model with his long, navy wool coat unbuttoned over a dark suit and tie, a light five o'clock shadow shading his jaw with roguish appeal, his full lips tipping in a hesitant smile... Ay, the suddenly frantic endangered butterflies warned that she was ready for more than what she knew was prudent.

"Of course!"

She waved the father-son duo into her classroom, all the while reminding herself that, along with her own "no dating the parents of her private students" rule, Saint Cecilia's principal had made it clear that parent-teacher fraternization was a commandment breaker.

"Sweet!" Luisito raced in with the exuberance most kids showed when exiting school. His father ambled behind him with a slow, rolling gait that amped up her anticipation.

"It's nice to see you again, Ms. Pagán." Héctor's voice was deep and rich, the bass note in a chord that echoed through her. His slight Spanish accent added a musical lilt to his words that reminded her of home.

He extended his hand politely. Cristina reciprocated and found hers engulfed by the warmth of his palm. His fingers wrapped around hers in what shouldn't feel like an embrace, but, coño, if her body didn't react like it was, going all tingly and heated in private places.

"My pleasure. And, por favor, call me Cristina."

She winced at the breathiness of her words. Clearing her throat, she focused on Luisito, the reason they were all here. "Did you fill in your dad about your big plans?"

"Uh-huh," Luisito answered. "He's here to sign the approval form and see what times are okay for you to come over to our house."

"Our house?" Brow furrowed, Héctor tugged at his navy-and-white striped tie uncomfortably. "Your lessons won't be here, after school?"

Luisito shook his head. His shoulders lifted and fell in an ambivalent shrug. Like his father's surprise was no big deal.

Héctor's throat moved with a swallow as he gave his tie another tug. She'd heard about his guarded personality. How he mostly hung out with Eneida Lucero or kept to himself at parent meetings and school events. Especially in the years since his wife's passing.

Cristina moved out from behind her desk, schooling her features into a reassuring expression normally saved for calming nervous students pre-performance.

"Because the lessons aren't organized or paid through the school, they can't take place on campus," Cristina explained. "If it's a problem and you'd prefer us to not meet at your house—"

"What? No! It's not a—no es un problema," Héctor assured her, though his frown said otherwise. "In the before-school rush this morning, Luisito didn't explain everything, so I'm catching up here."

"Oops, perdón, Papi," Luisito apologized, his brown eyes wide with chagrin. "I got so excited, I musta forgot that part. But it's okay, huh? Plus, practicing guitar will keep me off the drums. I figure you and the neighbors won't mind that." He waggled his brows playfully, clearly pleased with his reasoning.

Héctor's chuckle rumbled from his chest in a husky rasp that sent a delicious shiver shimmying across Cristina's shoulders.

"The silver lining in your adventurous plan." Héctor patted his son's shoulder, leaving his hand there in a show of support. "I'm excited for you, too, mijo. You're going to be great!"

The duo shared matching grins, Héctor's tinged with pride. His encouragement of his son's musical ambition made him even more appealing. Had this been a Broadway show, she imagined a delightful arpeggio playing in the background. In an old Rodgers & Hammerstein production, they'd break into a short dance number.

"Why don't you go grab your backpack from your locker while I discuss the logistics with Ms. Pagán?" Héctor told his son. "Then you can get to work on wooing your young lady."

"Wooing?" Luisito's face scrunched with confusion.

"Uh, enticing?" Héctor tried.

"Charming?" Cristina added.

"Impressing!" they said in unison.

Héctor flashed her a conspiratorial smile that sparked playfully in his dark eyes. A dimple winked in his left cheek, igniting lust in a swift line of fire that shot straight to her core. Dios mío, the rumors of this man's charisma weren't the run-of-the-mill chisme she had assumed them to be. The gossip about him was based on pure fact.

"Ahhh, like, blowing her mind. But in a good way, right?" Luisito asked.

"Exactly," Héctor said.

Luisito gave them a thumbs-up, then hurried out.

Seconds later, the wooden door slid shut with a soft click of its latch, leaving Cristina alone with the first man to have her pondering potential wintery date-night activities in the city. Foolish musings for a woman who didn't have time for distractions. Especially the kind that could get her fired.

"He's a good kid. Extremely talented," Cristina said, once again trying to focus on the reason why they were here.

"Gracias. He's also determined." Hands in his trouser pockets, Héctor ambled closer. "To be honest, in the months since you took over the band program, I've noticed the resurgence of his love of music. There's laughter in the house again. Mostly his, pero... bueno..."

Héctor trailed off. His gaze shifted to the piano off to the right. One corner of his mouth curved in a self-deprecating half smirk, and she wondered if he had revealed more than he normally would.

But... well, what?

His son was laughing again. Was Héctor?

The holidays were hard enough when distance separated you from loved ones, as it did with Cristina. But for this man—whose respectful, loving, and playful relationship with his son seemed to mirror the one he was known to have shared with his wife—the holidays must be extremely difficult.

"It's wonderful to hear that band class is helping Luisito heal," she said.

"I'm betting it's more the teacher than the class itself."

Heat seeped into her cheeks at the same time pride straightened her shoulders. "Gracias. I enjoy sharing my love of music with my students."

"It shows. At least it does with my son. Nothing against Mr. Lewis —whom I wish a full and speedy recovery—but he's a bit old-school. More symphony than rock 'n roll, if you get my drift."

"Believe me, you're not the first to mention that."

There went his raspy chuckle again. And again, it rubbed over her like a cat's rough tongue laving her bare skin.

Maybe her primas were right. How many times had her two closest cousins complained that she was too focused on work and her music? The lack of fun and relaxation time—her zero dating in recent years—was the only suitable explanation for this schoolgirl giddiness Héctor Gutiérrez made her feel. A reaction she'd have to figure out how to shut down or ignore.

Héctor slid his cell from his inside coat pocket. "With the talent show already a week away, I'm guessing this isn't a one-practice-a-week situation."

"Good guess." Cristina sank onto the front edge of her desk and reached for her planner. "It helps that Luisito's amazingly musically inclined. Along with the drums, I've heard him on our piano. And he says he's been teaching himself the guitar by watching online videos at home."

"My wife was his musical influence. My talents lie more in the kitchen. She bought him the guitar right before she got sick. I hadn't realized he had picked it up again." Worry lines creased Héctor's brow. His broad shoulders drooped, and her heart went out to him.

"I'm so sorry for your loss," she murmured.

He blinked, shook his head as if clearing away burdensome thoughts, then turned his focus back to her. "Gracias. Knowing how active the parent network—or as it's known in our casa, the nosy network—can be, I figure you've heard the pertinent details. Probably more." His tone lacked any censure or annoyance. Even the sorrow she had expected to hear was tempered by a remarkable sense of acceptance.

"We're getting by," Héctor continued. "Slowly figuring out a new normal. I think we're both ready to move forward. Although I was surprised to hear that Luisito's plan includes a solo number in front of the whole school."

His exaggerated shudder made her laugh. He smiled, and the dimple in his cheek winked at her again, knocking her heart out of rhythm.

She glanced down at her planner, open in her lap. Seeing her responsibilities and obligations was a visual antidote to the charming personality that had her temp rising like that old hit "La Bilirrubina."

"Speaking of Luisito, for liability reasons, another adult must be home during lessons. We can try to work around your schedule. Or, if there's someone you—I mean, if there's a family member who usually helps out?"

Heat suffused her cheeks at her near gaffe. Thankfully her brain caught up to her mouth before she asked about a potential new partner. No way did she want it to look like she was fishing for info about his dating life. A popular topic around the chisme mill.

"Usually my mami or a tía fills in. But with the holidays, they're busy volunteering with church and neighborhood events, so I'm scrambling a bit. What's your availability like?"

Héctor surprised her by moving to sit beside her on the edge of her desk as he opened the calendar app on his phone. His shoulder gently bumped hers and she sucked in a quick breath. A hint of cedar and spice assailed her senses. Desire curled in warm ribbons that floated from her chest into her belly. Lower.

Together they perused their calendars, with her privately noting his lack of social engagements despite the holiday season. Everything was either colored green for work or orange for Luisito and familia. No red for a special someone.

The wicked idea of inviting him to pencil in some adult time with her teased the tip of her tongue. She bit down on it. Her planner was full with teaching, career plans, and familia guilt trips, and now these two extra lessons with Luisito. The first, late afternoon tomorrow. That gave her about twenty-four hours to get this infatuation with Héctor Gutiérrez under control.

Closing her planner, Cristina made herself stand and circle behind her desk. A shield between her and the temptation he presented.

By tomorrow, she needed to walk into Héctor Gutiérrez's home like the consummate professional she prided herself on being. Keeping her distance from the enticing scent of his cologne, sexy broodiness, and heart-fluttering dimple.

But as he treated her to a friendly smile and waved goodbye, his deep "see you tomorrow" both a promise and a threat, Cristina knew she had her work cut out for her if she planned on ignoring her simmering attraction.

CHAPTER 3

"What do you think about something like this?" Cristina's question drifted from the sala at the front of the house to the kitchen where Héctor sat working on his laptop. Seconds later, the guitar strings hummed with the chord she demonstrated to his son.

Héctor had purposefully sat with his back to the living room. Still, he easily pictured her hugging the guitar close. Long, dainty fingers of one hand expertly pressing and releasing the strings along the instrument's neck while her other hand strummed lower.

She had arrived nearly thirty minutes ago, her tan cheeks and pert nose rosy from the frigid late December wind, eyes alight with pleasure as she greeted Luisito, pink lips tipped in a polite smile for Héctor.

Since then, he'd been sneaking glances over his shoulder at her. Telling himself he was only interested in Luisito's progress. Not the woman whose patient encouragement and bubbly laughter had Héctor wishing he was part of their fun.

Ha! He'd rewritten an email several times and finally minimized a document after repeatedly reading the opening paragraph without remembering a single word. No use denying it. If there was anyone he might be excited to meet under the mistletoe Luisito had insisted they hang in the foyer, it was Cristina Pagán.

"Hi, how's it going over here?"

Héctor started as the object of his infatuation sidled up to the opposite end of the kitchen island.

"Working away." He pushed his laptop screen closed to hide the proof of his distraction-driven online Christmas shopping and swiveled on the padded bar stool to face her. "Are you two done already?"

She shook her head, sending her brown, wavy tresses dancing along her shoulders. "Quick bathroom break for Luisito. Also gives his hands and fingers a rest before we run through what we covered. He's doing great. And his song is really sweet."

"'Christmas Crush'?"

"Catchy title, isn't it?"

"Makes his intentions clear." Héctor shot her a bemused grin.

An answering smile curved her lips, plumping her cheeks and dancing in her hazel-green eyes. His heart executed a cha-cha step of its own.

Chuckling, she leaned her right hip against the granite countertop edge. Her fingers toyed with a gold necklace that spelled out her name, two diamond specks accenting the *i*'s.

The motion drew his attention to her elegant neck, smooth skin, and delicate collarbones left bare by the wide neck of her pale pink cashmere sweater. His gaze trailed down to the deep vee hugging the hint of cleavage. Aware that he shouldn't be ogling her, he forced himself to look away.

"Based on the lyrics he's written, Luisito's a romantic at heart," Cristina said. "I couldn't help but 'awww' inside when I read them. Does he get that from you?"

The fingers toying with her necklace stilled and her eyes widened with shock. "Ay Dios mío, that was not meant to sound like a... a... fishing expedition. I am not interested in—I mean, you're an appeal—"

A mortified expression stamping her features, she broke off and pushed away from the counter. Her foot inadvertently knocked the bar stool next to his, and it teetered on two wooden legs. Héctor reached for the stool at the same time as Cristina. His hand closed over hers on the padded edge.

Their gazes met. Held. In a strange, slow motion, they set the stool upright, but neither moved to release it.

Warmth spread from his palm, up his arm, suffusing his entire body. The urge to pull her closer, drag in more of the faint floral scent that tinged the air around her, thrashed inside him like a racehorse anxious for the starting gate to open and let him run free.

His fingers flexed over hers, tightening their hold. Surprise mixed with awareness in Cristina's expressive eyes. The tip of her tongue slid across her bottom lip before she tucked the plump flesh between her teeth.

Lust and longing whooshed through him... a heady combination he hadn't felt in ages. The sensation swelled inside him, filling empty spaces he'd been loath to admit existed. Until now. Until her.

Out in the hall, the door to the half bath creaked as it opened.

Héctor snatched his hand away. Cristina gasped and stumbled back a step, as if they were two teens on the verge of being caught in an illicit act. She finger-combed her wavy tresses with a nervous glance in his direction. Coño, good thing he kept forgetting to WD-40 those hinges. Talk about a warning signal.

Seconds later, Luisito appeared in the sala. "Ready to wow you with my mad skills!"

"The kid's definitely got confidence," Cristina murmured, her startled expression giving way to a pleased smirk Héctor found far too sexy for his own good. Without another word to him, she strode back to the living room. "Show me what you got!"

Listening to her easy banter with his son, Héctor could almost convince himself that he had imagined the flash of shared attraction moments ago. Almost. If he ignored the fast cha-cha-cha rhythm beating in his chest and the tightness in the front of his pants.

Then again, maybe he'd misread her signals.

Dread soured the saliva in his mouth. Coño, he hadn't flirted with someone in ages. The last time he'd approached a woman about a date, there'd been no gray in his hair. No doubt his dating skills had passed rusty and moved into petrified.

What would he have done if Luisito hadn't interrupted them?

The truth taunted him.

Probably the same thing he'd done with the phone numbers of potential dates his mami and others continuously slipped him: nothing.

And yet, with Cristina, a titillating interest niggled at him.

Her and Luisito's shared laughter filled the open first floor. A spurt of jealousy surprised the hell out of Héctor.

Carajo, how had his son become the only Gutiérrez male confident enough to make a move on a girl? And what did Héctor plan to do to change that?

TWO DAYS LATER, Héctor continued puzzling over the same damn questions.

It didn't help that Eneida hadn't let up on her "Nochebuena plus-one or else" ultimatum. Her text reminders were like that old *Mission: Impossible* message warning about self-destruction. *His* self-destruction if he botched his friend's daring mission.

Luisito's excitement over his upcoming performance—plus his certainty that it would win his crush's affection—were tangible forces encouraging Héctor's newly awakened resolve to get back to the land of the living.

That's how he found himself in the kitchen, shirt sleeves rolled up, his fingertips coated with egg and spiced flour, preparing one of Luisito's favorite meals: chicken breast nuggets with truffle fries and mashed cauliflower. Relaxed and at home in his kitchen for the first time in ages.

If he timed things right, he'd have the food on the table just as Luisito finished his lesson. While his son washed up for dinner, Héctor planned to walk Cristina to the front stoop. Where he'd invite her for coffee.

No pressure. The type of date that could be cut short if he crashed and burned. Or extended into a meal if they hit it off.

The doorbell rang, followed immediately by Luisito's "¡Yo lo cojo!" His sneakers pounded on the stairs and hardwood flooring as he ran to answer it.

Like one of Pavlov's dogs, Cristina's bright "Hola, Luisito, great to see you" had Héctor's pulse pounding faster than his son's feet seconds ago.

"Oops, we got caught under the mistletoe," Luisito said with a laugh. "¿Abrazos?"

From the kitchen, Héctor couldn't see them hug in the foyer, but he easily pictured Cristina's laughing eyes, her full lips spreading in her wide grin. Exactly like in his dreams the last two nights. Only, with him, they had done far more than hug, and he'd woken in the morning with a boner aching for release.

Cristina and Luisito entered the sala, his son chattering away about chords and hitting high notes without his voice cracking.

"Buenas noches," she called to Héctor.

He lifted a flour-dusted hand to wave, but his greeting dissolved on his tongue when he saw her. A long-sleeved, cropped black sweater skimmed her torso. The hem barely reached the high waistband of her form-fitting black pants, their cuffs brushing the tops of her black combat boots. Her dark hair was slicked back in a smooth chignon, accentuating the sharp angles of her cheekbones, artfully arched brows, and angular chin.

She bent to set her brown satchel bag on the coffee table, and her sweater rode up, treating him to a flash of bare, tanned skin.

His mind skipped to a memory from one of his lust-filled dreams. His hands spanning her waist, gliding up her torso. The rasp of her quickening breath as his palms cradled the weight of her full breasts. Her pupils dilating with desire in the seconds before he bent to—

"Papi's making my fave for dinner," Luisito announced, jerking Héctor out of his wanton daydream.

Embarrassed by how easily he morphed into a prepubescent teen unable to control his impulses where she was concerned, Héctor ducked his head and got back to work.

"No one makes nuggets like he does," Luisito continued. "Hey, you should join us!"

The chunk of chicken slipped from Héctor's fingers to plop into the whipped egg bowl with a little splash.

"Ay, gracias, but I can't intrude," Cristina said.

"It's not intruding. Papi always makes extra so we have leftovers. Bueno, he used to. It's been a while since—"

"We'd love for you to join us," Héctor broke in, surprising himself as much as her, based on the quick double blink of Cristina's eyes.

"Are you sure?" she asked.

The hesitant frown wedging between her brows—so different from her easygoing smile with his son moments ago—bothered him. Made him want to do whatever it took to have her eyes sparkle with a similar joy when she looked at him.

"Positive," he answered.

Her frown faded. The corners of her full lips tipped upward, and her pointy chin dipped, then rose with a faint nod.

He grinned, pleased when her smile widened.

Moments later, Héctor caught himself humming along to his son's much-improved love song. Stealing glances at the patient, talented, engaging woman who seemed to be working her magic on both Gutiérrez men.

CHAPTER 4

"How many stormtroopers does it take to change a light bulb?" Luisito asked.

"None, because they're all on the dark side," Héctor answered without missing a beat.

Cristina chortled at Luisito's, "Aw man, I thought I stumped you with that one."

One hand pressed to her stomach—now full thanks to Héctor's delicious cooking but also aching from all the laughter—she wiped a tear from her eye.

Dinner had been a delightful affair.

Héctor and Luisito had such great rapport, their love and respect evident in their gentle teasing and easy conversation. Over dinner, the three of them had talked about the talent show, the latest holiday blockbuster movie Luisito hoped to see during the school break, and a new YA novel the father and son were reading together that also happened to be on Cristina's TBR list.

She'd been nervous about breaking bread with the man she hadn't been able to stop thinking about. Imagining the hand that had covered hers on the bar stool the other evening moving to touch her in places that made her pulse race and her insides melt with white-hot desire.

Despite her initial jitters, spending time with the father-son duo felt comfortable. Right.

Now that their plates were empty, Héctor and his son had spent the last few minutes engaged in a rapid-fire battle of bad jokes that made her head spin. And totally charmed her.

"Did you hear about the circus fire?" she threw out, entering the fray for the first time.

Two sets of obsidian eyes widened with astonishment as father and son turned to her.

"It was in tents," she finished, her tone heavy with mock trepidation.

Across the table, Luisito threw back his head and howled.

Héctor actually snorted, his shoulders shaking with his laughter. This was a side of him few had seen, based on the "silent and aloof but oh-so-sexy" description whispered among other parents and teachers. Relaxed and at ease, eyes crinkling with mirth, deftly rattling off silly jokes in a game the two must play often...

Coño, the man was freaking irresistible.

"Welcome to the bad joke club." Leaning toward her from his seat at the head of the table, Héctor patted her forearm where it rested between their place settings. But when he sat back, his hand remained on her arm. The weight and warmth gave rise to all kinds of "bad" thoughts that had nothing to do with jokes and would no doubt feel really, *really* good.

"Oooh, I heard one the other day and typed it in Notes on my cell. May I go grab it, since we're done eating?' Luisito hopped out of his high-backed dinner chair but waited for his father to give him permission.

Héctor's nod sent the boy hurrying up to his bedroom, leaving her alone with Héctor.

"This was nice. Gracias por la invitación," she said.

"My pleasure. Your dinner invitation is always open."

His quiet admission surprised her. Sent a thrill arrowing through her. She stared into his smoldering eyes, wondering if he felt it too. This intense connection. The electricity crackling around them. His thumb rubbed a sensual back-and-forth caress on her forearm, lulling her into forgetting all the reasons why this was a bad idea.

The wiser side of her brain prevailed, and she slid her arm out from under his grasp to pick up her empty plate and water glass. "It's getting late, I should help you clean up."

His chair legs scraped the wood flooring as he rose too. "Don't worry about it. Luisito's got kitchen duty tonight."

As if on cue, the preteen rounded the balustrade. A scandalized look blanched his round face. His arm outstretched, Luisito held out his phone like it might bite him. "Papi! Papi! She texted me! She asked if I could talk! What do I say?"

"Bueno, do you want to talk to her?" Héctor answered.

"Pffft. Yeah!" his son scoffed, punctuating it with an eye roll.

"What's the problem then?"

"What if I say something dumb and she writes me off before I can sing for her?"

Héctor crossed his arms with a *humph* and a stern scowl. Sure signs a parental answer was forthcoming. Probably not the man-to-man guidance Cristina figured his son wanted.

"Primero," Héctor said, "I highly doubt you'll say anything dumb. Second, if she reacts like that, then she doesn't deserve your song."

"Ugh, Pa, you're not helping."

Having witnessed many teen meltdowns thanks to raging hormones and young love, Cristina gently clasped Luisito's shoulder. "Odds are, she's at her house, nervously waiting for your response. Equally as worried as you."

"¿Deveras?" Luisito's face scrunched with hopeful worry.

"Yes, really. Believe me, I was once an eleven-year-old girl with a crush too."

"Sweet!" A relieved grin accompanied Luisito's favorite exclamation. "Papi, can I come down for dish duty when I'm done?"

"I'll cover you," Cristina offered. "As long as you practice before bed. The show run-through is tomorrow night. You wanna be ready."

"I will be," he promised. Luisito moved toward the stairs, but suddenly spun back around to throw his arms around her waist.

Giving her a tight squeeze, he mumbled, "Gracias, you're the best," before releasing her and running out of the room.

Warmed by his show of affection, Cristina splayed a hand over her heart, smiling as he disappeared up the stairs.

"Once again, you saved the day. How did you learn such magic?" Héctor asked. "And can you teach me?"

"Are you asking me to divulge my secrets?" she teased, pleased by his answering chuckle.

With an amused shake of his head, he stacked the plates and silverware, then carried them into the kitchen. She followed with their drink glasses, intent on keeping her promise to complete the chore, then copy Luisito's race from the room.

Only, she'd be running *away from* temptation.

"Seriously, parenting is not easy. Have you always been good with kids?" Héctor asked, nudging the faucet handle up to rinse off the plates.

Cristina set the glasses on the counter beside him and considered his question. "I guess so. As a preteen, I volunteered in our church nursery. Then, as my musical skills improved, I started giving beginner piano and violin lessons. My last semester of undergrad at the University of Puerto Rico, the musical director at our local parish decided to retire. It was kind of a given that I'd step in."

Héctor bent to open the dishwasher, setting the plates in the lower rack. She told herself not to look... to walk away and finish clearing the table... but por favor, the man's long legs, muscular thighs, and ass stretched the material of his Levi's in such a delectable way.

"So have you always wanted to be a music teacher?" He snagged the silverware from the sink, then bent again.

Damn, he had a great ass. Was he a boxers or a brief guy? Or... oof, commando! Ay, she bit her lip to keep a hum of appreciation from slipping out.

The metallic clash of forks and knives dropping into the plastic bin roused her from her horny musings to find him sending a quizzical glance over his shoulder.

"Wha—? Uh... no." She shook her head. "Teaching pays the bills. I'll stop working at Saint Cecilia's when I land a permanent chair with a Broadway show. That's my dream job. And the reason why I'm staying in the city instead of heading home to Puerto Rico to see my family for the holidays."

He straightened abruptly, spinning to face her. "You're not from one of the boroughs?"

"Uh-uh. Born and raised in Puerto Rico. Came to NYU for my masters a few years ago and never went back. Much to everyone's chagrin."

"So what are your plans for the holidays?"

"Cook my own Nochebuena feast, lamenting that it's not as tasty as my mami's, while hoping I get a call to fill in at a show. Every sub spot could eventually lead to a permanent one. You never know what's around the corner."

"You never know," he murmured.

His dark eyes flared with... sympathy that she was spending the holidays alone? A question, maybe?

They stared at each other, the light from the trio of blown glass globes hanging above the kitchen island bouncing off the window, blocking the darkened world outside to create the illusion that only the two of them existed. Them, and this awareness that shimmered and crackled and threatened to consume her.

"I should, um..." She stumbled over the words, torn between moving closer and backing away.

Give in to the tug of attraction or play it safe?

"I'm glad you stayed. We enjoyed... *I've* enjoyed your company tonight," Héctor said, his rich bass voice wreaking havoc with her ability to form coherent words.

As if he read her thoughts, sensed her inner turmoil, he edged closer. Not enough to encroach on her personal space. But if she dared to take a baby step toward him... toward temptation...

A temptation that could torch her job and everything she'd been working toward.

"I should grab th-the other dishes, so we can, um, finish."

Coward.

Héctor tucked his chin in a slow nod, and Cristina scurried to the dining room.

Her back to him, she dragged in a slow breath, willing the bongosero playing a fast martillo pattern in her chest to give his bongos a rest already.

Dios mío, the loneliness of spending another holiday by herself must be getting to her. Staying in the city was a necessary sacrifice, but that didn't lessen the pang of homesickness. Nor the desire to share her familia's traditions with a special someone.

All those holiday rom-coms she binged probably weren't helping either. It was one thing to daydream in your apartment. But to get all swoony and aroused in Héctor Gutiérrez's kitchen? Talk about embarrassing.

Better to keep her distance and her wits, quit ogling the man, and stick to mundane topics while they finished up.

"So, besides chicken nuggets, truffle fries, and the best mashed cauliflower I've ever tasted," she said, snagging the serving dishes, "what else is on the Héctor Gutiérrez menu?"

"Ooh, it's an extensive one."

"Really? I'm intrigued."

"You're good with music students. I'm good in the kitchen."

Imagining all the wickedly *good* things she'd like to do with him in the kitchen brought a nervous laugh bubbling up and out before she could stop it.

Héctor narrowed his eyes in a playful glare, softened by the smile tilting his lips. "Are you doubting my skills?"

"Me?" she teased in an innocent-as-pie voice. "Never."

His answering "pffft"—the same response Luisito had given him a time or two—had her chuckling.

After setting the serving dishes on the counter, she reached for a yellow-and-green sponge in a caddy near the edge of the sink to wipe off the table. Héctor leaned to his left, giving her room to hold the sponge under the open faucet. He didn't lean far enough, and her upper arm brushed his chest. Tingles of awareness skittered through her.

"Here, let me," he said.

The fingers of his left hand tangled with hers around the sponge. Warm water cascaded over their joined hands as he swung his right arm behind her to press his palm on the small of her back. His thumb tucked under the edge of her cropped sweater, teasing her bare skin.

It took all her willpower to not sink into him. Let her head rest against his shoulder. Turn to wrap her arms around his waist so they stood face to face. Chest to chest. Heat to heat.

She tried to focus on the tasks at hand: wet the sponge, wipe down the table. Ignore the desire pulsing in her body like lasers at a techno music fest. Leave before she got herself into trouble.

"Gracias," she mumbled, pulling their hands out from under the water stream and easing a tentative sidestep away.

The pressure from Héctor's palm on the small of her back increased, then relaxed. Not forcefully, but enough to signal his intent that she stay.

Conflicted, she tipped her chin and found him gazing down at her, tenderness softening his features.

"I meant what I said earlier. The invitation to join us again is always open. I'd love to cook something other than chicken nuggets for you. Maybe a meal that pairs better with wine and adult conversation?"

Her lonely heart fluttered at his softly spoken admission. His expectant question, paired with his nervous swallow, weakened her knees. And her resolve to quickly finish the chore and leave.

Oh, she could easily fall for this man if she wasn't careful.

Ha! She was halfway there already!

Releasing her hand, he shut off the faucet, then stepped aside to snag a blue hand towel hanging on the oven door handle.

Coño, if she didn't miss his touch. The solid feel of his chest against her left side. The tantalizing sensation of his thumb caressing a path along her back, above her waistband.

But with distance came clarity.

And clearly, she needed to go before she did something that might jeopardize her position at Saint Cecilia's.

Disappointed but resolute, she dropped the sponge back into the caddy. Time to make her exit. "I appreciate you indulging Luisito after his unexpected invite, and the extended offer of hospitality. It's always a pleasure getting to know my students and their parents better."

Héctor's brows angled together in a disconcerted frown.

She winced, realizing she might have carved out a moat instead of a mere line in the sand between them. However, firmly ensconcing herself on the teacher side and him on the parent provided her a polite escape route.

A truth her brain recognized, even while the rest of her complained.

"It's getting late, and I should go. Tomorrow'll be a long day with the full run-through for the talent show." Hurrying around the island, she strode toward the front of the house to grab her satchel bag. "Gracias, la comida estuvo rica."

True, the food had been delicious. Enhanced by the company.

Héctor's footsteps followed behind her. "You're welcome. If you're free—"

"Please tell Luisito I said goodbye," she interrupted, afraid Héctor was about to invite her for dinner on a specific date. More afraid she wouldn't be able to say no.

"Sure. Uh, sí, I will."

An awkward silence filled the foyer as she took her jacket off the coat rack, mumbling an, "Oh, I've got it," and sidestepping his attempt to help her with it.

"Cristina?"

She didn't have to see Héctor's face to know her brush-off confused him. It laced his tone, the thread of it tying knots of remorse in her chest.

One hand on the burnished brass doorknob, she paused, unable to do it. Unable to leave with him believing anything but the truth.

"I enjoyed dinner too. And the clean-up."

When he didn't respond, she peeked back and found Héctor standing a few feet away. Her gaze trailed up to the mistletoe dangling above him.

He craned his neck, then huffed an exasperated laugh when he realized what had caught her attention.

It was the perfect opening. A perfect reason to allow herself the kiss she'd been craving. A perfect lie if she told herself that one would be enough.

"Buenas noches," she said softly. Then she opened the door and stepped onto the stoop. Before she did something really foolish, like meeting Héctor under the mistletoe for what she fully expected would be a panty-melting kiss.

CHAPTER 5

"You did it, papito!" Héctor high-fived Luisito, who beamed so brightly you'd think he had swallowed the full moon.

Excited chatter filled the lobby area in front of the school's auditorium as students and family members celebrated the Christmas Talent Pageant's resounding success, in large part thanks to the direction of Saint Cecelia's famous alum, Broadway producer Antonio Sanchez. Especially Luisito, whose dedication to "the girl who has my heart" sent a wave of "awwwww" rippling through the large hall as he strummed his first chord. He finished to thunderous applause and cheers and was rewarded with a peck on the cheek and a shy smile from his crush, along with an invitation to join her and her parents for a post-show dessert.

Watching his son achieve his goal with such gusto and confidence filled Héctor with parental pride... and a determination of his own.

He hadn't spoken with Cristina since she'd left so abruptly the other evening. A decent chunk of the past few days had been spent thinking about her, wondering if he had come on too strong.

Tonight, he'd only caught a few glimpses of her in the wings backstage, assisting performers. According to Luisito, she was still in the band room, waiting for the last of the students to leave.

"Are you sure you don't wanna come have dessert with us, Papi?" Luisito asked.

"I volunteered for the clean-up committee." Not quite a lie because Héctor *had* told Eneida he was available if needed. "You go have fun. I'll meet you at home after."

Héctor thanked the girl's parents for the invite, then waited for the group to exit the building before he spun to cut through the remaining crowd. It took some bobbing and weaving. Even ducking behind a portly abuelo to avoid two single moms who'd made it clear they were available when he was ready. Finally, he made it to the dimly lit hall that ended at the band room.

A boy in Luisito's class and his parents headed in Héctor's direction. They greeted him warmly, and he thought he wished them Feliz Navidad. But he couldn't be sure. He was too busy praying that he'd find Cristina by herself. That she didn't already have her own post-show plans with someone else.

Reaching the wooden door, he paused. Listened for voices inside. Relieved at the silence, Héctor sent one final prayer for good luck and the confidence his son possessed. A deep breath later, he reached for the scarred knob and pushed open the door.

"Did you forget some—Oh, Héctor!" Cristina gasped his name when she spotted him. Uncertainty pinched her brow.

Blessedly, she stood near the upright piano—alone.

He stepped into the room as antsy and smitten as some of the students who walked the halls of Saint Cecelia's, craning their necks to spot their secret crush. Desperate to get up the nerve to start a conversation. Waiting for the perfect moment. Yet he was also mature and experienced enough to understand how fleeting life could be. How fast time flew by.

"Luisito left a while ago," Cristina said.

"I know. He's actually grabbing dessert with Jennifer and her parents. The kid wowed the crowd and the girl and got himself a first date all in one night."

Cristina grinned. Pleasure bloomed in her cheeks, turning them a rosy color that matched the wrap dress hugging her figure. Tonight, she'd left her hair down. It cascaded around her shoulders in loose waves that had his fingers twitching to run through their satiny softness.

But the other evening, she had backed away like the skittish colt he'd helped feed one summer on his tío's finca in Puerto Rico. He hadn't been to the farm in several years, but it held fond memories.

"Good for him. Luisito was amazing tonight," Cristina said.

"Thanks to your help."

She waved off his praise and reached for her purse on top of the upright piano. "It was my pleasure."

And his.

Her gaze slid to the closed door behind him. A polite signal that she was ready to leave.

It was now or never. He didn't have her phone number. Didn't really want to ask Eneida if she had it either. No telling what embarrassing action that woman would take to ensure his part in her plus-one plan came to fruition.

"I wanted to ask—"

"If there's nothing else—"

He and Cristina spoke in unison, both breaking off and gesturing for the other to continue.

When she motioned again, Héctor dug his suddenly clammy hands in his trouser pockets and stepped toward her. "There actually is something else."

Her head tilted in question, and one of her gold hoop earrings swung gently, peeking through her dark tresses.

"Since you mentioned that you're spending the holidays on your own, I wanted to invite you to Nochebuena dinner."

"Oh!" Surprise flitted across her face, and she drew back, bumping up against the piano behind her.

"Luisito and I celebrate with a large group of close friends," he continued. "Eneida Lucero and her familia will be there. And we'd love it—*I'd* love it—if you came with us."

One hand strangling her purse strap, the other fiddling with her name chain, she eyed him warily. "As... as friends? Like, parent-student-teacher?"

"Bueno, yes," he hedged.

Her shoulders sagged on an audible exhalation of breath, but he couldn't tell if it was with relief or disappointment. Her gaze skittered around the band room, landing everywhere but on him.

"And no," he added.

That earned her undivided attention.

Hazlo con ganas.

Words of advice Marielena had taught their son to live by. Luisito had certainly gone for it with gusto tonight. What kind of example would Héctor be setting for his son if he couldn't do the same?

Watching for even the slightest of back-off signs, he took a tentative step toward Cristina. Then another... stopping less than a foot away from her. Feeling every bit his nearly forty years and the fifteen it had been since he'd asked a woman out on a first date.

"Look, I might be botching this. I'm so out of practice, I wouldn't even make a junior league team." He huffed out a nervous laugh and rubbed the sting of embarrassment burning the back of his neck. "But I have really enjoyed our conversations and getting to know you. I admire your commitment to your career and your students. I appreciate the fact that you love your familia but also love yourself enough to not give up on your goal. Your sense of humor and smile brighten the room, and for the first time in a long while, I'm actually looking forward to a social event because you might be there. With me. So, yes, this is a friendly invite to Nochebuena dinner but from someone who's hoping that, at some point, we'll become more than friends. If you're interested."

The fingers fiddling with her necklace stilled, then slowly splayed to press her palm over her heart as if it might be racing as fast as his. She stared at him, eyes wide with shock. Mouth open in a little "oh" of dismay. Not quite the reaction he had anticipated.

"Héctor, I... I would... I don't—"

She broke off as the band room door opened behind him.

"Cristina, are you almost ready to—oh, excuse me!"

His stomach sank at the principal's astonished exclamation and the worry now thunder-clouding Cristina's eyes. Coño, of all the people who could have interrupted them, Olivia Perez was quite possibly the worst option.

Pivoting, he faced the statuesque Afro-Latina whose vibrant personality and stylish power suits set the tone and aided her in running a tight ship at Saint Cecilia's with the approval of the diocese, school board, and parents. Including him, most of the time.

"Hola, Olivia, Feliz Navidad." He dipped his head politely in greeting.

"Same to you. I'm surprised to find you both here. Everyone else has cleared the building." The principal's sharp gaze flitted from him to Cristina. "Is there a problem or something I should be aware of?"

"No! Not at all!" Cristina said quickly, waving her hands palms out, as if to ward off the principal's doubt.

"We're good here," Héctor assured Olivia. He'd be even better if the principal left and Cristina said yes to his invitation. "Ms. Pagán gave Luisito some private lessons in preparation for tonight's performance, and I came by to check on something before the holiday break."

"Bueno, if you're ready to go..." The principal made a noncommittal gesture with her head. Neither a nod nor a shake, but her subtext was clear—wrap things up.

"Almost," Héctor answered. "I'd like to see if we can get something on Ms. Pagán's schedule over the holiday break." He smiled benevolently at the principal, counting on his reputation as a respectable, long-time Saint Cecilia's parent to dispel any qualms she might have.

"No need for you to wait on our account," he continued. "I'm betting you've had a long day, Olivia. I'll escort Ms. Pagán to the subway station as soon as we're done. Or wait for her car service to arrive. We can never be too safe."

"Are you sure?" The principal directed her question to Cristina, who nodded mutely. "Fine, make it quick though. Oye, give Luisito a fist bump from me." She raised her fist toward Héctor, miming her request. "That boy's a charmer. Job well done tonight."

"Will do," Héctor answered.

"Cristina, I'll see you at the faculty meeting in the new year. Feliz Navidad to you both." With a loose-fingered wave, she left them.

As soon as the door clicked shut behind the principal, Cristina collapsed into one of the hard plastic chairs with a muttered groan.

"You okay?" he asked.

Her eyes closed, she shook her head.

Worried by her ashen complexion and the scowl wrinkling her normally smooth brow, he picked up one of the chairs and moved it next to hers. He covered her clasped hands with one of his in comfort. "Cristina, talk to me."

A soft sigh blew through her pink lips. When she finally looked at him, sadness and regret stared back at him. Disappointment pierced his chest.

The protective wall he had erected around himself after his wife's passing, which only recently had started to lower thanks to Cristina, rose again. The metal chair legs screeched as he sagged back against the hard plastic seat back.

Cristina grabbed hold of his wrist. "I am so sorry, Héctor."

"Está bien." *Lie.* He shrugged off her apology and stood, embarrassed that he had mistaken her friendliness for more. "I'm the one who's sorry. I didn't mean to make you feel uncomfortable earlier. Or at my house the other evening. That was never my intent."

"You didn't. Not in the least." She rose, her fingers still manacled around his wrist. "I'm... I'm flattered. More than flattered. And if I wasn't faculty here, or if Olivia hadn't made it clear that parent-teacher fraternization was seriously frowned upon—"

"What? Since when?"

"I'm not exactly sure. There's not an official policy, but she mentioned a specific situation that created some problems. A couple years ago or so? Either way, she was clear about where she stands on the issue."

Héctor frowned, trying to recall if he had heard anything about whatever Olivia Perez was holding up as rationale for this non-policy policy. But coño, in the past, Marielena would have been the one in the know. Only... two years ago, they'd been in the fight for her life, and he couldn't have cared less who was seeing whom or whatever chisme the parent portal was spreading.

"I can't afford to lose my job, Héctor. As much as I want to join you and Luisito, I'd be fooling myself, and you, if I said it was only as friends. And you deserve better than that."

The anguish on Cristina's beautiful face was like an ice pick to the heart.

Fuck. How could he argue with her reasoning? Knowing she wanted to say yes should have tempered his disappointment. It didn't.

They both deserved better than this.

Jabbing a frustrated hand through his hair, Héctor hung his head in disappointment. So much for a Christmas miracle this year.

CHAPTER 6

Nochebuena morning dawned with a light sprinkle of snow on the ground and low, billowy clouds in a crisp blue sky. The type of morning that usually enticed her outside for a walk in nearby Prospect Park.

Instead, Cristina stayed in bed, sipped an extra cup of café con leche, and binged *The Holiday*, followed by *The Family Stone*, followed by one that made her current depressive funk worse, *Love Actually*.

Their situations were different, but she couldn't help but feel a kinship with Laura Linney's lonely, pining character. Desired by a gorgeous, totally perfect partner, only to have insurmountable road-blocks barring a promising relationship. At the very least, a sexually satisfying one.

Okay, so Cristina had only fantasized about being with Héctor Gutiérrez. But she'd give her first violin—a prized possession—if she was wrong about him. Given his quick humor, the intent way he listened to her when they talked, the gentle caresses that left her swooning, and, por favor, his incredible body... No doubt he'd be an attentive lover.

A soft sigh escaped her again.

She hadn't heard from him since he had walked her to the Church

Street subway station after their talk in the music room the other evening. Him, repeating that he could drive her home. Her, convinced it was better to cut the thread binding them before she couldn't.

She had the entire break to get over this... this... Christmas crush.

Luisito's song title brought a sad smile to her lips. What was the father-son duo up to? Had Héctor cooked the special pancakes Luisito had raved about during their one dinner together?

A glance at her cell phone on the rattan nightstand told her it was nearly 2 p.m. Were they already getting ready for their fiesta? Was Héctor making a special dish for his friends now that his joy of cooking had been renewed?

Wistful jealousy crept over her at the thought of him whipping up something savory that she'd never get a chance to taste.

The aroma of garlic, spices, and roast pork wafting from her tiny kitchen lured Cristina out of bed to check on the small pernil slow-roasting in the oven. Even this depressed, she couldn't have a Nochebuena without a traditional pernil, arroz con gandules, and tostones. Unlike Héctor's gourmet meal, hers was pretty basic, and her mami would be scandalized to know Cristina planned to make the rice and pigeon peas in a rice cooker instead of a well-used caldero. She hadn't even bought herself a pot for the oven yet. And she'd never admit to buying frozen tostones. Peeling green plantains and going through the fry, smash, refry process required too much effort.

Today, she needed comfort food and a taste of home with as little hassle as possible. Especially since she'd be dining alone.

She was halfway down the hall to her kitchen when her cell phone trilled from the bedroom. Ooh! Maybe it was...

Spinning around, she raced to answer it, her socks slipping on the laminate wood flooring.

Hope faltered when she spotted a fellow violinist's name in the notification bar. Swiping her thumb across the screen, she rallied an upbeat tone to greet her friend. "Hi, Sheila. Happy holidays!"

"Oh, how I wish it was," Sheila replied, dejection coloring her words. "I just got some not-so-good news from my obstetrician."

"I'm so sorry, I hope everything's going to be okay."

"It should be. But I'm in a bit of a bind, and I'm hoping you might be my Christmas angel."

"Um, okay." Cristina lowered herself to the edge of her bed. "How can I help?"

CARRYING her foil-wrapped roasting pan with the small pernil in one hand and a bottle of homemade coquito in the other, Cristina sucked in a deep breath, squared her shoulders, and... froze on the first step leading to the Gutiérrez home's front stoop.

She had half a mind to pop the top and steal a swig of the creamy, coconutty concoction, Puerto Rico's delectable version of eggnog. A shot of rum-inspired bravery might be needed.

Halfway here, she had nearly told the driver to take her back home. But the cabrona in her—a stubbornness some had mislabeled as foolhardy—had gotten her this far in life. It refused to let her slink away without at least putting her cards on the table.

Moving to New York for grad school, then telling her parents she didn't plan to return, had been nerve-racking. But those decisions had been made with her professional goals in mind.

Showing up at Héctor's after she had turned him down? This was a personal gamble. One he might no longer be willing to take with her.

The knots of anxiety tangling her insides tightened.

He'd been brave enough to reveal his feelings with her the other night. If she couldn't bring herself to do the same, she wasn't worthy of him.

And she was. Worthy. Carajo, they both were.

Hurrying up the steps before she could second-guess herself—again—she pressed the buzzer.

Heart in her throat, she waited as the sound of footsteps inside grew nearer. Héctor peered through one of the decorative stained glass windows on either side of the ornate black door. She smiled, worried it might look more like a stressed-out grimace. The deadbolt clicked open, and she flinched.

"Cristina?" Surprise registered on his handsome face. His dark eyes blinked several times as if trying to clear his vision. "What are you... ? Come in!"

He draped a yellow kitchen towel he held over a shoulder and opened the door wider, stepping aside for her to pass by. She strode several feet into the foyer, stopping at a predetermined spot and turning to face him.

"I come bearing Nochebuena gifts," she announced, holding the bottle of coquito and the foil-wrapped pan aloft.

"Uh, gracias. I was actually sipping some coquito while cooking, but I never turn down a bottle."

"Wise move. And, um... bueno, I'm also hoping that your invitation to join you for the fiesta is still open."

Héctor's initial surprise gave way to befuddlement. It scrunched his face in a look reminiscent of Luisito's when she and Héctor had bandied synonyms for "wooing" during their first meeting in the band room.

"There's no one else I'm interested in bringing tonight," Héctor said, his words slow, measured... as if he were testing shaky ground.

"Ay, gracias a Dios, that's a relief." A huge one. She grinned, pleased that she hadn't arrived too late. "I got some good news today. Like, *really* good news. And you're the first person I wanted to share it with."

"Me?"

"Uh-huh. You."

He hooked a thumb in his front jeans pocket and flashed a sly smile that had his dimple making an appearance. Dios, she wanted to kiss that dimple so badly. Along with other parts of his hunky body. But first...

"You're looking at the new long-term sub and potential full-time string musician for Mateo Garza's Broadway production of *Clemente: Legend and Hero*! I start on the twenty-sixth."

"Are you kidding me?" Excitement kicked Héctor's deep bass up several octaves, and she fell a little harder for him.

"No. And it gets better." Giddy, still processing everything that

Shelia had thrown at her, Cristina rushed through the news. "The friend who called me to sub is pregnant and has to start mandatory bed rest for the next four months. She also has a full roster of private music students, many of them homeschoolers, so lessons are during the day, and she wants to hand over everything to me. For good. If I take them on along with my current students, I'll have to give notice at Saint Cecilia's."

"Give notice? The kids love you there. What will—hold on." His head shook in a quick double take.

Cristina held her breath, waiting for him to put one and one together, and hopefully come up with a sum that equaled the two of them.

A Cheshire cat grin split his lips, spreading across his face to crinkle his obsidian eyes, now shining with an elation that might almost match hers.

A second later, his arms wrapped around her waist, hugging her tightly.

"Ooh, wait. My pernil!" The heavy pan tottered in her hand.

He made short work of divesting her of both gifts, setting them on a decorative hutch nearby, then quickly slipped his arms inside her open winter coat and tugged her against him. She linked her hands behind his neck and gazed up at him, thrilled by the happiness shining back at her in the depths of his eyes.

"Congratulations," he murmured. "I can't think of a better Christmas present for you."

"I can," she teased, jutting her chin toward the ceiling.

Héctor glanced up, then let out a huff of laughter when he spotted the mistletoe. "We thumbed our noses at tradition once already."

"And I've been regretting it every day since! Why do you think I stopped in this exact spot?"

He shook his head with a raspy chuckle. "I am *so happy* to see you."

"Same. Feliz Navidad," she murmured.

His hands splayed along her back, drawing her closer. Slowly, he lowered his head, and she rose onto her toes to meet him halfway.

Longing coursed through her as his lips brushed hers. Once.

Twice. Then his tongue swept across her lower lip in a heated caress, and she opened for him. Their tongues parried and twisted in a sensual dance her entire body craved. She moaned low in her throat and delved her fingers into the short hair along his nape, wanting more. Needing more.

He obliged.

One of his hands slid down to cup her butt, hauling her against him. She gasped at the hard length of his erection pressing into her lower belly. Undulating her hips, she nipped at his lower lip with her teeth. Héctor groaned. His other hand moved to cradle her jaw, angling her head as he deepened their kiss.

He tasted of coconut and rum and deliciousness. Of lust and desire. Of home and possibility.

Of Nochebuena and Navidad and the gift of that special someone to share them with.

Footsteps pounded on the second floor. Luisito. A reminder that she and Héctor weren't alone.

Pulling back, Héctor grinned down at her. "I'm going to have to thank Luisito for nagging me to hang this mistletoe."

"Yes, you certainly are."

As if on cue, Luisito bounded down the stairs. His face lit up with excitement when he spotted Cristina. "Hey! Are you coming to the fiesta with us?"

"I sure am, if you don't mind," she answered.

"Sweet!" Jumping off the last step, Luisito circled around them and headed into the sala.

Héctor chuckled and drew her closer.

Cristina's eyes fluttered closed as he bent to press a warm kiss to her forehead. Joy filled all the lonely places in her heart, and she gave thanks for their Nochebuena miracle. And a sprig of strategically placed mistletoe.

ALSO BY PRISCILLA OLIVERAS

West Side Love Story

STANDALONES

Holiday Home Run

Resort to Love

KEYS TO LOVE SERIES

Island Affair

Anchored Hearts

MATCHED TO PERFECTION SERIES

His Perfect Partner

Her Perfect Affair

Their Perfect Melody

ANTHOLOGIES

"Lights Out" from *Summer in the City*

"Holiday Home Run" from *A Season to Celebrate*

ABOUT THE AUTHOR

Priscilla Oliveras is a USA Today bestselling author & 2018 RWA® RITA® double finalist who writes contemporary romance with a Latinx flavor. Her books have earned Starred Reviews from *Publishers Weekly, Kirkus Reviews,* and *Booklist* along with praise from *O, The Oprah Magazine, Washington Post, New York Times, Entertainment Weekly, Frolic,* and more. She earned her MFA in Writing Popular Fiction from Seton Hill University where she currently serves as adjunct faculty and also teaches the online class "Romance Writing" for ed2go. A long-time romance enthusiast, Priscilla's also a sports fan, beach lover, and Zumba aficionado, who often practices the art of napping in her backyard hammock. Find her online at prisoliveras.com and hanging out way too much on social media.

Sign up for Priscilla's newsletter here!

facebook.com/prisoliveras
twitter.com/PrisOliveras
instagram.com/prisoliveras

ALL I WANT FOR NOCHEBUENA

ALEXIS DARIA

When sparks fly between adult film stars Honey and Julie, Honey must work up the courage to invite Julie to her family's holiday party or risk losing what she really wants for Nochebuena—a chance at true love.

CHAPTER 1

Day 1

AFTER READING over the day's call sheet for the umpteenth time, I shove it back into my purse, then wipe my palms on my leggings. I sweat when I'm nervous, and I'm nervous as all hell right now, waiting to meet my scene partner.

The production team rented out a three-bedroom loft in Chelsea for the shoot. It has track lighting, a few areas of exposed brick that I'm sure we'll take photos in front of, refurbished hardwood floors that miraculously don't creak, and all-new kitchen appliances. Unfortunately, it doesn't seem like the windows have been updated, because the space is drafty as hell.

I'm currently hidden away in one of the smaller bedrooms, which already has lights and cameras set up. When they first put me in here, I tried to stay calm, but now I'm striding back and forth, checking the time on my phone every three minutes. I've only got about six feet of pacing room, but I'm making the most of it.

Doesn't matter how many times I tell myself that I'm a pro in this industry. That I've worked with some of the top-rated adult film stars, that I'm a star in my own right. Doesn't matter that I've done this hundreds of times.

I'm a *wreck*.

Hell, it's not even like I'm filming a real movie. This gig is all about recording promotional videos for Bad Kitty's new brand of intimate lifestyle products—sex toys, lube, lingerie, all kinds of stuff. I've been hired to test the products, demonstrate their usage, and review their effectiveness. Honestly, this job is a dream come true. I'm a *huge* fan of Bad Kitty, and there's even a chance I'll get to meet the Dominican rap goddess herself at some point.

But first, I have to meet my scene partner. Hence my sweaty palms.

I wipe them again and force myself to sit on the powder-blue armchair, but it's no good. I'm bursting with energy. A second later, I'm back on my feet, pacing again.

Misery loves company, so I pull out my phone and text my cousin Sarita. She's dealing with a work crush of her own, so I know she gets it.

I'm meeting her soon! I'm freaking out!

Before Sarita can reply, Ji-hae Kim, the director, sticks her head in the room. She's a petite forty-ish Korean woman with shoulder-length black hair, kind eyes, and a welcoming smile. "There you are, Honey," she says.

I jam my phone back into my purse and flash a smile at her. "Yes! Hi. That's me. Honey Grayson." After six years, the stage name rolls right off my tongue.

"You ready?"

Ready? Am I ready to meet my longtime crush, Just Julie, the young, pierced phenom who took the porn world by storm only two years ago?

Get it together, I tell myself. *You're twenty-nine, not twelve.*

I give Ji-hae what's probably a strained-looking smile. "Yeah! Totally ready."

"Are you mic'd up?"

"Uh-huh." A PA came through earlier and hooked me up with a lavalier mic. The battery pack is clipped to the waistband of my gray jeans and sits snug against the small of my back. The cord runs under my lacy sleeveless top with the mic attached to one of the straps, where it can easily pick up what I'm saying.

Ji-hae nods. "Let's go, then."

I wipe my hands on my thighs one more time before following Ji-hae into the biggest bedroom, where a camera crew is set up. Two of the PAs are carefully carting a giant framed mirror out of the room, probably because it'll show reflections of the crew while shooting. The bed is made up in white and gray bedding with lots of pillows. A few purple throw pillows show the logo for Bad Kitty's Boudoir.

It's too early to worry about the bed. According to the call sheet, we're just filming our first meeting right now. That's all.

The bed will come later.

This room is even colder than the other one, and I'm rethinking my outfit. I was wearing a heavy sweater and fleece-lined leggings when I arrived—hello, it's December in New York City—but I wanted to look cute for this meeting, so I changed after the style team did my hair and makeup.

Julie—a.k.a. @justjuliexxx—and I have been flirting online for nearly a year. Despite having watched all her videos and lurking on her feed, it still took me ages to work up the courage to reply to one of her posts. I'm bi, and I know Julie only dates girls because she's talked about it in interviews, but I'm so shy when it comes to these things. Finally, when I saw Julie post a picture of herself right here in New York City, I left a comment. All I said was, "My hometown!" but Julie had replied with, "Omg is that THEE @itshoneygrayson? Legend!" And from there, we commented on all each other's posts. Sometimes compliments, sometimes encouragement, sometimes just emojis.

But our paths have never crossed outside of social media. It seems like we're always on opposite ends of the country. If I'm in California, Julie's in New York. If Julie's in Vegas, I'm in Miami.

Until now. Bad Kitty handpicked two Latina adult entertainment stars—I'm Puerto Rican and Julie's Dominican—to create promotional material for her new brand.

Finally, Julie and I are going to meet.

147

And my palms will not stop fucking sweating.

AFTER CONSULTING WITH THE CREW, Ji-hae comes over to me. "Kitty wants this to feel as unscripted and natural as possible," she explains. "Part of that is letting viewers get to know who you are and seeing your dynamic with Julie. You've never met, right?"

I shake my head. "Not in person."

"But you know each other?"

"We've chatted online a bit." I'm proud of how nonchalant I sound, considering my enormous crush on Julie.

"That's good." Ji-hae checks her tablet. "Right now we're just going to ask you some questions and then film you two meeting, so we won't get into the products yet. Sound good?"

"Works for me."

"Ready to begin?"

Yes. No. Yes, *damn it*, I'm more than ready to finally meet Julie. I nod confidently. "Yes, I'm ready."

Ji-hae checks something with the camera and sound operators, then signals to me that we're starting. "So, Honey, what made you want to work with Bad Kitty's Boudoir?"

I give her a big smile. "Well, I love her music and her whole vibe. Bad Kitty is not just sexy, she's sex positive, in and out of her music videos. I appreciate her focus on sexual health and self-care, because in my industry, you can never have too much of either."

Ji-hae nods. "That was perfect. Okay, next question. Do you know who you're going to be working with today?"

"Yes." I try—and fail—to hold back a full-blown grin.

The director leans in. "Honey, are you blushing?"

"No. Maybe." I press my hands to my face. My cheeks feel hot, and not just because my hands are ice cold. I'm not playing coy for the camera, but I hope that Ji-hae thinks I am.

"Have you ever met Julie before?" Ji-hae asks, even though she knows the answer. "Or worked together?"

I shake my head. "We've never met, but we know each other. Kind of. On social media."

"Are you nervous?"

"A little, yeah." As if on cue, an awkward giggle escapes my lips.

"Why?" Ji-hae's tone is curious, but I know she's also digging for good content.

"There are always some nerves before working with someone new, you know?" I shrug. "Good nerves. Anticipation."

"All right, we're going to bring Julie in now. This is just for behind-the-scenes footage of you two meeting and chatting about the brand. Okay?"

I let out a slow breath. "Okay."

And before I know it, the cameras are moving back, Ji-hae is motioning someone in, and then...

There she is.

Julie.

She's beautiful, with light brown skin, heavy-lidded dark eyes, cheekbones that could cut glass, and a sleek, dark pixie cut. Piercings wink at her nose, dimple, lip, and eyebrow. We have similar coloring, but my hair falls in loose curls to my shoulders, and where she has multiple piercings, I'm covered in tattoos.

When I look at her, I can't even breathe. She radiates a cool self-assurance I could never begin to mimic.

Then she sees me, and her eyes light up. She gives a little scream and rushes over. "Oh my god, it's so nice to finally meet you!"

Her excitement unlocks something in me, and I giggle again. "I can't believe it's taken this long for us to work together."

"It's like we were never in the same place. Can I hug you?"

"Yeah, of course!" As if I'd say no.

She wraps her arms around my waist and presses herself to me, tucking her face into my neck. I'm taller than she is, but she feels strong and solid. I know she lifts weights because she posts videos from the gym, which I always comment on because I'm a thirsty bitch.

Julie lifts her nose to my ear and inhales deeply. "Mmm, you smell good. Is that your shampoo?"

"I used a coconut conditioning mask." Which I made sure to use today, specifically because it makes my hair smell amazing.

"Well, our people love using coconut on our bodies," Julie says with a laugh, and when she leans back to look at me, her eyes go a little soft. "God, you're even prettier in person."

"What? Stop." I can feel myself blushing, and I'm sure the cameras are just eating this up. "You're gorgeous."

"I'm serious. I love your curls. And your tattoos." Her hand skims down my bare arm, skating over roses, a wolf, and an owl. Her fingers leave a trail of goose bumps in their wake.

"I like your piercings," I say, and I can't help what slips out next. "They're so sexy." I mean it, but in this industry, flirtatious flattery is par for the course. It's hard to know what's real and what's for show. Sometimes, feelings crop up where they have no business being, and I'm determined not to put my heart in that position *again*.

Julie's smile widens. "Thanks! Do you have any?"

I touch the hoops in my ears. "Just these. Do you have any ink? I haven't seen it, if you do."

"Not yet. I can't decide what I want. Maybe you can help me?"

I get butterflies at the thought of ink decorating her skin. "I would love to!"

Julie asks me about my most painful tattoo—a sun and moon over my ribs—and I ask about her septum piercing before Ji-hae must decide there's enough footage of us examining each other's visible tats and hardware. She steps forward and gently interrupts us. "Is it safe to say you two are excited to work together?"

"Yes!" we say in unison, and my grin threatens to crack my face. Damn, I really have no chill where this woman is concerned.

AFTER OUR MEETING, we're separated to shoot scripted instructional videos and unboxings for each product. The plan is for us to film these on our own, and then the clips will be edited together to make one video for each item.

By the time I'm back in the main bedroom, I'm exhausted.

Julie's already there, lounging on the loveseat. "How'd it go?"

I roll my eyes. "Harder than doggy style on granite countertops."

She stifles a laugh. "It's a totally different way of being on camera. But I think this next part will feel more natural for us."

Her gaze drifts over to the bed, and I can't help but look there too. Because while this is old hat for me, there's always a little bit of nerves before having sex with a new person—mostly excitement, but also curiosity about what their energy will be like, or if we'll have good chemistry. With Julie, the nerves and excitement are cranked to an eleven.

Ji-hae bustles in and calls us over to the dresser, where an array of vibrators has been artfully laid out. Next to each is a discreet card with the product name.

"This scene's focus is on vibrators, so we have a few different items here," Ji-hae explains. "There's also flavored lube and massage oil, just in case. Don't feel like you have to use everything at once. It's more important to get an authentic scene, showing the two of you having fun using the products."

Ji-hae gestures toward the bed and the loveseat. "Feel free to take things as far as you like and use all the furniture. And if something's not working, toss it aside and we'll cut it. We want the reactions to be real."

"So we're just two friends playing with sex toys and trying to have orgasms?" Julie shoots me a grin. "Easiest job ever."

My heart pounds like a conga drum every time Julie turns that thousand-watt smile my way. But I just nod. "Challenge accepted."

"This was Kitty's idea," Ji-hae adds. "She wanted professionals to demonstrate the products, since lots of people want to try them out but don't necessarily know how. The videos will be behind a paywall on the website."

"Do you want us to narrate how we're using them?" I ask, wanting to make sure I get this right.

"Only if you want to. We'll get your official review afterward."

Before we get started, I turn to Julie and ask, "Is there anything you don't like?"

I always ask this. It just makes for a more pleasurable scene for everyone involved, regardless of how much scripting or directing we have.

Julie sends me a mischievous look. "I think I'll like anything with you."

That startles a nervous laugh out of me. "How do you know? We've never worked together before."

She gives a cheeky little shrug. "I know, but I've watched everything you've done."

Butterflies erupt in my belly. "Really? I've watched everything *you've* done."

Her eyes go wide. "What? No way!"

"Of course. You're amazing."

"But I'm so new. I was surprised you even knew who I was the first time you messaged me."

I roll my eyes. "Julie, everyone knows who you are. You're like the new It Girl right now."

She waves me off. "You're too nice."

"I'm serious. Everyone wants to work with you."

Her expression turns contemplative. "Then why did it take so long for us to get here?"

My stomach flip-flops. "Bad timing, I guess. But we're here now."

Julie sends me a soft smile. "Yes, we are."

Ji-hae steps forward, and after a few more equipment checks—and the removal of the lav mics clipped to our clothes—it's time to begin.

Taking a deep breath, I gather my on-camera persona around me like a cloak—shoulders straight, posture confident, grin dialed down to a sultry smirk—and join Julie next to the display. "What should we start with?"

Julie picks up a gold tube. "We should definitely try out this flavored lube. Do you have a favorite kind of vibe?"

"Can't go wrong with one of these." I pick up the cordless wand on the dresser and weigh it in my hand.

Julie leans over to read the name. "Kitty's Magic Wand. *Me-ow.*"

As I turn it on and cycle through the vibration settings, Julie picks up a silicone cylinder with a tapered end. It's magenta, with silver buttons. "This looks versatile."

"What's it called?" I ask.

"The Promise."

I raise my eyebrows. "A bold claim."

Julie winks and gestures to the bed with it. "Would you like to step into my office?"

I barely manage to hold back a giggle. "Okay."

We remove our shoes—motorcycle boots for Julie, heeled suede booties for me—and climb onto the bed together. I'm so jittery, it's a wonder I don't fall right off.

Julie sets the vibrator beside her and uncaps the lube. "It says this tastes like dulce de leche."

I raise an eyebrow. "Does it?"

"Let's find out."

Julie dabs some on her index finger and sticks it in her mouth. My heart flutters as her full lips close around the tip, and I want to suck her finger too. Her lips purse in thought.

"Hmm, it's hard to tell." She sends me a coy smile. "I think I need to try tasting it from somewhere else."

And even though this is a job and I've had sex with hundreds of other people by this point in my career, my mouth goes dry at the heat in Julie's eyes and the sexy smirk on her lips.

Then her voice lowers. "Can I taste this on your titties?"

My nipples tighten immediately, as if in preparation. "Yeah," I say. It's more of a sigh than a word. Full sentences seem like too much trouble right now, so I just lean back against the pillows and wrangle my lacy top over my head.

The air around us thickens the way it does when the chemistry is real. Yes, there are cameras, but sometimes it's like this with a scene partner—the heat flicks on like a light switch, and suddenly all my attention is on sex.

Julie kneels over me and gently grips the cups of my lacy black bra.

Her fingers brush my skin and I shiver a little, partly because her hands are cold, and partly because Julie's touching me and I can barely think past my need to have her touch me more.

She removes my bra, then uses her fingertip to paint a light layer of the flavored lube onto my nipple, which hardens into a tight bud. I can smell the sugary scent of dulce de leche, reminding me of the times my mom made the caramelized milk topping for desserts. Then Julie lowers her head to give me a lick.

At the swipe of her hot tongue on my breast, I suck in a breath and grip her arm, as if to keep her close.

She gives me a wicked smile before her plush lips close over the peak, making me moan.

Julie leans in more, cupping my full breast in one hand, and I shiver again. This time, when she lifts her head to look at me, her eyebrows are slanted with concern. "I'm sorry. Are my hands too cold?"

"It is a little cold in here," I admit, because it's true. I've been trying to ignore it, but there's a distinct chill in the air, and her fingers are like ice.

"Sorry, the building is having a problem with the heat," Ji-hae calls out in a stage whisper. "Unfortunately, the boom mic picks up the sound from the space heaters, but we can try to get more of them in here to warm it up between takes. Do you need us to turn them on for a bit before we continue?"

"Do you?" Julie asks me.

I shake my head. "I'm good. Besides, I know somewhere you can warm your hands up."

Julie's lips curve. I take her hand and draw it down between my legs, trapping it between my thighs.

"Mmm, it is warm here." Julie flexes her hand, rubbing her fingers along the seam of my dark jeans. Her eyebrow quirks, and then she asks, "Can I taste the lube on this pretty pussy of yours?"

God, I love this woman's dirty talk!

"Yes, please," I murmur, and Julie kisses me as she helps me slide off my jeans and panties. Our tongues tangle, and it's like the heat from her mouth somehow suffuses my whole body, because I'm suddenly warmer than I've been since we walked into this room.

Because I need to touch her too, and I know it'll look better in the scene, I tug her white crop top off. She isn't wearing a bra underneath, and I palm her small breasts, gently thumbing the silver bars in her nipples before she eases me back. I whimper, because I wanted to explore her piercings with my tongue, but her knowing smile says we'll get to that later.

Fully naked, I recline on the pile of pillows, gazing down my body to where Julie, who's still wearing her jeans, kneels between my legs. She licks her full lips like she's looking at something delicious.

Then she breathes on her hands and rubs them briskly together to warm them. Before I can laugh, she's pushing my knees up and, without further preamble, leaning in to give my slit a long lick. My eyes roll back in my head and I let out a soft moan as arousal zings through me.

Julie meets my eyes with a smile. "Sweet."

"You forgot the lube," I murmur, and her pierced eyebrow quirks.

"Did I?"

But she uses her finger to spread some of the lube over my labia and clit. That done, she settles between my legs and begins to lick in earnest.

I throw my head back on the pillow and moan at the sensations rocketing through me from Julie's hot little tongue. But after only a few seconds, she stops, resting her cheek against my inner thigh and wearing a dreamy smile. "You did it."

I blink at her, already a little delirious. "What?"

"That cute little noise you make when you moan. It's like a whimper and a giggle mixed together."

"Oh, that." My cheeks heat. I don't do that noise on purpose, and I was initially a little embarrassed by it, but fans and other performers seem to love it. "My claim to fame."

"I know. I've seen your videos. But it's different hearing it in real life, knowing *I* made you make that noise." Her dark eyes light up with challenge. "And I'm going to make you do it a lot more before I'm through."

She goes back to licking me, and it's so good, I forget what we're even supposed to be doing here.

There's something about sex that makes my mind shut off. It's the only time I stop overthinking everything, the only time I let my body lead the way. Physical intimacy is a kind of communication all its own, a connection of pleasure, of giving and receiving. My love life might be stagnant, but when it comes to sex, I know just what to do.

So, it seems, does Julie. Her finger teases my entrance and I moan even louder than I already have been. "Fuck, Julie. You're so good at this."

"I aim to please." Julie grins and holds up the magenta vibrator. "Should we test out whether the Promise lives up to its name? See how you like it with the lube?"

"I like anything you do," I say, with perhaps a little too much honesty.

"Good." Julie sends me a secret smile, turned away from the cameras.

I'm not sure what to make of her smile, but I reposition the pillows behind me and lean back. It's dangerous to read too much into things said or done during a scene, in the heat of the moment, because the cameras are on. It's a good way to get your feelings stomped on. I know, I've been there before.

But still... Hope isn't so easily ground out of me.

Julie slicks the lube over the tapered end of the vibrator. "Let's try it turned off first. Tell me how it feels."

I try not to jolt when Julie presses it against my vulva. "It feels cold," I say, chuckling.

"Shoot, sorry about that!" Julie's brows crease in concern. "I tried to warm it up with my hands first."

"It's okay. It's better now." I close my eyes as the toy slides into me, then let out my signature giggle-moan. "It's smooth. Has a nice shape."

"I'm going to turn it on the lowest setting."

I gasp as vibrations fill my channel and Julie continues to work it inside me. "That's nice."

"Let's see if we can do better than nice." Julie leans in to tongue my clit, then ups the vibration to the next setting and changes the angle of the vibe. Pleasure spirals through me. I twist my hands in the blankets, moaning and chanting "oh fuck," but then Julie pulls back, leaving me panting.

"Did you like that?" Julie asks, although her smirk says she knows the answer.

"Fuck yeah." I'm still trying to catch my breath. "That was really fucking good."

"We still have more to try, though." She holds up the wand I picked out, her long fingers caressing the smooth, round turquoise head.

"Both at the same time?" I ask.

"Well, I was thinking of putting this somewhere else." Julie gestures with the vibrator she slid out of me. The silicone shines with my inner juices. I visualize what it would be like to see her lick it clean. Then she brushes a lube-coated finger over my asshole and I jolt.

"Can I fuck you here?" she asks softly. "While you use the wand on your clit?"

I blink hard, nearly overcome just from imagining what Julie proposed. "Sure, if you want to. I'm prepped."

Her dark eyes all but glow. "I really, really want to."

"Then yeah. Absolutely!"

Julie turns to Ji-hae. "I know butt stuff is tomorrow, but this feels like a good opportunity to show that the product can be used in lots of different ways."

Ji-hae laughs and waves her on. "Whatever you like. You're both calling the shots here."

So Julie turns back to me and hands me the wand.

"Not yet," she says when I move to turn it on, a teasing tone in her voice. "I'm not done tasting you."

She proceeds to lick and suck my clit, fucking me gently with the Promise on a low setting. Then her finger teases my ass, and I lose myself to the sensations. I'm moaning and cursing by the time Julie removes the vibrator and places it, hot and wet, at my rear. There's a delicious pressure as the silicone tip pushes into me, followed by a fullness that makes my toes curl.

Julie's mouth drifts down to lap at my labia, so I lift the wand with leaden arms and turn it on before pressing it to my clit.

"Oh fuck," I gasp out, my hips bucking. "This combo is so fucking good."

"Yeah?" Julie gives my inner thigh a little nip, then presses two fingers into my pussy. "How about now?"

The vibrating pressure in my ass, the wand stimulation on my clit, and Julie's fingers stroking me inside—plus knowing it's *Julie* doing it —is more than I can bear. The orgasm rises up and slams me into oblivion. I don't know what kinds of sounds I make. Despite the cold, sweat breaks out on my brow and breasts. My thighs tremble and shake. Waves of pleasure threaten to carry me away.

And then Julie is turning off the devices and setting them aside. Her lips touch my clit to press a kiss there, and then she scoots up onto the bed to smile down at me.

"So, did the Promise live up to the promise?"

I can't think of anything clever to say in response. I just raise my head to kiss Julie full on the mouth. When we come up for air, I murmur, "Now it's your turn."

She's laughing as I tumble her to the mattress.

A PA HANDS US ROBES. They're super soft, tan on the outside and fuzzy white on the inside. The hoods have little reindeer horns and red Rudolph noses on them.

"Aww, these are cute," Julie says, pulling up the hood. "Let's take a selfie in them, since they're the only festive thing on this set and I'm not going to have time to see Rockefeller Center or anything while I'm in town."

We bundle into the robes and take pictures to post on our respective social media accounts while another PA rushes around, turning on the space heaters.

Julie sinks onto one end of the loveseat and I sit next to her, tucking my feet beneath me so I can wrap the robe around my bare legs.

"Well, that was... cold," she says with a laugh.

"Very," I agree. "But you were such a pro, no one would ever know. Meanwhile, I probably have icicles dripping from my nips."

"Sorry, I know my hands were freezing." Julie blows on them and rubs them together briskly.

"It wasn't too bad," I say, trying to reassure her, but Julie shoots me a "no bullshit" look.

"Sweetie, you jumped every time I touched you."

Okay, I did, and it was partly from the cold. But it had also been from nerves, although I don't want to admit that. "Maybe your hands were a little cold."

"I could run them under hot water before we start again," Julie muses.

"It's really okay," I tell her, not wanting her to feel bad. "You did a great job distracting me. And I'm pretty sure I shocked you a few times with my cold feet."

"I like your feet." Julie grins. "And yeah, that flavored lube was pretty great. I loved licking that off you."

My heart thumps as I remember the feel of Julie's tongue on me, and then the taste of her on my own tongue. I'll never see dulce de leche again without thinking of her.

"You're so good at eating pussy," I say, trying to keep my tone light and complimentary when it wants to go low and breathy.

"Aww, thanks." Julie flashes me another smile. "I was happy to finally see it in person. And god, those little noises you make. Hottest thing ever."

I can feel myself blushing. "Yep, it's what I'm known for."

"And your tattoos," she adds. "How many do you have?"

"Hard to say." I push up the sleeves of my robe, examining the black ink swirling down my arms. "I started with one, then three, and then I just kept adding to them until they all started to connect."

"Do they have special meaning?"

"Yes, but not in the way they might for some people."

"Can I take a closer look?"

"Of course."

She slips the robe off my shoulder, revealing a mass of ink. "You have a lot of flowers," she says, brushing her fingers over my collarbone and down my arm until the fleece blocks her movement.

"To remind me to bloom wherever I'm planted."

She hums in the back of her throat. "I like that. You've got animals worked in too. I see a lion, a wolf, birds... I could look at these forever. More reminders?"

I nod. "Each time I get one, I imagine invoking that animal's qualities in me. Strength, survival, flexibility, freedom. Stuff like that."

"And the celestial stuff?"

"A reminder to take a big picture view, to shift perspective when I get caught up in minor problems."

"So it's like having a bunch of symbolic 'notes to self' on your skin."

I laugh. "Something like that. The process of getting the tattoo grounds me, and then I carry the reminder of that with me."

"That's so cool," she says. "Can I see the dragon on your hip? I've always wanted to get a closer look at that one."

I slide the robe up to reveal the tattoo she's talking about. "He's my little friend. I got him done in Vegas."

"Cute! Does he have a name?"

"Nah, I just call him Dragon." I once again pull the Rudolph robe around me for warmth. "What about your piercings? Is there a story behind any of them?"

She opens the front of her own robe, revealing the little silver bars in her nipples and the heart-shaped crystal twinkling in her belly button. I get a rush of arousal at the memory of having my hands and mouth all over her.

"They mostly make me feel fancy," she says. "And each one is a reminder that I'm making my own decisions for myself and my body."

"I love that. How many do you have?"

"I've told myself I can't have more than my age," she says with a grin. "So I have twenty-four. If I get a new one, I have to take one out. At least until my next birthday."

"You've been doing porn for about two years now, right? How did you get into it?" I've always wondered but didn't want to ask. Everyone in the industry has a different reason.

She settles back into the corner of the loveseat, like she's getting comfortable. "I had just graduated college and a friend asked if I wanted to make some money as a PA helping out on a porn set. By the end of the day, I'd asked the talent a million questions, and decided I wanted to give it a try. I like sex, I like acting and performing, and I like traveling. This job lets me do all of that. Plus, I get to use my voice and my platform to demand better treatment for sex workers, and more diversity, equity, and inclusion in the industry."

"That was actually how you got on my radar," I tell her. "You did a video about ethical and fair trade porn practices that was spot on."

Passion infuses her tone. "It's so important that we speak up and demand better. Stigma says we should be embarrassed about what we do and not talk about it, but that's how bad and harmful behaviors persist."

"Totally agree."

She leans in a bit, her gaze on mine. "How did you start out? I mean, I've read your interviews, but I want to hear it from you."

It's so hard not to read too much into her words when she says things like that. But I focus on the question. "Well, I studied photography, and I was doing shoots for friends who were getting into modeling. They invited me to join them for a few gigs, and I couldn't believe the amount of money people would pay me to, like, stand next to a car in a crop top and booty shorts. It was so easy, it didn't even feel like working. From there, I started building up my own following. A friend connected me with a female porn director, and here we are, six years later."

"You were honestly one of the performers who inspired me to get into the business," Julie admits.

I'm floored by her confession. "I was?"

"Absolutely. I started following you on social media under my real name well before I got into the industry."

"That just makes me feel old," I joke, and she whacks me lightly with one of the Bad Kitty throw pillows.

"You're not old! I'm just a nerdy superfan."

"How did you get your stage name, anyway?" It's not something I'd ask everyone, but Julie's so easy to talk to, and I just want to know.

Hell, I want to know everything about her.

"It's so unoriginal," she says with a groan, covering her face. "My name is Juliana, and I couldn't think of a last name, so I went with *Just Julie*. How silly is that? I was only trying it out, and I didn't think I'd get so deep into the business so quickly, and with so many fans. And the name stuck. How did you pick yours?"

"Same initials," I say. "Honey Grayson. Helena Gomez. I figured it would be easy to respond to, since my mom calls me 'honey.'"

"That's really cute."

"*You're* really cute." I don't know where I found the guts to say that, but the words are out and I can't take them back. I don't want to, anyway. They're true. She *is* really cute.

Julie grins and opens her mouth to reply, but a PA rushes in, looking for something, followed by Ji-hae and the makeup team, and the moment is lost.

WE CLEAN UP, then the style team refreshes our hair and makeup. They record us chatting about the products we used, ask us what we liked best and why, and then we're free to go.

It's already dark outside, but New York City is bright and bustling at any time of day or night, especially during the holiday season. The lights and window displays sort of make up for the piles of dirty snow and sludge at the sidewalk curbs. Dressed in my seasonally appropriate attire and down coat, I'm warmer than I ever was in the loft.

"Where are you staying?" Julie asks.

I jerk a thumb in the direction of the downtown train. "With my family in Brooklyn. You?"

"I have the tiniest hotel room imaginable in Midtown." She rolls her eyes. "I guess we better go. We have an early call time tomorrow."

"Actually, I had an idea... " I say, and immediately worry I'm about to ruin whatever connection we're building.

But her eyes light up, even as she burrows more tightly into her jacket. It's puffy but short, and probably not warm enough to counteract the wind chill. I speak fast, before she can decide she'd rather just leave for her nice, warm hotel. "I was thinking about what we were saying earlier, about how the loft doesn't feel festive. So I was wondering...what if we go buy some decorations to liven it up? For us, and for the crew. I think they'd like it."

"That's a great idea!" She slips her arm through mine and cozies up against me. "Lead the way, since I have no clue where anything is in this city."

With Julie on my arm, I take us to Manhattan's equivalent of a 99 cent store, and we're delighted to find that the holiday decorations are already 50 percent off. We pick out a small, pre-lit Christmas tree and wreath, a light-up plastic menorah, beaded garlands, pre-cut paper snowflakes, glittery candy canes, a foam snowman, velvet bows, and a bulk supply of Santa and elf hats.

An older woman taps Julie on the arm as we're finishing up. "Excuse me. Your sister dropped this," the woman says, handing Julie one of the cardboard candy canes that's fallen out of the overflowing basket I'm carrying.

"Oh, thanks," Julie says, accepting the candy cane with a smile. "But she's not my sister. She's my girlfriend."

My breath backs up in my throat at the word, and I can't even begin to respond when the woman gives us a knowing smile and says, "You two make a gorgeous couple."

Julie slings an arm around my waist and grins broadly. "We do, don't we?"

I still haven't found my voice by the time Julie releases me. All I can do is replay her words in my head over and over. *My girlfriend. My girlfriend. My girlfriend.* What does it mean? Was it a joke? A declaration? A test to see if the woman was homophobic? A way to point out that Latinas don't all look the same? I can't tell!

"Ready to pay?" Julie asks, twirling the candy cane like a baton. Her tone is light, her expression open, just waiting for my answer.

So I let it drop. It must've been a joke.

Doesn't mean anything.

But I want it to.

CHAPTER 2

Day 2

My call time the next day is earlier than Julie's, so I bring the decorations to set them up before everyone else gets there. Ji-hae helps me, and I can tell she's touched that Julie and I thought to do this. The catering spread that morning also includes decorated sugar cookies and an impressive array of hot chocolate options. If we're all a little hopped up on sugar, well, maybe it'll make up for the fact that it's even colder in the loft than the day before.

I'm in the makeup chair, wrapped in my Rudolph robe, when Julie approaches.

"I have a gift for you," she says, her eyes glowing with mischief, as if she enjoys having a secret.

"You do?" I twist in my chair to look at her, and Calvin, the makeup artist, steps back to watch, a smile on his face.

Julie passes me a green-and-red gift bag with tiny dancing reindeer on it. My heart thumps as I rummage through the gold tissue paper. My fingers touch something unbelievably soft, and I pull out a pair of fuzzy socks in a blend of midnight blue and white. My jaw drops as I stroke the soft yarn, and my gaze shoots to hers.

"Julie, did you make these?"

She nods, a grin lighting up her face. "My abuela taught me to knit when I was a kid, and I'm pretty fast. I figured these would help you stay warm between takes. Do you like them?"

"I love them!" I press the socks to my cheek and snuggle them like I wish I could snuggle her. "They're so soft."

"They're made out of bulky alpaca," Julie explains, then pulls something out of her shoulder bag with a flourish. "I also brought my mittens with me so I can wear them before we film. Hopefully my fingers won't be as cold today."

I try to speak around the lump in my throat. "I think this is the most thoughtful gift anyone has ever given me."

Julie bites the corner of her mouth like she's trying not to smile too big. But her eyes twinkle. "'Tis the season," she says lightly. And then a PA comes to collect her.

Once Julie's out of earshot, Calvin leans down to speak in my ear. "Nena, sometimes socks are more than socks, you feel me?"

"I feel you," I murmur, but I'm scared to admit how much I hope he's right.

AFTER MAKEUP, I'm sitting on the loveseat in the main bedroom, wrapped in both my reindeer robe and an extra blanket, when Julie enters the room. She drops onto the cushion next to me.

"Is there room under there for me?" she asks with a hopeful note in her voice.

"Always." I lift one end of the blanket and Julie snuggles in beside me. She's wearing her mittens, and I've got the fuzzy socks she made for me on my feet. With all my tattoos, people think I'm really tough, so I can never admit that I teared up a little putting on the socks for the first time. Maybe it was my imagination, but they feel warmer and softer than any other socks I've ever owned.

"Tomorrow is Christmas Eve," Julie says, resting her head on my shoulder. "Are you flying out after we finish shooting?"

"No, my family is here. We're all going to a Nochebuena party together. What about you?"

Julie shrugs and shifts closer, tucking herself under my arm. "My mom is in Florida and my dad is in Texas. I'll just go back to Vegas and enjoy a few quiet days until New Year's."

That surprises me. "No Christmas plans?"

"Nah. Being in the desert doesn't feel Christmassy—not like here in New York, with the snow—and my roommate is away visiting her family. We didn't even decorate."

My eyes prick at the thought of Julie sitting home alone on Christmas. No matter where in the world I am, I always come home to spend the holidays with my family. Nochebuena is the big party night, but my parents and sisters—and now their families—always do Christmas breakfast together in matching pajama sets.

I suddenly picture Julie sitting beside me in the annual family photo, wearing the same green-and-white striped pajamas we picked out for this year.

The thought gives me such a start, I don't notice Ji-hae coming into the room until she launches into an explanation about the next scene. I'm only listening with half an ear because an idea is taking shape in my head.

What if I ask Julie to join me for the Nochebuena party?

CHAPTER 3

Day 3

OUR LAST DAY of filming is also Christmas Eve, and the crew is in a festive mood thanks to the decorations and endless supply of hot cocoa. They're all wearing the Santa hats we bought, the entire style team is dressed like elves, and everyone is wearing ugly Christmas sweaters. Before we left the night before, Ji-hae had announced there'd be a prize for the ugliest ugly sweater, and some of them are truly heinous. My money's on the sound guy wearing a sweatshirt featuring the poop emoji topped with a Santa hat.

Since I was already making my famous vegan coquito for the Nochebuena party tonight, I bring extra to share with the production staff. We pass around the Puerto Rican version of eggnog, minus the rum—we're all still on the clock, after all—and have a mini celebration in the loft's living room. Then we clean everything up and get back to work. We only have a few hours left to get all the shots, and then we're parting ways.

And I'm still no closer to inviting Julie to the party with me.

I'm a tangle of nerves, worse than on the first day. What had seemed like a mild internet crush is now full blown, and I dread saying goodbye to Julie.

At the same time, I still can't guess how she feels. Sure, she's flirty and we have great chemistry, but that's kind of the nature of this industry. There are some people you hit it off with, and some you don't. And I can't bear the thought of putting my heart on the line just for it to get trampled on again.

Over the course of my career, I've fallen in love three times. And every single time, the person hadn't reciprocated the depth of my feelings.

London just wanted to be friends. Kayla didn't "do" committed relationships. And Sergio just liked the extra sex. All were cases of "I like you but..." And that's not what I'm looking for.

I enjoy my job, but I want one person to come home to at night. One person to wake up beside, to share morning cuddles and movie nights, to commiserate with when things don't go my way or to cry on when someone says mean things to me on the internet. Despite the tattoos, I'm a marshmallow on the inside. Soft and squishy, sweet and easily burned.

I don't know if I can face being burned again.

And I like Julie. *Really* like her. I already liked what I'd seen when we were just flirting online, but after spending the last two days together, I can't deny that my heart is thoroughly involved.

I mean, what's not to like? Julie's funny and confident in a way that puts me at ease. She's thoughtful, as evidenced by the socks, which I will treasure forever. She's generous both in and out of bed. And she's full of praise in a way that doesn't feel fake or patronizing.

There's something here, I'm sure of it. But is it friendship? Attraction? Or something more?

I desperately want it to be something more.

Annoyed with my own thoughts, I pull out my phone to text my cousin Sarita.

Helena: *I like her. Like, really like her. What do I do? She leaves for Vegas tonight.*

Sarita: *What do you WANT to do?*

Helena: *I want to ask her to come with me to Gigi's Nochebuena party.*

Sarita: *Then you have your answer.*

I let out a breath and put my phone away. It's just a party, right? Maybe I can play it off like, *Oh, everyone comes to this party. No one will think anything if I bring a friend. Just so you don't have to spend Nochebuena alone. There's going to be great food, and I'm bringing coquito. And then maybe you can spend the night at my sister's house with me and have Christmas breakfast with my fam—*

Okay, this is getting out of hand. What's next—am I going to ask Julie to move in with me?

Totally ignoring the fact that this sounds like a great idea, I rein myself in with a little pep talk. *Calm your tits, nena. You've hung out for two days. So what if you've had more fun during these two days than you've had all year, even including the last convention's pool party? Don't get ahead of yourself.*

I'll play it by ear, and if the opportunity presents itself, I'll offer the invitation.

Or I'll chicken out. One or the other.

AFTER RECORDING a series of cutesy promotional clips, along with more arduous informational videos about lube, toy cleaner, Bad Kitty's signature antibacterial sex toy storage bag, and after-sex body care, Julie and I are lounging on the loveseat, which has become "our" spot, waiting to film a scene for the next and last product: strap-ons.

Now, I *love* strap-on scenes, and Julie has a reputation for being really great at them, so I'm excited. We're half naked already and arranging a big blanket around ourselves to stay warm when I have a silly idea. I push the blanket aside.

Julie gives me an incredulous look. "Aren't you cold?"

"Yes. But I need to do something first." I grab a couple of spare Santa hats that are sitting out of camera range. But instead of putting them on my head, I pop one on each of my boobs. Then I pose with my arms behind my neck. "Who am I?"

"The holiday version of Madonna with the cone bra!" Julie cracks up, then grabs her phone and snaps a picture of me. "Give me your number. I need to add this to your contact."

I pull the blanket around me—because it *is* cold in here, even with the space heaters on—and we swap phone numbers.

This is my chance. I could just say it. *Hey, do you wanna come to a party with me tonight?* Real casual. It doesn't have to be a big deal.

But damn it, I *want* it to be a big deal. I've liked Julie for a while, and being around her in person has only magnified those feelings. I want to know if she feels the same. I want to see where this goes.

Instead, I snuggle deeper under the blankets with her. "I think it's colder in here than it is outside," I mutter, annoyed at myself for chickening out once again.

"Aren't you from New York? This should be normal for you."

"Except I've lived in Los Angeles for the last seven years," I say with a laugh.

Julie shivers and huddles closer. "I've only lived in warm places. Florida, the Dominican Republic, Texas, Vegas, San Diego. Once it drops below seventy, I need a jacket."

I slide an arm around her shoulders and pull her a little closer. "I'll keep you warm."

She cuddles against me. We're quiet for a bit before I work up the nerve to ask, "What time is your flight?"

"At six. I'll clean up after we're done here, pack my stuff, and head straight to the airport."

This is it. The perfect moment to ask Julie to change her flight and come to Nochebuena with me.

Except the words won't come. Whatever is happening here is too easy, too casual. I'm probably reading into things. This is a budding friendship, nothing more.

But then Julie's hand moves under the blanket, sliding behind my back and around my waist. My skin tingles with awareness.

"I'm going to miss you," Julie murmurs. Her other arm reaches over my belly, and soon she's holding me tight, embracing me under the blanket with her head nestled in my neck. "Is this all right?"

I give a jerky nod, stunned at how freaking good it feels to simply be held like this. Just as I'm about to tell her that it's more than all right, Ji-hae bustles into the room, brandishing a sparkly purple harness with matching dildo.

"Ready for strap-ons?"

"ARE YOU OKAY?" Julie asks. She's rubbing her hands in slow, soothing circles over my back. The strap-on she wore has been discarded at the end of the bed.

I give a little laugh. "Oh yeah. Totally okay. I've never been this okay in my whole life."

Julie smiles. "Good."

"Yeah, you fucked me good."

It's her turn to laugh, then she accepts the water bottles and robes a PA hands us with a thank-you.

We put on the robes and sip the water, still coming down from the epic high of a really, really good scene. I ate her out like there was no tomorrow, and she went to town on me with the strap-on, her rhythmic hip action hitting all the right spots. Now Julie snuggles up against me, resting her head on my shoulder while the crew carries equipment out of the room.

"I don't want this to be over," she whispers.

Suddenly, the courage that has failed me for the past few days leaps to the fore, and before I'm even fully aware of what I'm doing, the words I've been wanting to say tumble out of my mouth.

"It doesn't have to." I sit up and take her hand. "Come with me."

"Where?" She sounds bewildered, but not uninterested.

"To a Nochebuena party. Tonight," I say. "And after..."

"And after... ?" she repeats, her curving lips prompting me to continue.

"Well, I'm staying with my sister and her family, which I know is not the most romantic of settings, but we could probably book a hotel, or—"

She presses her fingertips to my lips, which is a blessing, because I'm totally messing this up.

"Yes," she says. "To the party and after. I love the idea of spending Christmas with you."

I see the certainty of her answer in her eyes, hear it in her voice, and a full-body chill runs through me. And not the "this room is cold" kind, either. The "this moment is going to change your life" kind.

"I got you something," I whisper.

She beams. "A present?"

"Yeah. Wait here." Bundled in my robe, I rush out to the living room and grab the wrapped gift out of my bag. All around me, the crew is breaking down the set. It's Christmas Eve, and they all want to get out of here as quickly as possible. I hurry back to the bedroom where Julie waits on the loveseat. Everyone else has left the room.

"Here you go," I say, dropping onto the cushion next to her.

She takes the present, which is soft and lumpy and probably shouldn't have been wrapped in paper, but I couldn't fit a gift bag in my purse.

"What is it?" she asks.

I let out a nervous giggle. "You have to open it to find out."

She carefully slides a finger under the tape and folds the wrapping paper back, revealing a satiny red Christmas stocking embroidered with silver thread, forming a Christmas tree and snowflakes. On the top, in elaborate script, is the name *Juliana*.

She sucks in a breath and traces her name with her fingertip. "This is so pretty."

"You said you don't have any decorations at home," I say in a rush, nerves taking over again. "So I wanted to get you a little something to hang up. And if you said yes to coming with me... well, you can add this to the ones over my sister's fireplace."

173

"Like part of the family?" she murmurs, still fingering the embroidery.

The thought gives me a warm rush. "Yeah."

She squeezes the stocking. "There's something in here."

"Of course. I couldn't give you an empty stocking."

She takes a peek inside, but the things I put in there are wrapped. There's a Santa mug, a tin of peppermint hot cocoa powder, artisanal marshmallows, and an assorted package of gingerbread and short-bread cookies. She'd been so thrilled with the hot chocolate the day before, I thought this would be the perfect way to give her a taste of Christmas in Vegas.

Julie swallows hard enough for me to hear. "I think this is the nicest thing anyone's ever done for me," she says, echoing my senti-ment from the day before, when she gave me the handmade socks. Then she drops the stocking between us and throws her arms around my neck in a tight hug.

I hug her back, my heart nearly bursting with happiness. She said yes to Nochebuena. She said yes to staying with me for Christmas. There's just one more thing I have to ask.

"Julie, I—"

"I really like you, Honey," she whispers into my neck. "Like, *really*. Maybe it's not cool to say it, but—"

I pull back so I can see her face. "I really like you too, Julie. I've been wanting to ask you to stay with me for the holidays this whole time, and I almost chickened out."

"I'm glad you didn't." She cups my cheeks and kisses me, her full lips soft against mine. Her tongue dips into my mouth and I pull her closer. Considering how much we've already done together, this kiss shouldn't affect me the way it does, but it feels deeper, more intimate, than anything we've done before. We're not performing now; this is just us, kissing because we want to, because we like each other, because we want to continue exploring what's between us.

I rest my forehead on Julie's and whisper, "This."

"This what?" she asks softly.

"This is all I wanted for Christmas."

"Me?" Her voice is an adorable little squeak.

"You."

I kiss her again, and we don't come up for air until Ji-hae comes in to tell us we're free to go. Hand in hand, we get ready to leave, then head to the party.

Together.

ALSO BY ALEXIS DARIA

PRIMAS OF POWER SERIES

You Had Me at Hola

A Lot Like Adiós

STANDALONES

What the Hex (audio novella)

SOLSTICE STORIES

Solstice Miracle (short story)

Solstice Dream (short story)

ABOUT THE AUTHOR

Alexis Daria is an award-winning and bestselling romance author writing stories about successful Latinx characters and their (occasionally messy) familias. *You Had Me at Hola*, the first book in her Primas of Power series, was a national bestseller, *New York Times* Editor's Choice Pick and featured on several "Best of" lists from outlets like *Oprah Magazine*, *Buzzfeed*, *Kirkus*, and *Bustle*. Her latest release, *A Lot Like Adiós*, received starred reviews from *Publishers Weekly*, *Kirkus*, *Booklist*, and *Library Journal*. A former visual artist, Alexis is a lifelong New Yorker who loves Broadway musicals and pizza.

Sign up for Alexis's newsletter here! Or check out her author website!

 twitter.com/alexisdaria
instagram.com/alexisdaria

SANTA'S EAGER LITTLE HELPER

MIA SOSA

Sarita's plan to confess her crush on a colleague goes awry when she's tasked with playing the Sexy Elf to his grumpy Santa. Will she seize the opportunity to make Carlos's naughty list, or will she spend another Nochebuena alone?

CHAPTER 1

"Your brother's an asshole."

Sarita Barros looked up from the stack of papers she was collating and grinned. "Well, good morning to you too, sunshine."

Carlos Gonçalves, the test kitchen chef for Sabor Foods, scratched his scruffy beard and grunted. "Sorry. Good morning."

"Can you tell me what my brother did to piss you off, or have you reached your daily word quota? Because as much as I wish this weren't the case, I'm not fluent in Gruntish."

He grunted again, his dark brown eyes narrowing. Still, she caught the hint of a smile that teased the corners of his mouth. Despite his perpetually crabby demeanor, Carlos was an upstanding guy. She'd never forget his first order of business when he took over the position testing recipes in her brother's Latinx meal prep company three years ago: He'd familiarized himself with Sabor's business operations and the workings of the kitchen, then immediately arranged for unused packaged foods to be delivered to area homeless shelters at the end of each week. She'd fallen a little bit in love with him right then.

"He won't let me hire an apprentice," Carlos replied through gritted teeth as he rolled up the sleeves of his navy sweater.

Forearms. *Why* did it have to be forearms?

Shaking her head to clear it, she asked, "Why not?"

"Says the budget won't support an additional person in the kitchen. But the business is growing, and I only have two hands."

She knew he only had two hands. They were big, strong hands too. That kneaded dough with strength and finesse, as if he were massaging a lover's back—or, as she'd imagined it many, many times, Sarita's ass.

Gah. *Snap out of it, woman.*

"If Reynaldo says the budget won't support it, I believe him."

Carlos grimaced. "Of course you do. Listen, I get that he's your—"

The phone rang, and since she was filling in for the company's regular receptionist, who was stuck in midtown rush hour traffic, she raised an index finger. "Hold that thought. Feliz Natal and merry Christmas! You've reached Sabor Foods, where flavor reigns supreme. How may I help you?"

The man on the line sounded frantic, and after every few words or so, he coughed. "I need to speak... with... Lisa Hammond. She hasn't responded to the messages I left, and it's an emergency."

Yikes. Lisa Hammond, Sabor's *former* communications director, had quit on Monday, citing Reynaldo's unreasonable demands as the main reason for her unexpected departure. Sarita met Carlos's questioning gaze and bared her teeth nervously. The situation called for a bit of improvisation. "Unfortunately, Ms. Hammond is not available at the moment, but I'm sure we can find someone else to assist you. What—"

"Her boss, then," the man said in a raspy voice. "Tell them it's important."

That would be Reynaldo—or "Naldo," the nickname Sarita had given him when they were kids. As she dialed her brother's extension, Carlos pushed off the wall in front of the reception desk and waved goodbye.

"But we haven't finished talking," she whispered.

"You're busy," he said as he walked off, his shoulder-length wavy hair fluttering behind him. "And there's no point in discussing your brother. You'll always see things his way."

Well, that wasn't fair. When it came to Sabor, she always tried to remain neutral, taking the side of whatever argument made the most sense. Apparently, he disagreed. She wanted to respond to Carlos, but her brother picked up the phone, and she needed to get the anxious caller squared away.

"You have someone on line one," she told Naldo. "He's been trying to reach Lisa. Said he'd speak to her boss instead."

"Got it," Naldo said. "Everything's been so hectic with the holiday party planning, I forgot to deal with Lisa's loose ends."

"Is there anything I can do to help? As I told you before, I'm happy to step into her role, even if only while you find her replacement."

"It's a big title. And I like having you available for other things."

Meanwhile, she had no title at all. Sure, he wanted her around to fill in for a late receptionist. Or to make a coffee run. But any task that capitalized on her business degree and gave her substantive responsibilities seemed out of the question. Thinking it would pacify her, Reynaldo had presented her with a lovely corner office one year ago. She didn't do anything of consequence in it, though.

"Let me take this," Reynaldo said.

Sarita sighed. Perhaps Christmas Eve wasn't the best day to tackle her position within the company. "Fine. Transferring now."

She refused to let her work frustrations ruin her mood. Sabor's annual holiday party would begin in just a few hours, and Sarita had plans. First on the agenda: finally revealing her years-long crush on Carlos. After a cocktail or two, of course.

Per usual, she'd planned her strategy down to the tiniest detail— what she would wear (a form-fitting red dress), what she would say ("I've been in love with you for two years now"), and where she would say it (in front of the atrium's fireplace, which had been decorated with berries, poinsettias, and most importantly for her purposes, mistletoe). Even the gift she'd purchased for Carlos—two tickets to a Knicks game at Madison Square Garden—furthered her aims. With any luck, he'd invite her to join him, and they'd go on their first official date, perhaps eating dinner beforehand. Best yet, her cousin Helena, an adult film star, had approved her blueprint for the

evening, suggesting that Sarita invite Carlos to a Nochebuena celebration being hosted by a family friend. It would be an excellent
opportunity to explore their relationship beyond the company's
walls.

Unfortunately, this morning's exchange cast a shadow on tonight's
festivities. Carlos didn't like Naldo, and Naldo only tolerated Carlos
because he was a wizard in the kitchen. The two most important
people in her life couldn't stand each other. Wonderful.

Sarita knew she needed them both.

Her brother had practically raised her after their parents died in a
car crash when she was just fifteen. He was six years her elder and had
been finishing up college at the time. Thrust into a role he'd never
anticipated, Naldo had made sure they remained together, taught her
how to drive, and interrogated her date for senior prom. He'd also
helped put her through school, largely because he'd hustled to get
Sabor off the ground, convincing his former classmates to invest in
his idea to expand the existing market for convenient meal prep
services to include Latinx cuisine. Now, thirteen years later, Sarita
and Naldo were as close as two siblings could be, notwithstanding his
older brother complex. In short, he'd always been there for her, and
she wouldn't let any person undermine her bond with him.

As for Carlos, once Sarita had looked beyond his gruff exterior
and outright told him his grumpy persona didn't intimidate her,
they'd become close friends. He listened to her complain about
Naldo's inability to see her as an adult and offered advice on how to
assert herself in the workplace. She was always the first person to try
one of his new recipes. And she helped him navigate interactions with
their coworkers, all of whom ran the other direction whenever he was
around for fear of poking "the Bear." Carlos was *her* bear, though, and
tonight she wanted to take their relationship to the next level.
Tonight, at last, she wanted the Bear to poke *her*.

Still, she worried that even if Carlos returned her affections, they
were destined to fail as a couple. What chance did they have if he
couldn't stand to be in the same room with the most important
person in Sarita's life? Then again, what was the point of contem-

plating these questions when it was entirely possible that Carlos had zero romantic interest in her?

Sarita dropped her forehead to the desk and banged it repeatedly. Which was how Carlos found her when he returned to the reception area.

"Ahem," he said. "Everything okay?"

She kept banging. "Yep."

"Is there a reason you're banging your head against that desk?"

"Yep."

"Care to share the reason?"

"Nope."

"That's your Boricua side."

This was a running joke between them. Carlos was a Brazilian American of Indigenous and African descent. Sarita was Afro-Brazilian on her father's side. Her mother, on the other hand, was Puerto Rican. Carlos attributed anything she said or did that was strange or out of the ordinary to her Puerto Rican ancestry.

She narrowed her eyes at him. "Careful."

"Well, uh, I was wondering if you wanted to walk with me to the Starbucks on the corner. I'm in the mood for a cinnamon brown sugar latte. And... I, uh... wanted to apologize for being a dick earlier."

Sarita sat up and gave him a warm smile. "No need to apologize. We're good." She gestured around her. "But I can't leave just yet. Not until Sylvie gets here."

"Oh, right," he said, a flush creeping up the rich brown skin of his cheeks. "I don't mind waiting." Then he sat on the couch facing the reception area and plucked a magazine from the media rack. "So, are you planning to attend the party this afternoon?"

"I am. You?" His answer was critical to her plans, but she didn't want to be obvious about it. The one thing she couldn't do was guarantee that he'd be there.

"I don't know," he said, flipping through the magazine. "I'm not a fan of being around that many people."

"Let's be honest, you're not a fan of people, period."

He chuckled, then winked at her. "There are exceptions."

She was poised to ask him whether *she* was an exception, but Naldo appeared out of nowhere and skidded to a stop in front of her. "Sari, I need your help," he said, his chest heaving.

"Of course," she replied quickly. "What's going on?"

"Before she quit, Lisa arranged for a husband and wife duo to take over our Instagram account and teach dance lessons for the holiday party season. You know, like salsa, bachata, merengue, samba. They were going to advertise our foods as well, by talking about the meals they most enjoyed."

"Sounds fun."

"I think so too. But they can't do it. They've both come down with the flu."

"That's terrible," Sarita said. "You're going to cancel, right?"

"I can't," Naldo said, shaking his head. "As part of her communications strategy, Lisa wanted to show our investors how we're embracing social media, so she invited all of them to watch the takeover. If we cancel at the eleventh hour, we'll look like amateurs." He grabbed the back of his neck. "In short, we need a plan B."

"Why don't *you* do it?" Carlos asked from his place on the couch. "With a partner, I mean. Those spider legs must be good for something."

Naldo straightened, his shoulders nearly touching his ears before he spun around. "Shouldn't you be working?"

"I'm taking a break," Carlos said as he continued to flip through the magazine without even looking at its pages.

"Well, this doesn't concern you, so there's no need to make suggestions."

Carlos snorted. "Whatever."

These two. They were ridiculous.

Naldo turned back to Sarita, dismissing Carlos with a wave. "Any ideas, Sari? You're good on social media. Can you come up with something we can do instead of dance lessons?"

"I'm sure I can. Let me get back to you, okay? What time is the takeover scheduled to start?"

"At 1 p.m."

Sarita's stomach dropped. "But that's during the holiday party."

"Yeah, it is. Not sure what Lisa was thinking."

"So I'm going to miss it," she said glumly, knowing the answer and envisioning her plans going up in tragically metaphorical smoke.

"This is about our investors, Sari. It's more important than drinking champagne and snacking on hors d'oeuvres, wouldn't you say? C'mon, we all need to make sacrifices from time to time."

She heard the implication of Naldo's words loud and clear: We all need to make sacrifices like *he* had. Sarita slouched in her chair, then snuck a glance at Carlos and watched his nostrils flare.

He was right. Her brother *was* a bit of an asshole.

CHAPTER 2

Carlos tried to hold his temper in check as he and Sarita walked to Starbucks. He wished she would tell her brother to eat shit and fix his own mess, but he knew that wasn't happening. Not in this lifetime.

"Does it ever get tiring? Being at your brother's beck and call?"

"Don't start," she said as she strolled beside him. "It's not productive."

That was certainly true. They'd had similar discussions for two years now. None of them had led her to put her foot down when it came to her brother.

He understood that Sarita and Reynaldo were close. Appreciated that her brother had been there for her when their parents died. But Reynaldo used those facts to his advantage, convincing Sarita that she owed him... everything. Her allegiance. Her time. Her *life*. Carlos hated to see it. Especially since he cared for her. More than was wise, in fact.

Because Carlos had been down this road before. Well, not the exact same one, but a road that looked eerily similar. His ex-wife, Raquel, couldn't make a single decision about *their* life together unless her family weighed in as well. And whenever Carlos and her family had disagreed about an issue, her family managed to guilt Raquel into siding with them. They knew what they were doing, too, and he had no doubt Reynaldo was just as calculating. Carlos wouldn't put himself in a position to be manipulated like that again.

He turned up the collar on his charcoal pea coat and slid her a guarded look. "No, you're right. I spoke out of turn. Forget I said anything."

"It's forgotten." As they waited for the light to change, Sarita rubbed her hands together, then blew on her clasped fingers. "Damn, it's cold."

Carlos glanced at Sarita. She looked adorable in her cherry-red down jacket, a white knit hat with a lazy pompom covering her dark brown hair. Her cheeks were flushed, giving her medium-brown skin the barest hint of a rosy glow. Sarita was sweet and funny and tripped his heart into beating at double its usual rate every time he saw her. He yearned to fold her into his body, to give her his warmth. But he couldn't do it. Because being that close to her would drive him to want more. And more with Sarita would only lead to heartache. He needed a partner, not a person who'd let her brother get in between them. And Reynaldo *would* get between them. The man could barely look Carlos in the eye. So he would settle for being her friend and being there for her whenever she needed him.

"Where are your gloves?" he asked.

"I left them in my desk drawer, Papa Smurf."

"We should get you mittens. You know, the kind that attach to your coat."

She side-eyed him. "Ooh, and a Barbie lunchbox too!"

"Never mind," he said, shaking his head. "Point taken."

The pedestrian walk sign flashed, and they rushed across the street. Then he held the door to Starbucks open for her. As she passed him, he inhaled her rich vanilla scent. It reminded him of snickerdoodles from Mrs. Fields—his favorite cookies ever—and the urge to graze his mouth along her neck hit him hard. *Rein it in, Carlos.*

After ordering, they waited in a corner as other customers crowded the pickup area.

"So, what are you going to do about the IG takeover?" he asked. "Any ideas yet?"

"I'm still noodling through it in my head. Honestly, I'm not sure what Lisa was thinking when she scheduled a dance lesson on IG. Sabor's a food company, not a salsa club. It would make more sense if she'd arranged a cooking lesson." She jerked and clapped her hands excitedly. "That's it!"

"No."

She grinned up at him, her eyes twinkling like Christmas lights. "You don't even know what I'm going to say."

"If it has to do with cooking in *my* kitchen, then I absolutely know what you're going to say. And the answer is no. I'm not a presenter. I have no charm. I'd be too nervous."

"What if I joined you?"

"Tempting, but the answer's still no."

She pouted at him. "Fine. I'll come up with something else."

After picking up their drinks—a cinnamon brown sugar latte for him and a hot chocolate for her—they walked back to the building and slipped inside a waiting elevator.

"Hey, Adam," Sarita said to one of their coworkers.

Adam smiled at her. "Hey, Sarita!" Then he spotted Carlos, and his smile vanished. "Carlos."

He nodded. "Hey."

Carlos nicknamed all of his colleagues according to which store he thought best represented their personal style. Adam was Abercrombie & Fitch.

Sarita took a sip of her drink, then popped her lips softly. "Hey, Adam. I've been duped into doing an IG takeover this afternoon. But I need a partner. Was thinking about doing a cooking lesson. Kind of like a demonstration of how to plan a holiday date night. Would you be game for doing it with me?"

Adam perked up. "A date night? What would I have to do exactly?"

"Pretend to be enjoying my company," Sarita said, shrugging nonchalantly. "Clink glasses when we make a toast. Throw me a wink or two. Things like that."

What the fuck? She wanted to do all that with *this* guy? No. "Sarita, I already said I'd do it."

She whipped around to face him. "What? No, you didn't. You said—"

"I changed my mind, okay? It's *my* kitchen, after all."

"Actually, it's the company's kitchen," she said, her lips quirked up in amusement.

"As long as I'm at Sabor, it's *my* kitchen."

She threw up her hands in surrender. "Okay, okay. It's yours. For now. Anyway, thanks for having my back."

Carlos wanted to squirm, but he remained motionless. Her gratefulness made him feel guilty. He should have said yes the first time she asked, but he'd rejected her suggestion out of hand because he didn't enjoy public speaking and certainly didn't want to be the object of anyone's attention. Once Adam entered the picture, however, Carlos chose to make a complete and embarrassing one-eighty. Which made him an ass. A redeemable ass, perhaps, but still an ass. "No thanks necessary. It's nothing."

She rested her hand on his wrist. "Don't downplay it with me. I know you're not thrilled about doing this, and if it really makes you uncomfortable, I can find another way."

He swallowed. *Damn her for being so nice.* "It's all right. We'll get through it together."

"So you don't need me?" Adam asked, his mouth curved into a frown.

"No," he and Sarita said in unison. Admittedly, Carlos's reply sounded more like a growl.

A minute later, when they reached the office floor, Sarita turned to him. "I'm going to grab a pen and pad. I'll meet you in the kitchen so we can brainstorm what to do during the takeover. Sound good?"

"Sounds fine," he said, though his face probably suggested otherwise.

He watched her leave, trying not to notice how the bounce in her step did great things for her ass. Jesus Cristo. How the hell had this happened? Was he really going to make a fool of himself in front of strangers? Would they make comments? Would anyone even watch? Damn, he hoped not. With his head bowed, he trudged to the kitchen, unsure how he'd gotten caught up in this massive shitshow.

Ten minutes later, Sarita appeared at the kitchen door. She'd thrown on an oversized sweater that swallowed the top half of her wool dress, and she'd replaced her boots with flats. Her hair was now tied up in some elaborate knot on top of her head. He loved this about her. The ease with which she walked through the world. He wished he had a fraction of her confidence. Even as a kid, though, he'd been awkward and uncomfortable in his own skin. His height, his bulk, his facial hair—it always seemed to be too much.

Too intimidating. Too in-your-face. Too noticeable.

Next to Sarita, Carlos felt like the Hulk. Probably explained why Carlos had the green Avenger's quick-tempered personality too. And somehow, Carlos was going to have to bottle all that up and perform in front of a live audience.

For her, he reminded himself. He was doing this only for her. If anyone else had asked him to parade himself on social media, he would have told them to go fuck themselves. Not Sarita, though. Never Sarita. He didn't want to think too deeply about the implications of those facts.

"Okay, I have some ideas," she said as she climbed onto a stool in front of the kitchen's massive prep station. Then she scooted around to look at the room. "We should set up a small table for two. White tablecloth, flower centerpiece, maybe some candles. That'll set the mood."

He gestured at the storage closet behind him. "I'm sure we have all that stuff in there since that's how we stage the tastings."

Every month or so, Sabor invited food bloggers and editors to sample the latest menu items in the hopes of getting favorable media coverage. He cooked, and Lisa would host. Now that Lisa was gone, he didn't know who would take over the role.

"Great," Sarita said, jotting down notes in her pad. "Now, turning to your area of expertise, let's talk about the menu."

He rested his hip against the edge of the prep station and stroked his jaw. "Hmm. We should focus on easy dishes. If we're going to get people interested in Sabor, they should be able to see how approachable meal prep can be."

"Excellent point. But we should give it a holiday feel, right? Things we'd eat for Ceia de Natal. Nochebuena too. And it would be cool if we could talk about recipes from Puerto Rico *and* Brazil."

They settled on a menu consisting of two Puerto Rican recipes (arroz con gandules and coquito) and two Brazilian dishes (couve à mineira and rabanada). They also agreed that she'd serve as his sous chef for the live show.

As they took turns pulling the necessary ingredients from the pantry and refrigerator, they discussed how to bring all their ideas together.

"So it's a date night, right?" she asked. "You're cool with that?"

"Sure, that's fine."

"And you'll pretend to be a romantic?"

He stopped midstep, several bunches of collard greens for the couve in his hands. "Why do you assume I'll need to pretend?"

"Just a hunch," she said, her lips twitching.

He flicked her chin with a limp collard that he already knew was unusable.

"Oh, it's on," she said as she clobbered him with a loaf of bread.

He was frantically searching for another culinary weapon when Reynaldo strolled inside the kitchen and cleared his throat.

"Just checking in," he said as if Carlos and Sarita hadn't been horsing around. "Any ideas yet?"

Sarita straightened and hid the loaf behind her. "We're doing a cooking demonstration."

Reynaldo furrowed his forehead. "With *him?*"

"Yes, with him," she replied without hesitation. "We're doing you a favor, remember?"

"Right, right," he said, massaging his temples. "I suppose we *are* trying to sell our service."

"Exactly," she said.

Reynaldo blew out a breath, and his gaze landed on the floor. The hair on the back of Carlos's neck stood up. Reynaldo was hiding something, and if he was hiding something, Carlos knew he wouldn't like it.

"Something you want to tell us?" Carlos asked.

Reynaldo finally met his stare. "I forgot to mention one thing: the costumes."

"The *what?*" Carlos bellowed as he dropped onto a stool. He needed to sit for this.

"Now, there's no need to get upset," Reynaldo said, putting up his hands.

"Just explain," Sarita said, sounding exasperated with her brother's stalling tactics.

Reynaldo grabbed the back of his neck. "One of our investors is my old college roommate. He owns a costume and cosplay shop in the Village, on Houston Street."

"What does any of this have to do with us?" Carlos snapped.

"You see, I promised him he could showcase his costumes during the IG Live. Told him the couple would wear outfits from his shop and plug his business."

"Why didn't you mention this obligation before?" Sarita asked.

"Honestly, I forgot about it. I only remembered because the costumes were just delivered to the office."

"What kind of costumes?" Carlos asked, folding his arms over his chest. He was about to go Hulk on Reynaldo, consequences be damned.

Reynaldo gulped. "Santa Claus and one of his elves."

Oh, ho, ho, ho, the fuck no.

Now it was official: Carlos was trapped in a nightmare.

CHAPTER 3

Sarita pictured Carlos in a Santa Claus costume and did everything in her power to hold in her laughter. This day kept improving by the minute. It didn't matter that her plans for revealing her crush on Carlos had been disrupted. The scenario that was unfolding was better than any scheme she could have concocted on her own. She'd have him all to herself for the afternoon, and they'd both look so ridiculous, Carlos was bound to loosen up.

Still, she wasn't going to let Naldo off easy.

"Absolutely not," she told him. "I agreed to help you, not humiliate myself on social media."

"Exactly," Carlos chimed in. "There's no way I'm dressing up as Papai Noel."

"Gente, this affects us all," her brother said, throwing up his hands. "If we want Sabor to be a success, we need to keep our investors happy. We're a team, no?"

Sarita saw her opportunity and took it. "Actually, now that you mention it, Naldo, I *don't* feel like a part of the Sabor team. I have no true position here, and I'm basically your gofer. I'd like to change that."

"What are you asking?" Naldo said, his expression pinched.

Sarita took a deep, steadying breath and met his gaze. "I want to take over Lisa's position. As director of communications."

"But you have no experience in that role!" Naldo cried.

"Because you won't give me the opportunity to get any," she replied. "So if you want us to throw on ridiculous costumes and help you out of this mess, you'll need to make some concessions too."

Carlos shook his head. "Wait, wait, wait. I'm not agreeing to anything." He turned to her. "If you want to negotiate with him, go right ahead. But leave me out of it."

Sarita's face fell. Carlos had always encouraged her to stand up for herself. He'd often complained that she needed to be more assertive when she dealt with her brother. Now that she was heeding Carlos's advice, she wanted him to be proud of her. And if she were being honest with herself, she'd assumed she would get his support. "Didn't you say you would always have my back?"

Sarita had asked the question so softly she wasn't sure if he'd heard her. But when she looked up at him, he was staring at her through narrowed eyes.

"Oh, c'mon, Sarita," he said. "Me? In a Santa costume? Nobody wants to see that."

"You're right," she said glumly. "This is between Naldo and me."

Carlos threw his head back and let out a harsh breath. "Dammit, I'm probably going to regret this, but if putting on a silly Santa costume gets you a promotion, then fine, I'll do it."

"Not so fast, Bom Velhinho," Reynaldo said. "I never said she'd get a promotion."

Carlos rolled his eyes. "Then forget it."

"Hang on," Reynaldo said. He turned to Sarita, his expression pleading for her to be reasonable. "How about this? Do the Live tonight, and we'll see how it goes. If you handle the assignment to my satisfaction, we'll talk about you taking over Lisa's position on a trial basis. Fair enough?"

Sarita peered at Carlos and tilted her head in question; he nodded.

"Deal," she said.

"Excellent!" Reynaldo said. "I'll get my assistant to send down the costumes. Listen, I'll be making the rounds at the party while you're doing the Live, but I'll check in with you afterward."

"Sounds good," Sarita said.

Carlos grunted.

Once Reynaldo was gone, they stared at each other.

"Thank you," she said. The words seemed inadequate; they were heartfelt, nonetheless.

Carlos appeared to be forcing a smile, and his eyes were dim. "It's not an ideal situation, but we're in this together, right?"

"Right." Sarita could tell Carlos was still pissed, but she was sure he'd be singing a different tune by the evening's end. Wanting to lighten the mood, she grabbed his wrist and shook it playfully. "Oh, c'mon. They're just costumes. How bad could they be?"

HERS WAS BAD. Really, really bad. What little there was of it, that is.

If she were styling herself in preparation for a hot elf summer, then sure, this red-and-green polyester monstrosity would do the trick. But she was a half hour away from going live on Instagram, and her tits were pushed up so high her nipples looked like necklace charms. The matching hat was atrocious and sat affixed to her head with Velcro bows.

Sighing, she inspected the outfit's packaging and noted the "sexy Christmas elf" branding. Lovely. Once again, her brother's actions had screwed her.

Sarita could already envision it: Carlos would take one look at this catastrophe and double over in laughter. This was definitely *not* what she envisioned wearing when she revealed her crush on him. But there was nothing she could do about that now. She'd made a deal with her brother. Besides, she had more important matters to resolve —namely, whether or not to wear the red-and-white striped thigh-high stockings that completed the costume. Without them, the short length of her microskirt was hard to miss. With them, she would resemble a candy cane. After giving it some thought, she opted for looking like Christmas candy.

Remembering that Helena had asked for updates on her quest, Sarita sent her cousin a quick text:

The plan is a bust

Naldo asked me to help him out with an emergency

Carlos and I are going to do a cooking demo on IG Live at 3 pm

worse, I'm wearing a sexy elf costume (don't ask)

HELENA RESPONDED IMMEDIATELY:

doesn't sound like a bust to me

shake that ass and drive him bananas

I'll encourage my followers to check out the Live! good luck!

HER COUSIN'S optimism was misplaced. Helena was probably picturing an enticing dress and stockings; *this* was not *that*. She sent Helena a thumbs-up emoji anyway.

Resigned to her fate, Sarita threw on her down jacket so she wouldn't have to walk around the office with her ass on display. Opening the restroom door a fraction, she peeked out, then scrambled down the hall and scurried into the test kitchen. She didn't see or hear Carlos, so with her jacket still on, she began setting the table for two.

A few minutes later, she heard Carlos clear his throat behind her. "Before you turn around, I want to make something clear."

She straightened. "Okay, what is it?"

"If you laugh, I will walk out this kitchen and never return again. I'll just trek across the country like a Latinx Forrest Gump."

She burst out laughing, then stopped herself. "I didn't turn around yet, so that one doesn't count."

"Fine," he said.

"May I see what all the fuss is about?"

"You may."

She spun around—and nearly reached down to catch her eyeballs, which surely were tumbling onto the floor. Meu Deus, he looked sexy. And just a little ridiculous. Yet somehow the combination worked for him.

The outfit was... something. The red velvet pants reminded her of the stirrups worn by athletes competing in professional men's gymnastics. The top was essentially a sleeveless vest with a deep V, white trim, and a faux belt; it emphasized his bare (and broad) chest and his muscular biceps, the latter of which she'd never seen unclothed. If he were appearing on a *Dancing with the Stars* holiday special, he would get tens across the board for his costume.

"Actually, it's... fine."

"Fine?" he said, throwing out his hands at his sides in frustration. "I look like a marquee performer in the *Magic Mike Live Christmas Special.*"

Her mouth gaped, then she shook her head. "That's a thing?"

"How the hell should I know?" he said, raking a hand through his hair. "Focus, Sarita, focus."

She put out her hands to calm him. "Relax, okay. It's really not that bad. And I'll prove it to you too." She unzipped her coat and arced her arm in front of her in a sweeping gesture. "If you want to see bad, feast your eyes on this. Santa's Eager Little Helper at your service."

Carlos's eyes widened, and he staggered back. "Fuck. Me."

She gave him a saucy wink. "Is that a proposition?"

His body froze, and his ears turned red. "What? No, of course not. It's... uh... a figure of speech. I was just remarking on how truly bad your outfit is. Similar to saying *holy shit.*"

Well, damn. That wasn't the reaction she'd hoped for. Yes, she wanted to distract him from his train wreck of a costume, but she thought he'd at least be intrigued by the way her breasts seemed to be bobbing around like tube floats in a wave pool. Le sigh. "Okay, so neither one of us is happy about this. Let's just suck it up and focus on delivering an engaging and informative presentation. Deal?"

He dropped his chin and tugged on his Santa cap. "Deal."

"Okay," she said, feeling dejected but faking a smile. "I'm going to finish arranging the table, then set up my phone on the tripod."

He nodded. "I'll prep the station. You'll do the introductions?"

"Yep. Chime in whenever you're comfortable."

Sarita sighed on the inside. She was no longer confident of her plans to reveal her interest in Carlos. It was clear he didn't see her as a romantic prospect. Perhaps they were only meant to be friends. If so, she'd learn to accept that fact. He was a good guy, and she treasured their bond. Considering the tension between Carlos and her brother, any relationship between Sarita and Carlos would face an uphill battle anyway.

Sarita spun around and felt the air flutter against the backs of her thighs. She needed to remember not to make any sudden moves; the skirt's flouncy material created its own atmospheric system.

Behind her, Carlos whimpered.

She snapped her head in his direction. "You okay?"

"Yeah," he said, massaging his chest and stretching his mouth as if he had something stuck in his throat. "I'm okay."

Yeah, she'd be okay too. She just needed to get through this IG Live, then she could spend the rest of the evening celebrating Nochebuena with her friends.

And without Carlos by her side, of course.

CHAPTER 4

Carlos was *not* okay.

Because so many things about Sarita flustered him on the daily: her sweet smile, the soft expanse of skin behind her ears, her full-bodied laugh, and the way she nibbled on her bottom lip whenever she was deep in thought. The sight before him, however, didn't just confuse him; it scrambled his brain and made his chest tighten. Shit, he was so turned on, his toes were curled in his shoes to stop him from lunging forward and drawing her into his arms.

Seeing her this way seemed too intimate. Reminded him that Sarita was a sexy-as-hell woman with generous tits, a trim waist, and strong thighs he could easily picture wrapped around his shoulders. He was desperate to unleash all his unspent lust on her. Wanted to drive her so wild she'd spew curse words from those luscious lips. Damn, this was *not* the right headspace for him to be in, considering they'd be working in close quarters for the next half hour.

Jesus, take the wheel and my libido.

He snuck a glance at her. She was fiddling with the camera and tripod, arranging them just so. Each time she bent over, he caught a glimpse of her stocking-covered ass. It was just a sliver, but it was enough to make his hands clammy. If he wasn't careful, he'd slice one of his fingers during the demo.

She looked at her wristwatch and brought her hands together in a single clap. "Okay, camera's all set. Five minutes to show time. You good?"

He nodded. "As good as I'll ever be."

She gave him one of her sweet smiles, and it chiseled through the ice around his heart. "Remember, we're just two friends hanging out on Christmas Eve and cooking together. Forget there's an audience. Imagine us in your kitchen at home. Think you can do that?"

He swallowed. "I'll try."

"That's all I can ask of you."

EXCITED TO BEGIN, Sarita sidled up to Carlos, then reached over and opened the Instagram app. "Going live in five, four, three, two, one." She took a deep breath and went for it. "Olá, pessoal! ¡Hola, amigos! Sabor Foods would like to wish you a wonderful holiday season no matter what or how you celebrate. My name is Sarita Barros, and I'm here with Santa Claus, also known as Sabor's test kitchen chef, Carlos Gonçalves. We're going to share some of the foods that are a part of our Christmas traditions and show you how to make them step by step. Sound good?"

She smiled as several hearts zipped up the screen. Yay! People were watching. "Carlos, why don't you tell everyone a little about yourself?"

He stared at the screen and said nothing. Uh oh.

"Carlos?"

He jumped, then began to speak. "Right. Uh, hi everyone. I'm not much of a public speaker, but I'm happy to be here today to share my love of cooking with you. I'm a first-gen Brazilian American who grew up in the Bronx. I went to Bronx Science and wanted to be an engineer. But then I got the cooking bug in college, and I haven't looked back."

Sarita nodded. She was so proud of him. He was doing great, and although she knew he was probably nervous as hell, the camera couldn't tell. "We're so glad you caught the bug, Carlos, because the recipes you create for Sabor are outstanding. Y'all, the arroz con pollo is to die for."

The hearts flew up the page again.

"Okay, so let's talk about date night," Sarita said. "Now, as some of you know, many Latin American countries and Latinx people in the US celebrate Nochebuena, or as it's called in Brazil, Ceia de Natal or Véspera de Natal. Basically, it's a huge dinner and celebration with family and friends on Christmas Eve. Fun fact: In Brazil, Christmas Eve is basically you guys's Christmas. They go all out on the twenty-fourth and open presents at midnight. Christmas is for leftovers like the rabanada we'll be making later. So today, we're going to do a simplified version appropriate for you and your boo. Just to be clear, Carlos isn't my boo, but we're going to pretend that he is."

A shitload of hearts followed Sarita's statement, and Carlos smirked. People were leaving comments too.

He's handsome!

Could he be my boo?

Where'd you get that Santa costume?

Promote it on food_promotion_spotlights!

SHE QUICKLY DELETED that last one, then turned to Carlos. "What should we start with?"

He winked at her. "The coquito, I think. So we can chill it while we do everything else."

"Sounds great."

Sarita had no doubt the Live would be a big success.

CARLOS COULDN'T BELIEVE IT. The Live was going well, and he no longer had the urge to retch.

He attributed the smoothness of their delivery to Sarita. She was a natural. She knew how to be approachable and engaging, adding commentary to enlighten some reviewers while waxing nostalgic with others. At some point, he'd done as she suggested and pretended he was preparing a meal for her in his home—that settled his anxious brain.

What hadn't settled down was his libido, however. Mostly because, as she played the role of his sous chef, Sarita kept bumping into him or bouncing on her toes or reaching around him. Fortunately, they were almost done. He planned to head home after this and take a cold shower (or two or three).

"So, Carlos, tell us the difference between rabanada and French toast?" Sarita asked.

As he dipped the thick slices of stale bread in milk, he spoke to their audience. "Well, there are a few differences. We eat rabanada as a dessert or as an afternoon treat. It's not usually a breakfast item."

Sarita brushed her arm against his and winked. "But you can eat it the next morning too, right? After a long evening with that special someone."

She was killing him, and he was beginning to think she knew it. Well, two could play at that game. "Right. If it were us enjoying the morning after a long evening, I'd feed you pieces in bed. And lick the cinnamon off your fingers."

His eager little helper's eyes went wide, and she took in a sharp breath. Yeah, he knew the feeling. Imagining them together made him hot and edgy and restless. Sarita dropped her chin and focused on beating the eggs they would eventually dip the bread in.

"Sounds perfect," she whispered, seemingly to herself.

It did. It really did. Carlos could picture the scene in his head, and he wanted to make it a reality. *Their* reality. "I couldn't agree with you more."

Sarita jerked her head back and met his stare.

Because this wasn't the time or place to surrender to the attraction simmering between them, he chuckled, then grinned at the camera. "Rabanada is a PG-rated treat too. Any kids at your gathering will love it."

Sarita took his cue and returned the conversation to family-friendly territory as they finished the demo. Before she wrapped up the Live, she had the presence of mind to plug Reynaldo's friend's costume shop. Carlos waved at their audience as she blew a kiss at the camera, then she stopped the recording.

"We did it!" she said, jumping into his arms.

He groaned. This was torture. "That we did. You should be proud, and if Reynaldo doesn't give you a promotion, I'll kick his ass into next week.'"

"That won't be necessary," she said, playfully shoving him away. "Did you see how many people joined? And interacted with us too? Reynaldo's going to be ecstatic."

The literal devil they were speaking of chose that moment to rush into the kitchen. "One of the investors just texted me to say you two did an outstanding job. Bravo! I'll admit, I wasn't expecting much, but you surprised me in a good way. So thank you."

What a dick. Because Carlos didn't want to put a damper on Sarita's triumphant day, he walked away and busied himself by straightening up the kitchen.

Reynaldo didn't even wait for a response, though; he just dropped his head and started typing on his phone as he strolled out of the kitchen.

Sarita pursed her lips and shook her head. "You're welcome," she said to Reynaldo's back.

"Hey," Carlos said from his spot by the stove. "Even if he doesn't appreciate what you did, I do."

"I know," she said softly as she crossed the room. "I'll help you clean up, then I need to head home. I'm going to a Nochebuena celebration with some friends and promised to bring arroz con dulce."

"Sounds delicious."

"Would you want to join me?" she blurted out. "If you're not doing anything, that is. I mean, you probably are doing something, but I just wanted to offer. It could be fun."

He didn't want to be around a bunch of people, but he wanted to be around her. Maybe he could do some bending of his own. "I'd love to join you."

She exhaled a deep breath and gave him a tremulous smile. "Okay, great. Let's clean up, then."

They worked side by side as they washed and dried the dirty pots and pans they'd used during the demo, humming Christmas songs playing through his portable Bluetooth speaker. He was riding a high, excited about spending an evening with Sarita outside the office. Until Reynaldo returned to the kitchen and fucked it all up.

"Hey, Sarita. Just wanted to be sure you know I need your help dealing with the aftermath of the holiday party. Sylvie's calling Lyft rides for a few people, but it would be great if you could make sure the caterer gets their stuff out and leaves the lounge as they found it."

Sarita's shoulders dropped. "Really, Naldo? There's no one else who can do that?"

"Well, if you want to be a part of the team here, you can't act as if certain tasks are above you. That's not how we do things, Sari."

She sighed. "Right. Of course."

Carlos wanted to roar. He was about to channel his Avengers alter ego, burst through this stupid fucking Santa vest, and leave these itchy-as-hell pants in tatters. The urge to drop kick Reynaldo nearly overwhelmed him. But it wasn't his place to do or say anything. No, he was done getting between a woman and her family.

He didn't want Sarita to feel bad about their canceled plans, so he bowed out as gracefully as he could. "Listen, I'm beat," he told her. "Raincheck on hanging out?"

"Sure," she said, her voice reflecting none of the enthusiasm she had mere minutes ago. "Thanks again for helping me out today. You were a trooper."

"Anything for you, Sarita," he said. "Anything."

But that wasn't entirely true. He wouldn't fight her battles; no, she had to conquer those herself.

CHAPTER 5

Sarita caught up with Reynaldo in the hallway and tugged on the back of his jacket. She felt ridiculous asserting herself in an elf outfit, but she was not going to let a little polyester deter her. "*What* is your problem?"

He spun around, his eyes bulging. "Problem? What are you talking about?"

She wanted to strangle him. Yes, he had a lot of responsibilities. Yes, he was feeling the pressure of trying to build a successful business. But that didn't give him an excuse for treating her as if she were his lackey. "Yes, problem. Because unless you're absolutely clueless, you'd see that Carlos and I saved your ass today, and we deserve more than that halfhearted *thank you*. Also, you didn't even tell me where you stood on my taking over Lisa's position."

He blanched. "Yeah, about that... I'm thinking that's not a good idea. It wouldn't look good. Among the employees. Reeks of nepotism."

Absolutely not. She wasn't going to allow him to play that card. "If you weren't trying to grow a business based on your ancestry, one that could easily be a family business, you'd have a point. But that's not what we're talking about, right?"

He motioned for her to follow her into a conference room, then shut the door. "Look, this isn't the ideal place to discuss this—"

"We're discussing my role at the company. Where else would we have that discussion? Mars?"

"I'm just saying we can talk about it over dinner or something. Maybe next week."

"No. We're talking about this now. I'm not going to let you give me the runaround anymore."

"Shit," Naldo said, scrubbing a hand over his face. "I don't have time for your histrionics."

Sarita wanted to throw him in a headlock and pummel him. She chose to issue an ultimatum instead. "Here's the deal. Either you promote me to the position of communications director, on a trial basis if need be, or I sashay my histrionics-having ass out of this office for good. It's up to you."

"You'd quit?" he said, his brow knitted in confusion. "How could you?"

"Naldo," she pleaded. "You're one of the most important people in my life. I know how much you did for me. And I will never be able to repay you. But what I'm starting to realize is that I shouldn't have to. If you raised me out of love, then that should be enough for you."

"Is that how you feel? That I want you to repay me?"

"You've never used those words, but your actions certainly suggest that I'm indebted to you."

"I'm not perfect, you know."

"That's entirely beside the point. You can be imperfect and not treat me like crap. The two aren't mutually exclusive."

"That was never my intent," he said, staring at the floor. "I thought I was protecting you. From the strain that comes along with running this company. From the stress of making Sabor Foods a success. It's a lot, Sari. And I suppose I didn't want you to have to deal with it too. You've had enough ugliness in your life."

She walked over to him and bumped his arm. "You've experienced the same loss, and you're my irmão. We do this together or not at all."

Eventually, he raised his gaze to hers. "You'd really quit?"

She wasn't going to mince words here. "I would."

He remained silent for a long moment, then blew out a weary breath. "Okay, the position's yours." He raised an index finger. "But on a trial basis only. We'll revisit in six months."

"Fine," she said. "Oh, and I'm not helping you with the caterer. I have plans for tonight. With Carlos. And I'm not canceling them."

Naldo's eyebrows shot up. "It's like that?"

"It is," she said, giving him a no-nonsense expression.

He studied her for a few beats, then threw up a hand. "Whatever."

They left the conference room and strode in opposite directions.

"I'll see you tomorrow, right?" he called over his shoulder.

"Yeah," she called back.

That felt good. Really good. She and her brother wouldn't always see eye to eye, but she wasn't going to let him hold her back in life anymore.

Now she needed to get her man. But first, she wanted to update her out-of-office email message to reflect her new title.

AFTER CHANGING into his regular clothes, Carlos turned off the kitchen lights and headed in the direction of Sarita's office. He wanted to say goodbye before the long weekend and present her with the gift he'd been too chickenshit to give her earlier. Maybe she wouldn't use them tonight, but he still wanted her to know he'd been thinking about her.

He took a deep breath and knocked on her closed door.

"Come in," she said on the other side.

"Hey," he said, peeking in. "Do you have a minute?"

She clicked on her mouse, then closed a tab on her computer. "Sure. Come in."

He took a seat in a guest chair and set the wrapped gift on her desk. "That's for you."

"For me?" she said, pressing a hand to her chest. "How sweet." She tore through the wrapping like a kid on Christmas Day.

"You mentioned that you would be doing arroz con dulce before your brother..." He shook his head. "Anyway, I know your plans changed, but I remember you complaining a couple of weeks ago about not having bowls to serve pudding, so I got you those."

She lifted the box and inspected it. "Footed dessert cups. From Williams Sonoma. Ooh, fancy. They're perfect."

"It's nothing, really," he said, waving away her praise.

"No, it's something, all right," she countered. "It shows you were listening. And it shows you care. So thank you. Now accept my gratitude like a grown-up."

He laughed. "Yeah, okay. You're welcome."

She reached behind her and brought her purse to her lap. Grinning, she pulled out an envelope. "And these are for you."

He took the envelope, trying to ignore the way his hands were shaking, and opened it cautiously. "Knicks tickets? Against Minnesota, no less? Holy shit." Carlos had told her once that he'd never attended a Knicks game at MSG. Apparently, she'd been listening too.

When he looked up, Sarita was staring at him expectantly, no doubt hoping she'd selected the perfect gift for him. Little did she know the perfect gift was her friendship. And try as he might, he couldn't deny his feelings for this woman any longer. If she could accept his grouchy personality, he damn well could overlook that Reynaldo would always be a presence in their lives. He'd do it for her. Always for her. "You're joining me, right? We can make a date of it."

She blinked, then shook out her hands, her eyes bouncing around the room. "Is that what you want? To make it a date?"

"I want whatever you want."

She exhaled slowly. "Then I want you to kiss me."

Heat radiated through his chest, and his brain short-circuited for a moment. Now *this* was the best gift of all. "God, I want that too." He stood up and pulled Sarita forward by her furry collar, nearly toppling the guest chair in the rush to get to her. "I've been holding on to these feeling for years, Sarita. *Years.* Do you understand?"

"I do. Because I've been holding on to them too."

When their mouths met, they both groaned their appreciation. Just as he'd always imagined, her lips tasted like cherries and felt like silk and cream and all things soft and delicate. Her hands roamed over him, settling on his ass and drawing him flush against her. Warning bells sounded in his head. This was too much. Too soon. He should retreat now.

"Don't," she breathed against his lips as he began to pull away. "You can't leave me like this. Please. I need more."

He couldn't deny her, not when she was begging for the very thing he'd pictured in his fantasies. "May I lock the door, then?"

Her eyes grew cloudy. "Yes."

Once he'd closed them off from the rest of the world, he rounded her desk and swept her up in his arms to continue the kiss. And before long, he lifted her onto the surface.

"There's only so much we can do here," he noted.

"I know."

"But I'd like to make you come. Would that be all right?"

She squirmed, her hands massaging her breasts. "God, yes. I was hoping you'd say that."

He bunched up her skirt and tugged on her panties; she lifted her ass to allow him to remove them completely. Stunned by the enormity of his feelings for her, he staggered back onto her chair and drew her legs to straddle his shoulders. "I bet if I put my fingers here, you'd swallow them whole. You're so fucking ready. It's a shame we have to wait."

"For a man of a few words, you sure do talk a lot during sex."

"Are you complaining?"

"Yes," she said. "I'd like you to use that mouth for other things."

"Succinct and pragmatic. I knew there were a bunch of reasons why I fucking like you. Actually, more than like you."

He'd get into the specifics later. Tell her he wanted to be her boyfriend, her lover, and whatever else she desired. Explain that he would be more patient with her brother for her sake. Because he didn't want anyone but her. And he hoped she felt the same way about him.

"Baby, I'm dying here," she said. "I never imagined you'd be all talk and no action."

"I can't wait for you to revel in how wrong you are about that." Then he grazed her labia and massaged her opening. Slowly. Delicately. As far as he was concerned, he had all the time in the world to get this right.

"How's that so far?" he asked.

"Good. Can you feel how wet I am?"

"Yeah, it's wet and warm down here. Can't wait to press my lips here."

"My clit, baby," she said, falling back on her elbows. "Touch it, please."

He obliged her, settling two fingers against her nub and drawing tight circles there.

"Yes," she said. "Just like that."

He watched in awe as she undulated on the desk. She was so responsive. So uninhibited. He ached to fuck her senseless. Ached to be fucked senseless by her. Another time, he reminded himself. As it was, they were risking discovery simply by doing this. But he wouldn't leave her hanging. He wanted to know that when he left here, she'd be glowing from the orgasm he'd given her.

"What about my mouth? You want that too?"

"Yes, yes, yes," she said. "Please, please, please."

He lowered his head between her legs and pressed his lips against her pussy, taking one long lick to taste her sweetness. Fuck. She was writhing now. So he licked her like a man possessed. Over and over and over. Until his tongue was sore. Until his cock grew painfully hard and strained against the fly of his jeans. But he wouldn't stop. Not until she trembled in pleasure.

Sarita grabbed onto his hair and yanked him against her mound. "That's it, yes."

He fucking loved it. Her abandon pushed him to level up his game. He ate her pussy as if it were his only job in life.

"Carlos, I'm going to come soon," she forced out through clenched teeth.

He stood up and kicked the chair away, needing space to drive her over the edge. Then he slipped a finger inside her and nibbled on her clit. Within seconds, she spasmed under his lips, her legs locking around his back as she chased his face.

Damn. If this was round one, he wasn't sure he would survive round two.

He stroked her belly and thighs as she came down from her high. After a few beats, he helped her sit up and kissed her forehead.

"I'm speechless," she said.

"What a refreshing change."

She jabbed him in the stomach. "Careful." Then she jumped up and slipped her underwear back on. "Listen, I don't mean to get eaten and run, but I need to go."

"Yeah, I know. Your brother's waiting."

"No, he isn't," she said as she tucked herself back into the ridiculous elf skirt. "I told him I wouldn't be helping him this evening. I just came here to change my out-of-office email message to reflect my new position as communications director."

"You got the promotion," he said, his heart pounding.

"I did. After putting my foot down. So I was wondering if you'd still like to go to the Nochebuena celebration tonight."

His smile faded. "I'm not a people person. You're going to have to be patient with me."

"Good thing I'm like two people persons in one."

He chuckled. Damn, he was into this woman. A whole hell of a lot. "I'm all yours, then."

"Excellent. The sooner we get out of here, the sooner we can go to the party and leave. I'm thinking we're going to need a round two. At my place or yours."

He held her coat open as she slipped into it. "Great minds, Sarita. Great minds."

For the first time in a long while, he was looking forward to going to a party. Well, that wasn't entirely true. He was actually looking forward to the after-party. "Hey, let's stop by the kitchen before we head out."

"Why?"

"I need to grab my costume. I'm thinking about putting it on now so we can get to the *true* festivities faster." He winked at her. "Can't have a Santa's eager little helper without a Santa, right?"

Sarita pulled him into her arms. "Great minds, Carlos. Great minds."

ABOUT THE AUTHOR

USA Today bestselling and award-winning author Mia Sosa writes funny, flirty, and moderately steamy contemporary romances that celebrate our multicultural world. *Booklist* recently called Mia "the new go-to author for fans of sassy and sexy contemporary romances," and her trade paperback debut, *The Worst Best Man*, won first place in the romance category of the 2020 International Latino Book Awards; was named one of the best romances of 2020 by *Entertainment Weekly*, *Cosmopolitan*, *Oprah Magazine*, Buzzfeed, Barnes & Noble, and NPR; and received starred reviews across the board from *Kirkus*, *Publishers Weekly*, and *Booklist*. Before embarking on a writing career, Mia practiced First Amendment and media law in the nation's capital. Now she spends her days plotting stories and procrastinating on social media.

Sign up for Mia's newsletter here! Check out Mia's author website!

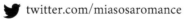 twitter.com/miasosaromance
 instagram.com/miasosaromance
 goodreads.com/miasosa

THE NOCHEBUENA
DATING DARE

DIANA MUÑOZ STEWART

Eneida Lucero takes a second chance on love with the handsome musical director at her school—even if it means causing some Nochebuena drama with her ex-husband and familia.

CHAPTER 1

It was a hard truth. Eneida Lucero enjoyed *shushing* people. Librarian power trip? Maybe. Sort of. But also…her life. With two loud kids, a loud extended familia, and a loudly confident ex-husband, she needed some quiet.

Scanning another return, she listened closely for the…*beep*.

Barely audible.

She smiled, placed the book on the cart, and grabbed another from the bin. Quietly. Just like the sign read. Library rules.

Not the rule on the subway she rode home. Or on the Brooklyn street where she lived. There, the decibels were staggering.

Dios, she even had a loud, yappy puppy. Pikachu the Chihuahua—awful name. She blamed her divorce for it. After, she'd been so eager to please her son, Lorenzo, and her daughter, Adelaida. Also Mami. Papa. Everyone, really.

Guilt did funny things to a mother—*if* one considered the fires of internal torment funny. *Enrique* was the one who'd cheated; why was her family disappointed with *her*?

Beep.

She supposed that, to them, months of therapy meant everything had worked out. Nope. All that effort had revealed two people with little in common—spiritually, emotionally, *and* intellectually. Admitting those truths out loud had been one of the hardest things she'd ever done. She'd been officially divorced for two months.

A crash of the library doors had her head jerking up. Four chatty, jostling boys, burgundy plaid ties askew, shoved through the entrance. Oh joy.

She lifted the obligatory finger, pursed her lips, and let out a softly stern, "Shhh."

They stopped talking. Silently rolled their eyes. Silently mimicked her by pursing their lips into excessive pouts. *Hashtag: #silently.*

It was all she could do to hold in her sinister, Jafar-taking-over-Agrabah laughter. Behold, the absolute power!

"Pero, I think you enjoyed that."

Startled by the deeply sexy voice, she turned. And blushed all the way to the tips of her long curls.

Midnight-black eyes, intense and challenging. Wavy, dark hair, chestnut-brown skin. A deliciously, naughty smile. Heart attack walking.

No introduction needed. Antonio Sanchez. Playwright, actor, musician, composer, producer, multiple Tony Award-winner, and the biggest thing to come out of Saint Cecilia's grade school in years. Which said a lot, considering the big names that had graduated from the school

"Mr. Sanchez," she said, "I've been warned..."

His incredibly suggestive eyebrows rose on the word *warned.*

Coño. Heat licked down her neck. She cleared her throat. "Uh, *told* that you'd be conducting play rehearsals here for the next few weeks."

Truth? She'd been WARNED. All caps. The superstar alum volunteering to produce the second grade's annual Nativity play—a traditional part of the Christmas Talent Pageant and a huge donor drive—was a *big* deal. With the auditorium temporarily closed for renovations, the library—much to the relief of the gym teachers—had been designated for rehearsals. So, yeah. She'd been *warned* to make him comfortable. *Warned* to be gracious. *Warned* that he could be unconventional.

And the charming—so charming it was sinister—way he grinned at her suggested she should've taken those warnings seriously. Why *was* he grinning at her?

Silence drifted between them like an ocean, something deep and formidable.

"Just admit you enjoyed the shushing." His award-winning voice was tonal sex, striking a chord so primal tingles slid down her body and zinged directly into the apex of her thighs.

Clenching said zinging thighs, she smiled without teeth. Best way to keep the drool from spilling out. And any inappropriate remarks. For example, the truth. "Library rules, Mr. Sanchez."

The way he shook his head suggested he didn't believe her. Suggested he saw her lying as proof of something. Or a challenge. "Call me Tony." He glanced at her blue-and-white plastic name tag. "Mind if I use this as a teaching moment, Eneida Lucero, school librarian?"

With his slight Spanish accent, her name, eh-NAY-duh, flowed like a song.

She shrugged. "O…kay?"

With no more encouragement than that, Antonio Sanchez—Tony —sprang up, vaulting onto the counter with a *thud* that knocked aside her turquoise stapler and toppled the acrylic LIBRARY RULES sign.

Shifting back in utter shock, she took in his long, long legs. The sure stance. The balanced and poised body. He was so comfortable in the spotlight, so comfortable demanding to be heard, so comfortable asserting his position. On top of her workstation.

Uh, oh. This was not good. But she could not look away.

Moth, meet flame.

CHAPTER 2

Shiny black boots slamming against countertops tended to get people's attention. Especially when the thick-soled Louboutin *thwack* came from the famous producer/performer now perched upon the library's circulation desk. Everyone in the biblioteca stood riveted, Eneida included. The man was a presence.

Satin black hair gleaming under the lights, Tony put a finger to his world-renowned lips. "Shhh!"

He propelled the sound out, directing it toward the boys she'd *shushed*.

Curious and smiling, they inched back past the Christmas tree that was decorated with present tags for needy children. The library's restrained atmosphere shifted as Tony dropped a recognizable beat: the title song from his latest hip-hop musical. She forced her head not to bop along as he freestyled.

> *Shhh... Society polices our silence.*
> *Demands each body's rigid compliance.*

He moved as if on a stage, gliding one leg out to bend dramatically toward his audience.

Don't rock the boat.
Don't own your gloat.

One of the students picked up the beat, blowing it through his lips and hands.

Ay. Dios mío.

Shhh. Tongue-tied or shackled hands.
Better not deviate the plan.

Tony waved one hand in the air like a DJ in a club. The kids and even some visiting parents followed suit. Carajo.

Words unchain the silence.
Break the past with nonviolence.
Shatter the thickest ceiling.
Send haters ducking and reeling.
Give voice and narrate your story.
Beyond their shushing lies your glory.

The kids erupted with cheers. *Loud* cheers. No-way-to-shush-them cheers.

Her face heated. Her stomach dropped. Mierda. Tony dismounted in an Olympic-worthy move that created a soft wind, brushing his cologne, a sage and leather combination, over her. He smelled so good. She began to straighten things with panicked hands.

As if to help, he reached for the stapler.

Hell no. She snatched it up first and clutched the cold metal protectively to her chest.

His already-moving hand shifted course and swept some mussed hair from his forehead. "You *did* say it was okay."

She gave him a no-worries, couldn't-care-less, no-skin-off-my-back sarcastic shake of her head. "Consider me the Hispanic Gale Nolan in your Dead Poetry Slam Society." She leaned forward

227

conspiratorially. "Think it will help me land the role of Ed Rooney for that *Ferris Bueller* remake?"

He burst into laughter, his grin rocketing past interested all the way to searing, open lust.

That was disconcerting because it wasn't a *Hey, I like your body* kind of leer. It was a *Hey, I like your brain* kind of leer.

Thank God for the anger that allowed her to push past the fluster and her own physical response. She pointed her stapler toward the part of the library cordoned off for his use. The section she'd painstakingly decorated with garland, stringing a silver-and-red FELIZ NAVIDAD sign along it. "Let's keep the drama behind those bookcases that were specifically placed there to create a private space for you and the students."

Something that had taken her and the school janitors a good part of two days.

Again, that charming grin. "Got it. All our drama shall remain behind closed doors." He winked.

Her heart fluttered. How annoying. "Perfect. Let me know if there's anything you need."

His eyes held hers, not moving a centimeter up or down. "You're upset."

"Not at all." She put down the stapler and picked up a clipboard, gesturing to it as if it weren't a sign-out sheet. "Having a powerful man demean my position is part of my job. Here. It's written into my contract."

He cringed. Face contrite, he turned, took note of the bookcases and the second graders now acting up outside it. "Oye, niños. Take this behind the bookcases. Respect the library rules out here."

The kids, laughing and joking, pushed happily behind the bookcases. Man was about to get what he deserved with that rowdy bunch.

"Sorry about that." He cast his gaze down, adjusted the stapler, turning it a hundred eighty degrees before looking back up, face sincere. And so damn handsome her chest ached. "Let me make it up to you? Take you out to dinner?"

Her heart, that sensitive, palpitating idiota, lurched in her chest. Not because he was handsome. Well, not *just* because. But also, because he'd apologized when she'd called him out. That kind of integrity was as irresistible to her as the most luscious chocolate.

She licked her lips and pictured them at dinner, chatting, laughing... and after dinner, kissing. It had been so long since she'd enjoyed the company of an adult. A man. And someone like him? Someone unlike anyone she'd ever been with. Could she?

The first-period bell blared, and she nearly bit her tongue. Lorenzo bounded into the library, pink permission slip in hand, not even glancing in her direction. His brown hair bounced as he skipped to Tony's rehearsal section.

Her hope went with him. Yesterday, it'd seemed wonderful that her son would be in the school play and get to meet Tony. But now? After she'd had--only for un momento--a fantasy about the hot producer, it seemed...well, too close for comfort. Too close to home. Too close to an unbreakable thread that wrapped around her soul. What had she almost done?

She was still getting Lorenzo to accept the divorce. And Adelaida. Not to mention her parents. She could not—*would* not—do anything to jeopardize their peace of mind. Especially this close to the holidays. Ahí vas. Tony Sanchez was off-limits.

She shook her head almost combatively, as if tossing out her own lascivious thoughts. "No. Nope. Nunca. Absolutely not. No way. Never. Don't ask me again."

Mischievous smile flattening into a somewhat chastened grin, he said, "A single *no* would've worked. Or even just the head shake."

Her face heated as she watched him walk away. Regret dropped like a stone into her roiling stomach. This felt wrong. But it wasn't. Putting her family above her own selfish needs was right. So why had that lump risen into her throat? And that pain speared her chest?

Eneida's cell vibrated under the counter. She caught sight of the screen. Her best friend, Héctor. She shouldn't answer. Shouldn't...

Fishing it out, she told him, "Ayudame."

"What do you need help with?"

"One sec."

She put out the cardboard ten-minute break clock with the red plastic hands. Scooting from behind the desk, she went to hide in the stacks and beg her best friend to help her make sense of these feelings.

CHAPTER 3

Scurrying down the Lives of Saints section—no one but nuns went down here—Eneida slipped a wireless earbud into her right ear and took Héctor's call. "I was just humiliated in the library by the school's coolest kid."

"I think I have the wrong number. Or the wrong decade. Is this 2021 or 1996?"

"I'm serious, Héctor. Antonio Sanchez rapped on my desk. And then he asked me out!"

A long pause, as if Héctor was watching the entire thing in his head. "And you said *no*?"

"Claro. Why would I say yes? I'm peanut-butter-sandwiches-in-reusable-bio-friendly-bags; he's a celebrity. A jetsetter. A night-lifer."

Night-lifer? Great. Now she was making up words.

She peeked out the end of the aisle. Three kids were lined up at her desk. Carajo.

"Honestly, Eneida, I think you're making excuses. Weren't you the one to tell me—yesterday, in fact—that dating was like riding a bike? You should take your own advice. Just do it. It's like jumping into a cold pool. Once you're inside, you'll get used to it quickly."

Whose pool was cold? Hers? Was she the cold pool? "Um, no. It's not. I'm..." Burning up. Definitely not cold. "I don't know. Insecure."

Héctor's disbelieving laughter was too loud—definitely not Library Rules. "Trust me. You're not."

"There's more than one kind of insecurity." She was great at being a mom, a librarian, situational comedy, but when it came to going for what she wanted...things got complicated. "Do you know how many men I've been with in the last twelve years?"

"One. As many as women I've been with in the last fifteen."

"Yes, but your wife died. She didn't cheat on you. Rejecting you. Making you feel... broken. Unable to connect."

"I'd rather my wife had cheated."

"Coño. I'm sorry." She cringed and lowered her forehead to the bookcase, inhaling aged ink and yellowed paper. Once again, her insecurities had rolled right into insensitivity. "Of course. Yes. I just meant...How am I supposed to handle someone so different from me, someone who makes me feel crazy with possibility?"

"Is that why you turned him down?"

She lifted her head, paced the aisle, pressing the spines of leather-bound books with a finger. She hated to admit the truth, but Héctor wasn't going to let it go. He always got to the heart of the matter. They'd made a promise after Marielena had passed: no hiding the truth. It was one of many promises they'd made as friends. And kept. "Not just that. Mi familia. They're not ready to see me dating."

He sighed. "You haven't shared a home with Enrique in a year. Sometimes, querida, you have to step up so others will step aside."

"Pero...the kids."

"Life happens, Eneida. Even to our kids." Héctor's voice had softened, reminding her that his son had lost a mother. "And yours are doing just fine. Trust them to adjust."

Maybe he was right. Maybe it was time. Time for her to step up. "Look, I've made a decision, and..." She exhaled the fear from her chest. She wasn't taking this big of a leap without him. Marielena would want her to bring Héctor along. She'd made a promise to his wife: one year of grieving. "I need a wingman. Don't make me go it alone."

Silence.

"¿Me oyes?" she pressed.

"Yes, I hear you. But how the hell did this become about me?"

"You have to get out of hermit mode, too. It's been two years since Marielena died. Let's do this together. We'll each bring a date to Nochebuena. That gives you time to work up the nerve. Or are you chicken? *Bawk.*"

"That's extremely childish."

"*Bawk, bawk.*" She laughed, imagining him shaking his head.

"Fine."

"Y no tu prima. No cousins for either of us. This dare is for bragging rights all year. No weak-ass dates. You bring someone who scares you as much as Tony scares me."

There was a heavy sigh. "There is no one else I would do this for but you. Challenge accepted. And good luck asking out Mr. Sanchez." He hung up.

She stared at the phone while her thoughts had a chance to catch up to her mouth. What had she done? She couldn't take a date to Gigi's first Nochebuena—this was a momentous year for her. She was sure to continue her parents' tradition and make it a big event. Everyone would be there. Many of Eneida's dearest friends. Her brother. Her kids. Her ex!

Taking a *first* date to that… What if it didn't work out? What if he was a jerk? What if they hated each other and the night was ruined for everyone?

Ay. Dios. What should she do? She couldn't back out. If she did, Héctor would back out. Maybe a test date? A first-date-before-the-date date. That'd work.

Estupenda. Now she needed to arrange *two* dates.

CHAPTER 4

A few days after her dating dare with Héctor, Eneida realized that, if she kept busy, she didn't have to think about it. So, she kept busy.

In fact, she was so deeply immersed in cataloging new books, it took a moment to wonder why butterflies filled her stomach and her hands were sweating. Then...she smelled him. Sage and leather. Vanilla, sugar, and...coffee?

She looked up. An undeniable electric surge hit her like a wave. First, the jarring impact and then the struggle to find air. She stared at him. No air. No words.

She *shushed* her body's urgent and definitive roar of desire with a *¡Cállate! He might hear you!* and said, "Did you need something?"

He placed a steaming cup of coffee, a white bakery bag, and what looked like a wrapped book onto the counter. "My way of apologizing again for the other day."

That voice... She could almost taste it. Caramelized butter.

Steadying her breath and trying for a calm she most certainly didn't feel, she slid the bag across the counter then peeked inside. It held pan de Mallorca—a soft, eggy Puerto Rican sweet roll dusted with powdered sugar. "One of my favorites."

"Mine, too," he said, then pointed at the coffee. "Didn't know how you take it. Figured plain black was safe and I'd leave the sweetener and cream up to you."

She took a sip. "That's how I take it." Smiling now, she slid a finger over the plain brown wrapper covering the package. "Let me guess. You realized a librarian has to like books?"

"Well, that, and I noticed the sign."

"Sign?"

"Taped to the end of the bookcase, there's a poem written in beautiful calligraphy. No secret I'm a poetry fan."

Oh no. She'd hung her poem there, thinking it was the only way it'd ever get into a library. And this Broadway producer—this Tony *winner*—had read it.

"Anyway, it spoke to me. No author credit, so I looked it up online."

Her face heated. She closed her eyes. Embarazosa. But, actually, *embarrassing* didn't even *begin* to cover it. She felt exposed, as if the secret things she kept bottled up, hidden behind humor or flip remarks, were naked and spread between them. "You've been to my blog?"

"I ravaged your blog."

Her gaze snapped to his.

Unrepentant, even a little gleeful, he pushed the package a smidge closer to her.

Fingers suddenly thick and ungainly, she ripped open the wrapper, then gasped a sound as joyous and light as a dove's feather. She ran a hand over the red leatherbound book. "I wrote my poem, "Love Is Possibility," after being inspired by this book of poetry." The poetry had spoken to her deepest desires, cracked opened needs she'd tried to suppress. Her poem had been her reaction to confronting those wants, her message in a bottle. Her way of letting out the truth she feared saying aloud.

"Open." He tapped the book.

Hope crashed against her chest, a solid hit that shattered the bones of resistance. Hands trembling, she flipped back the cover and froze. Eyes wide, she searched his face. "It's signed by the author to me?"

"A friend of a friend of a friend got me in touch with him. He was kind enough to overnight a signed copy. So am I forgiven? Did I give back what I took?"

Letting the book fall closed, she shook her head in confusion. "What you took?"

The brown skin of his cheeks reddened. For a moment, he looked uncertain and uncomfortable. "The day we met, I let my past experience with school librarians—particularly a librarian at this school—twist how I saw you."

She shifted closer as if to offer comfort to his discomfort. "I didn't realize you had an issue with Saint Cecilia's librarians."

"Just the one. You, however, are giving me a good feeling." He winked and a good feeling washed through her body. "But that one wouldn't let me take out books—"

"Wouldn't let you take out books?"

Her obvious horror seemed to tickle him. His black eyes gleamed with delight. "For the first two years I went here. After that, I'd learned enough to demand he let me."

She felt an intense surge of anger at that librarian, wanting to protect the boy Tony had been. "Why wouldn't he let you take out books?"

"I was a scholarship kid. Couldn't afford to go here otherwise. Apparently, he thought I'd go home and sell the books on the library-book black market."

"What a pendejo."

"Verdad. Anyway, I let that experience warp how I first saw and treated you the other day. I made you invisible. Something I find unforgivable in society and abhorrent in myself. I wanted to show you that I see you. I wanted to acknowledge you as a person, not an image from my past. So, did I give back what I took?"

"Yes. Apology accepted." He'd given her more—a reason to admit what she wanted out loud. "And there's something I'd like to ask you." Dinner? Movie? A club? Ayúdame. She had no idea where people went on dates these days.

Turning absently, she stapled something with her stapler. A hall pass. The niña who'd handed it to her looked at her with horrified first-grader eyes. *Whoops.* She dug out the staple, initialed the little pink box, then handed it back.

Tony leaned farther across the circulation desk. "You were saying?"

Oh, he smelled good. That cologne…it must be called "Temptation" or "Jump My Bones." Yes, please.

"I was wondering, if you'd like to have…" *Me.* She swallowed. How did people do this? "Maybe, um. Do you eat? Um, here? For lunch, I mean?"

"Tony?"

Olivia Perez—the school principal—entered the library, all curves, height, and wavy, silky black hair. That *hair.* Not even her best feature and it was insanely gorgeous. "I was hoping we could have lunch today. If you're free." Her sultry brown eyes ran over him with obvious intent.

Eneida's spine stiffened. *Back off, pendeja.* Kicking herself for her jokes and procrastination, she waited to see what he'd do.

Tony turned to Olivia.

Eneida couldn't see his smile. Or his not-smile. She listened intently. "Sorry, Olivia. I believe Señora Lucero was about to ask me to lunch."

Had Tony just openly suggested to the school principal that she'd been going to ask him out!? "I was not!"

He turned around, expressive eyebrows to his hairline. His mouth quirked in a somewhat puzzled expression.

Coño. *Why* was she self-sabotaging? "I mean, I was going to tell you that they have free lunches here for faculty and staff."

A long beat of silence. A beat Eneida had grown used to over the years. It was the space left in the wake of her turbulent awkwardness. That pause where everyone adjusted to her social spasms. When you weren't used to openly expressing what you wanted, dodging the truth became a lifestyle. An awkward lifestyle. Which was why she wrote poetry. She needed time to assemble her thoughts in a way that wasn't a shock wave. Otherwise, she resorted to her *go-tos*—one-liners and jokes meant to conceal the depth of her desires, distress, or fears.

Smoothing his features, Tony told Olivia, "Lunch sounds great."

Olivia's uncertain gaze bounced from him to Eneida. "Around noon?"

He nodded. Then, tapping lightly on the counter, he said, "Enjoy your breakfast, Eneida."

There was another beat of silence. A beat in which Eneida watched Tony's firm retreating ass. A beat in which she looked to see Olivia watching said fine ass. A beat in which their gazes locked. She stared into the long-lashed eyes of the woman who'd hired her nearly three years ago, the woman who was her boss. Each seeing what the other wanted.

Olivia frowned as Tony left the area. "Can I give you some advice? One divorcée to another?"

No. Shut up. "I guess."

"Brutal honesty, Eneida. Don't be such a coward. A man like that," she indicated Tony with a wave, "a man who knows his worth, has no reason to push you. Or *any* woman. Step up. Or someone else will."

"That's advice?" Her voice rose to Chihuahua-barking level. "It sounded like a threat."

Olivia's lips thinned, turned downward. "It was meant to spark your natural competition."

"I shy from natural competition. It makes my boobs sweat."

A trill of laughter as Olivia's hazel eyes danced with amusement. "Look, he obviously likes you. And I'm not interested in competing for a man. That was my marriage. Competing with women vying for my husband—the boss's—attention."

"Sounds miserable."

"It was. But I know my worth now. The question is, do you know yours?"

And with that, she walked her curvy ass and perfect hips away.

CHAPTER 5

"Do you salsa?"

Mouth suddenly dry, throat thin as a straw, Eneida's focus rose from the green leatherbound book, up a deep red, chest-hugging sweater, to a face hot enough to singe quivering thighs.

His expression—not bemusement, not confusion. An open and honest *I feel it, too.*

She swallowed, stomach muscles clenching against a knowing heat. She replayed the question, mentally groped the words, then finally produced an answer. "Not since my quinceañera."

"Bueno. Can I borrow your body for un momento?"

Yes! "Qué?"

"A demonstration for the kids."

It took her a full three seconds to dispel the image of him "borrowing" her body hard and fast up against a bookcase. *Hold your hormones, he's just asking for an assistant with his performance—uh, play.* And though she wanted to correct the verbiage—*borrow your body*—she could see the excitement in his eyes and understood he'd meant no offense. "Sure."

A grin broke across his handsome face. A grin so wide, she couldn't help but echo it. "Thank you."

Skirting out from her workstation, she followed him to the area set up for practice. Inside the open space, second graders stood backed up to bookcases, their little bodies aflutter with excitement.

Tony had had an incredibly positive impact on these kids. And Lorenzo. Her son, her video-games-and-computer-obsessed son, had told her that he wanted a career in the arts. Literally those words. Not *I want to do work like Mr. Sanchez*. A career in the arts.

But Tony hadn't helped only Lorenzo. She'd assumed the famous man would be here once or twice a week to organize the Nativity play part of the pageant. But he'd been here almost every day, giving his time to the students in the talent show part, too, organizing choreography, designing sets, and composing lyrics. He'd even played assistant to her friend Gigi, who'd shown up at Eneida's request to help with lighting for the play. The more she learned of Tony, the greater her regret over not accepting his first invitation.

He held out his hand to her. She took it.

"Okay, doubters. Watch this." He spun her into position. His free hand snaked under her arm, his palm pressing hot and heavy against her back, possessive and confident.

She placed her free hand atop his solid, tightly muscled shoulder. Even through his sweater, he burned her.

His left foot went forward. Her right foot stepped back. She followed his lead as smoothly as if they'd trained together, gliding to his other side as he guided her across his body. Despite the distance the dance form demanded, a taut electric current hummed between them, along her veins, and through her swaying hips. Her body rejoiced. This was fun.

He increased the pace to match the music.

Dios, she hadn't even realized music was playing. Their eyes stayed locked. She followed his lead flawlessly. And he, in turn, responded to every rock of her hips, mirroring her flow.

With a flourish, he ended the dance, spinning her away and holding up her hand. He bowed and she followed suit, grinning wide as her son clapped and hooted. "Bravo, Mami!"

Lorenzo's smile was wide and brilliant. So much like his father—

the golden-brown eyes, pin-straight brown hair, and tawny brown skin. She blew him a kiss.

Eyebrows rising, Tony dropped her hand. Told the class to think about how a Nativity salsa might work—to which a few called back that they still wanted a breakdance.

He walked her out. "I didn't realize Renzo was your son," he said when they exited.

"I recently divorced his father. Maybe, I changed my name back too quickly."

His step faltered for a beat. "How recent?"

"We were separated for nearly a year. Officially divorced two months ago."

Cringing, he rubbed the back of his neck. "I shouldn't have asked you out like that. The first day. You had every right to throw cold water over my head."

She laughed. "Cold water, huh?"

A smile dimpled his cheeks. "Claro."

This was it. Her chance. Her breathing increased. Her stomach pitched. Ay, Dios, she might pass out. The least sexy thing for a woman to do.

He put a hand on her elbow. "¿Estás bien? That was quite the workout."

Ay. Where was her word vomit when she needed it? "It's not the workout. I'm nervous."

Oh, there you are. Carajo. Why couldn't she keep her mouth closed?

His eyebrows rose. The corner of his mouth quirked, an almost hopeful gesture. "¿Por qué?"

Ready or not...

Definitely not. "Will you go out with me? Um, to dinner, maybe?"

A beat of silence.

What had she done? The man had just found out she had a son. And a daughter, because Adelaida had volunteered to help Lorenzo during her library time yesterday. He'd asked her out before knowing any of that.

Another beat.

Plus, she'd turned him down, then embarrassed him in front of the principal. To top it all off, she'd admitted to a recent divorce. *Way to sell yourself, Eneida...* She should flee, duck behind her counter, something...

Yet... something bright and hopeful flashed into his midnight eyes. "Sí. Yes. Sure. Ja. Oui. Definitely. Anytime."

Her heart floated out from her chest and into the air. It was so filled with possibility and hope, she imagined it bursting and spraying them with streams of brightly colored confetti.

For every *no* she'd given him, he'd given her a *yes*.

CHAPTER 6

Wearing a winter coat and spiked high heels, Eneida ushered her kids up the cement stairs to her family's Brooklyn brownstone. Lorenzo, puppy crate in hand, ran inside.

"Don't take Pikachu out of his carrier without asking Abuela," she called after him. Her mother would have a fit.

Adelaida hung back, chin jutted, long black curls—a match to Eneida's—falling from a face much too wary for a ten-year-old. "You'll be okay being all alone when we go to Papi's?"

The *all alone* concern was new. For a time, Adelaida had said the opposite during drop-offs. She'd tried to make Eneida jealous. Tried to tell her how much fun they'd have, and "poor Mami" would be missing it.

Knowing Adelaida had been hoping to entice her mother back into her old life had hurt as badly as any part of this divorce.

And now? Adelaida had obviously noticed the dress. Niña was no dummy. But the thought of telling her the truth—she had a date— made Eneida's jaw ache. Being honest with herself was one thing, but being honest with her daughter when she knew it would hurt her... why do it? This thing with Tony might not make it past one date. Her stomach twisted at the thought.

"I'll be fine, mija. Lots to do for Christmas. Go on now. Find Abuela."

Her deep-brown eyes doubtful and searching, Adelaida shrugged and turned, calling up to the man on the ladder. "Hola, Abuelo."

"Hola, querida. Ve a comer," he said, greeting her and sending her inside to get food without turning from putting up decorations.

Adelaida went into the house, backpack stuffed with clothes and toys for the weekend with her father, bouncing as she went.

Her throat thick with guilt, Eneida hung back in the biting night air, admiring the decorations. It was a spectacle of Navidad cheer, each window perfectly framed with lighted garland and dotted with a wreath. The brick of the townhome, lights, wreaths, and red front door could be part of a Christmas card.

"Oye, Papa," she called to her father, who was bundled up for arctic cold as he placed the last wreath. "Need help getting the house ready for the photo shoot?"

She was only partially joking. Her father, a professional photographer with a nearby studio—which was how the man knew everyone who lived around here—would most definitely be taking photos.

Laughing, he called back, "Have to keep up with Mami. She has high standards."

She answered before she could think better of it. "No one can keep up with Mami. Certainly not me."

Her childhood home had always been a place of safety and ritual and steadiness. She hated that she couldn't give that to her kids. That she'd taken that from them.

When her papa didn't answer, she looked up. Wreath in one hand, the other holding the ladder, he shook his head. "No es necesario. Se tú."

He was right. She only had to be herself.

Flicking his head toward the door, he said, "Go on in. Hace frio, mija."

Blowing him a kiss, she followed his direction and got out of the cold. She stopped in the front vestibule, slipped off her heels, and slid

Lorenzo's discarded sneakers under a poinsettia-stacked bench before walking into the family room.

Mami's tree was a thing of perfection. Mrs. Claus, herself, would weep. Tree lights twinkled white against red bows, silver-and-green balls, and a range of handmade decorations: red-, blue-, and green-colored antiques that represented precious familia history, including her mother's Puerto Rican and her father's Mexican roots.

The homeyness of it pierced Eneida's heart. She'd never spent a Christmas anywhere but here—not even after she and Enrique had Adelaida. At the time, their apartment had been so tiny, and Eneida had wanted her daughter to know the intense joy of waking up in this home, seeing these twinkling decorations, opening presents under a beautiful tree. It had been easy to get into a holiday celebration habit —going to the Baez's large Nochebuena party and later returning here.

What was she doing? How could she even consider bringing a date to Gigi's? This was a holiday for her dearest friends and family. Maybe she should cancel tonight, claim sickness.

She coughed into her hand. Her throat did itch. Should she go to Emergency Care?

No. She couldn't. Damn her Nochebuena dating dare with Héctor. She'd been text-harassing him about it every chance she got. She'd *bawk-bawk*ed at him. He'd never let her live it down. Besides, if she chickened out, *he'd* chicken out. She owed Marielena this. She'd promised not to let Héctor wallow in sadness for too long.

She'd meant to keep that promise. But discovering Enrique had cheated on her, the subsequent therapy, and the divorce had kept her busy the last year. No more. She had to try this.

And, in truth, not only for Héctor, but because she really liked Tony. He made her lady parts sit up and take notice. A feeling echoed by the rest of her body.

That salsa. She might never recover.

She moved back down the corridor and past walls lined with a hundred artful and exquisitely framed family photos. Inside the warm kitchen, the air thick with the smells of cooking meat, peppers, salt, and the sound of sizzling pans, "Blanca Navidad" gently played from the speaker in a corner.

Lorenzo sat on the floor in front of Pikachu's carrier, begging to let the yappy little puppy out. Adelaida sat beside him, wiggling her fingers through the bars. The dog licked and nibbled them. Her mother—work clothes visible under her apron, yet still in silver earrings and a matching necklace—refused and reprimanded them with, "No perros en la cocina."

Whining, they gathered up the carrier and went into the other room. Mami turned back to work, scooping an empanada from the frying pan, and placing it on a straining rack set over a pan. How *did* Mami do it? An artistic framer at Papa's studio, she also managed their entire business, and still did all of this perfectly.

Joining her at the stove, Eneida kissed her on her cheek and stole a way-too-hot empanada. She tossed it from hand to hand. "Dinner smells great."

"Hermosa," Mami noted, glancing at her dress. She took out another empanada, turned down the heat. "Enrique texted he'd be here in fifteen. We can all eat together."

Staying here, sitting down to eat, was tempting. And comfortable. It also wouldn't change anything. Taking a bite of her slightly cooler empanada—hot beef juices spilling into her mouth—she shook her head then swallowed. "I wish I could, but I have plans tonight."

Mami's eyes reevaluated her, the dress, and the makeup—which she'd probably assumed had been for Enrique. She drew closer. "Mija, you're going on a date?"

"It's dinner." Her shoulders rose defensively.

"What will I tell Enrique when he comes?"

"Why tell him anything?" She lowered her voice. "Dating while divorced doesn't require my ex's approval."

Heck, according to Enrique, neither did dating while married.

"Pero, los niños."

Despite the guilt tightening her throat, she managed, "The kids will have to get used to me dating."

A jewelry-thick hand rose to Mami's chest. "I tell you this so you can learn. Yolanda's daughter divorced her husband. And you know what? She found dating wasn't for her. Three months later and they're back together."

Eneida resisted rolling her eyes. Her mother was famous for telling cautionary tales painted over with the rosy hues of maternal hope. And she had no greater hope than to have her children in relationships as magical and steady as her own. "That's not going to happen to me."

Mami's gaze pleaded with her. "Give them a few weeks, mija. Give them the holidays. This is all so new. What if it doesn't work out? No need to shout it from the rooftops."

Was she being insensitive? Was it too soon? Would her kids be permanently scarred from her dating? Maybe. And the truth was, this thing with Tony might *not* work out. Why take such a big chance right now? Why gamble with her family's happiness?

Stomach turning, she put her half-eaten empanada down. "It's one date. Tomorrow it will be over." She kissed her mother. "Adios. Te amo."

One date was enough. Héctor would understand. He'd have to. Especially since one date was the most she could give herself without ruining her familia's holiday.

CHAPTER 7

Riding in the back seat of her Uber, a Kwanzaa-decorated Toyota Corolla, Eneida's emotions bounced between doubt and excitement.

The car inched toward the restaurant on a traffic-clogged street in Manhattan. She could walk from here. She could see Tony out front, scanning the incoming cars. He hadn't spotted her.

His full-length camel-colored coat hung open, revealing a brown windowpane suit jacket, a cream turtleneck, and slim-fitting dark brown pants. Wavy hair was slicked and tied back from a sharp jawline rimmed in stubble. His black eyes were mischievous and bright. Dear God. Sin walking.

Like magic, all her doubts disappeared.

The driver finally pulled up to Zoralie, a Dominican restaurant. "Estamos aquí."

"Gracias."

Spotting her, Tony smiled and headed to the car. Her spirit soared as he opened the door and helped her out. His cologne, a combination of vanilla, leather, and sage, hit her so vividly her knees almost buckled.

He leaned down, kissed her on her mouth. The kiss was fire. No tongue. All lips, soft and warm and wanting. Sizzling desire swamped her body. Heavy heat curled her toes.

He pulled back and traced his tongue along his upper lip with a smile. Their heavy breaths misted the December air. "Shall we go in?"

Had she answered? She must've because she found herself walking to the restaurant with his hand pressed warmly to the small of her back. Her head spun. Dios. What would happen if he'd actually put his tongue in her mouth? She might have combusted.

Inside, they handed off their coats, and Tony eyed her appreciatively. "You look spectacular. Navy is your color."

"Gracias." She *felt* spectacular, even in a four-year-old silk dress she hadn't worn in two years. It did highlight her best asset. Emphasis on *ass*. She ran her eyes down his suit. "You, too."

"Thanks. I don't dress up for everyone."

She'd read that about him, that he was extremely casual. Laid-back, even.

Again, they shared a look.

Again, the heat and longing.

Again, the inability to break eye contact.

A loudly uttered, "This way, *please*," from the hostess shattered the spell. The hint of amusement indicated she might've said it a couple of other times.

Hyper-aware of her skin, her pulse, the silk sliding across her ass, the eyes of her date she could feel watching her ass, Eneida headed to their table.

It smelled fantastic in here—seared meat, onion, peppers, and cilantro. She could almost taste the sofrito. She sat. "I've always wanted to try this place."

He leaned down to her ear as he pushed her chair forward. "I have a feeling it's going to surpass all our expectations."

The heat of his breath; the timbre of his voice… She repressed her moan.

It did. And then some.

But more impressive than the delicious salt-and-plantain-mashed mofongo, delicate arroz y frijoles rojos, and thickly satisfying potato-and-meat-rich sancocho was the conversation.

"Prometheus," Tony continued, pushing away his empty plate, "is one of my favorite mythical stories."

"Why? His story has a pretty gruesome ending."

"Sí. But he dared to go against the gods to give men fire. All of my work, my plays, center around that kind of idea. Not just the themes, but the characters."

He leaned forward and, captured by his intensity and the passion with which he expressed himself and his ideas, so did she.

"People like Isabel Rosado Morales, who went against impossible odds—not always successfully—to stand up for what she believed was right."

She, too, admired the Puerto Rican freedom fighter one of his plays had been based upon. "Own your gloat," she said, repeating his lyric from that first day in the library, and lifted her wine glass.

He lifted his beer bottle. They clinked glasses.

Remarkably, this was only one of a dozen things they'd clicked on tonight. Music. Books. Poetry. Social issues. Politics. Her kids. Was there anything better than a person who saw your kids? Really got them? His genuine affection for Lorenzo was beyond endearing.

They'd been animated and thoroughly engrossed in each other all night. So much so that each kept leaning across the table, making contact—a touch of a hand, a brush of a face, a grasp of an arm. It was the most sensual conversation she'd ever had. Actually, before this, she hadn't known conversations *could* be sensual.

When the busser cleared away the dishes—silverware, plates, and glasses rattling—Eneida finally had a moment to regroup. She sat back, dazed and shaken. The intensity, emotions, ease, and electric joy of this night startled her. This kind of connection between people wasn't possible—or so she'd always thought.

She'd heard of it. Like she'd heard of mythical unicorns. Of weird people connecting and marrying weeks or months later. But those people were flighty and probably easily impressed. She was neither.

The busser left and the server appeared, dropping off two dessert menus.

Leaving his on the table, Tony took a sip of his beer. "You look so serious now. What are you thinking, cariño?"

The soft endearment made her blush. Along with the question. Did he feel it too?

Suddenly self-conscious, she picked up the dessert menu, but then put it down without opening it. "This night... it's good, right? I mean, talking to you is so easy. Being with you feels so right."

She held his gaze, uncertain if she wanted him to deny the connection or support it. Denial would make her life a heck of a lot easier. It would also hurt. But only her. Acceptance would hurt her family.

His hand slipped overtop hers. "Feels like we're relearning each other. Not getting to know each other."

"Exactly." Pulse jumping under tender skin, she delighted in his touch and this shared feeling. "But it... can't be real, right?"

"Feels more real than anything I can remember."

A tremor of fear sliced down her spine. It couldn't be. She'd told her mother what she thought to be true. It was one date. It would be over tomorrow. But what if... it wasn't? What if this feeling was something more?

Worse, what if *she* wanted more?

Could she risk her family's happiness on one hot date?

Sliding her hand away, she dropped it into her lap. "It's the drinks."

He picked up his brown beer bottle, twisted it so she could see past the label to see how much he'd drank. "I've had less than one beer." He tipped the bottle's neck to her wine. "You've had half a glass of wine."

Ay. He was so logical. "It's hormones."

He laughed. "You got me there." He winked at her. "But I'm not a teen. I don't feel this attraction for just any partner." He frowned. "Do you?"

"No." Never had. She fiddled with the napkin across her lap, twisting it with both hands. She couldn't do this to her family again. Lust did not a lifetime make. "But it can't last. Right?"

He leaned forward. Close enough that his lips were a breath from hers.

Moisture pooled in her mouth. And lower. His gaze was a deep stroke of awareness.

"I don't know. Truth is, we won't know unless we risk it." His words brushed warmth and possibility across her lips. "Do you want to risk me, Eneida?"

"Yes." The truth popped out before she could process all the implications. Before she could curtail it, hide it, tuck it behind a joke.

Taking her declaration for the invitation it was, he swept his lips against hers. Even that light touch seared her. She *wanted*. Wanted to want without the guilt. At least for tonight.

Tossing inhibitions aside, she reached around his neck and dragged him into full contact.

The kiss erupted with bold hunger. There was nothing shy about her tongue mingling with his, about her deep sighs and desperate hold. About her throbbing sex.

Realizing their breathing had grown embarrassingly loud, she released him. Not okay in a restaurant, even if they *were* in a dark and secluded corner.

He sat back, grinning wildly and running a finger along his kiss-swollen lips. "You don't want dessert, do you?"

He said it like he hoped she'd say no.

Not happening. One night. She'd give herself what she wanted without hurting anyone.

Tonight's memories would have to last.

She ran her eyes down him with a ravenous leer. "Tonight, I want to taste everything. First cake. Then you."

His arm shot up. She laughed as he quickly got the server's attention.

When dessert arrived—a torta de tres leches—they shared the delicious, milky, multilayered cake. So good. The texture and taste had her closing her eyes and moaning out loud.

When she opened them, Tony was staring at her. He licked his lips. "Cariño, I'm feeding you cake every night."

The hunger in his eyes captured her, took hold of her body and her tongue. "Want to have sex?"

His eyes widened.

Her mouth dropped open. Of *course* this would be awkward.

For a long moment they sat there, the truth between them, big and hard and waiting.

He closed his eyes. "Have you been with anyone since…"

The obvious end to that sentence was *since the divorce.*

Awkward bombs away. "I haven't been with another man in twelve years."

His eyes popped open. His gaze drifted down to her cleavage. He swallowed. "And you're ready for this?"

Like Prometheus, she was willing to risk the fire. For tonight, anyway.

She put down her fork. "Can we go to your place?"

She didn't need to ask twice.

CHAPTER 8

Entering Tony's Astoria townhome, Eneida had a moment of surprise. She thought his home would be on the Upper East Side or someplace less family oriented.

Her flash of surprise was replaced with white-hot lust when Tony took her coat, kissing her lightly on her exposed shoulder.

Fire.

Sex with him couldn't happen fast enough for her.

He took off his coat and, to her hormone-addled mind, it was an erotic striptease.

She shifted in her heels, hyper-aware of how wet she was.

He guided her into the gleaming black-and-white marbled foyer with his hand pressed possessively to the small of her back. She shivered under the scorching touch.

Her breathing became labored. This night—hell, the whole time they'd known each other—felt like one long round of foreplay. She needed… Coño. She needed to act like a normal person. "It's beautiful."

"It's taken me five years to restore, replace, or refab the first three floors." His gaze flicked down to the soft curves of her breasts. He swallowed. "I'm working on the fourth and a rooftop—"

She cut him off mid-sentence by pressing her greedy lips to his. Then she slid her tongue into his warm, welcoming mouth.

His tongue tangled with hers, slick and probing. The fire Prometheus first brought to the world didn't burn as hotly as Tony's kiss. He singed all thought, all inhibition, all reason from her brain.

She leaned into him, and he grasped the sides of her dress with both hands, pulling it up and pressing himself firmly against her. The hardness that greeted her core sent a ripple of shock and pleasure racing through her.

He wanted her. And she *desperately* wanted him.

She was still processing the surge of need and want, still wrestling with the way her hips ground against him uncontrollably and the way his hands clung to her sides, when he broke from the kiss.

"Upstairs?" he breathed.

Not tonight. She didn't want to play nice. She didn't want soft sheets and pillows. She wanted fast and rough and satisfying. She wanted a memory to singe her gray hairs. When she had some.

She glanced about the opulent entryway. Below the heavy glass chandelier sat a round, white marble table. She could picture all sorts of dirty things happening on that table. But did she dare speak that truth out loud?

Hell yes she did.

She pointed. "There."

His eyebrows rose to his hairline. She saw him work moisture into his mouth, then swallow hard. "Sí."

In a flash, she swept aside a stack of mail, hitched up her dress to reveal a lacy thong, and positioned herself strategically on top of the table. Chest pressed to cold marble, she looked over her shoulder at him.

He choked out a sound like appreciation and moved up behind her. His large, hot hand cupped her ass. Squeezed.

Ay, Dios. This was, by far, the sexiest man she'd ever sleep with.

Whispering in Spanish of his sinful desire, he slid her panties down her legs. On his way back up, he nibbled lightly on her ass cheek. She cried out, gyrating her hips to let him know playing with her ass was a definite yes. Understanding her encouragement, he slapped one of her cheeks with a firm hand and squeezed. *So good.*

Bending to her ear, he groaned, "You are so beautiful."

She thrust back, feverish, losing her mind at the nearness of him, the heat. "Hurry."

The sound of his zipper going down and the soft *thud* of his clothes hitting the ground had her body rejoicing.

And then his satiny, hard length nudged against her saturated core. She almost came. "Sí. That. Inside."

"Mmmm," he said, pulling his erection away to glide a hand between her legs, then he slipped a finger between her labia.

He. Was. Killing. Her.

He moved another finger inside her, rubbed her clit with his thumb.

She lost all conscious thought. Almost blacked out. She was beyond saturated. Beyond ready.

She moaned. As good as that felt, she wanted him inside her pussy. *Now.*

She writhed. "Por favor, apúrate."

The desperate *please hurry* sent him into action. He pulled a condom from his pocket, sheathed himself, then, slow and thick, he glided into her. They moaned, and he began to thrust his heavy length.

Blissfully filled with him, she let out a series of sharp, pleased cries.

He leaned down to run his tongue inside her ear, then whispered, "You sigh so sweetly."

Her body bucked. No one had ever told her the ear was *that* erotic. Thirty-six years old... How was she just discovering this now?

He increased his pace, whisper-moaning, "Increíble. Tan buena."

The roughly spoken words, *incredible* and *so good*, had the muscles in her thighs clenching and her core tightening. He drove her toward the edge—so close. She encouraged him to go faster, the words falling from her lips like a prayer. "Más rápido."

He answered her prayers, and she lost her mind, overcome by the relentless, deep push of his cock driving into her.

Their heavy breaths echoed in the foyer. The table scraped against the floor. Each thick thrust coiled a heavy tightness between her legs. Hot, aching pleasure mounted higher and higher. "So close," she panted, needing the release, maddened by the tingling nearness of it.

"Be there," he whispered, and reached around to rub his thumb forcefully against her clit.

She came, a breathtaking orgasm, a wave of clenching muscles and electric shocks that had her crying out sharply, shamelessly.

His thrusts continued with an unremitting rhythm that outpaced her pounding heart. A pace that nearly had her coming again.

And then he groaned.

Hot.

Long.

Primal.

His thrusts slowed. His body stilled. He collapsed over her. Kissed her cheek. Whispered soft words. Her hair mingled with the sweat on his face, sticking to his mouth and he breathed it in, panting by her ear. "Want to try the bed next?"

She recognized the joking tone but also the sincerity. And, yes, she wanted. Because she *got* it. All those irrational, easily impressed, flighty people... She got it. The tingles in her body, the weight of him, the feel of him *this* close, and the rightness of it was no joke. And yet, she was afraid. Terrified. Steamy, wild table sex was a fling, but a bed?

That was one step from sleeping over. And that seemed like the start of a relationship—*not* one date.

CHAPTER 9

Entwined with Tony in the center of his big bed, Eneida luxuriated in being with this incredible man. Moonlight streamed across the California king. Her core still tingled from a series of earth-shattering orgasms. Her limbs were as liquid as soup and her inner thighs raw from the stubble on his chin.

Tony reached down and pulled off the condom, dropping it into the bedside wastebasket. The room smelled of their coupling and the faintest hint of his cologne.

She snuggled against his warm, sweat-slick body. Listened as his pounding heart rate started to slow.

He brought her closer, squeezing her to his side. "Enrique has the kids until Sunday, right? So can you stay tonight?"

The question under his question dislodged her casual ease. This was supposed to be one night, but his tone invited more.

She glanced at the clock on the nightstand. 2 a.m. What if Enrique called in the morning? What if her mother called? "I can't risk it. My kids aren't ready for me dating." She huffed. "Neither are my parents."

There was a slight tightening of his eyes, a frown line on his forehead that she wasn't sure she understood.

Exhaling, he ran a hand along the soft stretch marks along her belly. "You know, I think your kids are the best."

"Thanks. You're great with Lorenzo."

His hand trailed up her stomach, tickled across her breast and nipple, then brushed down her arm in little, exploratory touches. So why did it feel more like a remembering than a getting to know each other?

"He's clever and interested, creative, and he gets my jokes. Even the ones that go over most kids' heads. I'll look at a bunch of blank faces, but Renzo will be laughing."

That was the second time he'd called her son that. "You gave him a nickname? Renzo?"

His eyebrows went up. "He asked me to call him that."

He had? Her little boy was growing up, making his own changes. "Renzo. I like it. And he was born funny. Full of a curiosity that is absurd. He's obsessed with frogs."

"Ah, that explains him choosing to be a hip-hop coquí in the school play."

A loud Puerto Rican frog, that was her boy. She shifted closer, inhaled Tony's masculine scent. "You let him pick?"

"I told the kids they could pick whatever animals they wanted for the manger, but if they picked something too out there, they had to help make up their own lines. And they had to rhyme." He grinned. "You're going to love the lines he came up with."

"I can't wait for this play." She leered at him. "Though it might be a bit awkward pretending I'm not undressing you with my eyes."

The joke fell flat. In fact, he tensed under her. There was a long moment of silence before he exhaled and relaxed again. He brought her hand to his lips, kissed her fingers. "I really like you, Eneida. And I get the feeling you like me."

She laughed, draped a leg over his body. "What gave me away?"

He sucked on the tip of one finger. "Mmmm, that's definitely part of it." He released her finger from between his teeth. The moonlight streaming through the blinds slashed shadows across his face. Or was that darkening something else? "Pero I've learned not everyone who shares my bed wants to be part of my life. And vice versa."

"What are you trying to say?"

"The sex…"

She leaned on an elbow. "No good?"

He burst into laughter that lasted for several uncontrollable moments. Finally, he wiped a tear from the corner of his eye. "Dios, I really like you."

She slapped his chest. "Say it!"

His smile quieted and his expression became serious. Uncertain. "The sex was amazing. I'm seriously considering bronzing that table."

"And yet?" She could feel the *and yet*.

"The choice of that table felt… safe."

Safe? She rubbed at her forehead. "Please. Be direct. My ESP has been giving me such a hard time this week."

A snort of laughter. "Honestly, I was worried that table would be as far into my home as you got. When I helped you stand back up, I saw your eyes dart to the door. I got the feeling you wanted out. And that's not a feeling I'm used to. Not a feeling I like."

She had thought about leaving. Not because of him. He was great, but she had anxiety about becoming entangled with him. "I didn't bolt." Only considered it.

He ran a hand along his stubble. "It's not just tonight."

A creeping feeling of dread began to butterfly in her stomach. Was it butterflies when the fluttery feeling came from dread? She pressed a hand to her stomach. "Go on."

"When I first asked you out, I thought you'd said no because I'd been a jerk. The second time, when you almost asked me out, I thought it had been nerves. That's why I made a point at dinner to say —to ask—if you were ready to risk me."

"And I said yes."

"Is it still a yes?" His direct gaze met hers. "Because you not staying overnight not because you need to be there for the kids, or not because you have something to do or somewhere to go, or not because you don't have a toothbrush or have to get home to your dog, but because you're worried someone will find out about us... Damn it, Eneida, that hurts."

The air between them was suddenly alive. Drawing in breaths ached like swallowing bees. She'd hurt him? Of all the things she'd considered about this date, about this night, hurting him had never occurred to her. He was a jetsetter, a night-lifer...

No.

She shook herself. That was her not seeing him, her assigning him a character role. Just as he'd done—then made up for doing—the first time they'd met. Plus, he had a point, calling her on the table sex. She'd wanted it to be scandalous. She'd wanted it to be a memory she took into her old age. Not something sweet and languid that they shared as a forever memory.

Dios. *She* was the asshole. How did she fix this? "I really like you. Kind of wish I liked you less."

There was that familiar awkward rocking pause. "Qué?"

"If I liked you less, I wouldn't have to face doing it again."

"Doing what?"

"Making that drastic choice between speaking up and saying nothing."

"Drastic?"

"In this instance. Carajo, in a lot of instances."

"But you're not thinking of a lot of instances."

True. She exhaled deeply, as if she'd been holding her breath for a year. "I told you that Enrique cheated. But I didn't tell you how I found out." She blanched at the memory. Could feel him waiting for her to explain. "We always open one present before heading to a friend's Nochebuena party. Last year, when I opened Enrique's gift, I was stunned. He never bought me jewelry. Ever. And it was actually lovely. Something so stunning and obviously expensive that, for a moment, I could only gape with this big goofy smile. My son and daughter were *oohing* and *aahing*. I looked at Enrique to thank him. And his face was stricken with fear. I looked into the box and noticed a note. He made a strangled sound, reached for it. I opened it. It was a love note. With another woman's name on it. He'd mixed up our gifts."

"Cabrón." Tony looked into her eyes. "What did you do?"

"I... pretended everything was fine. The kids were there. My parents were there. So I pretended and we went to our party."

Tony frowned, puzzlement and a bit of surprise crossing his face.

She grasped his bicep. "Don't bother trying to make sense of it. It took months of therapy before I realized my marriage was just like that moment. That I'd been shoving down all I needed—support, affection, and friendship—to be what Enrique needed. Loving myself enough to put me first was the hardest thing I've ever done. I'm not really recovered from hurting my family so I can be happy."

He drew her back into his arms and kissed her on her head. "I'm sorry you had to go through that. Pero you shouldn't feel guilty. Your family, the ones I've seen, are survivors."

She rested her cheek against his chest and stared up at him. "Yeah, they've adjusted. But do I really want to throw another thing at them? Do I need them to adjust again? Especially around the holidays? I don't want to... what were the words you said that first day? Rock the boat, own my gloat?"

He leaned in and kissed her. Expertly. Passionately. Heat swamped her body, taking her mental faculties prisoner. His tongue tangled with hers, coaxing a response that was uninhibited and aching. And then he pulled away. He put his forehead to hers. "You forgot the rest."

"Hmm?"

"'Beyond their shushing lies your glory.' Take what you want, Eneida. I'm here. I'm offering you this—me. Us. If you value it, value what *it* is, and the possibility of what it might be, I'm going to need you to own that gloat. Love is possibility. It extends and expands and enhances life with every full breath."

Her chest tightened with an ache that was both affection and hope. He was reciting her poetry to her. It had mattered that much to him. Could she? Could she show her family who she was and what she wanted even though it meant causing them more pain?

Her cell blared. Startled, she flipped over and reached for it on the nightstand. *Enrique.* Heart thudding, she answered. "What's wrong?"

"She'll be fine." Enrique had on his manager voice. His smooth and controlled voice.

She knew that voice. It lied.

She bolted out of bed. Cold washed down her body. She gripped her cell. "What happened?"

"Adelaida got up in the night. I had no idea. She fell down the stairs at my new house."

Those stairs were incredibly steep. Adelaida's head. Her little body. "Oh God. Is she okay?"

"We're at the hospital. No head wound. But I think her leg is broken. Your parents are on their way."

Eneida was already sliding into her panties, then picking up her shoes. "St. Vincent's?"

"Sí."

"I'll be there as soon as I can."

She hung up and turned to Tony. She expected to find him watching her, expected to have to explain what was happening, but he'd listened, caught on, and was already dressing. "I can drive you."

"No." She slashed a hand through the air. "My parents will be there. My ex. My kids."

He froze, one arm inside the sleeve of his shirt.

They stared at each other, a distance as deep and wide and cold as the ocean opening between them.

Her breath hitched. Tears pricked the corners of her eyes. "It's not what you think."

"Isn't it?"

"I... I can't deal with their reactions when I need to be there for Adelaida. Please understand."

Pink patches rose up his neck. He swallowed and began to button his shirt. "Claro. But I wouldn't feel right just letting you go. Let me drop you off. I won't go in."

"No." She watched that word slap him—eyes going wide, an indrawn breath, the rising of his shoulders. And then his face went slack, emotion blinking away, becoming as invisible as a black pen on black paper.

He picked up his cell. "I'll call you a ride."

"Gracias." She had to get out of here. Away from his hurt. Away from her guilt. And to where she should be, by her daughter's side.

Avoiding eye contact, she shoved on her shoes and left without kissing him. Without letting him kiss her. The hollow sound of her shoes clicking on the floors, traveled up and burrowed into her chest carving out an empty, lonely space.

CHAPTER 10

Eneida arrived at the ER in full panic mode and ran headlong into her parents, their pajama pants visible beneath the hems of their long winter coats. Papa held Lorenzo, who was also wearing a coat over his pajamas. His head rested on Papa's shoulder. Despite the harsh fluorescent lights, the boy slept. She rushed over to them.

Papa shook his head, whispering, "He was very upset. Let him rest. We're taking him home."

Shame suffused her body. She hadn't been here for him. She'd been… She closed her eyes, opening them to find her mother's gaze flitting down Eneida's open coat and seriously wrinkled dress.

Ay. Caught. And this was why she'd been right not to let Tony come here. How could she handle Mami's reaction to him *and* her injured child?

Pushing past embarrassment and guilt, she said, "Where's Adelaida?"

Mami pointed. And said nothing. Arctic ice was warmer. Had more give.

Papa glanced at Mami, then whispered a series of quick directions and a room number.

She thanked him, then kissed Lorenzo lightly on his soft cheek before making her way to Adelaida's room. She avoided eye contact with Mami.

Enrique was outside the room, lean and tall, bleary-eyed and bedraggled, dressed in T-shirt and sweatpants. He spoke with a doctor, a dark-skinned woman with salt-and-pepper hair.

He put an arm around Eneida when she neared, squeezed once. "She's fine. This is Dr. Álvarez."

After greeting the doctor, Eneida leaned far enough over to look into Adelaida's room. Adelaida was smiling and talking to a nurse. She *seemed* fine.

Pulling off her leather gloves, Eneida shoved them into the pocket of her black wool coat and faced the doctor. "What's going on?"

The doctor answered, "As I was telling your husband—"

"Ex," Eneida and Enrique said in unison.

The doctor's eyebrows rose. She checked her digital pad, as if that held the information that they were divorced. It probably did. "Yes. Well. There's nothing wrong with your daughter. Nothing I can find on her X-ray or tests. I was asking your—Enrique—if there might be a reason Adelaida pretended to be hurt."

Enrique dropped his arm from around her shoulders and stared down at his black running shoes. He looked back up, all amber-brown eyes and guilt behind black-rimmed glasses. "And I was explaining we're recently divorced, and Adelaida has taken to trying to parent-trap us back together. She's tried a couple weekends in a row to get me to call her mom about a stomach ache or a scary dream. That kind of thing."

Dr. Álvarez frowned. "Did something happen to cause her to try this more drastic idea?"

Eneida blanched. "I had a date tonight. I think she suspected."

Enrique's gaze flowed down her body, noting her dress. He rubbed a hand through his bed-mussed hair. "That would do it."

His tone held no judgment, but Eneida still felt awful. "What's your medical opinion, Doctor? Should we run more tests?"

"I could, but if you two have noticed this behavior before, I'd say she's safe to go home. Unless you'd prefer I run more tests."

"No," they said again in unison.

"We're so sorry, Doctor." Eneida gestured toward the room. "I can't imagine how frustrating it is to deal with a child faking being hurt. We'll explain to her exactly how wrong and worrying this is for us, for the hospital, her grandparents, and her little brother."

Dr. Álvarez dropped the hand with her digital pad to her side. "It was a slow night, thankfully. And I've seen adults doing this kind of thing, too. It's the ones who are really sick that you can't get to take illness seriously." She let out a breath. "If you don't mind, I learned a few things from my own divorce, and I think I can offer some advice."

When neither Eneida nor Enrique objected, she waved at the door to Adelaida's room. "If we try to protect our children from life, we often do more damage than good. The divorce happened. You dating will happen. Think of these situations as an opportunity to teach her about life, to give her life skills. To show her that her parents are human, and that's okay. Show her that change happens and hurt happens, and she can survive both.

"Because, and I'm sorry to say, this won't be the first or last time she is hurt by life. Teach her how to acclimate, how to adapt. Give her life skills, not platitudes. She will be better adjusted and a lot happier. And so will both of you."

CHAPTER 11

The atmosphere inside the SUV on the way to the Christmas Talent Pageant was tense. Mami barked at Papa to drive faster so Enrique wouldn't have to wait too long. She wasn't giving up on Enrique and Eneida getting back together, no matter how many times Eneida explained it wasn't happening.

She got it, though. Her mother wanted for Eneida what she had: a wonderful and devoted marriage. She wanted what had worked for her, for her family. Still, Eneida wished her mother would listen and see the undue stress she was causing everyone.

Papa took her warning about being late to heart, driving through the light snowstorm like a NASCAR driver. He turned the corner too fast, jostling Eneida in her seat between her children. "Papa, slow down."

In the seat next to her, Adelaida leaned forward, bursting into laughter for the hundredth time since Lorenzo had come out of his room green-faced, wide-mouthed, and googly-froggy-eyed.

With his green soccer goalie–mitted hand, Lorenzo tried to reach across Eneida to slap his sister. Eneida grabbed his green-felt arm and pushed it down. She'd spent hours sewing a coquí costume for him, and she could imagine it tearing before they got into the auditorium.

"You'll rip a seam."

Still grinning wide, Adelaida said, "So, Renzo, why are there so many songs about rainbows?"

"Renzo?" Mami said from the front seat. "No es tu nombre."

Was it possible for someone with green on their face to blush? Because Eneida swore she saw pink under the face paint. "He likes the nickname. I like it, too."

"Lorenzo is the name of a king," Mami said regally. "Renzo means nada."

Now her mother had a problem with nicknames? "Dios, when did you become so set in your ways? That's not how you raised me. Despite your traditions, you've always accepted the differences in our large group of family and friends."

Her mother turned in her seat, wrapped in a white wool coat like a queen, something like a queen's pointed surety present in the way she held her head. "Porque I realized I was wrong. I had to have been. Because, what I taught you has led to so much pain."

The *whoosh* of windshield wipers brushing soft snow was the loudest thing in the car as Eneida's understanding of her mother's rationale did a backflip, landing with a staggering *thud* in a completely different place. Her mother felt guilty. She'd been blaming herself.

Shaken with the realization, Eneida uncrossed her legs, pressed the tips of her pumps into the car's rubber mats, braced her hands on her knees, then leaned forward. "Mami, parenting isn't a forcefield against life, and change isn't always a bad thing. Despite the pain, Enrique and I are better co-parents now than when we were married. If you'd just let go of the way things were and embrace the way things are, I think you'd see that."

Her mother's regality collapsed, washed away by the tears brimming in her compassionate brown eyes. "Vas a estar bien?"

Warmth flooded Eneida's own eyes. She sat back and lowered her heels. "Sí, Mami. We're going to be fine. All of us."

With a soft and wistful sigh, her mother turned back around.

A small touch had Eneida looking down. Adelaida's hand rested atop hers. Eneida threaded their fingers together. Her daughter's eyes held a new kind of trust, a rebuilding.

A lump rose in her throat. No matter what happened tonight with Tony, he'd already helped to make things better. He'd given her a reason to make what she wanted a priority. Given her a reason to step up, so others knew to step back. That honesty was a lesson, a skill she knew benefited her children. It already had.

Something had shifted after Adelaida's dangerous and inexcusable stunt at the hospital. The child had been remorseful, as much as she'd ever been, but, also, she'd been deeply honest about her fears during their family counseling session. This time, when Eneida and Enrique talked with her about the divorce, telling her again that they'd always be a family, but a different kind of family, she'd begun to believe it and to be okay with things changing.

A screech of tires. Everyone jolted to the side as Papa took a sliding turn into the parking lot. Mama gasped. "Ay. Dios. There's no reason to go so fast. Slow down, mi amor."

"Sí, cariño. Yo soy."

Like he had a choice. There were fifty cars pulling in to drop kids off early. Her nerves were on edge, but not about the play. About who would be *at* the play. It seemed like years, not days, since what the familia now called the "Niña crying loba episode." Years since she'd left Tony standing in that bedroom.

She hadn't called. Hadn't texted. She hadn't wanted to do anything that would require more words. She'd hurt him, had shown a cruel lack of regard for him and for the possibility of them. It was the opposite of what she'd professed in her poem—*and* to him directly. Words mattered very little in the face of those actions.

And since she'd requested a few days off to get ready for Christmas, there'd been no chance to see him in person. Tonight, at the play, would be the first time.

Nervous didn't cover it.

But nervous was okay. Safety wasn't always found in the comfortable and familiar. Bone-deep, soul-deep safety was found in growth and accepting challenges because you understood and trusted yourself to handle them no matter what happened. That's why, tonight, Eneida was risking the fire. As she'd already explained to Lorenzo and Adelaida, tonight, action was where it was at.

SEATED in the third row of the newly renovated auditorium with her parents, Enrique, Héctor, and Adelaida, Eneida was riveted by the Christmas play. The performance was unique and engaging, informative and inspirational. And fun.

The place was packed. It was a huge success. The school had raised more money with this one pageant than all the others combined. Everyone wanted to see what a famous producer did with the play. Even the local and national media were here.

The laughter in the auditorium quieted as Lorenzo stepped up and delivered his croaking lines: "And everyone was quiet. The sheep and the cows, the pigs and the hens. The sleeping Lord and visiting wisemen. All except the coquí and the drummer boy, who played music and danced with joy."

The drummer boy began to play. Lorenzo threw his body to the ground and began a twirling breakdance that had everyone laughing and hooting.

Baby Jesus, the smallest kid in the second grade, sat up in his straw-laced trough and watched, clapping in time to the drums.

When the play ended, Eneida jumped out of her seat, fist-bumped Héctor, hooted and clapped loudly. She wasn't the only one. The auditorium erupted in applause.

Tony had told her that all his plays were about facing the fire, about speaking up even when it didn't seem appropriate. This play kept to his premise.

The deepest core of her being curled in on itself. She *hadn't* spoken up. Her cowardly actions had hurt him.

No more.

Following her family backstage—where the parents were supposed to pick up their children—she braced herself to follow through with her plan. Tony was the man she wanted in her life. Hopefully, he still wanted to be in hers.

Adelaida held Mami and Papa's hands as they maneuvered past groups of families. She scanned the area for her frog. Lorenzo ran to Enrique, who scooped up his little coquí-clad son. Lorenzo flapped his green goalie mitt hands. "Mami! Did you see my breakdance?"

"Sí, mijo. It was spectacular." She kissed him, wiping green dye from her lips with a laugh.

As Mami and Papa praised Renzo, she gazed around the packed area and spotted Tony. The moment their gazes locked, pain flooded his eyes. She put a hand to her heart. Oh, she'd thought the ache of these days without talking to him couldn't get worse.

With deliberate purpose, she moved past a rather large family there to pick up their twin cows, only to get sideswiped by a llama in red pajamas. Feeling a hand gripping hers, she looked down. Adelaida, her face serious, shoved past the llama, past a pig, and pulled Eneida along.

Best wingman ever.

Her insistent little legs got them outside the crowd gathered around Tony, who was taking pictures with each of the performers. Mami, Papa, Enrique, and Lorenzo caught up. Tony signed another autograph and took another photograph before saying, "Un momento, por favor."

A hesitant smile lit his face. Enrique and her parents were already praising the show. Loudly. Demonstratively.

Fear danced into her throat, carrying a pitchfork of doom. Swallowing that spikey fear, she squared her shoulders just like she'd practiced.

She waited for a break in the chatter then said, "Tony, I truly enjoyed our date the other night, and I would be so happy if you would join me, as my date, for Nochebuena."

There it was. That awkward silence where everyone adjusted to her social spasms. This time, however, it wasn't because she was hiding the truth. She knew what she was saying, knew what she was doing. She just hoped it wasn't too little too late.

"Why, Eneida," Tony said, matching her serious and practiced tone, a gleam in his midnight eyes. "I, too, was delighted with our date. And I would be thrilled to join you for Nochebuena."

He winked at her, a wide and priceless smile on his handsome face. Lorenzo flapped his coquí limbs. "Yes! It worked, Mami!"

Enrique pushed up his glasses and extended his hand. "Hola, Tony. Yo soy Enrique. Glad you'll be joining us for Nochebuena."

"Nice to meet you," Tony said. "Renzo said you were the person who taught him to breakdance."

Enrique swiveled his hips. "Verdad. I've got the moves."

Adelaida laughed at that. Her amazed, almost hopeful gaze bounced between her father and Tony. And because Enrique had set the tone, Mami and Papa followed suit, both shaking Tony's hand and telling him he was welcome for Nochebuena.

Her heart was light as air as she mouthed, "Thank you" to Enrique. This could've been a lot harder—as difficult as the years they'd spent living a make-believe life, each wanting something different.

Fear had kept her from seeing the truth about her marriage for a long time. Fear had kept her conforming to a family ideal that no longer worked for them. The way they were learning to co-parent now might not be perfect, but it was honest.

Another person came up to ask Tony to take a photo with their child. Much to Eneida's surprise, Mami, perhaps warming up to Tony, asked if he'd take a photo with her little coquí afterward. Tony's smile was bright and beautiful as he moved to take the pictures.

Enrique leaned over and kissed her lightly on her cheek. "Te ves feliz."

"I *am* happy."

"Bueno." Looking back to see if Mami and Papa were still occupied with the photo—they were—he whispered, "I was going to bring a date tonight, but was too afraid to face your mom."

She repressed the laugh. She'd suspected he was dating. "Are you bringing her to Nochebuena?"

He blew out a long breath, glanced back at Mami and Papa and

Tony and the kids, then shrugged. "Perhaps I should sit this one out? It would be so awkward."

She grasped his hand, squeezed. "A good kind of awkward. Our way of finding a new pattern, a new way of being. And, frankly, I can't think of any better place than a Baez Nochebuena. You know Gigi will carry on her big family tradition. One where everyone is welcome."

Enrique nodded. "Bien. I'll call Amanda. She was upset at not being invited."

Before he could make the call, Mami waved him over. "Come now, Enrique. We want a picture with you and the kids."

Eneida smiled. Her mother. She always wanted everyone to know they were loved. Including Enrique in this photo was her way of doing that. It was her way of making room for everyone.

With a nod and a smile, Enrique went to take the photo.

Tony returned and swiped a thumb across her cheek. He showed her the green he'd wiped away. "I'm thinking this could be my new favorite color."

"Really? Not cherry red?" She ran a tongue across the cherry-red gloss on her lips.

His eyes bright with joy, he moved in to give her a hot, possessive kiss. There. In front of everyone. And she kissed him back, a kiss that showed she was ready for whatever this brought.

It was worth the risk. Because now she understood. The miracle of life was that it happened and kept happening, ready or not. She wasn't going to hide from it. Or from the possibility of love ever again.

ALSO BY DIANA MUÑOZ STEWART

THE BAD LEGACY SERIES
Broken Promises

BLACK OPS CONFIDENTIAL SERIES
I Am Justice
The Price of Grace
The Cost of Honor
The Edge of Obsession (Novella)

ABOUT THE AUTHOR

Diana Muñoz Stewart is an award-winning author who writes diverse characters with a focus on justice, family, and love. Her stories reflect the optimism of a growing and inclusive society. As *Booklist* noted about her unflinching look at today's relevant issues in her Black Ops Confidential series, the author, "gives these topics hope."

Diana Muñoz Stewart's work has been a BookPage Top 15 Romance of 2018, a Night Owl Top Pick, an Amazon Book of the Month, an Amazon Editor's pick, a Pages From The Heart Winner, a Book Page Top Pick, Golden Heart® Finalist, Daphne du Maurier Finalist, A Gateway to the Best Winner, and has reached #1 category bestseller on Amazon multiple times.

Diana lives in an often chaotic and always welcoming home that—depending on the day—can hold husband, kids, extended family, friends, and a canine or two. A believer in the power of words to heal and connect, Diana has written multiple spotlight pieces on the strong, diverse women changing the world. Find out more about the causes Diana supports at her website here.

Sign up for Diana's newsletter here!

facebook.com/DMSwrites
twitter.com/dmunozstewart
instagram.com/dianamunozstewart

LOVE IN SPANGLISH

ZOEY CASTILE

A heartbroken romance writer gets snowed in with a novel-worthy hero who may just make her believe in love again.

CHAPTER 1

Eight Days Till Nochebuena

CALISTA CALDERÓN WAS LATE. Not in an "I missed the subway" kind of way. Not in a "Did the condom break?" kind of way either. God knew she'd been on birth control for three years, about as long as she'd been with Angelo Castiglione, DDS.

No, this kind of tardiness was somehow worse—a deadline.

She stood in front of Bloomingdale's with her bags of last-minute gifts and shot out her hand. A yellow Lincoln taxicab cut across the gray slush of Third Avenue and braked in front of her. She climbed in, gave the driver the cross streets of the spa near her apartment, telling him to take the Queensborough Bridge, not the Triborough. She let the round vowels of her Queens accent slip through, so he knew she was not one to play with.

When he hit the gas, Callie's cell lit up with the call she'd been dodging. But she couldn't avoid it any longer.

"Hello?" she answered sweetly.

"Seriously?" Janie asked. She'd been a smoker for half her life and sounded like it. "You send me to voice mail for four weeks, put on your out-of-office, and then answer like I'm not on your fucking caller ID?"

Callie smacked her hand on her forehead. "I'm sorry."

"Callie..." There was shuffling. Slurping. Probably cold black coffee. "You're late. You know you're late. We can make it work. But you have to, you know, *communicate*."

Callie took a deep, steadying breath and grabbed the handle on the ceiling of the taxi, usually reserved for hanging dry cleaning or for use in case your driver was Dominic Toretto. *Or* if your editor called, telling you the thing you didn't want to hear.

"Callie?"

"I know, Janie. I know. I'm sorry."

"Look, I've cut you as much slack as I can, kiddo. But it's been five months."

If anyone other than Janie called her kiddo, Callie would've rolled her eyes. But Janie wasn't patronizing. She was a sixty-year-old Black Puerto Rican woman who had been an editor for over three decades and knew how to handle every personality in the book. She'd launched more bestselling romance authors than anyone else in the game and made diamonds with that pressure.

Callie was lucky. She knew she was. But she was also just one person trying to have it all. And the thing about trying to have it all was if you cracked, you might end up having nothing.

"Talk to me," Janie said, softening. "We can push the book, but next season's crowded and there's shipping delays. That puts you a year out."

"A *year*?" Callie's throat squeezed with anxiety.

"I'm not going to have my most promising star crash and burn. Even if we're on a hot streak from *Eleven Eleven*. Preorders are triple your debut. If we push the date, Sales is worried about losing momentum. So let's cut the bullshit. What's going on in that brilliant head of yours?"

Callie hated letting people down. She hated being the thing that was not dependable. The rogue variable in a routine experiment. Even in kindergarten, Callie had objected to a seatmate change because it upset the delicate balance she'd become accustomed to. *A creature of habit*, her brother called her. *Anal*, her dentist boyfriend liked to tease. That's what made asking for help so difficult.

"Honestly?" Callie asked. "You'd tell me if the book sucks, wouldn't you?"

"I would."

"So, does it suck?"

Janie didn't even hesitate. "It's a good book, Callie."

"But is it a *great* book? Is it good enough to follow up *Eleven Eleven*?"

Janie cleared her throat. Every compliment she gave was hard earned. And she wasn't an ego-stroker, so that *breath* of hesitation was the answer Callie needed to validate the sneaking suspicion that burrowed at the back of her thoughts the entire time she'd eked out every painful word.

"I knew it," Callie said.

"Listen to me. I don't publish basura, and I wouldn't let you walk out there with spinach in your teeth either. And here's my tough love. I've worked with hundreds of writers. Enough to know that you're your own worst enemy. Get out of your head and get down to the root of why you're telling this story in the first place. Starting with the fact that there's no catharsis from their love."

Janie was right. Callie knew Janie was right. Only, she thought she'd already done that. "The catharsis is that he got over his amnesia and went to find his true love who thought he'd died in the plane crash. I think it's clear."

"Yes, but do you remember the part in the edit letter when I point out it can read as emotional guilt? Not love."

"Catharsis," she exhaled.

More paper shuffling. "You've got a week, kiddo. Or we're pushing to next year."

"But—it's Christmas."

"I've got a calendar."

Callie lightly hit her head repeatedly on the window. "Okay. I'll get it done."

Janie, economic with her greetings and farewells, clicked off.

Callie Calderón had wanted to be a writer since she wrote her first biography in second grade. She'd put in the work and sacrifice, buoyed by her lovably obnoxious Ecuadorian family through college and her buzzy debut. She had the career she'd dreamed of... and she was blowing it.

Callie watched the city roll past from the backseat of the taxi. The icy Hudson cleaving between the boroughs. The flurries hailing from a pale gray sky. There was a blizzard warning upstate, but down here it was the perfect New York holiday greeting card.

Slowly, a game plan began to take shape. It went as such:

Skip her mani-pedi appointment and go straight home. She could begin rereading the manuscript before her anniversary dinner with Angelo. Then she'd send him home and work on pacing herself, tackling fifty pages a day until Christmas Eve. She absolutely couldn't miss Gigi's Nochebuena party, not after the year she'd had. Even a looming deadline couldn't mess with tradition.

WHEN THE CAB pulled onto her street, Callie paid with cash, and the driver blessed her and her family.

She hefted her shopping bags into the elevator and rode up to the third floor. At her door, she stopped at the sound of a moan. She rolled her eyes. Ruby was a yoga teacher at the local gym, and her sculpted body was just one of the reasons people carouseled through their apartment during the week. Sometimes Callie envied her roommate's sex life, since she and Angelo hadn't had sex in weeks.

She stopped, the key half-turned in the keyhole. She counted on her fingers and realized that it had been months. *Five* months. Perhaps they were overdue for anniversary sex that night...

Callie let herself inside, hoping Ruby had at least kept her sexcapades to her own room. She'd once caught her in the throes of passion with two of her yoga students. Talk about a downward doggy-style train. The living room really was more spacious for that sort of thing.

Callie swapped her stylish leather boots for hideous but comfortable knock-off Uggs, then dropped her bags of gifts in front of the Christmas tree. She grabbed a bottle of wine and empty glass to bring to her room just as Ruby's moaning orchestra began to crescendo.

But as Callie slid across the polished floors, Ruby's door swung open.

The lean, muscled man covered his junk with one hand and stepped out into the living room without looking, knocking into her. She began to slip, but he caught her, freeing his semi-erect dick in the process. For a moment, all Callie could think was *Don't touch me with your wet penis hands!*

But slowly, painfully slowly, she registered that those hands had already touched her. All six feet of that lean, muscular Tower of Pisa was Angelo. Her Angelo with the gold cross she'd bought him for his birthday, the tattoo with his deceased father's name over his right pec.

For a moment, she doubted herself. Angelo must have been coming out of *her* room to surprise her. Denial was an insistent bitch, and she did a double take from her door across the living room to Ruby's.

Ruby, who was sprawled on her pink faux fur rug, her mouth turning from a sex-drunk smile to an O of sheer horror upon seeing Callie.

"What the fuck?" Callie blurted, her traitorous denial catching up with the logical part of her brain.

And all he could say was, "You were supposed to be at the spa until five."

She supposed that the cruel irony was that she, Callie Calderón, who was late in every other aspect of her life, had chosen that very moment to arrive early.

WITHIN HALF AN HOUR, Callie had shoved her manuscript, laptop, and wallet into the first travel tote she could find and left the apartment, dragging a carry-on she hadn't unpacked from her business trip five months ago.

She ran down the three flights of stairs. She hadn't stopped moving since Ruby and Angelo had hovered around her, pleading forgiveness.

I'm sorry.

We're sorry.

We didn't mean to but—

—it just kept happening.

Come on, Cal, you haven't wanted to have sex for months.

It hurt that they were a royal we and already finishing each other's sentences. It hurt that it hadn't been just one time. But most of all, it hurt that Angelo's apology relied on her blame.

Somehow, Callie had tuned it out. She was numb. On autopilot.

Pack, she thought.

Flee, her instincts shouted.

She could barely feel her limbs as she left Ruby and Angelo in the dust.

The same cab driver who had dropped her off was drinking coffee and smoking a cigarette and was likely on his break when he saw her tripping on the patch of ice in front of her building. Her things fell everywhere.

He flicked the cigarette to the ground and didn't ask questions as he helped her put everything back in the tote and then stowed her carry-on.

With tears threatening to spill down her face, she returned to the back seat she'd been in not half an hour prior and said, "Amtrak. Penn Station."

Callie vaguely remembered buying a train ticket on the app, then booking an OurB&B for that night and receiving the confirmation email with instructions.

When they arrived, the driver rejected her payment. And the thing was, it wasn't seeing her boyfriend of three years and her roommate naked with his come running down her back that made her cry. It was the driver's kindness. The hand he gently placed on her shoulder with a wordless goodbye. That was the thing that broke her.

Thankfully, New York City wasn't a stranger to people openly weeping on the streets. And as she boarded the train to the Hudson Valley with one minute to spare, the man who checked her ticket only gave her a sympathetic smile and said, "Don't worry, it'll get better tomorrow."

BY SUNSET, Callie stood at the Hudson train station, and it was snowing harder than in the city. She'd sent her #CalderónLegion family group chat a short message of her breakup and deadline situation but left out the part where Angelo cheated. She didn't want her brother and cousins arrested during the holidays, as old-fashioned as the sentiment was. *And* she didn't need to listen to her dad telling her that he "always knew" that hijo de puta cabrón was no good and his teeth were too white like a demon's.

She needed to work. Deadlines didn't care about heartbreaks. Besides, they were used to her leaving on solo retreats to work on her book.

Her new problem was that there were more passengers than there were cab drivers, and she had absolutely no service to call the taxi company or get a ride share.

"When it rains, it pours," she muttered.

She waited for a new round of taxis to circle back, but the next train wasn't due to arrive for another hour. Good thing that on the ride down she'd mapped the route from the station to the OurB&B.

The map estimated forty-seven minutes, but she walked like a New Yorker. A *city* New Yorker. And so, Callie dragged her suitcase, regretting not having taken the time to put her leather boots back on.

An hour later, she was on an unmarked road surrounded by trees, shuffling her cold feet through the snow. That's how she discovered she had a tiny hole at the back of her fake Uggs. And yet she pushed on, all the while making a mental checklist of the things she'd forgotten in her haze of anger. First and foremost was her common sense. But she was in survival mode, so she'd forgive herself.

Then there was the matter of a winter jacket. She'd left the apartment wearing a pair of black jeans and a merino wool sweater. Warm in most instances, but not after an hour of walking in steady snowfall.

Her stomach rumbled. She'd skipped lunch in anticipation of her anniversary dinner. The memory of the last hours slammed into her. She winced and let loose a groan of humiliation, followed by full-body shivers.

How could she have been so stupid?

Heart racing, Callie continued uphill in the dark. At the very least, her suitcase was obnoxiously pink and could be seen from space.

Everything she'd felt up until that moment was pushed out of the way as fear and panic crept their way in. She hadn't seen a car in miles. She wasn't even positive how many miles she'd walked, but it felt like a hundred city blocks.

"Don't panic," she said to herself.

The flicker of headlights and hum of an engine signaled that she was no longer alone on the road.

As the red pickup truck slowed beside her, her first instinct was to run. But she was too cold to move faster than a Galápagos tortoise. She practically saw the news coverage: CUCKOLDED WRITER FOUND FROZEN IN A DITCH WITH UNFINISHED NOVEL.

He tapped the horn, then rolled down the window and shouted. A snowy gust ate up his words.

She walked faster.

"¡Oye! ¿Estás perdida?" the strong tenor voice tried again.

She knew enough of her kindergarten Spanish that he was asking if she was *lost.* Yes, she was lost, but why admit that to a virtual stranger on the side of the road?

"Fine!" she blurted, tucking her head down, though nothing could avoid the harsh snow.

The driver stammered. She hadn't gotten a good look at him. It was dark and he let the truck crawl beside her.

"Sorry," he said in accented English. "Por favor."

She stopped. Surely a serial killer wouldn't apologize and then say *please*. Though she didn't know any serial killers to compare.

Then he said the words that caught her attention: "Hour bee bee."

Cold air bit at her cheeks. The wind, which had been behind her, had whipped around with a vengeance. Suddenly, she was aware that she was dragging a wheeled suitcase *up* a hill, and only arms toned by years of yoga (thanks, Ruby) were preventing the thing from rolling away. She was Sisyphus hauling a boulder, and she was *not* about to get into an eternal loop of misery. She also was not about to get murdered by a stranger who was waving his phone at her.

Despite her New York survival instincts clawing at her insides, Callie got closer to the driver's seat window, holding up her hand, which made a useless visor against the sleet.

"OurB&B?" she repeated.

The back of his head hit the headrest with a disgruntled *thump*. He flicked on the truck's cabin lights. Frustration marked his face. A face illuminated by the hazy yellow light, unflattering on 99 percent of the population. But not him. She registered deep brown eyes and darker eyebrows. A rippled brow—frowning, of course, which made it so much hotter.

"¿Hablas español?" he asked, a hopeful edge to his words.

She swallowed the guilt that lived on the fringes of her entire life as an immigrant to the United States. She shook her head.

"Comprendo," she said, and cringed at the sound of her own pronunciation. *I understand.*

"Ah. Okay. Soy Ángel Valenzuela. La casa es de mi hermano. Estoy buscando a…Mira…"

As he handed her his phone, she did the mental calibrations of translating a language that was as familiar to her as the stretch marks on her hips and the freckles on her décolletage. She thought of it like running strips of dough into a pasta maker. Or beef into a meat grinder. You start with one thing and then it takes an entirely different shape even though the composition is still the same.

The message read: *Hi Calista! We're in Ibiza but happy to squeeze you in on such short notice. My brother-in-law, Ángel Valenzuela, will be making sure the cabin is squeaky clean for you and get you all settled in. If you want, he can swing by and get you, no trouble at all. The cabin is hard to find in the dark. I'll have him text the number on your profile. Keep a look out for a cherry-red Ford pickup truck.*

Relief washed over Callie's nearly frozen body. He *was* from OurB&B.

Her heart gave a lurch. *Of course* his name was Ángel. Of course. Of all the storm-tossed streets in all of upstate New York, a man named *Ángel* had to be the one to rescue her when the last thing she wanted was a reminder of Angelo.

Callie pulled up her phone. She'd lost service so long ago that the message hadn't come through on her end.

She worried the inside of her cheek and glanced at Ángel. He had on a puffy winter coat and he was definitely in a red truck. By then, she couldn't feel her ears, her toes, or her knees. She had very bony knees. As a matter of fact, every part of her was just short of getting frostbite. Between hopping into a car with a stranger with the hope it wasn't some elaborate kidnapping scheme and a snowstorm nipping at her heels, she decided she'd be dead either way.

In one scenario, she'd be warm.

She nodded and said, "Okay."

He blew out a sigh of relief and got out to unceremoniously toss her suitcase in the bed of the truck. She climbed up into the passenger seat, and he even came around to get her door. She'd literally never had someone do that for her, except the time her publisher had sprung for car service during her book tour.

"Thank you," she said.

He gave a wordless nod and then returned to the wheel, blowing heat into his fists before putting the car in drive. The radio station played Latin pop. She recognized the song as Ricardo Arjona, her uncle's favorite singer.

Despite the music, an awkward silence settled between them.

Callie glanced at him in surreptitious intervals. He stared intently at the road, dark and covered in fresh snow. Trees flanked the road like shadowy sentries. Every second they spent driving made her realize he'd found her in the nick of time.

"I didn't know you were coming," she said, breaking their silence. "I'm sorry."

He took his eyes off the road to give her a once over, and she didn't miss the way his eyes fell to her general mouth region. Then he cranked up the heat. Right, she was Melty the Snowman and dripping all over his truck.

He did this thing before he spoke which reminded her of her uncles and mother. "Ehh—" Like he was preparing himself to do the pasta pressing and meat grinding of translating his words.

She saw the moment that he gave up, squeezing the ten and two positions out of frustration.

"Perdóname," he said. "No vi el mensaje de Susana. Fui a recogerte pero llegué tarde. Pasé por el pueblo y cuando no te vi me di la vuelta a buscarte. Y bien. Aquí estamos."

She caught about a third of that. But she understood that everything was all right now. She also noticed he had a slightly different accent than she was used to, having grown up with mostly Puerto Ricans and Dominicans, in addition to her own family. It was her favorite thing about Spanish, one of the languages that had been forced on Latin America but that every country had made their own.

When they turned into a path of narrow trees she most *definitely* would have missed had she been walking, she gave a little gasp. The headlights illuminated the wooden A-frame house surrounded by nothing but woods, giving the illusion that they were in the middle of nowhere. They parked right up front.

This was what she'd needed. "It's beautiful."

He smiled at her, and it totally changed his face. The frustrated, slightly annoyed man who'd picked her up on the side of the road morphed into someone who liked to laugh. He had pronounced laugh lines and a sweet dimple. That smile felt like a fresh start. She supposed people were always pleased when their family home was complimented, even if it was a cabin in the woods.

"Vamos. Hace frío." He tipped his head outside and shivered to prove his point.

"*Mucho* frío," she repeated, and he chuckled.

In moments, he'd retrieved her luggage and was walking through the front door. The heat of the cabin enveloped her. She hardly had time to take in the seasonal decorations, but she noted the unlit fireplace. A coffee table. Big glass windows and high ceilings. An untrimmed pine tree. Narrow steps leading up to a loft bedroom.

"It's the perfect mix of old and modern," she said, craning her neck to look at the exposed wooden beams.

His cheekbones were so pronounced when he smiled at her that way. "Gracias. Es mi diseño."

She didn't know the word, and so they stood there, letting in the cold and staring at each other.

"I...make," he said, pointing all around.

Then it struck her. Diseño. *Design.*

"Oh, wow. I love it."

He waved her deeper into the cabin, shutting the door against the howling wind. He gave her a tour of the half bathroom downstairs, the storage closet, and the kitchen. He opened the refrigerator, and she gasped.

"You got me groceries?"

His smile gutted her. For the second time that day, a complete stranger was taking care of her in a way her boyfriend never had. Why was kindness overwhelming? It was the season of giving, after all.

Do not *cry*, she mentally scolded.

Perhaps he was thinking the same thing because he waved his hands in front of himself. "Tranquila. Todo está bien."

Relax. Everything is good.

"Thank you. So much." She blinked so she wouldn't cry. "I've had the worst day."

They stood that way, him glancing worriedly between her and the door. He probably wanted to run for the hills, far away from the bananapants city girl who'd tried to walk five miles in a fucking snowstorm.

He bit his bottom lip and demonstrated with his thumb. "Me tengo que ir."

She definitely knew that phrase from one of her mom's favorite songs. *I have to leave.*

"Yes, of course. Thank you, again. I'm sorry about thinking you were trying to pick me up to murder me."

His eyes went wide, followed by a delayed laugh and smile that brightened his whole face again. She released a slow breath as he began to let himself out and pointed at his phone. He made the universal sign for *phone call* or *cowabunga, dude.* "Si necesitas algo..."

If she needed something...

She needed several things. A memory lobotomy so she never had to imagine—them. A magical solution to her writer's block. She needed to be alone but feared it at the same time. She needed the strange sense of peace that Ángel radiated. She needed to see his smile again because it was like pure sunshine.

She shook the thoughts and walked him to the door. She'd been single for a handful of hours. Wasn't there a moratorium on dating? Kissing? Fantasizing about beautiful Latin men with dimples and soft black curls?

Not when your boyfriend fucks your roommate, her lizard brain responded.

Ángel opened the door and was walking out of the cabin when lightning struck and illuminated the surrounding woods. A deep, rumbling clap shook the darkness. It was far enough away that they weren't in danger of getting hit, but then Callie felt his body cover her, enveloping her like a shield as something cracked and crunched. She grabbed onto him out of sheer fear. His puffy coat collapsed where her hands gripped his solid arms. She wondered if he could hear her heart race the way she heard it in her eardrums.

When the darkness resumed and there was only the whistling wind, Ángel released her. Cold filled in the place where his body had been. The motion sensors came on and illuminated the damage—a tree had fallen over the front of his truck, denting the hood. There were too many leaves to see any damage to the windshield.

They both let loose a string of curses, and the dark sky answered with a rumble of its own.

AFTER MUCH DEBATE, Callie convinced Ángel to sleep on the couch. He rubbed his head and glanced at the door. She tried not to take it personally. The cabin had room for them both, but it was a strange situation. Made stranger still by the fact that he had the Spanish version of her ex's name. Only, his name was *Ángel*. Ahn-hel. All soft pretty vowels that felt like sighing. Angelo was hard guttural sounds, Aaayn-jell-o.

At the very least, Ángel knew where everything was and made himself a little nook on the leather couch in front of the fire, which he'd lit while she showered. The only other weird thing was sharing a shower with him. He had the bathroom downstairs, but the only shower and tub were upstairs. Despite the language disconnect, they made it work. He carried a toothbrush and towel to her bathroom and gave a closed-lipped nod as he shut the door.

Callie noticed the way he tried to make himself smaller. To not make much of a sound. To not be in her way. He was about five eleven, and muscular in ways that were earned by getting your hands dirty. She imagined him hauling the slats that lined the ceiling. Sanding, then nailing the railing that boxed in the loft.

Stop it, she growled at her thoughts, then took a couple of painkillers and brought a paperback to bed with her. Not that she had the bandwidth to read. Sometimes she needed to sleep with a book nearby for comfort.

When the bathroom door opened and linen-scented steam billowed out, she told herself she wasn't going to look.

She looked.

He was in boxers that should have been shapeless but hugged muscular thighs dusted with dark hair. The white shirt he'd been wearing clung in wet spots on his strong shoulders. He glanced back at her and gave a quick goodnight.

While she felt relatively safe with Ángel sleeping just downstairs, only a railing separating them, she couldn't help but wonder—what if she snored in the middle of the night? What if she farted in her sleep? Why hadn't she worried about those things with Angelo? Was *that* why he'd sought comfort in her sexy, free-spirit roommate who was the antithesis of everything Callie was? Free-spirited where Callie was orderly. Toned where she was curved and soft. Sexual where Callie was on deadline and didn't have time for anything but a quick kiss.

And so, instead of dreaming, she twisted and tossed, and she relived the worst five minutes of her life. Instead of resting, she stared at the ceiling and wondered if every shadow was a spider.

By the time the sharp howls of the storm finally lulled her to sleep, the sky had brightened into a new day. The thing that snapped her awake was the light metal creak of couch springs. His soft groan, probably from having slept on a couch. The whisper of a door being closed, followed by running water moving through the pipes. She listened carefully to the beautiful softness of him, every sound he made unlike the slamming doors and passive-aggressive shouting she was used to.

Callie gave up on the task of rest and was determined to hit reset on her life. The thin plaid curtains did little to block the white sky. She sat up on the unfamiliar bed, rubbing her puffy eyes. She hadn't had so much as a drink of alcohol, but she felt hungover on sadness.

She opened her suitcase and rummaged for clothes. Washed up, dressed, and with her work in hand, she crept down the stairs.

Ángel poked his head out of the kitchen.

Her heart lurched at the sight of him. His white T-shirt clung to his thick torso. His nearly black hair was mussed and adorable, and she ignored the little flutters in her belly as he flashed a crooked smile.

"¿Cafecito?" His voice was still scratchy from sleep.

Little coffee. Though she knew it wasn't actually *little* little. More like a cute way of saying coffee.

She nodded eagerly and didn't know what else to do but follow.

Yes, he took care of the OurB&B, but he wasn't there to wait on her hand and foot, and she felt guilty. He'd already done enough.

He poured them two mugs, and when he went to add sugar and milk to hers, she waved him away. He raised his thick eyebrows in surprise and scrunched up his nose, still grinning as he added two spoonfuls of sugar and plenty of milk into his.

"¿Cómo te sientes?" he asked softly.

"Bien," she said, grateful she remembered the word for *good.* "Thank you again for yesterday. What about your truck?"

"No te preocupes. Llamo a Bob y me ayuda con la camioneta."

She nodded. Processed. "Who's Bob?"

"Ah." He mimed something that looked far too much like milking a cow, then she realized Bob was a mechanic. "No quiero dejarte sola pero..."

"Oh, no, don't worry. I came to be alone. I'm way okay alone. You know. Alone." She cringed at how many times she'd said the word *alone.* "I have to write." She mimed typing. "Mi trabajo." *My job.*

She drank deeply from her coffee as he studied her. Her messy bun and oversized white sweater that read I LIKE BIG BOOKS AND I CANNOT LIE. No one saw her this way. Not even Angelo.

"¿Trabajo?" He made a sound with his lips, like he couldn't believe she was working. "¿Y no disfrutas las vacaciones?"

"Oh, no." She snorted. She had no idea how to stand in front of him without fidgeting. "No vacations. I have a deadline. Um, como se dice *deadline?*"

When he pressed his lips together, his dimple appeared. Why did Sweet Latino Baby Jesus have to give this ridiculously beautiful man even more cuteness? It was one thing to be hot. But to be adorable and hot was a crime.

He nodded, squinting once at the tiny window at the back door, then at the wall clock. It read six in the morning, but the sky was already bright and white. He probably wanted to run, and she really couldn't blame him.

Callie's only relief was that she could get down and focus. Buckle in and *work*. She needed to forget the humiliation and hurt of Angelo and Ruby. She had to find the emotional catharsis in her love story.

I got this, she thought.

Somewhere out in the galaxy, someone must have been laughing. Because as she and Ángel walked out into the living room, she noticed his face go still with worry.

Alarmed, she set her mug down and followed his gaze. "That's weird. There's no trees."

Then she realized it wasn't the sky that was white or the trees that were gone. It was snow. Snow packed so high it blocked out their view from the windows.

Ángel rushed to the door and cracked it open.

"No!" she shouted.

But it was too late. An avalanche of snow pushed its way in, covering his feet and the welcome mat.

She didn't need her mental meat grinder. In any language, she knew the beautiful, kind stranger who had rescued her in the middle of a blizzard and made her coffee wasn't going anywhere. Neither of them were.

They were snowed in.

CALLIE LAUGHED. It wasn't the kind of situation you laughed at, but she laughed. She understood a concerned Ángel asking why she was laughing, but her abdomen contracted too hard to be able to give him a Spanglish answer. She laughed until he laughed with her, and soon they were sitting on the hardwood floors, which still smelled polished and new.

When her cackling tuned into a soft chuckle and she could finally sit up, they stared into their coffee mugs and finished drinking.

"I think the universe is trying to tell me to finish my book."

He watched her in that way of his, like she was the most curious thing he'd ever seen. She was pretty sure she'd looked at rare species of jellyfish at the aquarium that way. She didn't exactly mind, since jellyfish were her favorite.

"¿Qué tipo de libros?" When *he* mimed the word for "write," he ghosted a pencil over his hand. She found herself wondering if he was used to holding a pencil because he designed things like this cabin.

"Love stories," she said, and when he shook his head, she drew the shape of a heart with her index fingers. "Romance."

"¡Ah! ¡Romance!" How was it that the roll of an r and an emphasis on the middle of a word could change its entire sound? "¿Algo que he leído?"

She usually hated that question. Even though five hundred thousand people in the world had bought a copy of her debut novel, *Eleven Eleven*, she didn't think he was one of them. Though it *had* been translated into Spanish, along with fifteen other languages.

Still, she shook her head. "I don't think so. But that's why I'm here. Well, one of the reasons."

They were quiet for a little while longer. It didn't make sense that she should enjoy being alone with him. He brought her comfort, like he was the peace at the eye of her hurricane. Or snowstorm, for that matter.

Callie was so used to feeling on edge. Like she needed to be doing something. On a call or making sure she kept herself in shape in order to be the ornament on Angelo's arm at his stupid dentistry society foundations. She pinched the bridge of her nose, pushing at the stinging sensation at her tear ducts. She would not cry. She wouldn't. There was nothing she could do about Angelo and Ruby and the storm, and the beautiful man stuck in a cabin with her. She was, after all, a creature of habit and that habit was working. "Keep calm and write on" had been her motto for the decade before she sold her debut novel. It needed to be her motto now too.

Callie did what she always did—she attacked the problems one by one.

First, she turned on her phone. She had one hundred three missed messages. The only text she answered was her mother's.

Me: Safe at the cabin. On deadline. See you at Gigi's.

Her mother had grown accustomed to Callie's schedule. Even if she always reminded her that it wasn't too late to become a lawyer.

Next, she needed a workstation. Thankfully, there was a sweet wooden desk tucked beside the Christmas tree. It faced a window but was close enough to the fireplace that she wouldn't be too cold. She arranged her laptop, the printed copy of her manuscript, her unnecessarily large bag of multicolored pens and highlighters, and her coffee.

When she heard the *Avengers* theme song chirp from her phone, she froze. She'd assigned Angelo that song. Her throat constricted with a strange pain.

"No," she managed.

Her body's reaction was alarming. She couldn't even think or see past the red haze. He'd ruined her beloved *Avengers*. So, she shuffled a few paces and threw her phone in the fireplace.

"Oye. ¿Qué pasó?" Ángel said, alarmed.

The haze cleared and she stared at her phone screen cracking and turning black in the fireplace. "Oh, fuck."

Ángel knelt and tried to use the iron clamps. But the fire was hot and roaring. The flash of WTFuckery passed quickly and the feeling that followed was—peace.

She put her hand on his shoulder and squeezed. He whirled around, and they were on their knees facing each other. There was soot on his knuckles and on the slope of his cheekbones. Without thinking, she reached out and brushed it away.

"It's okay. Really. It's better this way."

"Qué locura." He chuckled, low at the back of his throat. His brown eyes flicked to her lips again.

She noticed the way he swallowed. Then the outline of his penis against his jogger sweatpants. Thank the fútbol gods for those pants.

"Mira," he said. *Look.* "Sé que tienes que trabajar y no te molestaré, lo juro."

She understood that he was promising to stay out of her way. She ignored the concern in his voice and extended her hand. "Deal."

He smiled that dizzying smile of his, too wide, silly, perfect. "¿Tienes hambre?"

She squinted. Why did squinting feel like a faulty x-ray for translation?

He rubbed his belly, which could have meant pregnant or hungry. She decided on hungry.

"Sí," she said, and headed to the kitchen. She snatched the bag of cereal she'd seen on the top of the fridge and brought it with her to her desk.

Though visibly horrified that her breakfast was fistfuls of Lucky Charms, he did as promised and left her alone.

Callie concentrated for hours. She highlighted and marked up her manuscript. Her wireless earbuds canceled out the noise, but after a while, she found she preferred the lo-fi sounds of the cabin. The crackling fire, the tin whistle of the wind outside, Ángel tidying up a bookshelf, the percolating chug of the coffee machine. In some ways, she felt like she was inside a snow globe, protected from the outside world by a barrier.

Miraculously, her coffee cup refilled as if by itself. That is, until she looked up and Ángel was there, emptying out the pot into her mug.

Her stomach gave a pleasant squeeze. "Thank you. I can get my own coffee. You don't have to—"

"Ehh, tienes—" He pointed to her face.

She rummaged through her mental catalog and found the translation.

Tienes. *You have.*

She grinned through her humiliation. There were cereal crumbs on her face. On her sweater. All over her paper. He reached forward and plucked a tiny shamrock marshmallow that had somehow gotten stuck on the corner of her mouth. And he ate it.

He made a face as if to say *Not bad.*

She barked out laughter. "I'm sorry. This is really a disgusting side of me."

He bit on his bottom lip. "No te preocupes. Es un look bien sexy."

Was he making fun of her? Like calling her disaster-mode sexy as a sarcastic joke? It *had* to be a joke.

Definitely a joke, she decided, and got back to work.

Problem was, the book wasn't writing itself, and the issues her editor had pointed out were not easy to fix.

She stood every hour, on the hour, and touched her toes.

She walked in circles.

She bit the end of her favorite pen, which looked more like a dog's chew toy.

She felt dizzy at some point, and only looked up when her nose caught a whiff of something delicious. Garlic and salty goodness. She hadn't eaten since her cereal. Hadn't even heard him chopping anything.

She slid across the polished floor to where Ángel was removing a roasted chicken from the oven. "You cooked?"

"Espero que tengas hambre," he said, removing the oven mitts. "Sólo has comido pura golosinas todo el día, eh."

"If you're saying I'm hungry, you're right." Her face scrunched with a smile, and she ignored the dig at her sugary cereal.

He pointed to the living room and shooed her out of the way.

A warm sensation spread across her chest when she realized he'd set the coffee table while she was working. She took a seat on a floor pillow. Despite her best efforts, familiar doubts began to edge themselves into her thoughts—Angelo. Naked. Ruby. Naked—she pulled the fleece blanket around her. It smelled like sunscreen and pine and something she couldn't quite put a name to, other than the scent of a man. That's when she realized she was sniffing *his* blanket.

She threw it off her body just as he waltzed into the living room with two plates of food. Roasted chicken and potatoes, with green beans topped with shaved almonds.

As he sat across from her, her mouth watered. She told herself it wasn't because of the way his body strained the already-thin fabric of the shirt but because of the thick, juicy thigh in front of her. Chicken thigh.

They ate in their easy silence, and she couldn't help but make delighted noises as she did.

"Ah, olvidé." He tapped a napkin on his lips. He walked across the room and opened a small cabinet to reveal a cleverly integrated bar. He retrieved a bottle of wine, an opener, and glasses. He winked at her. "Espero que te guste vino Chileno porque es lo único que tenemos. The best."

"Oh, this isn't spicy," she said, picking up on the *chili* part of his sentence.

His deep laugh rumbled as he uncorked the wine. "No. Chile." He searched for the word. "Ehh, my country."

Callie smacked her forehead. "Fuck. Duh. Sorry."

He laughed as he poured two glasses and offered her first. She smelled it and was positive it was a red wine. That was where her taste buds ended. "You're from Chile?"

He nodded, his face brightening with something like pride. "¿Tú?"

She pointed at her heart. "Ecuador."

"Ah, ¿sí?" He thumbed at himself. "Viví en Quito por unos años."

"I was born in Guayaquil. But we moved here when I was three and I just lost my Spanish."

He nodded along. Squinting. Language processing. "My brother... same."

She loved the shape his mouth took when he sounded out jagged English vowels. The way his tongue scraped against the back of his front teeth.

"Not you?" she asked.

He shook his head. His eyes were cast toward the fire, and she recognized the signs of someone falling into a memory. When he was done speaking, she understood the sad truth—his mother had gotten a visa to Canada, and then New York with his brother, but he and his father hadn't been able to follow.

She wished she could respond. Tell him that she knew how he felt. She hadn't seen her own father for her entire young adulthood. Callie wanted to know why Ángel had lived in Ecuador's capital, and ask where else he'd traveled, and tell him in her very broken words that today she'd felt her stress melt away and it was all because he made her food and let her breathe. *Just* breathe. But she couldn't. She couldn't and it frustrated her. It always had. In the past, there had been someone there to translate, or someone who could communicate with her.

Now she ached for her mother tongue in a way she hadn't in so long.

"Pero hace unos meses, me llegó la visa y por fin nos reunimos."

She sipped and gleaned that he'd only been here for a few months. She imagined Ángel reuniting with his family. She felt herself wanting to fill in more of his story, the little details that made up a person's whole life. Their anecdotes, their playlists, their closets, their snacks, and snack caches. Their wishes. She wished she had the words.

"Do you miss it?" she asked. That's what people always asked her about her first home.

He nodded slowly, almost pained. Slowly he said, "I... miss my brother more."

She drank and let the wine roll across her tongue. "Why aren't you in Ibiza?"

He grimaced and made the immortal sound of *untz untz untz*. He didn't like EDM, which made him nearly perfect. He pointed to the ceiling. "Quería quedarme aquí a terminar este projecto."

"Have you always been a designer?"

"Arquitecto. Estuve en Madrid unos años antes de aquí. Pero no sé..." He shrugged. "Quería algo más."

Más. She knew that. He wanted *more*.

"Es una locura," he continued. His posture was relaxed, the honey-tan of his complexion gold in the firelight.

"What's crazy?"

"Un hombre de treinta y nueve con ganas de empezar su vida de nuevo."

"Oh, come on. You're never too old to start over. Thirty-nine?" She would have guessed a few years younger.

"¿Me veo viejo?"

And because he leaned forward and batted his lashes in a silly way, she ran his fingers along the corners where fine lines creased at the corners of his eyes. His humor turned into something darker. Something she could only call hunger. The spell broke, and he forced a smile as he reached for his wine.

"No, you don't look old. I'm thirty-one, but I feel a hundred. Everyone's always resetting."

He shook his head. That's where their translation chain broke.

"I mean, I understand. Wanting to start over."

"¿Como así?"

"Muy largo." *Too long.* She hated that she couldn't remember the word for story. She was a storyteller!

He chuckled low and deep. His eyes roamed the cabin, as if to highlight their situation. "Creo que tenemos tiempo."

He was right. They did have time.

She was about to speak, but there was a low, whining sound all through the house. His eyes snapped skyward as every light went out.

"¡Qué cagada!" he swore.

She knew he wasn't calling her shit.

But yes, *what the shit?*

Together they searched the cabin and found every single appliance and light was out. He reset the breakers, but still nothing. He took out his phone and typed out a message.

"You have service?"

Ángel shook his head and showed her the screen. Nothing had gone through.

"Maybe the storm took out a tower. Is there a backup generator?"

Ángel rested his hands on his narrow hips. He was a powerful silhouette in the dark, and she felt a little guilty that she wasn't worried or scared. Oddly enough, she felt safe.

"No llega hasta la próxima semana."

"Next week? I'll be gone."

Heat radiated from his body, as well as the crackles of anxiety, worry. He snapped his fingers, like he'd just remembered. He vanished into one of the closets and returned with a box of tall votive candles. Bless Latino Catholics. There were twenty-four in total, and they made quick work of distributing them throughout the living room.

When they were lit, Callie sucked in a sharp breath. It was like being in an old cathedral with nothing but candle flame. She glided across the room and spun at the center of their own little retreat away from the world. It made her giddy in a way she never let herself be, out of fear of not being taken seriously or of being seen as childish.

"Por fin," he said, catching her as she spun on her socks. She hadn't even meant to, but her body pulled into his gravity like she was a moon to his planet's orbit. He gently tapped her chin. "Te ves feliz."

Happy. Was she happy?

Her emotions had been all over the place for thirty-something hours. She was hurt. She was anxious. But with him, just in their snow globe, she wasn't sad. Was the absence of sadness happiness? Or was joy something else completely? Something like brown eyes searching her own in the dark?

She blushed under his stare. "What?"

"Creo que tú sabes mucho de mí. Pero yo no sé mucho de ti."

She smirked. "You're right. I haven't told you anything about me. You know I'm a disaster but not *why* I'm a disaster."

He walked around to the couch and patted the empty seat beside him. Her throat went a little dry and she took a sip of her wine.

"Cuéntame," he urged her softly, like spring encouraging a flower to bloom.

Tell me.

And a tiny thrill ran through her as she remembered the word for *story*. Cuento. He wanted a story. Her story.

And maybe it was the flickering candlelight or her full belly or the way he just looked at her with his impossibly dark eyes—no pressure. Just patience. But she told him everything. To her surprise, it wasn't about Angelo and Ruby. It was everything else.

She told him the things she left out when talking to her cousins and brother and her mom. How she'd spent a decade trying to make a dream come true. She'd been rejected by every publisher in existence. She wrote book after book and then, finally, one stuck. All of a sudden, she was a debut darling. Her life changed so drastically in two years, and she had spent every day trying her best to be perfect. Have the perfect social media presence. Look like the perfect girlfriend. Be the perfect daughter. Give the perfect interview, lest her words be dissected and twisted. Somewhere along the way, she stopped doing the thing that she was supposed to love, which was *writing*. And she had a week to remember how, or else that dream would slip from her again.

When she was done, they'd come close together, slumped on the couch with their thighs and arms touching.

"I don't know if you understood any of that. I'm sorry."

He bit his bottom lip. She read shock across his face but wasn't sure at what. He snapped his fingers, then ran off. This time, he went to the bookshelf and returned with a hardcover.

"¿Eres tú?"

She snatched the book he held in front of her. It was her Spanish edition of *Eleven Eleven*. Apparently, he *was* one of the five hundred thousand people in the world who had her book after all.

She buried her face in her hands. "Seriously?"

"¿Qué pasó?" He took up his seat beside her, letting her fall plushly against him. His fingers stroked the ends of her curls.

"I'm embarrassed." Her cheeks hurt from smiling. She couldn't remember the last time that had happened.

"Lo compré en el aeropuerto cuando estaba en ruta a New York." He riffled through the pages, and something moved inside her when she noticed that there were several bookmarks. Little scraps of paper torn here and there. Heat spread through her at his smile, his near-ness, his—joy.

"Well, you don't have to tell me if you like it." She'd been with Angelo for three years and he had never read her book. Neither had most of her family.

"Wow," Ángel said. "Ahora me siento responsable de que termines el segundo libro, ¿eh?"

"You're definitely not responsible for me meeting my deadline. Honestly..." She took a deep breath and said the thing that she'd been avoiding since she ran out of her apartment. "I don't know how I'm supposed to write another love story after catching my boyfriend having sex with my roommate."

She watched as Ángel processed her words, translated, and understood.

"Calista," he said. His brow was furrowed. His beautiful mouth twisted into something like anger. He didn't even know her. How could he feel so angry for her when she just wanted to forget? She wanted to be in her snow globe. She wanted to have his soft silence and beautiful calm. She wanted him.

So, she leaned up and kissed him.

And he pulled away.

"I'm so sorry." She swallowed hard. Alarm ran through her. She got to her feet. "I shouldn't have done that."

"Calista," he said, trying to grab her hand, but let go when she shook her head.

"It's fine. I'm tired. Thank you for dinner. It was amazing."

With that, she ran upstairs, washed her face, and crawled into bed.

This time, exhaustion won, and not even the worst of the storm woke her.

CHAPTER 2

Six Days Till Nochebuena

ON THE SECOND day of being snowed in, Callie came downstairs in search of coffee and her box of cereal, and instead found Ángel dancing in the tiniest shorts she'd ever seen. He didn't notice her, but she leaned against the open frame and felt her grumpy morning pout unfurl into a smile.

The shorts in question barely covered his thighs. The tank top, because it could only be called a tank top, read *FLUSHING'S FURIA* and had a soccer ball set aflame. He was a '90s workout video, sauntering out of her teenage Mario Lopez wrestling fantasies. All he was missing was the headband.

She knew the song he mouthed along to. A classic from Los Enanitos Verdes that her cousin had put her on to. It was, as the kids said, a bop.

"Buenos días," she said, and couldn't help the chuckle that bubbled out.

He whirled around, holding the spatula like a mic. "¡Calista! ¿Te desperté?"

She chuckled and forced herself to look at anything. His knees—
no, not his knees. They were sexy knees. Who knew knees could be
anything but bony sockets that held your legs together?

"Oh, you didn't wake me," she assured him.

The good thing about their translation escapades was that neither
of them tried to address the ill-attempted kiss or how she'd revealed
more than she normally would.

"Nice shirt," she said. She was certain if he stretched, she'd be able
to see his nipples. Jean-Claude Van Damme wore bigger shirts in his
heyday.

Ángel lined a pan with bacon, and her stomach made an embarrassing sound. He flashed his irresistible grin. "Es de mi hermano.
Dejó una bolsa de ropa extra."

"Your brother's clothes?" She worried her inner lip.

"Es muy flaquito." He laughed.

"I can see that." She could see many things, and it had nothing to
do with Ángel's skinny brother. The sight of him was making the
wires of her mind fray and spark. This wasn't like her. She didn't run
away, and she didn't try to kiss strangers. Her previous breakups had
been mutual, cordial, and far less dramatic. Perhaps all her feelings—
Angelo, Ruby, Janie, the book, and now Ángel—were impacted, and
that's why her skin felt too tight. Like she was unsettled.

Or she was overthinking it, and she had to face that the random
chance of winding up with Ángel had left her uncertain. No, not
uncertain.

Horny.

Callie tried to remember the last time she'd had sex, five months
before. She and Angelo had taken advantage of the hotel during a
book festival in Las Vegas. And she hadn't even come.

She needed to snap out of it. Ángel wasn't there for her ogling. He
was smart and capable and strong and kind.

He opened the back door and revealed a makeshift refrigerator
where their perishables were stacked in the mountain of snow accu-
mulated on the deck. He grabbed four eggs, then shut the door and
reached for the salt on a high shelf. And there it was—his exposed

pectoral, the dark chocolate drop of his nipple hard in the slight chill of the kitchen.

Fuck. Now that she was aware, it was impossible to deny that yes, she had a desperate crush on Ángel. She organized a mental list of why it was a bad idea. First of all, he was stuck with her against his will. Second of all, she was an emotional train wreck. Third—she'd just dumped her boyfriend. Fourth, and most importantly, was that he'd recoiled from her the night before.

And sure, she had a book to edit. That was important too.

It was the dread of her deadline and her editor, more than anything, that brought her out of her reverie, and she accepted the mug of piping hot black coffee Ángel offered.

"You don't have to feed me," she told him.

"Claro que no. Pero quiero." His lashes were unfairly long.

She drank to quench her thirst but burned her tongue instead. Though having him admit that he *wanted* to feed her exacerbated a different thirst. She would kindly accept his meals, even if it confused her. She was a Jenga tower of emotions with too many blocks stacked on top. The slightest breath or tap could send her crashing, and she couldn't have that. She just had to make it to the new year. The eternal symbol of a fresh start.

Ángel set a sriracha-drizzled bowl of hash browns, runny eggs, and bacon right at her desk. She thanked him and he nodded, lingering like he wanted to tell her something. Instead, he turned on his feet and stalked to his side of the cabin. She blinked slowly at the way the nylon fabric of his shorts did little to hide the curvature of his ass.

She ate her breakfast bowl in unladylike bites, and she wasn't even self-conscious when she heard him laugh softly.

Slowly, they regained their delicate equilibrium. She pored over her pages and kept coming back to the question her editor had left: Why should we love this man?

And she wanted to answer, "Because that's how I wrote him! Because he's the *hero*. Because he overcame amnesia to crawl his way back to her!"

But she knew none of those were complete answers.

With her first book, she knew the answer. It was a novel about high school sweethearts separated by war, and when he returned, they were both changed. They made each other better.

Callie grunted her frustration and set the pages down. Her coffee mug was empty. She was getting up to refill it when she glanced at Ángel. The sight of him nearly knocked her senseless. He was sprawled on the couch with a blanket draped over his midsection. Strong legs propped up on an arm of the couch. His index finger twirled one of his unruly curls. The other hand held her book, *Eleven Eleven*.

Or *Once Once* in Spanish.

"What are you doing?" she asked, standing right in front of him.

He rested the open book against his chest. "*Leyendo.*"

She rolled her eyes. "I can see that you're reading. It's weird."

He smirked. "*Nunca he leído algo cuando la autora está frente a mí.*"

"Well, I don't make it a habit of watching people read my book. My *family* hasn't even read my book."

He arched his brows. He had the most perfect "shock" face. Like everything was surprising, everything had wonder. He had earned the "shock" lines across his forehead.

"*Entonces, hay una primera vez para todo.*" He resumed his reading.

There clearly *was* a first time for everything. The last few days proved that. When she returned to the living room with her fresh coffee, she made it a point not to look at him. He was a car crash, and she was a lonely driver on the BQE rubbernecking at him.

She almost made it.

But she was only human.

And she looked.

One look was all it took.

"Are you—crying?" she asked.

He sat up and quickly wiped at his eyes. "*No. Tengo alergia.*"

Something pleasant and warm spread through her. She brought her coffee to where he sat. He moved and made room for her.

"Chillón," she teased.

He barked a laugh because at least she knew how to call someone a crybaby. Then he schooled his face into something serious. But his eyes were puffy and a little red, scrutinizing her. He pointed at her desk, then at the book. "¿Así creas?"

It was strange to her that "creas," when conjugated in certain ways, meant *believe* and *create*. To Callie, writing was both. It was how she believed. It was how she created.

"There's usually less snow," she said. "When I wrote this book, I was thinking of a story my grandmother told me about her first boyfriend who never came back from war. I kept thinking about what would have happened if he *had* come back, and what if it took place during a war my generation knew, like Kuwait or Iraq instead of Peru."

He nodded, his eyes flicking toward her lips. She told herself it was because he was trying to understand her. Trying to read her lips. Her heart gave a hard thud with palpable want.

"¿Y el segundo libro?" he asked.

"That's the big question." She explained the problem she was having with her editor and did her best to describe the plot. A woman agreeing to a loveless marriage, then her boyfriend returns from the dead after a plane crash. Her editor didn't like either man.

"We love the hero because he came back from the dead. Not literally. He had amnesia."

Ángel tapped his chin. He said something she understood as "But what did he do to keep her?"

And she didn't have an answer. It didn't help that she felt like her emotions and her words were trapped in a bottle. She didn't want to feel hurt, and she didn't have her mother tongue. Now when she needed both, she had nothing.

Yet somehow, Ángel managed to evoke several feelings from her, *and* make up their own form of communication.

"Los dos suenan como hijueputas." He shrugged. "Perdón, pero no debería casarse con ninguno de ellos."

She stared at him. "They're not motherfuckers. They're just—"

Why was she defending a character that didn't exist? Because one was supposed to be her leading man. And, if she was honest with herself, because he was based on Angelo. Subconsciously, she'd written him the same way. The character just showed up and expected his presence to be enough. She'd met Angelo through friends, and they went on a nice date, and they repeated that for nearly three years. Along the way, her life changed. She got used to *nice* when she wanted more. But she'd never let herself ask for more. And he—he did something else entirely.

But what did he do to keep her?

She felt Ángel's words move in her mind, tugging on a feeling she'd had for a long time. Restless. Fine. Good, but not great. At some point she wasn't sure if she was thinking about her book or her ex.

But she knew. Deep down, Callie knew what was wrong with her novel.

"¿Calista? ¿Dije algo?"

"You're brilliant." Emotion filled her up. Anger and joy and frustration. She knew what she needed to do. It was the moment when lightning had struck in their woods. The moment when she'd realized they were snowed in. The moment all their candles had been ignited. It was the dawning.

She gathered the manuscript. It had every note, every line edit, every new word she'd agonized over the last several months. The entire thing was heavy in her hands as she carried it to the center of the cabin.

"¿Calista?"

She took the five steps to the fireplace, and she dropped the book in the flames.

"*Pucha,*" he said, which was more an onomatopoeia than a word. He ran his fingers through his hair and watched her with concern.

She took a deep breath. There was a backup in her email and her hard drive, but she needed to burn the words. She had to start over from the very beginning. Her heart kicked up at the thought of calling Janie and explaining. At the thought of disappointing her team. But that same freedom she'd felt when she'd burned her phone only intensified. She wasn't sure what she was going to do, but Callie knew she was on the right track.

She reached out for Ángel, and he took the hand she offered. She said, "Thank you."

He seemed to understand something intrinsic about her had shifted. It was the moment a bud begins to flower, or when a shaft of sunlight illuminates a dark room.

He kissed her knuckles. His lips were warm on her cool skin. She held her breath as he ran his fingers up her forearms. His hands were rough and calloused, but she didn't mind them. She liked how rough and solid he was. How unexpected.

This time, when he looked at her mouth, she knew he wasn't trying to read her lips.

This time, he kissed *her*.

As the pages for a year's worth of work curled and burned in the fire, she parted her lips to welcome him. His tongue searched for hers, and she answered. Kissing had always felt like such a strange act to Callie. It was putting your mouth on someone else's, yes. But it was opening yourself up for more. It was a soul-deep kind of hunger.

She was the first to break the kiss. He touched the furrow on her brow, and she understood *he* was confused at *her* confusion.

"I thought you didn't want me."

He threw his head back, scrunching his face because he didn't have the words. "Tomamos demasiado vino. No quería que te arrepintieras."

"Oh," she said. There *had* been a lot of wine. He didn't want her to have regrets.

She wouldn't have regretted it, though. She didn't regret it now.

Ángel kissed her again. He grabbed her waist and pulled her against his chest. She felt just how much he did want her.

"*Oh*," she whispered, breathless as he reached down and traced a finger along the thick erection bursting out of his skimpy little running shorts.

He chuckled at her surprise and guided her to the couch. He sat back and she climbed atop him, never parting their lips for more than a few seconds at a time. She clung to his neck. His calloused fingers explored under her shirt and drew a line along her spine, pressing on her lower back to seek the friction of their lower extremities, rubbing and rubbing.

She felt the first spark of her orgasm as he raised his hips and lined up his cock with the heat soaking through her sweatpants.

She hadn't come from dry humping since junior year of high school when she and her crush had played seven minutes in heaven in their swimsuits. But with Ángel touching her, kissing the sides of her neck, tugging her earlobes between his teeth, and rocking himself against her, she was buoyed by a feeling she hadn't felt in forever.

The spark.

The spark she wrote about but had forgotten to feel herself. The spark she'd longed for when she'd settled for *fine*.

As the feeling pooled in her belly, she fisted her fingers in his hair and kissed him like he was the only man she'd ever want to kiss from then on.

Sensation broke through her. He pressed soft kisses over her cheeks, her throat, as she came down from her climax.

She covered her smile behind her hands, embarrassed at the noises she'd made. "I'm sorry."

He hurried to appease her. "Nunca te disculpes por eso. Eres —divina."

He kissed her slow and long, like he was memorizing the way she felt and tasted. She toyed with the flimsy ties of his shorts and tugged on them. They both watched his cock spring between them.

He was perfect, with pale veins and a rosy wet tip. He watched her trace her finger along the head, under the ridge of his frenulum. He let out a string of curses and shut his eyes. She cursed, too, when she took hold of his base and could barely make her fingertips meet.

He swallowed, panting as he spoke. "Tengo que decirte algo."

She froze. What did he need to tell her? Her writer brain filled in dozens of horrible scenarios—STDs, married, secret baby daddy to ten children, tentacle appendage.

The seconds were never-ending.

Instead, he said, "No he hecho esto en cinco años."

She processed her language meat grinder and settled on "anos." *Anuses*. Five anuses. No, años. The little mustache over the n was *very* important. Años meant *years*.

Five years.

She kissed his cheek. His forehead. His throat. "We can stop."

Please, don't stop, she thought.

He shook his head frantically. "*No*. No sabes cuánto te deseo. Pero no estoy acostumbrado a traer protección."

"Protection!" He also said he desired her, which she hadn't forgotten. She was simply marinating in the feeling.

"Un momentito," she said.

She ran upstairs and opened her suitcase. She'd already missed two pills from her birth control and was not about to add *knocked up* to her list of things that could go wrong that year. For all the mistakes Past Calista had made, keeping a sleeve of condoms in her suitcase was not one of them.

Instead of rushing downstairs, she stripped off her sweatpants and threw them over the railing.

Ángel seemed to catch on to the idea as she peeled off her shirt. Before it hit the floor, he'd climbed the loft stairs and picked her up by her thighs.

She squealed at the sensation of falling on the mattress. She held the condom up and he seized it. His hands trembled and his hips gave a little thrust. Like he was already fucking the air in preparation to be inside her. His desperation made her want him more.

Callie watched him roll the condom down his shaft. He fisted the base. She couldn't remember the last time she'd had a penis that big, and she pressed her thighs together in anticipation.

He got on his knees and nuzzled his face between her legs, smoothing patient hands up and down her thighs until she opened for him. She felt his mouth on the mound of her pelvis, kissing his way down until he parted her labia with his tongue. Long strokes wound her up, hitching her breath until all she could think of was that she needed him. Needed him with an urgency that surprised her.

"Please," she whispered.

He gave her clit one final stroke before returning to her. She kissed him, wrapping her hands behind his neck. She liked holding him that way. Holding him close as he lined his cock up at her entrance and nudged in. Watching his lips part in pleasure as he inched inside her. She felt her inner walls squeeze, and gasped sharply at the sensation.

He stopped, lowering to take her breast into his mouth. Every one of his movements was passionate in how measured and deliciously slowly he took his time.

It was Callie who writhed against him impatiently. Running her nails down his back, tugging on his hair. She needed more of him. All of him.

"Please," she whimpered. "More."

He stared into her eyes and seized her lips with his own. He pulled out, then entered her again. This time a little harder. He did that again, and again until he was seated deep inside and the pleasure of it made her skin crackle with expectation. It had never felt that good before, that wet.

Ángel fucked her slowly at first. Exploring her. Caressing her breasts. Kissing the gasps from her mouth. She reveled in the feel of him. It was all too much, too good to be anything but her own imagination.

But when he whispered, "Mírame," she did as he asked. She opened her eyes and knew it was very real. His hand dropped to her throat, and she stayed his fingers. Showed him exactly how she liked the pressure there. How she wanted to keep kissing him as he held her with his calloused palms and fucked her hard and fast, so close she was sure they'd fuse into a single being if they were together any longer.

When he came, he rutted through his pleasure until her climax pooled deep in her belly and her inner walls contracted around his pulsing cock. He rested his forehead between her breasts and kissed her as she toyed with his hair.

She protested as Ángel left her to take care of the condom and get them water. And when he returned to her side, she protested as he patiently waited for her to hydrate. The naked sight of him, hard and leaning against the headboard, was incentive to drink every last drop.

Later that night, as she drifted, she sank into her post-sex high. This time, when she thought of Angelo, there was no haze of anger, no bitterness, no anything. She still had a lot to work through, but for now, she didn't want to be anywhere else. She wanted sweetness and warmth. She wanted Ángel.

CHAPTER 3

Five Days Till Nochebuena

THE FOLLOWING DAY, they created a rhythm that was entirely their own. He woke up with the sun and she groaned when he tried to leave the bed. He kissed her throat, a promise of what would follow later.

Callie eventually made her way down for coffee, food, and sex. In that order. They fucked in front of the fireplace, where she straddled him and relished the heat of both his touch and the flames. Every time he came, he held her so tight he left marks on her thighs, and later he kissed and massaged them.

Sex became their own language. One they both had to pay close attention to. He was so aware of whether her cries were of pleasure or pain. When the pain was good. When a nudge of her finger meant that he should slow down. She became aware of the tells of his face, when she took his cock in her mouth and licked him until the tiny furrow between his brows became so pronounced it meant he was going to come.

Callie didn't write. She didn't miss her phone, now a metal scrap among the coals. She told him the full story of her breakup, and he left abruptly to go to the downstairs bathroom. He returned with a bottle of pink nail polish he said his sister-in-law had left behind. He painted her toes, since she'd missed her mani-pedi, and told her of the dozen cousins he did the same for, and he missed them all. They were scattered all over the world on asylum and work visas.

She kept thinking about how they were all starting over, in big and small ways. That it was easier for some than other. That there wasn't a limit to starting over. Her first time had been when she'd immigrated to New York City as a little girl, even if she couldn't remember it. She *could* start over—a story, a life. Something that felt like the first tendrils of love.

CHAPTER 4

Four Days Till Nochebuena

ON THE FOURTH DAY, when the snow began to melt and the first patches of blue appeared in the sky, Ángel showed her the hot tub, heated by logs. Naked, they plunged into the cold of the deck and into the tub. He warmed her with his slow, hard kisses. He lit her up with the things he whispered in her ear and fucked her with his fingers. She came, her breath frosting between them and flurries kissing her cheeks.

CHAPTER 5

Three Days Till Nochebuena

ON THE FIFTH DAY, he dug out his truck from the snow. There was a knot in her stomach as she watched from the window. He hefted the fallen tree and tossed it to the side. Only a small crack marred the passenger side of the windshield. It was a Christmas miracle. He opened the hood of the truck and spent a few minutes surveying for possible damage. He turned around to give her a thumbs-up and smiled.

She should have been relieved that they had a ride out of their little snow globe world. Part of her wanted this, whatever this was, to last longer. Ángel's smile always gave her the same heady rush, and before she could think through it, she stripped off her sweater. Her flannel leggings. By the time she got to her bra, he did a double take and dropped the wrench in his fist.

Then he bounded inside, peeling off his hideous puffy coat and fucked her against the window, always, always holding her like she was precious and his. He was a dichotomy of soft and strong. Patient and urgent. And she wasn't sure if she was ready to let him go.

CHAPTER 6

Two Days Till Nochebuena

WHILE ÁNGEL MADE pasta and sang in his off-key but enthusiastic way, Callie sat at her desk. Her laptop's battery had died. It was cold from being near the window, and she couldn't find the charger anywhere. If she remembered that awful day correctly, she was pretty sure she'd lost it after she fell on the ice and her things fell everywhere.

Thinking of that cluster of moments, Callie only saw flashes. But what she found was that she wasn't heartbroken that Angelo and Ruby had found each other. She was hurt that they'd done it behind her back. Was love messy because people made it messy? Or was love simple and people were the messy ones?

With two days left on her retreat, she was certain that she wasn't going to meet her deadline. She'd rather write a book she'd be proud of. Even if she had to start from the beginning. Even if she had to face Janie, though she knew she'd have her back in her own cranky editor way. All she'd needed was a snowstorm and a breakdown to force her to take a rest.

Callie stowed her laptop in her suitcase, then cleared the clutter on her desk, not that Ángel allowed her to keep the seven mugs of half-finished coffee she was used to.

She found her favorite fountain pen, opened a notebook she always carried in case of emergencies. She'd never quite imagined the emergency would look like this—but for the first time in so long, Calista Calderón, bestselling author and debut darling with so much to prove, let go.

She wrote. And wrote. And wrote.

She wasn't sure the shape it would take, but she put one word in front of the other until she had a sentence, a paragraph, a page, a stack of pages. She wrote until her fingers cramped and were smudged with ink. Until she felt Ángel brush her hair away from her neck and press a kiss on the place that made her toes curl. A week ago, she might have made the excuse that she had to work. But she found it impossible to stay away from him, to say no when he was trying to take care of her.

She clung to the moments they had left.

CHAPTER 7

One Day Till Nochebuena

CALLIE CALDERÓN and Ángel Valenzuela stayed in bed. They had coffee and she made them two bowls of cereal. She let him steal her marshmallows because his kisses tasted all the sweeter.

CHAPTER 8

Nochebuena

THAT MORNING, Callie woke before him and packed. She made the coffee and she tidied up. She looked around the cabin and felt a strange tug against her bellybutton. She wasn't ready to leave, but she had to be her own bird mama kicking her baby bird self out of the nest.

She'd spent hours agonizing over the things she still wanted to tell Ángel. *I want to stay. I want us to stay. I want you.* In every language and every comfortable silence and in between.

But as they got in the truck and drove to the Amtrak station, she began to lose her nerve. A group of passengers hurried inside, and she lingered, clutching her tote bag and biting at the pink polish he'd painted on her nails.

He kissed her softly. There was that frown. That exhale. The frustration at not having the right words.

He didn't need them.

She grabbed his coat and pulled him harder against her. As they kissed, a taxi driver whistled, and she gave them a thumbs-up. Then she turned around and began her journey home. She dragged her carry-on to the platform and trembled despite the jacket he'd found in the closet for her.

She swallowed the emotion choking her, and not in the good way that she liked from him. This feeling stung. Burned. She ached in a way that was impossible. How could she feel so much for a man she'd known for a fistful of days? How could being away from him feel like something was breaking and tearing? She tried to rationalize the things everyone said—hormones and pheromones and yay science and a dick so good it made her senseless and brown eyes and a true smile.

Then there were the things she knew, as someone who believed in love. Created love stories. The only thing that mattered—everything they'd shared was real, and what she was still feeling was real. She didn't need to rationalize anything beyond that.

Callie Calderón cried the tears she hadn't let herself shed for a man who didn't deserve her. She simply couldn't get on that train.

When she ran back out to the lot, the taxis had scattered and only a couple of cars were left. None of them were a cherry-red truck. She had no phone, and the next train wasn't for hours. She plopped onto the concrete and covered her face with her cold fingers.

"Oye. ¿Estás perdida?"

She snapped up at the sound of his voice. He had barely put the truck in park before he tumbled out of the front seat and gathered her into his arms.

"Calista," he said, breathing hard and fast. "Don't go."

She shook her head. "I have to. But—"

He looked so vulnerable, so scared of what she was going to say.

"Pero...necesito ir a Nochebuena. ¿Ven con mi?" She knew she was conjugating something wrong, but she got the gist of it. She wanted him to go with her.

And she knew he understood her meaning the moment he smiled hard and kissed her harder, warming her with his calloused hands.

As he put away her suitcase again, he said, "Bueno, alguien tiene que asegurarse de que no comas puro Lucky Charms todos los días."

"Sorry, the Lucky Charms is part of the package." She hopped into the passenger seat, and he kissed her hand before peeling onto the street.

Callie and Ángel had many things to figure out. Language. Location. Jobs. Families. There were a million ways to make love work, a million types of love, each one as probable and rare as lightning during a blizzard. Theirs was love in Spanglish, love in touch, love in breakfast, love in coffee, love in snowstorms, love in Christmas.

Their love had its own language.

ALSO BY ZOEY CASTILE

THE HAPPY ENDINGS SERIES

Stripped

Hired

Flashed

ANTHOLOGIES

"Far Side of the World" from *Best Women's Erotica of the Year Vol. 6*

WRITING AS ZORAIDA CÓRDOVA

The Inheritance of Orquídea Divina

ABOUT THE AUTHOR

Zoey Castile was born in Ecuador and raised in Queens, New York. She started writing in her teens and pursued that love in her studies at Hunter College and the University of Montana. For nearly a decade, she worked as a bartender, hostess, and manager in New York City's glittering nightlife. She is the author of the Happy Endings series. When she's not writing, she is the co-host of the podcast Deadline City. For more of her fiction visit zoraidacordova.com. Sign up for Zoey's Newsletter!

twitter.com/zoeycastile
instagram.com/zoeycastile

TO US, YOU ARE PERFECT

ALEXIS DARIA & ADRIANA HERRERA

Newlyweds Pasquale and Yamilette's Christmas is just short of perfect. The missing piece is their best friend Marcelo, who has loved them from afar for years. This Nochebuena, they'll finally complete their happily ever after.

CHAPTER 1

Marcelo

ONE MONTH until Nochebuena

"THEY'RE PERFECT TOGETHER."

I cringe. It's the fifth time one of the guests has said that while we watch my best friend, Pasquale, and his new bride, Yamilette, do their first dance as a married couple. They *do* look perfect, though. They fit together just right.

Pasquale is in a bespoke tux of midnight blue velvet. His beard is perfectly groomed and his dark brown skin is flawless. The man's mouth is what should appear in the dictionary next to the word *luscious*. He's always been beautiful, but tonight, he's glowing.

Yami looks like a queen in his arms. As expected, she went for something nontraditional for her dress—a strapless chartreuse gown with a dip in the back that almost reaches that perfect ass of hers. It's got a long train that swishes around her as Pasquale moves them around the room. My heart lurches and my face heats as I take in all that golden brown skin.

They are the very image of "made for each other." One has only to look at them to see it's true. And I am the worst kind of bastard for wishing for things that I have no right to want. They've earned this moment. Those two have been through it together, and no one deserves their happily ever after like they do. But as I look at them, I can't help the feelings that bubble up.

You've been there for every trial they've faced. It was the three of you against the world.

I shut down that insidious thought and instead focus on capturing their moment with the Nikon DSLR slung around my neck.

"Hey, man." The hushed greeting yanks me out of my thoughts, and I turn to find one of my other college friends standing next to me.

"Hey, Yeison," I whisper, my eyes still on the couple on the dance floor.

"Where the fuck have you been, tiguere?"

Despite myself, I smile at the Dominican word that I've rarely heard over the past twelve months I've been in California. But Yeison's not done.

"I don't think I've seen you since last Thanksgiving."

I grimace and shrug in a "I know, crazy, right?" gesture, but keep my mouth shut.

"I couldn't believe it when Pasquale said you weren't coming to his stag party."

I resist the urge to shush him, because he isn't actually being loud —I just really don't want to talk about this. I continue to avoid looking at him, with my eyes trained on the viewfinder like a douchebag, because Yeison has known me long enough to know when I'm full of shit, and I'm about to lie my ass off.

"You know how it is, man," I mumble. "Just been busy with work."

I catch his frown in my peripheral vision and see that he's not buying it. Not that I blame him. Pasquale and I have been inseparable for over a decade. If you were a friend of Pasquale's, you knew me too, and if you spent more than ten minutes with me, you'd hear about my best friend Pas. So of course Yeison's surprised I wasn't at the party. Since college, Pas and I have *always* been there for each other. Like when his dad died unexpectedly, or when my sister got sick and I had to move back home to help her. Pasquale had done the hour drive up to Westchester every week to hang out with me even though he was working two jobs and going to grad school. He wasn't just a friend, he was my ride or die, my Day One, and I'd totally ghosted him because I was too much in my feelings.

"Now that I think about it, you weren't even at the Nochebuena party last year." Damn Yeison for being so observant. But he's right—I wasn't. Because that was when Pasquale was planning to propose to Yamilette, and I got the fuck out of Dodge before that. Except I can't exactly say, "Here's the thing, Yeison. I sort of slept with both the bride *and* the groom two days before he was going to propose, then freaked out and went to hide in California until, like, three days ago," now, can I?

"I left for LA before the party," I say, not wanting to get into the details.

"At least you made it to the wedding," Yeison muses as I chew on the inside of my cheek hard enough to draw blood.

The song they're dancing to is almost over. It's "All Night" from *Lemonade*, because even after we teased Yamilette about it, it's still her favorite. I tighten my mouth to kill the smile blossoming at the memory of a salty Yamilette flipping Pas and me off for dissing her Queen Bey and force myself to look at Yeison.

"You going to Gigi's this year, right?" Yeison never could leave well enough alone.

I shrug and hold the camera to my face again. "I might not be able to get back to New York this Christmas. Things are mad busy at work."

Which was technically true, but I don't actually have any shoots booked at the moment that would prevent me from being here for the Nochebuena party. Hell, there's a high-end studio that just opened an office in Manhattan that's been begging me to work for them. Like everything else in my life for the last year, I've avoided thinking about it.

"No te pierdas, mi hermano," Yeison says, finally abandoning the idea that we're gonna catch up. I give him a dap with my free hand, and he heads in the direction of the bar.

The song ends and both Yamilette and Pasquale turn to face the crowd of guests gathered around them. People clap and hoot, but Pas and Yami barely crack a grin. It seems like they're both looking for something, someone, in the crowd. I instinctually step back, but their eyes keep roaming over the clusters of bodies. I can see the tension in Pasquale, the set of his mouth that tells me something isn't right.

Me. I'm the thing that's not right. I came to this wedding and have acted like an asshole the entire time. I've barely exchanged ten words with my best friend or his wife. I want so badly to go to them. To let Pasquale take me into one of those strong embraces that, over the years, have been my safe harbor. To feel the scratch of Yamilette's nails on my skin. I want them both and they are not mine.

Yamilette freezes when she spots me, then whispers to Pasquale, and his head snaps in my direction. He smiles at me, and I die a little inside. Instead of raising my hand, I step further back into the crowd until I'm completely hidden from view. Heart racing, I scurry into an alcove like a damn coward and close my eyes. All I can see are their faces when they saw me. The flash of delight, then the disappointment when I walked away. I don't know what the hell is going on with me, but I need to get out of here before I ruin their fucking wedding with my bullshit.

Over the sound system, I hear Pasquale's gravelly voice, and my entire body tightens. I am a fucking mess.

"That last song was only the first half of our dance," he says, and I can practically see the wistful smile in his voice. I can't help myself—I sneak out of my hiding place so I can see him. They're up on the little stage on the dance floor and I have a perfect view of him. Tall and strong and gorgeous... and I really need to quit this "mooning over my married best friend *and* his wife" shit.

"This next one is the other part of our first dance. This song is important to both me and Yamilette for a very special reason. We wish—" He clicks his tongue, catching himself like he was about to say too much, then hands the microphone to his cousin, who's been serving as emcee for the reception. Yamilette shakes her head and gives him a sweet little kiss on the lips. The music starts and he takes her in his arms. As soon as the notes of a familiar beat float around the room, my heart starts pounding. I have to put the camera down and press my fist to my sternum, breathing through my mouth.

My throat closes as I hear the lyrics of the "Avant Toi" kompa remix, Pasquale's favorite version. The deep, sultry voice in the duet sings about how before they met their perfect person, they didn't have anything: no colors, no history, no heart. That he has found his life, his passion... finally. A feminine voice responds by saying that finding this love has rewritten her life, that she is ready to embark on their new path... and I can't take it. I hide again, leaning against the wall and squeezing my eyes shut, but it doesn't help. Instantly, the song takes me back to the last time I heard it.

"ARE you ever going to give me the recipe, or what?" Yamilette teased me as I wiped the counter. We'd just finished making pasteles in Yamilette and Pasquale's tiny kitchen in Brooklyn. Their place was nice, bigger than my Manhattan studio anyway, but there was still barely five feet of space between us. I looked up to where she was leaning back against Pasquale. He had his arms around her waist, his cheek resting on the top of her head, and I felt a pang at how perfect they looked together. To cover it up, I scoffed and made a joke.

"You know damn well that's my abuela's secret adobo mix. I have no idea what she puts in it. She just gives me a jar whenever I run out."

"I don't believe you," Yami said with a grin.

Pas gave her a squeeze. "It's true, baby. Abuela Tomasa likes me more than him, and even I don't know the secret recipe."

I flicked the washcloth at them. "See, back me up!"

Pas laughed at my clowning, then licked his lips. I made myself turn away before I started drooling or worse, putting way too much attention into hanging the kitchen towel on the little hook next to the fridge.

Since college, it had been our tradition to get together to cook pasteles for Christmas. First Pasquale and me, and then in our senior year, when he started dating Yamilette, our duo became a trio. Our little tradition was extra special this year, in a way. I knew that Pasquale was planning to ask Yami to marry him on Christmas Eve. Since he'd told me a few weeks before, I'd been oscillating between being really glad for him, to wondering how everything would change.

And then there were the messy, complicated feelings about them I barely let myself acknowledge.

I was in love with my best friend and fairly certain I felt the same way about his future wife. Like I said, messy. So messy I wasn't even sure it was a good idea to go on our annual New Year's trip to Pas's family cabin in Lake George. Like the pasteles, it was something the two of us began doing first, and then Yami joined. I looked forward to it all year. Just us, holed up in a snowy mountain getaway for five days. Even in the last couple of years, when my emotions were getting more and more muddled with the two of them, I loved our time in the Adirondacks. But now everything was going to be different. They'd be a married couple and would probably start hanging out with other married friends, and I'd finally have to admit that I'd been the third wheel for a very long time.

"Cel." Pas's sharp tone brought me out of my shitty thoughts. When I looked up, his dark eyes were full of concern. "You all right?"

"Just tired," I lied with the ease of someone who hasn't let himself think too much about his feelings for years. "Maybe I should head out."

Yami shook her head. "No way, you guys promised you'd teach me how to dance kompa tonight."

She'd insisted Pasquale and I teach her the Haitian dance together, even though everything I knew about it, I'd learned from Pas, who could've taught her anytime. But the thought of Yami being the queso frito in a Pasquale and Marcelo sandwich was something I wasn't strong enough to say no to.

She extended her arms to me. "Come here."

"We're still cleaning up," I protested, and Yami gave me an exasperated look.

"Marcelo, the kitchen is spotless. It's time to dance."

While Pasquale barked at Alexa to play his kompa playlist, I took a very deep swig of the Malbec we'd been drinking. Did I want to dance with them? Hell yeah. But there were also a thousand reasons why I shouldn't. And the biggest one was the ring hiding in Pasquale's sock drawer.

Still, as the first notes of the "Avant Toi" remix began, I closed the short distance between us. I fucking loved this song. Kompa was foreplay music. The rhythm forced you to move your hips into your dance partner. To tighten your arms around them. To stand face to face with barely a breath between your bodies.

And the three of us were about to do it together.

I put one arm around Yami and snagged Pasquale's side with the other. He had one arm on her waist and the other on my hip. If anyone were watching, we probably looked ridiculous, but the moment we started moving, it worked somehow. The low rumble of Pasquale's voice issuing instructions grounded us in the moment, kept us moving as one.

It was warm in the tiny kitchen, cramped with all three of us in it, and the music filled whatever space was left. I was trying to be, I don't know, respectful of Yami, but then she shot me a heated look.

"Muévete, Marcelo," she urged, circling her hips into me, and my dick got hard. If she felt it, she didn't say, but she didn't stop moving on me either. The beat of the music picked up, and Pasquale had stopped giving us directions some time ago. He was grinding into Yami while she and I rubbed on each other. The only light came from the Christmas tree and the stove hood. It was a mood in that fucking apartment. And I was on fire. It was fucking *hot*. Yami looked up at me and licked her lips while I basically fucked her with clothes on, and I had to bite my lip to keep from moaning.

Something about tonight was different. Every look, every touch felt like it was burning my skin. Suddenly she turned around to face Pasquale, and the way he was looking at me sucked the air out my lungs. His hand slid down to my ass. I groaned, so turned on my head was swimming, while Yami worked my dick with that thick ass of hers.

"Fuck," I moaned, and Pasquale took his hand off Yami and clapped it on the back of my neck. My heart thundered in my chest, and the way he was devouring me with those brown eyes made me dizzy and giddy all at once.

"Kiss him, baby," Yami urged my best friend, and I decided this had to be a dream. That was it, I'd fallen asleep watching whatever Hallmark movie she'd put on after the pasteles, because there was no way my wildest dream was coming true.

"Cel." Pasquale sounded winded, but then Yami was slipping out from between us, shifting behind me, her front pressed to my back while her man and I stood just shy of kissing.

"Are you sure about this?" I asked, as blood rushed between my temples. We'd kissed before, back in freshman year of college, hooking up a few times before we'd settled into the rhythm of being best friends instead of friends with benefits. But whatever was happening here was totally different, and I didn't know what to make of it.

"Yeah," he said, breathing the word out on a sigh.

"Yami?" I didn't even know what I was asking.

"We want you, Marcelo." Her hand snaked down to my crotch, stroking my dick through my jeans. It was a trip to have Pasquale's huge, rough hand on my neck, and Yami's smaller one on my dick. "Do you want us?"

Words failed. I could only nod.

Pasquale pulled me closer. "Can I kiss you?"

A strangled cry was my answer before I crashed my mouth onto his. Fuck, then his tongue pierced the seam of my lips, and he was inside fast, hot and hungry. There are things you dream about, want for so long that you tell yourself they can never be as good as you've imagined, but this... this was better than anything I could've imagined. Tangling my tongue with Pasquale's while Yami touched us both was a fucking dream. An overwhelming, brain-blitzing miracle.

"You are so hot together," Yami purred, still stroking me while I kissed her soon-to-be fiancé. And I was almost coming just from those sweet caresses and this life-changing kiss. Pasquale was a gentle giant, but he kissed like a fucking warrior—teeth scraping, his tongue lashing against mine, and that hand at my nape keeping me in place as he plowed my mouth. Yami made these sweet little mewling noises as she rubbed each of us, and I was seconds from blowing. Then Pasquale pulled away. I chased after him, not wanting to stop, but he just gave me this sexy-as-sin grin.

"So greedy." He nipped at my bottom lip. "Don't you want a taste, baby?"

Yami made a sound of approval like he'd just presented her with her favorite treat, and she slid into my arms once more. I eagerly lowered my head, and we were reveling in the feel of each other's mouths the next second. I sucked her tongue as Pasquale touched us both, his hands everywhere. It was perfect.

God, this is going to ruin me.

I don't fucking care.

We came up for air a moment later, and Pasquale tugged on my hand. "You want to take this to the bedroom, Papi?"

Fuck... did he just call me... ? *Don't question it.* "Yes, yes I do."

It was the best night of my life.

Being with them was like being burned down to blood and bone, to the purest essence of who I was, beyond my name, beyond boundaries. Just pure sensation, pure emotion. With them, I finally felt whole. At peace. Like I had found my home.

So I ran. I made love to the two people I cared for the most on this planet, then left their bed like a thief in the night.

It seemed like the right thing to do. I didn't want to ruin things. I didn't want to complicate their perfect relationship over some one-time, spur-of-the-moment thing. So I went to my apartment, packed a bag, and took the next flight to my place in LA.

It's a year later and I am still as fucked up as ever. I hoped the distance would make things easier, that I could come to the wedding and it would be just like old times.

It's not. I'm still just as in love with them as I was when I left.

As the song that changed everything comes to an end, I open my eyes to find Yamilette and Pasquale standing in front of me.

"We thought you'd left without saying goodbye," Yami says, and she looks so fucking unhappy. It's her wedding day and I'm making it about my sad, thirsty-ass feelings.

"Of course I didn't," I say, pointing to the camera. "I was recording your first dance." Pasquale makes a pained sound and steps closer to me. Yami is sandwiched between us, like she was when we danced. And later...

"We were looking for you for the second song," he says. "We wanted you there."

I bite my tongue, misery swirling inside me. "It's your night, P, and Yami's. I'm just a guest."

Pasquale shakes his head. "You are never a guest in my life, Marcelo."

The way he says it makes the hair on the back of my neck stand up. I know what that tone means. He is deathly serious.

"I know," I tell him. And I do. I know how he feels about me. It's just that it's not the same way I feel about him.

"Are you coming to Lake George?" Yami asks, and I blink in surprise.

"Aren't you guys doing your honeymoon?"

"We'll be back before then, and we want to spend time with you," Yami says stubbornly, but I can't do it. I can't be snowed in with these two as newlyweds. It'll destroy me.

I can't even look at Pasquale when I open my mouth to answer. "I don't know."

Pasquale is gazing at me in that broken way, like he's scared I'll run off if he pushes me. Yami's brows are creased in sadness, her eyes full of concern.

"Vamos a bailar!" Yami's mom shouts, saving my sorry ass by ushering everyone onto the dance floor. The chaos that ensues allows me to make my escape, and I return to my lonely apartment with their present—the recipe of my abuela's adobo mix, still folded in my pocket.

CHAPTER 2

Yamilette

NOCHEBUENA

SOMETHING ISN'T RIGHT, no matter how much I try to pretend it is.

I raise the half-formed pastel to my nose and take a deep sniff. Just to be sure, I pick up a bit of the pork filling and pop it into my mouth. As I chew slowly, my taste buds compare the flavor against years' worth of memories, confirming what I already know.

"This isn't right." I peel off my disposable gloves in disgust.

My husband Pasquale comes over to take a look, examining the parchment paper and banana leaves laid out before me. "It looks fine to me."

"Not the wrapping. The pasteles themselves. They suck."

His expression is patient, but there's pain in his eyes. Pain that has only gotten stronger over the past year. I'm sure he knows what I'm getting at, but it's like he doesn't want to speak the words aloud, like that will make the situation too real. But I'm tired of holding this in.

"We need him," I say, and as I predicted, Pas lets out a weary sigh.

"Yami," he begins, but I cut him off.

"Hear me out. Please." I take his hands, turning him to face me. "It's not the same without Marcelo. And you know it."

His eyes flicker at the name, and he looks down at our joined hands. At the matching wedding bands on our left ring fingers.

Two bands. Two people. But we were never just two, we were a trio. And we've been missing a piece of ourselves for a full year.

"I thought everything would go back to normal after he came to the wedding," Pasquale mumbles.

"I did too," I say softly. "But look at us. Making Marcelo's pasteles without him. Without his abuela's adobo."

"You're right," Pas agrees. "They don't taste right."

I look around our tiny kitchen. Every available inch of counter space, along with the top of the stove and the square dining table, is covered with our pasteles-making attempts.

Pasquale sighs again. "We're going to have to tell Gigi we can't bring them."

"Fuck that." I drop his hands and pull out my phone, opening the text app. "This has gone on long enough. I don't know what bug crawled up Cel's ass, but he's our friend. He can't keep ignoring us like this."

"Come on, Yami." Pasquale's voice is quiet. He stands in the kitchen with his shoulders slumped, arms hanging limp at his sides. His strong, beautiful features are etched with sadness.

"Come on what?" My tone is exasperated, but a ripple of unease tenses my stomach.

He raises an eyebrow. "You know why."

It's my turn to sigh. "I guess I do."

The last time we saw Marcelo was for this very event—our annual tradition of making pasteles together. Earlier that day, Pasquale and I had been cleaning the kitchen and talking about how much Marcelo meant to us. And I... well, I'd told Pasquale that I wanted to try something. I knew he and Marcelo had hooked up a few times back in college, well before I came into the picture. It didn't bother me that my husband and his best friend had been together—quite the opposite, in fact. I'd been intrigued, and the image of them kissing, touching, and more had stayed with me, lingering in my thoughts.

Until one year ago, when I'd told Pasquale I wanted to know what it was like to kiss Marcelo. What it was like to see the two of them kissing each other.

Maybe that wasn't a typical thing for a girlfriend to say to her boyfriend, but it felt right to me, and the beauty of my relationship with Pas was that I could say anything to him, tell him anything I wanted, and he'd listen.

As soon as I'd suggested this, something in Pas changed. He seemed excited. He assured me he was on board, and he thought Marcelo would be down for it too.

So after the pasteles were fully wrapped and packed, after the kitchen was clean, I'd made my move. We started with a dance lesson to see what would happen, to see how Marcelo responded. And the chemistry between the three of us flared hotter and brighter than I could have ever imagined.

It was amazing. And I hadn't regretted a second of it. Not that night, and not the next day, even though Marcelo had disappeared from our bed while we slept.

No, the regret came later. After Marcelo never showed up at the annual Nochebuena party last year, after he ignored our calls and only replied to texts with a belated, "Sorry, busy."

Pasquale proposed to me and I said yes. We planned a simple wedding and of course invited Marcelo, even though we hardly heard from him for months.

But he came to the wedding. And I hadn't realized until then that his appearance was what I'd been waiting for. Maybe he was just really busy with photography gigs. He was traveling a lot, he at least told us that much. And yeah, we missed him, but we were busy, too, with work and wedding planning.

In my heart, I'd told myself that if Marcelo came to the wedding, it meant things were fine with us. That my curiosity, my need to have more than any one person could ever deserve, hadn't ruined things between my husband and his best friend.

But Cel seemed off at the wedding, and since then, we hadn't heard a single word from him. No texts, no emails, no calls. And now, even though we texted him all the details for today, he's not here making pasteles with us.

Pasquale has never once complained, never made me feel like I'm not enough companionship. But I know he misses Marcelo. And shit, I miss him too. After I met Pasquale, I knew I wanted forever with him. But I'd pictured Marcelo there too. The three of us. A team. We're incomplete without him.

Pasquale turns away to tackle some of the dishes in the sink, and I stare at my phone. At the long line of unanswered texts I've sent Marcelo over the past month. Switching to the photo album, I scroll through some of the pictures our friends uploaded from the wedding. When I find the one I'm looking for, I bring it over to my husband. It caught my eye the other day, and I haven't been able to stop thinking about it. Pasquale pauses with a bowl in his hands and looks down at me from his greater height.

"This," I say, holding up the phone. "Do you see this? The way he's looking at you?"

The picture was taken at the wedding by our friend Gigi. We're supposed to be bringing these shitty pasteles to her Christmas Eve party tonight.

In the photo, Pasquale has his arm around me, and we're chatting with a group of our friends from college. Marcelo is off to the side, at the edge of the frame. This must have been taken before Gigi urged us all to stand closer and do a silly pose. Marcelo's gaze is on Pas, and it's clear he doesn't know Gigi is taking the picture. If he had, there's no way he would have revealed such... wistfulness. Longing. *Desire*. It's all there, plain as day.

Or maybe I recognize it because I've seen that look before. I've seen him look at Pas that way in the past. Maybe I mistook it for fondness, for friendship, or on that one night, attraction. But seeing Cel captured like this, completely unguarded in a public setting, broke my heart. Part of me wished Gigi hadn't sent the photo because it hurt to see it. But it's also the missing puzzle piece, the thing that shows me without a doubt why Marcelo has avoided us for a year.

It's my fault.

Pasquale's brown eyes flick over the image on the screen. His expression softens, but a second later, his mouth firms and he shuts his eyes.

"I see it," he says, sounding almost resigned, like he doesn't want to admit it.

"He's in love with you," I blurt out. "And I ruined it. I ruined *us*."

My voice breaks, and Pasquale quickly shuts off the water in the sink. He grips my shoulders gently, his hands still wet, and peers directly into my eyes.

"No, baby. You didn't ruin anything."

"I did." Tears gather in the corners of my eyes. "If I hadn't brought up that stupid idea about wanting to see you two together, about knowing what it was like to be with him too—"

Pasquale kisses my forehead. "It wasn't stupid. It was genuine. And I always want you to feel comfortable asking for what you want."

"But he's in love with you, Pas. I should've seen it sooner. The way he looks at you..."

"Baby."

I sniffle. "What?"

"He looks at you the same way."

"He... what?" I peer at the picture again. And it's true, I saw something similar on Marcelo's face when he was inside me, and at the time I thought... I hoped...

I shake my head. "If I'd know the three of us being together would have meant losing him, I wouldn't have suggested it."

"But you wanted it. I wanted it. He wanted it. And it was amazing."

I rub my hands over my face. "I know. It was stunning and beautiful and revelatory. And it felt..."

"What, Yami? How did it feel?"

"Right," I say, dropping my hands. "It felt right."

He takes me in his arms. "It felt right to me too. I wasn't sure if you just wanted it to be a one-night thing, or what."

"We should've talked about this a lot sooner. I just thought Marcelo would be around and we'd discuss it together. But he disappeared. And I didn't know what you wanted."

He blows out a breath. "I don't think I knew either. Not then, anyway. Not until he was gone. And then... I guess I was so hurt that I didn't want to talk about it."

"I just kept hoping he'd come back, that his busyness wasn't related to us. So I didn't want to talk about it either."

"We've basically been the miscommunication cliché for the past year."

That pulls a little laugh from me, but I sober quickly. "This still doesn't explain why he's hiding from us. If he can look at us like that, if this is an indication of how he feels, then why is he being like this?"

Pasquale's tone is hesitant. "Cel is... weird... about relationships. We had some friends who brought a third person into their marriage, and it imploded."

"But we don't have to be like that," I insist. "Why would he think that?"

"Forget what I feel, and what Marcelo feels," Pas says urgently. "What do *you* feel, Yami?"

"I love you," I say firmly, because that was never in doubt. "But... I miss Marcelo. We felt, I don't know, more complete when it was the three of us."

"And what about that night?" The look in his eyes is intense and unreadable. I don't know if talking about this is going to ruin everything or make us stronger. I pray it's the latter.

"What about it?" I whisper.

"Would you do it again?"

I suck in a breath, let it out quickly. "Yeah. Is that okay? Is it okay to want both of you?"

He kisses my forehead. "More than okay. I want you both too."

In another relationship, for other people, these confessions might be strange, but for me, they make everything click into place. I want

Pasquale and Marcelo. Pasquale wants Marcelo and me. We just have to let Marcelo know how we feel, and then...

"Do you love him?" Pasquale asks, and when I search his eyes, I see the steadiness and strength that drew me to him from the moment we met. I love this man so fucking much, and there is enough room in this relationship for me to love his best friend too.

To love him the way I know Pasquale does.

"Of course I do," I say softly. "Don't you?"

He nods. "I love both of you with everything I have," he says simply.

The ring of truth in his words floods me with energy, and I suddenly can't take a second longer of being separated from our missing piece.

"What the hell are we waiting for?" I pull out my phone and dash off a quick text. "This has gone on long enough. We need to get him back."

Pas shrugs. "We don't even know where he is."

"Leave that to me. First things first, we gotta break the news to Gigi about these pasteles."

Yami: *Sorry, we're not gonna be able to bring the pasteles. They suck.*

Gigi: *What! Why? What's going on?*

Yami: *We don't have Marcelo's secret adobo. The pasteles don't taste right.*

Gigi: *Tell him to get his butt over there with the adobo!*

Yami: *He's not answering our texts. I guess he's still out of town.*

Gigi: *Nah girl, my uncle saw him at the barber shop this morning. He's home!*

When I read her text, some feeling I can't name floods my body. Or maybe it's a mix of feelings—relief, anticipation, longing, and...

Love.

I shove my phone in my pocket. "Gigi says he's home."

Pasquale's brow creases. "We told him we were doing this today, and he didn't show."

"That's why we're going to go get him. We can figure out the logistics later. I just know the three of us are meant to be together. But first, we have to hit up the 99 cent store."

Pas chuckles and drops a kiss on my forehead. "All right, baby. I know better than to question your plans."

His faith in me melts my heart, especially since it was my brilliant idea that fucked things up with Marcelo in the first place.

It's okay, though. I have a plan to fix it. Since Marcelo wants to be in this all-or-nothing space with us, we just have to show him that *all* is on the table.

And hope like hell he accepts what we're offering.

CHAPTER 3

Pasquale

"BABY, TRAFFIC IS A NIGHTMARE RIGHT NOW," I tell Yami as she comes out of the neighborhood dollar store. I do a double take when I see her arms are full of rolled-up poster board—the kind you use for school projects—in various shades of neon. "What did you do, buy every single one they had in stock?"

"Yes, actually, I did," she says with a sniff. "I have a whole speech planned. Did you already schedule a car, or do I have time to hit up another store?"

I shake my head and show her the rideshare app on my phone. "Nah, there isn't anything for less than a hundred bucks."

"What the hell?"

I shrug. "It's Nochebuena."

Yami glares at the subway station entrance across the street, but she shoves the neon boards into my hands and squares her shoulders. "We're taking the subway."

I have to bite my lip because she looks mad as hell about it. My wife does not fuck with the subway.

"Wait until I tell Cel you willingly dealt with the MTA on a holiday for him," I say, transferring all the poster board to one arm so I can pull her in for a quick kiss. "We're really doing this?"

"I didn't just buy forty dollars' worth of arts and crafts supplies for nothing, Pasquale. This is our grand gesture!"

The subway is packed, but Yami manages to squeeze into a seat. She spends the whole ride carefully writing out her "speech" in block letters, much to the amusement of the other passengers. The doña to her right goes from nudging her aside to helping her hold the poster board flat. By the time we get off at Second Avenue, the other riders are cheering us on and wishing us a merry Christmas.

I'm glad she has something to occupy her thoughts because I'm a nervous wreck inside. I have no idea if this will work, if Marcelo will even be there, if he'll even let us in. Our friendship has always been easy, something I could always count on. The uncertainty is fucking me up, but I don't want Yami to see. She's so sure this will work, I don't want my doubts to bring her down.

We're literally spelling it out for him on bright-ass poster board. If this doesn't work...

I shake my head. It *has* to.

We arrive at Marcelo's Avenue B apartment building as someone is on the way out, their arms full of wrapped presents. We hold the door for them, then slip into the lobby without buzzing up. My heart is beating out of my chest, and when I grab Yami's hand, it's like ice.

"You okay, baby?" I ask her, and for a moment, she looks unsure. I've known this woman for ten years and have never seen her second-guess herself once she's made up her mind.

"Do you think he'll let us in?" I don't know if she's asking about his apartment or his heart, but I nod and reach for the stack of poster boards in her hands.

"He's ours, babe." I gently pluck at the signs, but she doesn't let go. She's nervous, afraid he'll reject us. Afraid that she'll ruin my friendship with Marcelo. But I know these two people were made for me, and I'm not giving Marcelo up without a fight. "You know how I think about you and Cel?" I ask her, real low in the quiet of the lobby. She just shakes her head.

"Mi luna y mi sol," I tell her, and her eyes get a little shiny. "You are everything to me, and so is he." I tug on the signs, and this time, she lets go and comes in close for a kiss. I taste her, sweet and slow, needing this to ground myself, to give me strength.

"We got this," I mutter against her mouth, and she nods, eyes closed. She must believe what I tell her. "He won't come to us, so we are here for him. To bring him home."

When she pulls back, the fire in her eyes has returned, and she's smiling.

"Let's do this." She turns around and I heave a sigh as we head to the staircase. Because leave it to Marcelo to be a photographer to every A-lister in Hollywood and still live in a fourth-floor walk-up. By the time we reach the fourth floor, Yami is cursing under her breath and I'm thanking the gym gods that I haven't been skipping leg day. This must be why Cel's thighs are like granite.

The thought dredges up old memories and I ruthlessly tamp them down again. If this goes well, I'll let myself relive that one glorious night as many times as I want. But if it doesn't? If he still sends us away? Then I'm better off keeping those memories locked down tighter than Abuela Tomasa's adobo recipe.

But this is part of what got us into this mess: my own reluctance to think about or discuss the things that hurt. And for the past year, Marcelo, my best friend in the entire universe, has been one of those things. Trying not to think about him has been almost unbearable. The only reason I could get through it has been Yami. And I know Marcelo's hurting too, but he's always been like this. So damn stubborn, always believing he is expendable. I suspected he'd get skittish after the night we all finally got together, and I was prepared to have a heart-to-heart the next morning. Except I never got a chance. He ran out on us. But I am not letting one more day go by without that man knowing he owns half my heart.

We're huffing and puffing by the time we reach his door, and I can see Yami's shoulders tense.

"No wreath or anything," she whispers, gesturing like this is Exhibit A that Marcelo desperately needs us back.

"You want me to ring the bell?" I sound calmer than I feel. She nods, her eyes fixed on the signs in my hand. There are a few other Latinx families on his floor, and I can hear the chatter and music that usually accompanies Nochebuena preparations. I take in a breath as I lift my finger and press the doorbell, sending up a quick wish to have both my loves by my side this year.

"Get ready," Yami instructs, and comes to stand next to me. She looks so damn cute in her green, red, and white hat. We hear footsteps and we both stand straighter as the locks click. Then, after a breathless moment, they stop.

"He probably saw it was us," Yami says, and I nod. But I'm not going to holler at Marcelo to let us in. We've come all this way. It's on him to open the door for us.

I can almost feel the hesitation coming through the door. Marcelo does not like confrontation and he is a fucking expert at hiding and licking his wounds. But I also know that he's brave and he loves hard. I know that he wants what we are here to offer him. I *know* he does. But he has to take the final step.

I reach for Yami's hand and hold it tightly in mine, and right then, the door finally opens.

Seeing him again hits me like a punch. He's tall and lean, built from hours of swimming and running, and wrapped up in fitted jeans and a sweater. His face is tan with a square jaw, softened by a dimple that used to flash relentlessly but is now nowhere in sight. His dark, wavy hair is shorter than usual, and I remember Yami said Gigi's uncle spotted him at the barber this morning. There's a wariness in his beautiful eyes that was never there before, and it kills me a little to see it.

I hope we can clear it away.

I'm holding the cards in order with the first one flipped around so Marcelo can't read it. Yamilette and I talked about how we'd do this on the walk from the train, but now that we're here, I can't help but feel a little silly, standing in the hallway holding a giant stack of poster board.

No, not silly. *Vulnerable.* Scared. I'm holding my heart in my hands in the form of a pile of cardboard, hoping this man will accept it. And not just my heart, but Yami's too.

If he rejects us now, it won't break us, but it'll be like a piece of us is missing for the rest of our lives. A loss like death, one that lessens over time but never fully goes away.

That's how the past year has felt, dealing with Marcelo's avoidance and absence.

That kindles a spark of anger in me, of betrayal. I'm sure some misguided part of him thought he was doing us a favor by staying away, but why the hell was he the only one who got to make that choice? We're a team, damn it, and he shouldn't have made that decision for us.

Yamilette's dark eyes search mine, and I can almost hear her asking me, *Are you sure about this?* And I'm suddenly surer than I've been about anything else in my whole life. Except for the decision to propose to her. This feels on par with that. This is a declaration. A statement. A plea. As Yami said, it's our grand gesture.

Love us. Let us love you. Please.

I nod, and she flips the first poster board over, revealing the beginning of our missive.

DON'T SAY ANYTHING...

His brows drawn together, Marcelo's eyes flick over the words. He gives us both a confused look, but the corner of his mouth quirks a little, and he nods. I imagine he's got some joke bubbling up behind those perfect lips, but he holds it back, obeying the message.

Yami takes the first board from me, revealing the next one.

BECAUSE YOUR NEIGHBORS ARE MAD NOSY.

Marcelo leans forward, squinting as reads. Probably because "mad nosy" is squashed in the bottom right corner of the board. Then he makes a choked sound in the back of his throat, like he's suppressing a laugh.

Yami sends me a sidelong look and mutters, "I told you I needed more poster board."

I speak through my teeth. "And I told you we could do it on the iPad."

Her lips purse in annoyance, but she grabs the card, showing the third.

LAST YEAR WE MADE HOT AND SPICY...

Marcelo's eyebrows shoot up, and Yami yanks the card aside.

PASTELES.

Cel's shoulders shake a little with an internal laugh, and he smiles, but his eyes are wistful. Yami reveals the next card.

AND THIS YEAR WE MADE...

She pulls that one aside quickly.

NOTHING.

There's clear sadness etched on Marcelo's gorgeous face, and that tall, toned body of his is slumped against the side of the door frame. But Yami isn't done. The next card is the kicker.

BECAUSE WE DIDN'T HAVE YOU.

Cel's nostrils flare as he sucks in a breath. I can see his hard chest rise with the inhalation. We hesitate, Yami and I, waiting for his reaction. For a second, I think there won't be one. Or worse, that he'll just slam the door in our faces. But then he releases the breath he's been holding, and it's like the weight of the world has been lifted from his shoulders. His face creases in a smile—a small one, a tired one, but it's a smile nonetheless. And then his eyes shift from the words to my face. Our gazes lock, and a thousand words pass between us in an instant, and then he looks at Yamilette, and it's like I can see the same connection shared between them.

We've all been so fucking stupid, acting like there was only one way to be together. It's all so achingly clear now. And Yami's next words will let him know the truth.

As if she can hear my thoughts, she takes the card and slowly pulls it aside.

YOU'RE THE ONLY ONE WHO CAN MAKE PASQUALE LOL...

His mouth cracks into a grin because he knows it's true.

AND GET YAMI TO ADMIT SHE'S WRONG.

Yami makes a show of rolling her eyes, which makes Marcelo's smile broaden. And damn, it's so fucking good to see him smile again. It's been so long.

Yamilette flips through the next three quickly, barely giving Marcelo a chance to respond. But I watch his face as she pulls aside each card, my throat tightening at the naked emotion I see there. These are all things I thought he knew, but I'm realizing you can't take anyone you love for granted. You have to tell them how you feel, and why.

That's what we're here to do.

YOU'RE OUR CONFIDANTE...

OUR SUPPORT...

OUR MISSING PIECE.

Yamilette shoots Marcelo a look, and I know she's nervous about this next one. Truthfully, so am I. We're laying it all on the line here.

TO US, YOU ARE PERFECT.

Marcelo is crying now, tears streaming silently down his face. He holds a fist to his mouth as he reads the words. My own eyes are feeling a little misty, and Yamilette looks distraught, but she grabs the top card to reveal the next.

OUR HAPPILY EVER AFTER ISN'T COMPLETE WITHOUT
YOU...

Yami pauses, letting this one sink in. It has taken us a year to realize it, but as much as we both love each other, we need Marcelo. For ten years, he's been part of us. *Us*, as a unit, and us, as individuals. We work together as a couple, but we work even better as a trio.

I hate that it took us so long to figure it out.

Slowly, Yami takes the card.

AND NEITHER ARE OUR PASTELES.

That shocks a laugh out of him, and he shakes his head, wiping his eyes. Yami takes the pasteles card and makes a point of clearing her throat when the next is uncovered.

AND IN CASE IT WASN'T CLEAR...

We're both staring at him now.

WE LOVE YOU, MARCELO.

The three of us pause, frozen in the hallway in some kind of weird rom-com tableau, the declaration hanging between us. My heart stutters in my chest and I don't have to look at Yami to know she's holding her breath. We both watch Marcelo, waiting, waiting...

He lets out a choked sob and nods.

With a flourish, Yamilette reveals the final message, written in huge letters, the lines thick from the number of times Yami went over them to make them stand out. There's so much ink on the board, the scent of the marker stings my nose.

NOW LET US IN!

Marcelo lets out a long, long sigh. His eyes are still wet as he takes us in. Then he nods at the cards. "Can I talk now?"

Yami jumps, as if startled by the sound of his voice. "Oh. Yes, that was the last one."

Cel's mouth quirks. "Is this like that movie—"

I shake my head and give him a warning glance to cut him off. This was a big topic on the subway ride here, and I know if Yami hears the movie title one more time, her head is going to explode.

"¿Puedo entrar, Marcelo?" I say, and something about the tremor in my voice makes the smile on his face disappear.

He flinches at the question. It's been a long time since I've asked permission to walk into Marcelo's home. I was with him the day he signed the lease to this apartment. He opens the door the rest of the way, his gaze flicking between Yami and me. It's fucking painful that we can't talk to each other anymore. It hurts to look at him.

"Okay." He moves to the side and waves us in.

Yami shakes her head and takes the boards from me. "No, you two need to talk first. I'll wait here."

Her face is pinched with worry. But there's also fiery determination in her brown eyes. "Don't take too long though, if your neighbors see me out here with these cards, they're going to be all over me."

That pulls a reluctant smile from Cel. I walk into the apartment, and I can't help looking for the pictures of us hanging on his walls.

They're all there. The two of us with his family in Rio, with my mom and dad in Las Terrenas in the DR. With Yami in Lake George, and the three of us in New Zealand that time he flew us in while he was shooting for a magazine there. We're on a beach and Yami's standing between us, tucked under my arm, with her arm slung around Marcelo's waist. We look so happy there. So right.

"I'm sorry." He says it so quietly, I wonder if I've imagined it. I can feel him behind me, and I'm scared that he won't want this. That I'll lose him.

"I've missed you," I tell him, and I hear a pained sigh from behind me. "*We've* missed you." I shake my head, trying to bite down all the questions I've asked him in my head for the past year. "I thought you were going to skip my wedding, Cel."

There's a shuffle of feet and I feel the heat of his body on my back, not touching me, but close.

"I didn't want to get between the two of you." His voice is heavy with sorrow.

I turn around, because I have to look him in the face when I tell him this.

"You could never do that, Cel. We both love you. We both want you. If this year has made anything clear, it's that we are lost without you. It has to be all three of us. The two of you are the loves of my life, and it's not a happy ending without both of you."

There's pain in his eyes. He doesn't fully believe us yet. "You and Yamilette have a good thing going. I don't want to ruin that just because I caught feelings I had no business having."

"We had a good thing going when it was the three of us doing everything together. The past year, it's felt like something is missing. Not just for me, for Yami too. And the missing piece... it's you, Marcelo. It's you."

He hangs his head. "I'm just going to fuck it up. This stuff never works."

"Why? Because Juan and Macia's open relationship didn't work?" I wave my hand in a dismissive gesture. "They're a mess regardless of the scenario. And this is not *open*. It's only the three of us. Together."

I can see that sinking in, the kindling of hope in the dark depths of his eyes. "And Yami's okay with this?"

I let out a snort. "Dude, it was her idea to come over here."

At that, the door opens, and Yami sticks her head in, making it clear she's been listening.

"Can I come in now so you can tell me how incredibly romantic and perfect this grand gesture was?"

Marcelo gazes at her with open love in his eyes, and I wonder how he ever hid it, how I never saw it before. He nods and she comes over to join us, ditching the pile of poster board on Marcelo's trendy glass coffee table.

"Do you believe us?" I ask, because this is the key point. If he's still unconvinced...

After a long moment, he lets out a breath. "I do," he says, and then his voice gets stronger, laced with laughter. "Fuck, I do. And I don't know if it's because this is all I've wanted, or because you two are just too damn irresistible, but I fucking do."

I grab him in a tight hug, and there's a tremble in my chest. I have Marcelo back. My best friend, my love.

"Maybe it's both," Yamilette says softly, coming up beside us. "Maybe you *can* have what you want, and maybe we're *also* irresistible."

Cel laughs and pulls her into the embrace with us, and for the first time in a year, everything feels right with my world.

Then Yami, bless her, turns her pretty little face up to Cel and asks in a voice gone husky, "Can we kiss you now?" And that "we"... Fuck, I feel it in the marrow of my bones.

Cel's eyes search her face, then mine. There's heat there, but also wonder, like he can't believe how fucking lucky he is.

Or maybe that's me, and I'm just seeing it reflected in him. Either way, he nods.

"Yeah, baby," he says, lowering his head to her. "You can kiss me now."

The second their lips touch, I'm hard. There's something so fucking hot about watching them lap at each other's mouths, especially knowing what they both taste like. My wife and my best friend. The loves of my life. I'm holding them both in my arms while their tongues tangle together, and this is all I need in the whole fucking world.

I can't help the moan that slips out when Marcelo nips Yami's lower lip with his teeth, and then they're both turning to me, lips slick with each other, and Marcelo is kissing me hard while Yami urges us on. His tongue is in my mouth, her hand is slipping down my pants, and I'm about to lose myself to the moment when there's a buzzing sound and Yami gasps.

We break the kiss to look at her, and she's staring at her phone.

"What's wrong, baby?" Marcelo and I ask in unison, and she turns her stricken expression our way.

"It's Gigi," she says, grimacing. "She's asking when we're showing up with the pasteles. She's going to kill us if we show up empty-handed!"

"But we threw them out," I say.

Marcelo rubs the back of his neck. "About that..."

We both turn to him with hopeful gazes.

"I actually made a whole batch."

I stare at him in surprise. "You did?"

"Yeah, I was going to bring them to your apartment. But then I started to worry that you only want me for my secret sazón..." His grin shows that he's joking.

"Silly, *you* are our secret sazón." Yami pulls him down for another kiss.

I squeeze them both. "No more secrets between us."

Marcelo raises his head, and his tone is solemn. "None."

I give him a smacking kiss on the cheek to lighten the mood. "Then you better give us that recipe."

He laughs and pulls a folded paper out of his pocket, which Yami pounces on. "This was supposed to be your wedding gift," he says.

"You're the best gift of all." I kiss him again, and Yami's arms wrap around both of us, holding us tight. Before it can get too hot, we pull apart.

"Lake George?" I ask, and Cel nods. Then we all grin like Cheshire cats, knowing we'll have all the days between Christmas and New Year's to spend together, making up for lost time.

Yami's phone buzzes again with a text from Gigi, and we begin the mad dash to pack up the food and leave for the party. Somehow, on the way there, I end up holding hands with both of them, which is when it hits me: *this* is my family. No matter what happens, I will fight for us. For the three of us. Together.

And for the first time in a long time, I feel perfectly complete.

THE GREAT HOLIDAY ESCAPE

ZOEY CASTILE

Gigi is always hustling to make sure her little sister has everything she needs, including a big Christmas Eve fiesta with all their friends and family. When her loved ones surprise her with a luxe getaway, she meets not one, but two beautiful strangers who fulfill all her wildest fantasies. But as the vacation wraps up, Gigi can't bear the thought of leaving her heart behind in South Beach.

CHAPTER 1

THREE DAYS BEFORE NOCHEBUENA

GIGI BAEZ LIVED by two creeds: *hustle hard* and *love harder*. At twenty-seven she had a full-time job, two or three side hustles, and was currently getting her little sister ready for college. So, when her family and friends had bought her an all-expenses paid vacation to South Beach a few days before Nochebuena, she felt too guilty to do anything but spend the morning before her flight working.

She sometimes slept in the unused greenrooms of the Madison Square Garden after long shifts running light tech for concerts. The pay was mediocre, but she gobbled up the energy from the crowds. Vibed from the musicians belting their little hearts out. Plus, she could put Lily on her health insurance. That mess was *expensive*, and so was college.

Gigi was just in the middle of a dream in which Maluma noticed her backstage, and serenaded her just before kissing her up against—

She grumbled awake at the caterwauling of her alarm and rubbed the exhaustion from her eyes. *Technically*, napping at work, even if she wasn't on the clock, was frowned upon. But it saved time on her commute. One glance at her phone confirmed it was the ass crack of dawn, or four thirty in the morning, and she was already a few minutes behind. She tossed the disposable orange earbuds into the trash, washed up in the bathroom, and yawned her way into the cold Manhattan morning.

Last night's concert still had her teeth vibrating as she trudged past the yellow cabs dropping off passengers to the Long Island Railroad. The city was covered in muddy slush, and fresh flurries transformed the streets into one of those holiday postcards her mom had liked to collect. Gigi popped into a deli for a piping hot café con leche, extra sugar, and a bacon egg and cheese on a roll.

"Thanks, Gus!" she shouted to the large Greek man setting up for the day. She ate the sandwich in three giant bites.

He chuckled. "Chew your food, you're going to choke on your bacon."

She grinned sheepishly. "I got a couple of gigs before I can go home."

"You work too hard, kid." Gus clucked his tongue. "You're a beautiful girl. You gotta enjoy yourself while you still can. Otherwise, you'll be like me, too tired to have a life."

Gigi had heard that a million times. Friends, family, coworkers, and even her favorite deli guy always reminded her that she was a catch. She *knew* she was a catch. She just didn't think she was quite ready to be caught.

"I *do* enjoy myself!" she said. "And I'll sleep when I'm dead."

Every single job she got outside her main gig at the Garden was because of her wide network of friends and family. Gigi had the rare gift that she could turn a stranger into a new friend. It was a quality she'd gotten from both her parents, which was how they'd ended up hosting the biggest, loudest, funnest Nochebuena party on the block for years. On the first holiday season without them, Gigi was afraid she'd bomb the whole tradition. It was why her loved ones had insisted she get a little R&R and come back refreshed for the party.

Gigi never took a sick day. She never declined an opportunity for a side job. It had been so long since she'd had a date, she barely recognized when someone was flirting with her anymore.

There was no rest for the wickedly ambitious, as they said.

Gigi polished off her breakfast, then split before Gus could try to set her up with his nephew again. She didn't have time for romance. Not the kind that she dreamed about. The kind that surprised you and left you feeling like your heart had gone a round in the Tea Party ride at Coney Island. And besides, after a string of disastrous and disappointing dates, Gigi had stopped trying to make something happen. Instead, she focused on making sure she could afford her sister's tuition and save for a future that felt ever-changing.

With her new caffeine rush, she hurried to catch the train to Midtown, where the Park Central Vista hotel was waking up with early bird guests coming and going. Martha Weinberg, the hotel's night shift manager, was waiting for her in the glittering lobby. Gigi had gone to Hunter with Martha's daughter where they'd dreamt about producing Broadway shows. Katie was doing exactly that, while Gigi had gone down another path. Martha always threw extra jobs her way, and Gigi did what she did best. She talked to the wires and bulbs. Not every job was as easy as unplugging and plugging it back in. This wiring was simple enough but required the patience Gigi had honed over the years. Sometimes Gigi thought people were just like light fixtures—veins instead of wires, blood instead of electricity, souls instead of light. Only sometimes, she preferred one over the other.

Half an hour later, Martha handed Gigi a red envelope with her cash fee. In her rush to get to her next stop, Gigi raced out the lobby and collided into a plush winter coat at the front steps.

"*Oof!*" she said as she bounced back. She felt someone grab her arm and keep her steady.

It took her a moment to truly get a look at the man in front of her. She registered his eyes. Rich and brown and fringed by thick lashes which caught the dusting of flurries like some startled winter prince.

His face shifted from irritation at being bumped into and slowly moved into pleased shock.

He was something right out of her fantasies, dressed in an extravagantly embroidered beige coat, a wide flat-brimmed fedora, and sleek black dress shoes that were not appropriate for the cold. The drip was exquisite. *He* was exquisite. Her heart gave a soft squeeze as he kept smiling at her.

"Sorry," she mumbled, and hurried away.

He took a step toward her and extended his hand, but she was already out of reach. If he was some Latin Pop Star Prince, she was no Cinderella. Still, she glanced back once to see him folding himself into the back of a black Lincoln.

Gigi hurried through the rest of her morning. She swung by Saint Cecilia's in Brooklyn for a quick job arranging lighting cues for the school's Christmas Talent Pageant, and then by noon she'd missed the F train and instead took the G to the 7 and walked the rest of the way instead of waiting for the bus.

When she passed Astoria Bookshop, she knew she was almost home. The year her parents had moved into the redbrick house with a narrow front yard, they'd put all their savings into it. Back then, it had been worth under a hundred thousand dollars. Now, she was getting offers from eager gentrifiers for a million bucks. As tempted as she was—she didn't think she could do it.

"Finally!" came Lily's cry from the kitchen as she opened the door. As a senior in high school, it was her final winter break, and naturally the one time she didn't want to sleep in. "You have to pack! Your flight leaves in four hours! And Leila said if you miss the spa appointment Vivi will kill you..."

As Lily buzzed around, ticking off the things waiting for Gigi in South Beach, Gigi shrugged out of her jacket, and realized she'd been walking around all day with ketchup on her shirt. Not to mention she hadn't deep conditioned her curls in a month and her warm golden-brown skin looked sallow.

Her biggest worry was leaving Lily alone. But she reminded

THE GREAT HOLIDAY ESCAPE

herself that Lily was a good kid, and Leila and Héctor would swing by and check in on her to make sure she hadn't burned down the place.

"It's only two days," Gigi reminded herself as she shoved toiletries and chargers in her carry-on. She'd get some sun. Have some cocktails. Then come right home. With every second, she was finally on board with her vacation in...*forever.*

What was the worst that could happen?

CHAPTER 2

TWO DAYS BEFORE NOCHEBUENA

GIGI HAD NEVER BEEN on a real vacation. Day trips to Jones Beach and Coney Island over the summer were just reserved for sticky New York summers. Still, she adapted to her stay at the Lux Revel hotel fairly well.

A chauffer had waited for her outside baggage claim and taken her to a junior suite where gifts had been waiting for her: a bottle of champagne that read "Take a fucking break, please!" She was positive her cousin Callie had written that, though she was one to talk with her non-stop writing schedule.

Gigi unwrapped two more boxes containing a blue silk slip dress she could never have afforded with a note from Leila and Vivi. Gigi rolled her eyes. They needed to stop playing and *get together* already.

The final gift came from Helena, and Gigi was sure she'd gotten it on a film set. It was a sexy white swimsuit and a card decorated with doodles of dicks and read "Get some vitamin D!" The hotel staff must be sick of her friends and family and her stay had barely started.

On that first night, she'd ordered a giant plate of fancy pasta, wine, and slept like the dead.

When she woke up, she forgot where she was, for a moment, and had a hot flash thinking she was late for work.

But after a long day of pampering, Gigi had been twisted, massaged, waxed, manicured, and polished into a version of herself she hadn't seen since her college graduation. She wiggled into her swimsuit, which accentuated her narrow waist and curvy hips. The gold accents burnished her sun-starved skin.

Gigi made her way through the lobby of couples and families on fancy holiday getaways, and though she had the feeling that she didn't belong, she still strutted her way through the massive pool area and claimed the cabana reserved for her under Vivi's name. She was surprised she was actually looking forward to doing nothing but sunbathing and reading all day.

She had a copy of her cousin's novel *Eleven Eleven*, which she'd swore she'd start when she had a moment to herself. Well, she finally had a hundred moments to herself. She swam in the pool. Downed a piña colada. Reapplied sunscreen. Threw herself into the ocean in front of the hotel. Ordered another piña colada. Read. Napped so hard she was pretty sure she woke herself up with a loud snore.

When she wiped the corner of her mouth, she felt eyes on her. In the cabana directly to her left was one of the most beautiful men she'd ever seen. Familiar, but couldn't quite place how. Tawny brown skin glossy from sunscreen. Lean, long muscles. Smiling lips that were too full and pouty and dangerous for anyone to have. His eyes were light brown, almost honey, and his curls were artfully tousled with saltwater. Despite his young aura, the lines at his forehead and the silver at his temples showed his age.

She glanced behind her, but the other cabana was empty. Nope, he was *definitely* smiling at her.

Her body flashed hot under his stare. Was she violating some sort of fancy cabana etiquette by snoring? Was she supposed to wear big sunglasses and sit in an uncomfortable pose like the toned models across the pool?

"I love this song," she said, because their staring contest was becoming too much for her.

He squinted and made a show of listening over the waiters chattering and the families in the pool. "You look a little young to know this song."

"'The Piña Colada Song' is a *classic*." She held up her drink. She bit her tongue to stop herself from blurting out, *I'm twenty-seven, but thanks, Cabana Daddy*.

Cabana Daddy chuckled and leaned across the big empty cabana bed. She imagined she could fit under his arm. "Ah, but the name is 'Escape.'"

She made a smug face. "Technicality. *Technically* it's "Escape (The Piña Colada Song). So, we're both right."

He chuckled and began to say something when his phone rang. Frowning, he gave her a smile, like he was apologizing for taking a call.

Gigi shook her head. What did she imagine? A handsome older man would just so happen to be at the cabana beside her and think she was adorably cute? That he'd ignore everything just for her? She watched *too many* telenovelas. It was rotting her expectations of romance, even if she loved love stories.

She buried her face back into her book. If the couple didn't get together, she was going to kill Callie.

Chancing one last glance, just a tiny one, at her neighbor, she found Cabana Daddy was gone. A waitress was cleaning up his unfinished drink and towel. Disappointment made Gigi pouty. She had no business being pouty. Though as the sun set and she went back to her suite to change for dinner, she thought of the handsome stranger and imagined bumping into him in the elevator. Maybe at the sauna. Or at the sultry lounge on the rooftop.

Gigi rolled her eyes at her own imagination. "You're being ridiculous."

But she was on vacation! She was allowed to fantasize. Gigi had always been prone to day-dreaming that way. When she was in school, she thought she'd be working on stages or movie sets. She thought she'd have traveled half the world by now. But Gigi's Achilles' heel was her self-doubt and fear of the unknown. As she got dressed for her dinner reservation, she wondered how different her life would have looked if she had taken the big scary opportunities that had come her way instead of staying at the same safe job.

She walked to her window and stared at the mammoth clouds drifting across the sunset, and the blue ombre ocean lapping against the beach. Was it time she made a change? She didn't even know where to begin. All she knew was that she felt restless, despite the most relaxing day of her life. It was like she was holding her breath because she was getting ready to leap into some wide unknown. Like somewhere out there, the stars were shifting just for her and she wasn't sure which way her luck would turn.

For a moment, Gigi couldn't help but think of the man she'd bumped into the day before and was unable to stop her smile. Then, while she dressed, she remembered the hot Cabana Daddy, and queued up "The Piña Colada Song" on her phone just for fun. She spun in her royal blue silk dress and gold heels, singing off key. Her mom's gold earrings glinted at her lobes, and she dabbed on a mauve lipstick. She looked like the million bucks she didn't have and felt the spark of hope she hadn't in so long. Who knew all she needed was a little bit of rest and sunshine?

Gigi arrived early at the hotel's steakhouse. It was packed and her table (for one) wasn't ready, so she parked herself at the bar. Outside, palm trees were decorated in red and green lights, which was bizarre to her New York City brain.

"Dirty martini, extra dirty," she ordered.

The bartender winked at her. "Blue cheese olives?"

Her eyes flared. "Uhm, yes *please.*"

She spun on the swivel barstool, and when she returned to the starting position, she came face to face with someone familiar. Her heart stuttered. It was the man she'd bumped into the day before outside the midtown hotel. Instead of his soft wool coat and fedora, he was in a tailored gray marble suit and red suede loafers with gold buckles. The whole thing was extremely over the top, but he made it look effortless.

He glanced around, unbuttoning his blazer in that confident way some men had. She noticed the signet ring on his middle finger, but no other jewelry. He grinned, trying to place her, then gestured at the empty seat to Gigi's left.

God, two unbelievably beautiful men had sat beside her in one day? She'd won the South Beach vacation lottery.

Red Suede Shoes rapped his knuckles on the bar counter. "Oban 18. Please."

Within seconds, a highball of near amber whisky was set before him. He picked up his glass, tipping it to his lips but not drinking.

"You're the girl," he said.

She was aware that she'd been watching him since he sat down and ordered. She swallowed and sipped her dirty martini. "Girl? The last time I checked I was an adult."

He opened up his posture. Everything about him was easy but effervescent. Like wherever he went he knew he was going to enjoy himself. "Well, the dress is certainly...different...than the Spider Man T-shirt you were wearing yesterday."

It took all of her not to choke on her drink. She swiveled to match his stare and was hit with his playful grin. Oh, he was *trouble.*

"I was wearing a Blink-182 shirt, thank you very much. From their last show together."

He raised his hands in mock surrender. "Well, I'm fascinated."

"By?"

"How you went from practically shoving me into the snowy sidewalk to this. I mean—" He drank and lightly shook his drink at her. "Of all the whisky joints in all the towns in all the world..."

She loved the play on that line. *Casablanca* had been her mom's favorite movie. The thought wrapped around her heart and squeezed. The sensation only doubled when a man entered the busy steakhouse, walked past the hostess stand, and made straight for them. Fire alarms went off at the sight of him.

Cabana Daddy. He'd ditched the linen pants for a sleek matte black suit with a red silk tie.

Gigi swallowed and finished the *Casablanca* line, but found she was almost breathless. "You had to walk into mine."

Cabana Daddy shoved his hands in his pockets. The gesture was so confident, like someone who was used to showing up and letting the entire room know he meant business. Gigi crossed her legs together and squeezed against the flutter that started at her core.

Fuck, she thought. It had been so long since she'd been with anyone that even being surrounded by these two men was enough to rile her up.

"I leave you for two seconds and you're already making friends?" Cabana Daddy said, his deep voice pitched low with amusement.

The two men clearly knew each other, and very well at that.

"Oh, we're old friends," Red Suede Shoes said. He polished off his drink and signaled to the bartender for another.

"Are we?" Gigi asked. She couldn't stop herself from lightly swiveling from side to side. "I don't even know your name. I've been calling you Red Suede Shoes."

"Pedro Bernal," he said. "I've been calling you the girl who pushed me outside the hotel."

"I did not *push* you."

"She's the one?" Cabana Daddy asked, a tilt of surprise to his words. "In that case, I've been calling her Ms. Piña Colada."

"*Oh?*" That, as well as Pedro's pleased expression, piqued her attention. They'd talked about her? They'd talked about her to *each other*? A fuzzy feeling spread across her chest. She tugged on her bottom lip to stop herself from smiling like a fool.

Gigi leveled her gaze to Cabana Daddy. "I prefer Giselle. Or Gigi if you're lucky. And you?"

He leaned in toward her, stepping on the bottom rung of her chair to stop her from swiveling. "Don't I get a nickname?"

She wanted to be the confident girl in her sexy blue dress, sipping her fancy big-olive cocktail. Instead, she was blushing. Actually blushing. "I'm not telling."

Pedro whistled, accepting his replacement drink with a nod at the bartender. He took a step closer, and it was like they were lions cornering her, a gazelle in their sights. Her heart raced with the thrill of it.

Pedro took a sip, then whispered, "It's probably something filthy."

Gigi regained some composure and made a gesture like she was shooing them away. "The only filthy thing about me is this martini. Don't you guys have hot dates or something?"

Cabana Daddy checked his gold watch. "That depends."

"On what?"

"On who you're waiting for."

Gigi stirred her drink with her skewered olive. She didn't want to sound lonely or desperate or like an easy target. But she felt herself opening up to these men. What were the chances that she'd brushed paths with them in the span of thirty-six hours, and now they were together and right in front of her?

"I'm flying solo," she finally said.

Cabana Daddy took her hand and brushed his fingers across her knuckles. "Giselle. Would you do us the immense pleasure of joining us for dinner?"

Her first reaction was to say no. The safe thing to do was to keep her reservation for one and have a quiet night in, much like every other night for the last few years. She was already acting like a girl with a crush. A double crush. She was afraid she'd make a fool of herself. But then she remembered that feeling she'd had in her room while she was overlooking the ocean. It was just dinner with two charming, gorgeous men, wasn't it?

"I'd love to," she answered.

Perhaps it was the way they looked at her, stripping her down with the desire in their eyes. Perhaps it was Pedro's playful smirk. Or the way her Cabana Daddy gripped her *and* Pedro's shoulders as he guided them toward the private booth overlooking the turquoise sea. Or the twinkling lights around them, the utter freedom that came with being away from home. But Gigi Baez was certain that she was about to have a very good vacation.

GIGI ORDERED THE PRIME RIB, medium rare. Pedro asked her to choose the wine, and she picked one she'd seen her cousin order at fancy restaurants. They seemed pleased with the selection.

Gigi had a million questions. *Are you together? If you're together, why do you keep looking at me like you're seconds away from ripping my clothes off? Why are you in a hotel for the holidays?* She decided to start off easy.

"Wait," Gigi said. "I still don't know your name. I've been calling you Cabana Daddy."

"See?" Pedro smirked as the waiter brought over the wine and poured a tasting into her glass. "I knew it was filthy."

She drank, tasting the velvety, dry cabernet, and offered her glass for more. "It's great. Thank you."

When the waiter left, Cabana Daddy cleared his throat and said, "Isaac Aguilar."

Gigi was struck by the same familiarity as the first time she'd seen him. Isaac watched her face as she searched for the connection until it clicked. She almost choked on her wine and Pedro nearly doubled over in delight.

"Isaac Aguilar—" Gigi pressed her hands on her warm cheeks. "Like from *Angeles del Mar?*"

Isaac scrunched his features, embarrassed. "I thought you might be too young for that telenovela."

Gigi nearly squealed at him. *Angeles del Mar* was about a group of angel pirates who protected the seven seas. Isaac had been the youngest cast member and a dreamboat. Unlike the other actors, he'd vanished from the limelight halfway through the series. But the soap played on reruns at least once a year.

"I can't believe I didn't see it right away," she said. "I *love* that show."

"It was a long time ago." Isaac did that humble nod famous people did. She'd seen Vivi do it all the time when she was getting fawned over in public.

"What happened?" Gigi asked, then reined in her enthusiasm. "I mean, unless it was traumatic, and you don't want to talk about it."

Pedro snorted. "Oh, he loves it. You should see the shrine at our apartment."

"I did love it once. I was fifteen and being called a heartthrob in international magazines. Fans followed me everywhere. I was in talks of doing a pop album. But then, when I was eighteen, I started dating a boy I met in Puerto Vallarta." Isaac's frown softened, like it made him sad to remember. "The paparazzi was all over us. Was I gay? Was I bisexual? Was it for publicity? You name it. The studio tried to squash the headlines, of course. Half of the executives wanted me to be their queer poster boy. The other half was worried about the *demographic*. Things aren't much better, but fifteen years ago they were worse. I didn't want to play by their rules, and I didn't want anyone I dated to be caught in the crossfires. So, when they killed off my character that season, I decided to go to college. I bought an apartment and invested the rest of my money. I never looked back, and I've never been happier."

He looked at Pedro adoringly and said, "I *did* steal my costume from set, which is the shrine he's referring to."

Gigi didn't have the right words to convey how much she hated what he'd gone through as a kid. Instead, she rested her hand on top of Issacs's and squeezed. He didn't pull away from her touch, only linked his fingers with hers, which ratcheted up her heart rate.

She turned her attention to Pedro who glanced at the gesture, and Gigi couldn't help but think he looked *pleased* instead of jealous.

"Are you an actor too?" she asked Pedro. "Wait, let me guess… reggaeton upstart."

"Upstart!" Pedro clapped a hand over his chest like he'd been hit by an arrow. "I should be insulted."

"Serves you right," Isaac said, taking a drink of his wine. "Those shoes are truly ridiculous."

"You *bought* me these shoes."

Isaac winked at Gigi and leaned in conspiratorially. "He sent me the link six times with a reminder that Christmas is around the corner. Plus, he's very persuasive."

Pedro scooched over to her a bit, and she welcomed the way they felt on either side of her, like sturdy pillars of muscle and devastating smiles. "I'm good like that. It's what makes me so good at my job."

"Gigolo?" she teased.

His laughter boomed and people turned to look at them. "I fundraise for non-profit organizations. My best qualities are that I am shameless and devilishly handsome, which comes in handy when getting rich snobs to hand over their money for good causes." Pedro smiled up at Isaac. "That's how we met."

Isaac shook his head slightly, like he was used to Pedro's antics. "And we've been together ever since."

They were a stunning couple. So beautiful it was like looking directly into the sun, especially when they gazed at her so intently. It was easy to get swept up into their rhythm. Pedro with his exuberant energy and Isaac with his attentive calm.

"What about you, Gigi? How did we get so fortunate to have you all to ourselves?"

The way he said *all to ourselves* sparked something in her belly. Isaac had to know what he was doing by brushing her bare arm as he talked. Pedro, in turn, was close enough that his knee was touching hers, and though there was plenty of room in the booth, he wasn't moving away. She didn't want him to.

"It's a funny story." She told them about her family and friends, their surprise early Christmas gift. Explained how the final nail in the coffin was when she'd fallen asleep going home and had ended up riding the subway all the way to Coney Island and back to Jamaica. She'd woken up with her phone jacked and a crick in her neck. "And yes, I know better than to fall asleep on the subway in the middle of the night. But I barely know what to do with myself when I'm not working. I feel—" She stopped herself. One of the reasons that she was able to always keep moving, always keep focused on her jobs, was because she didn't stop to talk about her feelings. But here she was with these men, and they had shared slivers of themselves. Why was it so hard to do the same?

"I feel afraid of what will happen if I stop moving." She washed down the knot of emotion with a sip of wine. "I know that I don't have to *earn* my rest. But what if one day work is scarce? What if something happens to Lily and I'm not there? What if something happens to *me*? Lily has already lost so much..."

"So have you," Isaac said softly.

Just that acknowledgement was more than she could have asked for. It was something she didn't remind herself of because she was afraid to be weak, soft. To let go.

Their food arrived in a flurry of sizzling plates. Juicy steaks and pan seared sea bass, bubbling truffle mac and cheese and charred greens. The way Pedro offered her a bite of his filet mignon made her think of meals with her family. The way they reached across the table to snatch buttery dinner rolls and share morsels of flaky fish. For a moment, she pictured these two men at her Nochebuena table. For a moment.

"Is the vacation working?" Isaac asked her.

She tucked an errant curl behind her ear. "I certainly haven't thought about stage cues in twenty-four hours, so I think it is. Though I am now."

Pedro waved his arms in a big X. "No more work talk. So, you're not staying in Miami for the holidays?"

"That's a big no. I leave tomorrow night to make sure I'm home in time for Nochebuena." She explained how this was her year to uphold her family's tradition. "What about you guys?"

"We've sort of become our own family," Isaac said. "We've been together for three years."

"Four," Pedro amended. "The year we were *just friends* counts."

"Fine." Isaac laughed, and when he did, his whole face transformed with happiness. "Then, since you're leaving us tomorrow night, I want to know everything about you, Giselle."

"There's not much to know," she said.

"I doubt that." Isaac watched her with his keen golden eyes.

The truth was in recent years she hadn't let many people get too close. But as the night went on, and they listened to her stories of her family, her attraction turned into serious crushes. They were so easy to talk to. Isaac had visited almost every country Gigi had on her wish list. Pedro quoted movies and songs at every opportunity. They plied her with questions about the celebrities she'd had encounters with at work, which weren't many considering she worked backstage. With every passing minute, she felt like she was just catching up with long-time friends. Ridiculously charming and heart-stoppingly beautiful friends. There was something familiar in Isaac's honey-tinged eyes, and the way Pedro cozied up beside her as he fed her a spoonful of passionfruit crème brûlée. Like they'd had this dinner a dozen times. Like she'd known them her whole life.

She refilled her wine, her insides bursting every time Isaac's shoulder brushed against hers, every time Pedro tucked a loose curl behind her ear.

When the waiter came by with the check and announced last call, Gigi blinked. They were the only table in the restaurant that hadn't cleared out.

Isaac charged the meal to their suite even though she tried to shove her credit card into the waiter's apron.

"That wasn't necessary," she said, and shivered in the air-conditioning chill as they made their way to the elevators. "But thank you."

"A small early Christmas present." Pedro draped his gray blazer over her shoulders and took a long moment to admire her from head to freshly painted toes. Whatever he saw, he seemed pleased.

She felt light, buzzy, but not yet drunk. Happy, even. Maybe she needed breaks more often. Maybe the world wouldn't fall apart if she just slowed down a tiny bit.

The doors opened and the three of them filed in. For the first time she noticed how big they both were. She wanted to bury her face into Isaac's strong chest and feel Pedro's hands at her waist. She sighed and settled for leaning against the glass wall.

She noticed the boys exchange a look she couldn't quite read, then Pedro pressed the penthouse button because *naturally* they were in the penthouse. She asked them to hit the level just below theirs with the slightly less fancy suites.

"Gigi," Isaac whispered. "Giselle."

She wanted to tell him that they could call her Gigi. But she loved the sound of her full name on his lips. "Yes?"

"We're not quite ready to say goodnight." Isaac's dark gold eyes were full of emotion, like he was bearing a part of himself that he didn't always show. "Would you like to come back to our room?"

"What would we do?" she asked, even though she knew. She knew by the way he undressed her with his stare, and the way Pedro flashed that devilish smile. But she wanted them to say it.

"We want to make love to you."

"Oh," she said breathlessly. Her mind was racing a hundred miles a minute. The elevator beeped the floors, ascending closer and closer to hers. But Pedro drew her attention with a tap of his finger on her chin. "Do you—?"

"No," Pedro said. "We don't do this a lot. We've tried...it's never been *right*. But I felt something when I saw you yesterday, and then to find you here today, to know you're the same person who caught Isaac's attention too... It feels like fate, doesn't it?"

The elevator came to a stop. The doors dinged open at her floor. Gigi needed to think. But she didn't have time. She *did* want to follow them. And then what? What happened the next day and the one after? Her body was screaming to chase the flutter gathering low in her belly just at the thought of both these men. But her heart and her mind steered her out the elevator as the doors were closing.

Pedro began to follow, but Isaac calmly eased him back. Her Cabana Daddy flashed her a small smile, like he understood that it was too much. Too much. They were too much, and it didn't make sense that she felt so tangled up over two men she barely knew.

Fate, Pedro had called it. The word tumbled in her mind as she hurried to her room and pressed her head against the door.

"You idiot," she told herself.

Hadn't she wanted Isaac?

Hadn't she wanted Pedro?

Was it enough to simply *want?*

She picked up the bottle of champagne her family had sent. The metal bucket full of ice had melted. She reread the note attached. "Take a fucking break, please!"

Gigi deserved a break. She deserved fun.

She'd had more than fun with Pedro and Isaac. They were beautiful and funny. Kind and sweet. Every moment with them had felt like a small gift from the universe. Those were the things she craved from a partner, the things that had felt missing from so many failed attempts she'd stopped trying. Gigi had never considered that she could find those things in two people, so diametrically different, but who fit around her like missing pieces.

She kicked off her heels to get ready for bed, then remembered she was wearing Pedro's blazer. In one of the pockets, she found a heavy black keycard.

"Fate," she said.

Barefoot, and with her champagne bottle in hand, she turned around, and before she could talk herself out of it, Gigi Baez ran back to the elevator. She wasn't ready to say goodbye to them just yet.

THE ELEVATOR DOORS opened up right into the penthouse suite. Gigi had never been anywhere like it. Modern, sleek furniture all in white and blues that made her feel like she was stepping into Miami's version of heaven.

"Hello?" she called out, making her way into the living room.

Isaac was pouring himself a glass of whisky and Pedro was halfway done with unbuttoning his shirt. Both froze at the sight of her.

"I—" Now that she was in front of them, she was beginning to lose her nerve. She shrugged off the blazer and held it out. "I wanted to give you this."

"Is that all you wanted to give?" Pedro asked, smirking as he crossed the wide room. He towered over her, and she watched the muscles of his throat work as he swallowed. Was he nervous? She hoped she wasn't the only one. That she wasn't still dreaming in the Garden's greenroom. And if she was, she didn't want to wake up.

"No, that's not all." She tugged at the end of his loose tie. Every part of her body was molten steel, ready to be transformed and shaped into something stronger, sharper. "I've never done this before. But you have?"

Isaac walked up behind her. His strong fingers traced her bare arms. She was aware she was still holding her bottle of champagne. Pedro chuckled and took it from her, setting it on the coffee table.

"Yes," Isaac admitted. "We love each other, but sometimes there's a spark with someone we both admire and want. It has never lasted. Or felt as natural as this with you. I wanted you the moment you walked into that pool and smiled at everyone, even the sun. Like you were grateful for everything around you. I wanted you since I saw Pedro leaning toward you at the bar."

"Do you feel it too?" Pedro asked, tapping the underside of her chin so she looked up at him.

"I do. I feel all of it." She reached up to finish undoing his buttons, his heart was racing as fast as hers. When she ran her palms over his hard abdomen, her voice quivered as she said, "Now, feel me. *Please.*"

Behind her, Isaac brushed her hair away from her neck, and Pedro closed ranks and kissed her throat. That kiss alone made her dizzy, sucking at parts she didn't even know were so sensitive. She was grateful that she was being embraced by them, supported by their strength and desire.

Pedro cupped her face and kissed her. As his tongue parted her lips, Isaac pushed up the hem of her dress to caress her hips, toying with the elastic of her panties. Their cocks were hard, a rod against her belly and another resting at her lower back. They pressed tightly against her, and that eagerness shifted something inside. She wound her hips and felt Isaac moan kisses along her shoulder, as Pedro explored her, tasting of whisky and passionfruit. Gigi had never been in the spotlight, but she could only imagine this was what it felt like. As if she was being illuminated from within. Adored from every side.

She pushed the threadbare straps of her dress away, past her full breasts. Her nipples hardened from the exposure. Pedro shut his eyes and groaned a "fuck" as he ground his cock on her belly, grabbing her hips and spinning her around to face Isaac.

She was nearly breathless as Isaac took her nipples into his mouth, lapping his tongue in a way that made her tremble with want.

When her knees nearly gave out, Pedro guided her toward the couch where they feasted on her body. A tangle of desperate kisses and exploratory caresses. She rucked up her dress and revealed her ridiculous red panties. She didn't think anyone would actually see her in the holiday-themed underwear. They had candy canes and reindeer printed on the front.

"I didn't expect company," she laughed.

"They're perfect," Pedro said, his voice deep and lust drunk. He bunched the fabric to the side revealing her tight, trim, black curls.

Gigi and Isaac watched as he split the cleft of her pussy with his thick finger. She wanted to squeeze her thighs together, but Isaac held her knees apart as Pedro found the aching pearl of her clit and rubbed her slowly. So slowly she raised her hips to chase the sensation building at the pit of her stomach, wriggling and matching the concentric rhythm of his fingers until the orgasm surprised her, sharp and sudden. Pedro smiled and leaned down to suck her nipple as she came down.

Gigi fell back on the plush couch. Turned her face and found Isaac there, offering a kiss that soothed her hunger for both men. But only for a moment.

"You are both far too dressed," she said, delighted as she shimmied all the way out of her dress. It fell in a crush of blue silk.

As both men stood, the chill of the air-conditioning filled the space they had occupied. She busied herself opening the champagne bottle with a *pop!* she felt in her core. Fizzy champagne overflowed down her wrist. Since they didn't have glasses handy, she took a drink straight from the bottle and restlessly watched them undress. She needed them to come back to her because they weren't finished. They might never be finished. The thought was overwhelming, but it had taken root.

Pedro undressed in the blink of an eye and returned to her, licking at the trail of champagne running down arm. He eased her onto her back on the couch, spilled champagne into her navel, then drank it. Gigi tried to bite down on the ticklish sensation of his tongue there, but soon they abandoned the bottle, too entranced by Isaac undressing.

He undid his cufflinks and set them aside. He finished unbuttoning the mother-of-pearl buttons and folded his shirt over the armchair. He watched Pedro and Gigi as he undid his belt, shoved off his pants. His erection peeked out of the waistband of his black boxers, the dark head glistening, ready and wet.

Gigi smiled because Isaac kept his socks on. He stood in front of her, proud and strong and thick. She tugged his boxer briefs down. His cock hung heavy between powerful thighs. He could crush her with those thighs, and she'd thank him, ask him to do it harder.

"Holy shit," she hissed as he sat beside her.

Isaac tilted his head back as he stroked himself in front of them. She leaned forward, her body arching like a cat. Behind her, Pedro smoothed her rump with his palms as he pulled her panties down. She felt too exposed, her labia still slick with her orgasm.

She looked over her shoulder as he positioned his face at her opening. He parted her wet pussy with his tongue. She bucked lightly, a natural reaction to the surge of sensation, but he steadied her hips hard and kept her in place.

"I will never get enough of you," Pedro said, his voice husky as he lapped her up. She shut her eyes as he slid a finger inside, then another, exploring her soft folds and stroking at her inner walls.

It was too much, too good. She wanted to keep that feeling forever. She wanted to share it with Isaac, who was fucking his own hand while he watched them.

She flashed him a smile full of promises and took his crown into her mouth. Dragged her tongue in circles under his frenulum and felt him shiver, restlessly thrusting into her mouth.

"Fuck. Giselle. Fuck me," Isaac growled.

She took him deeper still, letting the flared head of his cock graze against the back of her throat. The sensation was uncomfortable at first, but she wanted more and more of him. Of both of them.

"Oh God," Isaac moaned. "I need—" He stopped himself.

Gigi gave his cock a long lick, then pulled back. "What do you need?"

Behind her, Pedro kissed his way up her spine until he was at her shoulder, biting harder than before. She wanted him to do it again.

"He needs to fuck you, querida."

The way he said it, the way he could so clearly see what his partner needed thrilled her. It made her eager to share in that connection. To learn what they wanted and desired with a simple look and touch.

"Please. *Please* fuck me." She eased back into Pedro's hold, sitting between his legs. Together, they watched as Isaac vanished into the bathroom and returned in a flash, sheathing his cock with a condom.

Gigi pressed her knees together. "It's so big."

Pedro kissed her lower ear. "Wait until *I'm* inside of you, querida."

"Fuck," Gigi exhaled and opened her legs, her wrists held by another man while Isaac readied to enter her. It felt delightfully dirty. Vulnerable in a way she didn't let herself be often, perhaps ever. And yet, she'd never felt safer, wanted. Ready to plunge into the unknown of this new, scary, beautiful feeling.

Pedro ran a finger through her pussy as Isaac climbed up on the long sofa. He kissed her, then Pedro, then her again, notching his tip at her entrance. She reached back and held onto Pedro's neck as Isaac pierced her.

She cried out in pleasure, her inner walls squeezing against him.

"You're so fucking tight," he rasped, his arms braced on either side of Pedro's thighs as he pulled out completely.

"Harder," she whispered at Isaac's ear.

Pedro nuzzled her, reaching down to stroke her clit. "Let him in, querida."

Her thighs melted around Isaac, like they were molding around the shape of him, taking him in with every stroke until he was seated deeply inside.

There was a moment when she wasn't sure whose hands belonged to whom. Pedro and Isaac kissed as Isaac drove into her, and then they were kissing together, three hearts beginning to tangle in a way that was going to change everything, the three of them tugging and thrusting and gasping until Gigi couldn't stand it. She came in fast, crashing waves. Her beautiful, open-hearted men tipped over the edge, chasing her in ragged pants. Pedro's warm semen spilled between them, as Isaac filled the condom with a strangled grunt. Pedro tugged on Isaac's hair, and they shared a final, deep kiss between the three of them as they squeezed the dregs of their pleasure.

For a moment, they lay there, sharing in the heat of their bodies, electric with the heady spark of this new feeling.

Eventually, Isaac left to dispose of the condom, and Pedro brought cool towels to clean up with. They finished the champagne, naked on the couch, Gigi resting against Isaac's chest and her legs draped over Pedro's thighs.

"Do you know what's weird?" Pedro asked, toying with the little scar on her knee she'd gotten from when she fell learning to ride a bike.

"The fact that Isaac likes to wear socks during sex?" she teased.

"My feet get cold," he said, defending his socks stance. He tugged gently at her earlobe.

Pedro shook his head and flashed that perfect smirk of his. "It feels like we've done this forever."

"This is new to me. But I know what you mean." She nodded and accepted the kiss he offered as he moved on top of her.

He rested his forehead between her breasts. His sigh was pouty, almost distraught. "Stay with us, Gigi."

Gigi had never spent a holiday without her family, or most of the friends they'd made over the years. That house that her parents had made was her safe place. But perhaps, there was a way she could have it all.

It was crazy, and too soon. But it hurt to imagine waking up in the morning and saying goodbye. Even the thought of leaving the room and going to her own suite alone felt wrong. She belonged with them, in their arms.

"Why don't you two stay with me?" she said softly. "I mean come back with me."

Pedro sat up. His brown eyes cut to Isaac, then back to her. "To New York?"

"To Nochebuena." She swore she could hear her blood pumping in her ears as she waited for an answer.

Isaac smoothed a thumb absently on her knee. His frown spoke more of confusion than dislike. "With your family?"

She sat back, pulling a pillow over her body. "I'm sorry, that's too fast, right? I just thought—"

Pedro chuckled lowly. "No, querida. We're only surprised you'd want us to meet your family. Would they be okay with...*this?*"

Gigi couldn't imagine what they'd been through in their past. Her heart swelled with the need to soothe. To assure them that they would be safe. It was a promise no one could make, but she knew her loved ones. "I actually think everyone that I love would love you. Both of you."

"I think we could change our tickets. I do prefer a New York City Christmas to Amsterdam," Pedro said.

Gigi shook her head, laughing her nerves out. "Damn, I didn't know I was competing with Amsterdam."

Isaac took her chin in his strong fingers. His face was serious, full of fear and sweet, sweet happiness. "It's not even a contest, amor."

"So, you'll come?" Gigi sat up, clapping her hands together.

They nodded, and Pedro sat forward to kiss her first. It was hard and passionate, his tongue sweeping against hers in a way that made her so wet. She reached down and rubbed at her needy clit.

Isaac grew hard watching them, and soon, he carried Gigi to the bed where she straddled Pedro while Isaac watched them fuck, a spark of possession in his amber eyes.

"You are both perfect," Isaac said, stroking himself into release, pearlescent ropes of semen spilling across his abdomen. "You are *both* mine."

It was too soon, too crazy, too much. It could have been pheromones or fate, or something completely new. But whatever it was, it belonged to the three of them, wholly and unabashedly. Gigi could see the beginning of something she'd craved for so long. Something she wanted to keep.

There was no question about it. She wanted to be theirs. Start the New Year with them in her life.

"Yours," Pedro said, thrusting his sheathed orgasm into her.

She eased her head back, rocking fast against his cock and seizing the friction between their best parts. As she came, she repeated it. "Yours."

Isaac kissed them, together, at once. "Always."

CHAPTER 3

NOCHEBUENA

Nochebuena was the time of year Gigi loved the most. Back when their parents were alive, Mama started decorating the house the day after Thanksgiving until it was ready for the big party. Papi played old salsa records, which he said was a requirement to make his food taste delicious.

Gigi had no aspirations that she could make her father's Panamanian-style pernil, or her mother's Ecuadorian stuffing, but she tried her best.

She queued up her dad's favorite record—*Asalto Navideño*—and stared at the ready living room. Part of her felt that her short stint in South Beach had been a sex-starved dream. But as Isaac hung the final ornaments on the tree, and Pedro helped Lily stage the dining table, she knew it was real.

Dressed in a forest green velvet suit, Pedro matched the massive pine tree that filled the corner of the room. Trimmed in white lights, and the decorations her mom had lovingly wrapped in tissue paper and bubble wrap. She said that's how things stayed new. All anything needed was a little time, a little care, a little love. Gigi wondered if that's how you cared for love, too.

Lily and Isaac came up beside her, smiling proudly at their impressive dining table full of succulent dishes that truly made it feel like home. Strings of delicate lights were strung along the large windows, giving them an impressive view of the snowy day.

When the three of them had arrived the night before, after a day of piña coladas and sex, and a red eye flight that had Gigi twisted into anxious knots, Lily had greeted them with the biggest hugs. Gigi had never questioned that her sister would adore them, but she'd never brought a boyfriend home, let alone *two*. The biggest night of their year felt like a moment that might make or break them, and Gigi had already decided that there was only one outcome. She was theirs. They were hers.

"Everything is perfect," Lily said. "I think mom and dad would be proud of us."

Gigi wasn't sure if it was because she missed her parents fiercely or because of her sister's words or because Pedro and Isaac had made themselves right at home—maybe a combination of it all—but emotion wrapped around Gigi's heart. Happy tears stung at her eyes.

"Last thing," Gigi said, holding up four index cards and pens.

"Wishes?" Lily's whole face scrunched up with excitement.

Gigi nodded. "Wishes."

"What wishes?" Isaac asked, readjusting his red tie for the hundredth time.

"It's a tradition," Gigi explained. "I don't know where I got it from but ever since I was a kid, I would write down wishes on pieces of paper and burn them on Christmas Eve. I made my parents play along and Lily, too."

"Now you," Lily told them.

Pedro and Isaac looked deep in concentration as they scrawled on their index cards. In previous years, Gigi had written down things like a unicorn, magic powers, straight As, for Antholyn Rodriguez to like her back. Then there were the real things born out of a desperate love —for her parent's failing health to get better, for the strength to raise Lily, for love.

Love had been her wish several years prior.

The realest kind of love. The kind of love that took her by surprise and stayed. The kind of love that would not ask her to slow down but that would catch up with her.

She wrote down, *I wish for things to always remain this beautiful.*

It felt foolish, like still believing in birthday wishes and Santa Claus, but it was her tradition and her heart's desire. She knew, of course, that nothing ever stayed the same. But with a little time, a little care, *a lot* of love, Gigi could sure as hell try.

"What did you wish for?" Isaac asked.

"You're not supposed to ask," Lily rolled her eyes.

Pedro tugged on his chin and winked at her. "Blue suede shoes."

As their wishes caught fire and burned, the doorbell rang with the avalanche of guests. There was a chorus of "Eyyys!" and "¡Feliz Nochebuena!" and "Happy Christmas!" Everyone enveloped Pedro and Isaac with bone-crushing hugs. One of her aunts recognized Isaac from *Angeles del Mar* and nearly fainted before peppered him with questions about the show.

"I'm sorry," Gigi mouthed, but he only kissed her temple and humored the middle-aged aunty doused in Chanel Number 5.

Sarita arrived with bags of presents, a tray of arroz con dulce, and the sexiest Santa anyone had ever seen. Carlos's serious face broke into a small, shy smile as Sarita introduced him.

Behind them, Helena kicked snow off her heels at the front door. She waved a giant bottle of her family's famous vegan coquito in the air, and a gorgeous date she introduced as Julie.

Gigi's neighbors swung by for a bit and dropped off a tray of tiramisu, while a gaggle of children ran in chasing a boy in what looked like a frog costume.

"Is that...Baby Yoda?" Pedro asked, wrapping an arm around her waist.

"He's a *coquí*," Eneida said, dusting snow off her coat before hanging it on the rack as she introduced Tony Sanchez to the rest of the family. Gigi had met the charming Broadway producer a few days before, and was glad to hear the talent show went off without a hitch.

"Baby Yoda would make a dope musical," Tony said, winking at Eneida, who blushed. While he and Pedro shook hands, Gigi realized she couldn't remember the time she'd seen Eneida *actually* blush since her separation.

"Okay, food, drinks, extra coats in the guest room," Gigi repeated with every wave of guests. She felt like she was directing her own chaotic orchestra. Eventually, she could hardly keep track of the people in her house.

Thankfully, Lily's godfather Héctor took charge of the kitchen, something they hadn't seen him do the last couple of years. Meanwhile, his date, Cristina, had pulled Isaac into a geek-out session over Gigi's father's record collection.

Sarita placed a glass of coquito in Gigi's hand and told her to relax. Sarita grinned behind her glass. "So. *Details*."

Gigi's face felt hotter than the oven keeping the pernil warm. "Tomorrow at brunch. For now, let's just say if I knew I was going to meet them, I would have taken a break sooner."

"Get it, girl," Sarita winked, then hurried to rescue Carlos from the onslaught of aunties fascinated with his scandalous Santa vest.

As Mayor Lucero arrived, Gigi completely lost her cool and gave him a tight hug. There was a fresh wave of excited greetings. Her parents had been prominent volunteers for his campaigns throughout the years, and he embraced the Baez sisters with a warm hug. Eneida greeted her brother and the beautiful date he introduced as Natalia Menendez. The mayor's bodyguard positioned himself near the dessert table. They brought a giant tray of cookies, a cold bottle of champagne, and a soccer ball which immediately got put to use.

"No balls in the living room!" Eneida reprimanded.

"That's always been my motto," Julie snorted into her glass, and Helena playfully nudged her.

"Can't quite relate." Pedro cackled and clinked his glass to theirs.

Gigi had barely closed the door when Marcelo, Yamilette, and Pasquale showed up together—their smiles wider than Gigi had seen them in months.

Soon, the house was warm with the fireplace and residual heat from the oven, plus the bodies dancing from one side of the living room to the other. Gigi pulled Isaac onto the dance floor.

"I don't remember the last time I danced," she said, swaying too slowly for the rhythm of the salsa. It just felt good to be held by him. "Are you having fun? I know we're a lot."

"You're everything," Isaac whispered in her ear. She pulled back because she did not need to get horny in front of her friends and family. But she did press a sweet kiss on his lips. Isaac spun her and she came face to face with Pedro. Together, their movements were aligned, the push and pull of the salsa in perfect harmony.

When it got too hot, Gigi stepped outside for a second to feel the flurries kiss her cheeks. She shut her eyes and whispered, "Thank you," knowing in her heart that somewhere, somehow, her parents were blessing them all.

That's when a giant red truck rode up and blocked the driveway. Out tumbled her cousin Callie and an extremely good-looking man who hugged Gigi like they were long-time friends. Gigi had a ton of questions, like "where did you disappear to?" and "What happened to Angelo?" and "Did you smash?" But all of that felt like conversations for after the kids went to sleep piled into the guest room.

"I like him," Gigi whispered, and Callie's face crinkled with unfettered happiness as she said, "Me too."

Back inside, after hours of food and music and nosy, but loveable, prying into the lives of new friends and loves, Lily dragged a chair to the center of the room and climbed up. Gigi didn't have time to be alarmed as her sister tapped a plastic fork on her glass, calling for attention. It didn't do much, but Tony whistled between his fingers like he was hailing a taxi in Times Square.

"Thank you." Lily dipped into a curtsey. "I wanted to say a few words—"

Just then, their cousin Leila barreled through the door with mega pop star Vivi Guerra, their hands tightly entwined. Leila shoved a bottle of Don Julio 1942 at Gigi and winked. "What? We're right on time."

"Maybe, in Latino Time," Callie giggled.

"As I was *saying*," Lily continued.

Gigi linked her fingers with Pedro and Isaac. Lily hadn't told her she was making a speech.

"This past year without Mom and Dad has sucked," Lily said. "I was afraid that because I was underage, the city wouldn't let me stay with my sister. But Gigi did everything she could to make it work. She busted her ass at a million shitty jobs on top of her normal job just to prove to the social workers that she was responsible. And to make sure I can pay for school next year. I just want to say—"

Lily turned to Gigi and held up the single glass of coquito she was allowed. "You always tell me that you want me to make something out of myself, so I don't end up like you. And don't worry. My fashion empire *will* blow you all away one day. But I just want you to know that I hope I am *exactly* like you. You care and you love people, and you work harder than anyone I know. I miss Mom and Dad, but I know they'd be happy that you and I are together, and we're not alone because we have literally everyone here."

Gigi didn't realize she was crying until she felt lips pressing against her wet cheeks. She reached out to hug her little sister, everyone clapping and hugging each other as the train of kids chasing the coquí returned.

"All right, I was told this party had to be memorable," Tony shouted. He flipped a vinyl between his fingertips before laying it in place and setting the needle.

There was a scratch, then the boom of horns and raspy crooning of the salsa song, which everyone sang and danced along to until they were the loudest house on the whole block, perhaps all of Queens.

Surrounded by pure love, Gigi Baez had everything she'd ever wished for, and more.

"Yours," she whispered to the men who'd caught her heart.

"Yours," Pedro said.

Isaac watched them with a promise of everything that was to come, and added, "Always."

FIN

ALSO BY ZOEY CASTILE

THE HAPPY ENDINGS SERIES
Stripped
Hired
Flashed

ANTHOLOGIES
"Far Side of the World" from *Best Women's Erotica of the Year Vol. 6*

WRITING AS ZORAIDA CÓRDOVA
The Inheritance of Orquídea Divina

ABOUT THE AUTHOR

Zoey Castile was born in Ecuador and raised in Queens, New York. She started writing in her teens and pursued that love in her studies at Hunter College and the University of Montana. For nearly a decade, she worked as a bartender, hostess, and manager in New York City's glittering nightlife. She is the author of the Happy Endings series. When she's not writing, she is the co-host of the podcast <u>Deadline City</u>. For more of her fiction visit <u>zoraidacordova.com</u>. Sign up for Zoey's Newsletter!

Printed in Great Britain
by Amazon

74829281R00246